Amanda Prowse

Will You Remember Me?

HEAD
of
ZEUS

First published in the UK in 2014 by Head of Zeus Ltd

9 7 5 3 1 2 4 6 8

A catalogue record for this book is available from the British Library.

Trade paperback ISBN: 9781781856512
eBook ISBN: 9781781856499

Typeset by Palimpsest Book Production Ltd,
Falkirk, Stirlingshire.

Printed and bound in Germany
by GGP Media GmbH, Pössneck.

Head of Zeus Ltd
Clerkenwell House
45-47 Clerkenwell Green
London EC1R 0HT
WWW.HEADOFZEUS.COM

I dedicate this book to the man who believes that family is everything. He would give me his last penny (and often has!) and I know that no matter how old I am or where I am in the world, I only have to pick up the phone and he will come running. With a safety net like that, it is very easy to climb mountains... My dad, Ken x

Prologue

I often think about the day we got married, replaying the best bits in my head. I picture us laughing as we walked to the pub afterwards and the way he held my hand, tightly, possessively, stepping slightly ahead as if leading me. I was happy to follow. It felt safe and comforting. The bloke that owned the local café drove past in his van and shouted out of the window, 'Oi oi! It's Mr and Mrs!' It was the first time we'd been called that and we exploded with giggles. I thought I looked very average – dreadful, really. It wasn't like I had the posh frock and all the trimmings. But when I look at the pictures now, of the younger me, I can see that I looked far from dreadful. I was glowing, as if my joy shone out of me; no fancy dress could match that.

Later that night I climbed into the rickety bed alongside my husband. The gas heater hissed, doing its best to take the chill off the damp room. My face ached from all the laughing and the permanent grin I'd worn. We were both tired. I was about to drop off. My eyelids were drooping and I was really, really comfy, when suddenly he flicked on the lamp and sat up. I opened my eyes, wondering what was wrong, thinking that maybe those seven pints of Guinness and the kebab on the way home had finally caught up with him.

He lay back down and turned over, positioning himself on his side, with this head propped up on his elbow. And then he said, 'I love you so much. I want to give you the moon with a bloody big bow tied around it. My wife! I've got a wife and not just any wife but the best bloody wife in the whole wide world!'

I laughed as flames of happiness flickered inside me.

'Tell me,' he said. 'Tell me what you want and, one way or another, I'll get it for you.' He reached out and knotted his free hand with mine.

I remember looking at the bumps of our knuckles side by side, with our little wedding bands sitting next to each other, shiny and new. 'I don't want anything, only you,' I whispered, which was the truth.

He shook his head. 'Nah, that's not the answer, girl. If you could have anything, and everything was possible, what would you want?' His expression was bright, hopeful and child-like.

I lay back and closed my eyes, trying to picture a world for us where I could have anything, and everything was possible. 'Well...' I swallowed. 'I'd like two kids, a boy and a girl, who are happy and secure. I want them to be like us, but smarter and cuter.'

'Well that wouldn't be too difficult!' He laughed.

I didn't open my eyes; I stayed in that world that he'd created for me. 'And I'd like a swimming pool shaped like a kidney—'

'Why like a kidney?' he interrupted again.

'Because, apparently, rectangular pools are the cheapest design, but a kidney takes some doing, with all them curves. Costs more. So everyone would know how much dosh we've got, just by its shape.'

'Gotcha. What else?' He moved closer. I could feel his minty breath against my face.

'I'd like a diamond ring. Not just any old diamond, mind, but one the size of an ice cube. And I'd show it to everyone from school and on the estate who has ever laughed at me or made me feel like I was nothing.' I felt his lips graze my neck and a shiver of joy travelled down my spine. 'And I want to lie on a tropical beach and feel the soft powdery sand slip through my fingers and the hot sun on my face.' This was the wish of a girl who had rarely left the postcode of her childhood.

'So, not Southend?' He kissed me again.

I opened my eyes and turned to face him. 'No, not Southend.'

'Are you done?' he asked as his hand travelled up under my nightdress and rested on the flat of my stomach.

'Nearly.' I placed my hand on top of his. 'I want to dance with you in the rain, wearing a lovely dress, and I want it to be a proper dance, like a waltz, old fashioned and romantic.'

He rolled over then until he was lying on top of me, resting on his forearms. He smoothed the hair from my forehead and kissed me gently on the mouth. 'Then a dance in the rain you shall have.' He covered my chest and neck with tiny kisses, making my heart beat faster.

'And what about you?' I managed. 'What would you want if you could have anything, and everything was possible?'

His expression was suddenly solemn. He looked into my eyes and spoke in a soft voice. 'I want us to live in the countryside, just like we've always wanted, and I reckon if we lived somewhere nice, everything else would fall into place.'

I nodded agreement against his shoulder. The countryside was our dream.

He wasn't finished. 'And I want to give you everything that you've asked for. That'd be enough for me: to make you happy. That's a world I'd like to live in.'

'Well, congratulations!' I beamed. 'You do make me happy, so maybe we've arrived there already!' I laughed and wiggled down the bed with my arms wrapped around him.

'There is one more thing...' I added softly into his ear.

He paused his kissing and gave a small sigh. 'You're sure it's the last?'

I nodded. 'I'd like to know who my dad is.' I had felt the absence of this special man on this, my wedding day. Unexpectedly, a tear found its way to the surface and trickled down my cheek, which he kissed away.

'Don't be sad,' he whispered. 'Not tonight.'

I sniffed and smiled. He pulled the duvet over our heads and it felt like we were in our own little bubble, sheltered from the world; like no one could get to us and we were safe. And I remember thinking, if I get to feel like this every night of my life, lying in bed with the man I love, knowing that nothing can touch us, then we *have* arrived at that place, we really have. And I was right.

One

'Bye, Granny Claudia!' Peg waved her hand over her head, ensuring her farewell would be drawn out until the last possible moment, and watched as Granny Claudia got smaller and smaller in the rear window. 'I've had the best Christmas ever!'

These were the words they wanted to hear from their daughter every year.

Peg settled back on her booster seat with her baby brother, Max, dozing in his seat by her side.

Poppy smiled at her husband as he turned the car out of Clanfield, the Oxford village where they had spent the festive holiday in the dear company of the mother of their late friend Miles. Gracious and well-educated, Claudia was a surrogate grandma for the children and a welcome voice of guidance for Poppy and she relished the role. Her only son, Miles, a journalist, had been killed by a car bomb some years earlier, and she had been widowed for a long time now.

Poppy closed her eyes and pictured the Christmas Day just passed: a golden turkey with all the trimmings, a brisk walk with the kids in the snow as dusk bit on the day, and dark port in crystal glasses that had sent her into a glorious sleep in her husband's arms as they sat in front of the roaring log fire. Peg was right; it had been the best ever.

'What's the best Christmas you ever had, Mum?' Peg whispered.

'Ooh, I think this one will take some beating.' She squeezed her husband's thigh across the central console of their Golf. The joy of his surprise return, early from tour, still lingered.

'What's the best *present* you ever had?'

'Definitely Daddy coming home.' Poppy beamed.

'What about when you were little?' Peg shook her head to get her toffee-coloured fringe out of her eyes; it needed a trim.

Poppy looked out of the window at the snow-spattered hedges and the wheelie bins crammed full of Christmas packaging, awaiting collection. She only ever gave her daughter diluted accounts of the deprived conditions in which she had grown up, not wanting to upset her with the image of her mum wanting.

When they were children, Poppy and Martin had routinely gone to bed on Christmas Eve in their respective damp flats with tummies full of butterflies and expectancy. Neither knew whether, the next day, all their dreams were going to come true, or whether it would be a rubbish day like any other. It was nearly *always* a rubbish day like any other, but that didn't stop them being excited. There was always the smallest possibility that the rumours were true, that if they had been good, they would get lots of great stuff. Poppy was a smart child, quickly learning that the whole Santa thing was a rotten lie, but for an hour or two before bedtime, the antici-pation would be almost painful. She liked the possibility that there might be some magic, somewhere.

The disappointment of waking on Christmas morning to find it was just another shitty day, albeit with a bit of cooled turkey, a couple of roasted spuds and a string or two of balding tinsel thrown in for good measure, didn't wane. That was until she married and had kids of her own. Now she and Martin could give Peg and Max the sort of Christmases they could only have dreamt of for themselves, erasing the miserable memories in the process.

Poppy turned to face her daughter. 'Well, I don't remember too much about my presents, but one year, when my nan and grandad were asleep in their chairs—'

'Nanny Dot and Grandad Wally?' Peggy interrupted to show she knew who was who.

'Yep.' Poppy smiled. 'Anyway, my mum had gone out somewhere.' An image flashed into her head of Cheryl arriving home, giggling as she slid down the wall with a defunct paper blower between her lips and the smell of booze hanging over her in a pungent cloud. 'I curled up on the sofa and watched the movie *Miracle on 34th Street*. It made me feel very Christmassy and I remember thinking how lovely it would be to have your wishes come true. That was quite a special day for me.'

'I think wishes do come true. I wished my dad back and he came!' Peg clapped.

'That's true,' Martin confirmed over his shoulder.

Poppy tucked the shoulder-length layers of her hair behind her ears. 'Well, as I said, that film was very special for me.'

'I like that movie too, Mum.' Peg beamed.

'I saw the black-and-white version though, Peg. The original.'

Peg considered this. 'Black-and-white films make me really sad.' She spoke to her hands, folded in her lap.

'Why's that, Pickle?' Martin asked in the rear-view mirror.

'Cos everyone in them is dead.' This she delivered with her palms upturned and her voice doleful, as if she was standing on a West End stage.

For some reason this struck Poppy as funny. She snorted

her laughter into her palm and Martin followed suit.

Peg folded her arms across her chest. 'You two drive me crazy!'

This was fuel for their already giddy state. The two of them laughed until their tears spilled and they wheezed for breath.

'I really missed you.' Poppy gazed at her husband, the one person who could make her giggle even harder just by giving her a well-timed glance.

'I missed you too.' He grinned at his wife, who reclined in the passenger seat.

'It's New Year's Eve,' Peg stated.

'Yes, love, it is, and tomorrow is a whole new year! It's exciting, isn't it?'

'Are we going to have a party?' Peg sat forward, eyes wide.

'No, I don't think so, we are far too boring.' Poppy pictured a night alone with her man, the kids tucked up, a glass or two of wine, and hours and hours in which to make up for their long, lonely months of separation. She felt a stab of excitement at the prospect. Her soldier was home.

'Jade McKeever says her mum and dad always have a party and they drink champagne and beer and cocktails. Last year, her dad's friend got drunk and weed in the downstairs cupboard because he got mixed up and thought it was the loo.'

'Well, that certainly sounds like fun.' Poppy grinned at her husband.

'We don't have to have a party, Peg. I could just wee in the downstairs cupboard anyway.' Martin winked at her.

'Oh, Dad, that's gross!' Peg stuck out her tongue.

'You started it.' Martin laughed. 'Is Jade McKeever Ross's

girl?' Martin had worked with Ross, a fellow mechanic, in the past.

'Yep, and Jade is Peg's new life-coach, apparently.' Poppy rolled her eyes.

'We *never* have parties. I'd like you to have one so I can sit on the stairs and watch everyone getting drunk!' Peg was on a roll.

'You don't have to get drunk at a party, Peg. Sometimes it's nice to go and have a dance and chat to your friends—'

'Wee in the cupboards,' Martin interjected.

'Yes, that too.' Poppy slapped his arm. 'We didn't even have a proper wedding reception, did we, Mart?'

'Nope. Didn't need all that fuss, I was just glad to get my girl.'

Poppy pictured Jenna and a couple of Martin's mates from the garage singing 'Ta da da da…' repeatedly to the tune of 'Here comes the bride' as they arrived at the back bar of their local.

'Who caught your bouquet then, Mum, and tied ribbons and tin cans to your lovely white car?'

Poppy smiled. Peg had definitely seen too many wedding-themed movies. 'I didn't have a bouquet or a fancy car. It was just Daddy and me and a few of our mates in the pub near where we lived. I had a lovely day, even without the fuss.'

'Would you have liked all that – tin cans and a fancy bouquet?' Martin asked, his face now serious.

Poppy considered this. 'Sometimes I think it would have been nice, but if I picture a reception or a big party, then I see the kids there, so I guess I didn't miss not having one. But maybe a party one day would be good. We could do it for our silver wedding or something?'

Martin nodded. That sounded like a plan and was sufficiently far off not to send him into a panic over finances and organising. 'Am I *really* your best present?' he asked.

She nodded. 'Yep. Although when I'm rich and famous and have my kidney-shaped swimming pool, am wearing a diamond on my finger the size of an ice cube and have danced in my evening dress in the rain, that might change.'

'You'll still need me to pick you up and carry your bags though, right?' He leant towards her.

'Always. That's your job, to pick me up when I fall and carry my bags.'

'And kill baddies!' Peg piped up from the back. They'd quite forgotten she was listening. It set them off giggling again.

Finally, as Peg dozed and Max snored, Poppy turned to her husband. 'How was it? Out there?' She looked straight ahead.

Martin exhaled through bloated cheeks. As usual he would spare his wife the reality of life on tour, the crushing loneliness, the boredom. 'Oh, busy. Hard work, a shitty place, the usual. I've had enough, really, Poppy.' He ran his hand over his face and rubbed his chin.

She nodded. *Me too.* 'Well, if you can stay here for a bit, that'll be okay, won't it?' She tried to offer a small flicker of consolation.

'That'll do me, mate. It's all I want, to come home to you and the kids every night. Trouble is, I don't know how long it'll be until I'm off again, and it's the uncertainty I don't like.'

'I know. I know.' She placed her hand on the back of his and thumbed his tanned skin.

'I hate being away from you and the kids, but it also

makes me realise how lucky I am. Imagine all those blokes like me who are away and don't have our heartstrings.'

Poppy smiled and squeezed his hand. It was their thing and always had been, the belief that they had heartstrings that joined them across time and distance. Linking them as one, no matter what.

Poppy gave a long yawn.

'Am I keeping you up or are you just bored?' he joked.

'Sorry, I can't help it, I'm permanently knackered.' She sank back into the seat.

'Ha! It's me that's travelled across the globe, hopping on and off planes and sitting up half the night and it's you that's yawning!' Martin tutted.

'I know. I think I've found it harder work than I realised, having you away this time. But you're back now and that changes everything.' She grinned, wrinkling her nose in the way that Peg had inherited.

An hour or so later they were back in the rolling Wiltshire countryside.

'It's bloody beautiful here, isn't it?' Martin grinned, leaning forward against the steering wheel to take in the bright sky and snow-covered fields.

Poppy nodded. They'd traded the concrete of East London for all this green, open space and the novelty was still acute for both of them.

As she stepped out of the car, Poppy looked across at their army quarter, one of twelve identical houses that had been built in the 1970s for the MoD. It was flat-fronted and rather ugly on the outside, but inside, the lounge/diner was quite spacious, the large windows let in lots of natural light and the kitchen was a useable square. There were two good-sized bedrooms and a third that people used either as a study or, like Poppy and Martin, allocated to their second or third child.

Martin lifted the bags from the boot of the car. 'God, it's bloody freezing! Hope you left the heating on.'

Poppy tutted. 'Of course I did. Can't risk a pipe freeze in this weather. I do manage, you know, when you're not here. It's a case of bloody having to!'

Martin smacked her bum as she walked past and made her way inside.

Jo, their neighbour, ran down her front path in her slippers, blushing as she patted her hair, which had been hastily shoved into a band. 'Mart! Oh God, wasn't expecting to see you. What you doing home? Thought you had another couple of months to go?'

'I did, but they cut the tour short.' He smiled. 'I didn't want to say anything to Poppy in case everything changed. You know how it can.'

Jo nodded. 'Don't I just.'

'It was all very last-minute, but I got to Oxford on Christmas morning in the early hours.'

'You lucky sod.' Jo wrung the tea towel in her hand; she wanted her husband home too.

'Danny all right?' Martin asked after his drinking buddy and fellow armchair Spurs supporter; he had been one of the last to be deployed to Afghanistan.

'Yeah. Y'know.' Jo shrugged. She didn't need to elaborate on how horrible it was to be separated, especially over Christmas.

'Give him my best.' Martin nodded, sincere.

'Will do, mate. Tell Pop not to worry about tonight. We were going to open a bottle of plonk and watch a bit of telly, but tell her I'll catch up with her in the week.' Jo hovered.

Martin nodded again in her direction. He had no intention of allowing Poppy to honour this engagement; tonight he wanted her all to himself.

Poppy stood in the kitchen and watched as her man lumbered through the door, laden with bags of laundry, presents and the detritus that gathered in the car on any journey.

'You're home,' she whispered.

'The place looks lovely!' Martin grinned, taking in the immaculate leather sofa, shiny laminate floors, cushions plumped just so and dust-free surfaces. He smiled at the tiny Christmas tree in the window and the Santa statues on the side table; he was glad they had made the effort even though they were away for Christmas itself. It made the place feel like home. He loved how Poppy cared for their house; he felt a sense of pride every time he opened the door. 'And bloody huge! Living inside a tent and washing in a communal block every day makes this feel like a palace!'

'Is that right? Better get me a tent then. I'll kip in that for a couple of weeks and then come in and be as chuffed as chips with this grotty quarter.' Poppy slipped her arms around her husband's neck and kissed him on the mouth, running her fingers over his shorn, fair hair. He knew she loved this house and loved looking after it, finding it far from grotty.

'How soon can we get the kids off?' he whispered gruffly into her hair.

'Well, that depends. If I had a hand with cooking tea and getting them into their PJs, it would all happen a lot quicker.'

'Consider it done.' Martin clapped his hands, loudly. 'Right, Peg, Maxy, who wants what for tea?'

The two thundered into the lounge. 'Chicken nuggets, chips, peas and chocolate mousse please, Dad!' Peg shouted.

'Yes, nuggets!' Max nodded his agreement.

'Coming right up.' Martin bowed. 'Is that on the same plate?'

The kids giggled. 'I love having my daddy home!' Peg pogoed up and down, Max joined her.

'Tell you what, babe, why don't you go have a shower, have a moment to yourself,' Martin said to Poppy as he headed for the kitchen.

Poppy smiled. She liked having their daddy home too.

She kicked her pants on top of the jeans and T-shirt that lay in a heap in the corner of the bathroom, and let the water splat against the shower tray. She usually jumped into the slightly chilly deluge and started scrubbing as it warmed, but not tonight. Instead, she carefully laid out her silky nightie, dressing gown and only matching set of bra and pants, then positioned her perfume bottle ready for a quick spritz before she went downstairs. *He's home!* She grinned into the mirror and practised her smouldering pose: hair over the shoulder, cheeks sucked in slightly, eyes fixed. She laughed; she was rubbish at that stuff and she knew that, after eighteen years together, Martin would only find it comical, not alluring. She felt sexy enough without trying to do sultry as well.

Steam engulfed the space as she let the hot water wash over her. She squeezed a blob of her new, expensive shower gel into her palm – a gift from Claudia that she had been determined to save for special occasions. Well, this was certainly a special occasion: it was New Year's Eve. Again she smiled at the thought that her man was on the floor below her instead of miles and miles away, across a sea or two.

Poppy inhaled the shiny, amber-coloured liquid. It smelt of vanilla and honey; lovely. She rubbed her hands together to make lather and ran her palm over her arms, neck and chest. Like most people, she had a familiar ritual for her washing routine, doing it in the same way and soaping her body parts in the same order. To deviate would feel odd. She considered this and smiled, wondering how long it had taken for this sequence to become habit. Did other people for example start at their feet and work upwards? Poppy grimaced; that would be entirely wrong.

She began to sing, loudly. 'Let your love flow...'

'Mum! Mum!' Peg banged on the bathroom door, then tried the handle and realised to her delight that it wasn't locked. She strolled in and gathered up Poppy's silky nightie with its lacy edges and side split. 'What is *this*? Mum, is this a dress? It looks fancy! Are you going to a party after all?'

Poppy turned her face to the shower nozzle and let the water cover her blushes. 'Oh no, that's just a very comfy nightie – it's nice and cool when it gets hot.'

Peg ran her fingers over the silky material. 'But it's a bit snowy outside, Daddy's freezing!'

Poppy turned off the shower, knowing that her allocated 'me-time' was over. 'Yes, I know, but it can sometimes get a little toasty if we leave the heating on.'

'Why don't you just turn the heating off?' Peg stared at her with her head cocked to one side and her nose wrinkled.

'Good point, love. I shall do just that.'

As Poppy wrapped herself in the large towel and ran her fingers through her hair, Peg slipped her mum's nightie on over her head and tucked the bottom of it into her jeans. 'Dad says we can go on the trampoline!' She clapped her hands.

If anything good happened or they were celebrating an anniversary, the whole family always took to the trampoline, deciding beforehand how many bounces were appropriate, ten being the most. The impending arrival of Max two years ago had merited a ten, and so had the loss of Peg's first baby tooth. The occasions weren't always the most traditional.

'Really? Tonight?' Poppy tried to hide her slight irritation; this wasn't how she'd seen their evening of passion beginning.

'Yes! It's New Year's Eve! And we've got a lot to look forward to.'

Poppy kissed her little girl's forehead. 'Yes we have, my darling.'

'I mean, I'm going to be nine next year and I'm getting a new pet, aren't I?'

Poppy nodded as she reached for her toothbrush. She was still hoping that acquiring a guinea pig might lose its appeal, even though Martin had readily agreed to the idea.

'And I'm going to try and be register monitor next term. I'm going to be really good, Mum, and not talk too much when Mrs Newman is talking, and use my ruler for drawing lines and not hitting people, and this time next year I might be on the *X Factor*!'

'Why, is Mrs Newman on the panel?' Poppy mumbled as she spat her toothpaste foam into the sink.

'No!' Peg tutted. 'But Jade McKeever and me are doing a dance routine and we've learnt a song and we're going to audition.'

'But you'll only be nine!'

Peg rolled her eyes. 'We are going to lie on our application form.'

'Ah, of course, they won't be expecting that!' Poppy tapped the side of her nose. 'Well, good luck with your bid for stardom, Peg. What song are you going to sing?'

'It's Miley Cyrus, but I haven't learnt the words yet. Jade's going to teach them to me.' Peg coughed and placed her hands on her hips, as if just by knowing the name of an artiste she was elevated to that auspicious rank of teenager.

Poppy sprayed her perfume onto her neck and wrists. Peg breathed in deeply. 'I love your perfume, Mum. You smell all chocolatey.'

'Chocolatey? Oh good.' Poppy laughed.

Martin did a double-take as Peg trotted down the stairs with his wife's silky nightie pulled on over her hoodie and Poppy following in her comfy tartan PJs and bed socks.

'What the...?' he began.

'Peg came to chat to me while I was getting ready and she found my nightie.' Poppy gave a wide, false grin.

'Mum only wears this when it gets hot,' Peg stated matter-of-factly as she sat at the table and poked a large chip into her mouth.

'Err, last time I checked, we used cutlery at the table, love.' Martin tried to look stern.

'Oh, Dad, you are so funny!' Peg chuckled as she picked up a chicken nugget with her fingers and dunked it into the little puddle of ketchup on the side of the plate.

'I believe we are trampolining after tea?' Poppy quizzed.

'Well, it is New Year's Eve and we are getting a new pet.' He winked.

'Mart, she's got you wrapped around her little finger.'

'Can you get me a drink please, Mummy?' Peg mumbled between mouthfuls.

Poppy jumped up.

'Oh, hello, kettle!' Martin called after her.

Poppy ran the tap and smiled. This was a good feeling: back to normal, family life, everyone where they should be, snug and safe under their little roof in Larkhill.

17

She opened the fridge and saw a bottle of champagne and two glasses cooling on the top shelf – perfect.

With the tea things washed and put away and the kids in their padded snowsuits, the four laughed and squealed as they made their way out to the little square back garden. Martin was the first to climb onto the trampoline; he was in his jeans, sweatshirt and socks, and his wellington boots were placed neatly side by side on the ground. Poppy handed him Max, who was wrapped to resemble a little Michelin man; he giggled, finding the whole exercise hilarious. Peg made her own way up and stood resplendent in her snowsuit with a neon-green tutu skirt over the top and her face almost entirely covered by her hood and scarf. Poppy clambered aboard in her pyjamas, dressing gown and thick socks, with a fleecy top zipped up under her chin and her striped bobble-hat securely over her ears.

Martin held Max as they all stood in a wobbly circle and held hands.

'Okay, Cricket family.' Martin spoke in a whisper as his breath blew smoke into the chilly December air. 'How many bounces? I vote four.' He smiled at his wife.

'Four?' Peg screamed. 'No way! Ten! And Maxy wants ten, I can tell.'

Max clapped and shouted 'Duck!', his word of the moment.

'Okay.' Martin looked at each member of his family. 'So that's a four from me, a ten from Peg and a duck from Maxy. Mummy, you have the deciding vote.'

Poppy gasped and placed her hand on her chest. 'Oh, gosh, that's a huge responsibility. Well, let's have a think…'

'Ten, ten, ten!' Peg chanted, causing waves as she jiggled that threatened to topple them all.

'I vote... ten!' Poppy shouted.

Peg screamed and commenced her bouncing, which caught Poppy off guard and sent her sprawling; she squealed as Martin lay down next to her, holding Max's mitten-covered hands while he bounced in the small space not filled by his parents. Peg finished her bounces and jumped on top of her mum, landing with a thump. Max copied his sister and pretty soon all four were in a heap on the trampoline, laughing, fighting for breath and staring at the clear winter sky.

Their breathing slowed and the noise hushed. Martin slid his palm across the thick woven base and gripped his wife's hand.

'There is nowhere on earth that I would rather be than right here, right now.'

Poppy raised his hand to her mouth and kissed his fingers. 'Me too.'

'It's going to be the best year, Poppy. I just know it.'

She smiled into the darkness. 'Yes it is, my love. The best.'

Two

Martin turned his attention from the pan on the stove to his wife. 'Well here she is, my beautiful hot bird.'

Poppy held the folded newspaper up to her face.

Joan May Williams, aged 84. Wife, mother, grandma and great-grandma. Died peacefully after a brief illness. Donations to any Alzheimer's charity in lieu of flowers.

She looked up from the paper and over her shoulder at her husband, who was wearing her 'I kiss better than I cook' apron as he flipped fried eggs that popped and sizzled in the pan. She pointed at her chest. 'Do you mean me? Or have Tesco delivered one of them rotisserie chickens you like?'

'Yes, I mean you.' Martin held the spatula up and grabbed her around the waist with his free hand, pulling her towards him. After any time away, he was drawn even more strongly to his wife's pale skin, with its smattering of freckles across her nose, and to her clear green eyes and shiny, shoulder-length hair, now layered and hanging in reddy-brown loops around her face.

'You make me sound like some leggy model. I think we might need to get your goggles upgraded.'

'I don't need no leggy model, I just want you.'

'Well that's lucky, cos that's what you've got, mate, and you are well and truly stuck with me.'

'What's that you're reading?' Martin watched as she turned her attention back to the newspaper, studying it intently, devouring the contents.

'Nothing.' Poppy haphazardly collapsed the paper into an awkward parcel and shoved it next to the bread bin.

'Are you looking at the obituaries again?' He waited for her reply, wanted to see if a lie would pass her lips.

She nodded, trying not to laugh.

'I hate you reading them,' he whispered.

'But I've always read them.'

'I know and it creeps me out!' He shivered.

'Why? I think it's lovely to see what people have said about their loved ones.'

'I tell you what it is, it's an excuse for people to wallow in their sadness and for the newspaper to make a few quid! What's the point? Grief should be a private thing. The person they're writing about is brown bread, it's bloody pointless.'

'It's not pointless, Mart. At least I don't think it is. It's like wishing them a fond farewell.'

'A fond farewell? I just don't think it's very jolly.'

Poppy threw her head back and laughed loudly. 'Not very jolly? Have you been mixing with them officers again, Mart? Jolly?' she taunted. 'Not very jolly?'

He kicked his leg out, trying to catch her with his foot as she wriggled out of reach.

They both smiled as Poppy stood behind him at the stove and ran her fingers over the tan line at his neck. She felt the slight bulge of flesh against the pad of her finger. Martin had always been solid, stocky, and she could now see the extra pounds that would pad him into his middle age.

'I love having you home.' She kissed his neck.

'Well that's lucky too, cos I'm not going anywhere either.'

'Although I must admit, I find it easier to keep my kitchen clean and tidy when you aren't here.' Poppy picked up the empty egg carton and flung it in the recycling bag she kept by the back door, then reached for her cloth and sprayed it with Cif.

'*Your* kitchen? Blimey, there are women burning bras all over the world so the kitchen won't be considered "theirs".' Martin laughed.

'Not me.' Poppy smiled as she swiped at the sink drainer. 'I like looking after my house. Plus I've only got a couple of bras; I'd be in all sorts of unsupported trouble if I started burning them.'

'I sometimes think you'd rather we didn't eat and then you could keep *your* kitchen immaculate at all times.'

Poppy carried on cleaning, not willing to confess that sometimes that was exactly what she thought. 'Well, if you don't like it, you can always move into the shed in the back garden, where the dirt and mess might be more to your liking!'

'I'm only teasing you, babe. I love being in our shiny house. I'm not going anywhere.'

'Not yet.' Poppy crinkled her nose, hardly able to think that this happiness might be subject to a countdown. The supposed two-year gap between deployments seemed to be commonly ignored these days, as numbers dwindled and campaigns continued. She knew it wouldn't be long before he came home looking sullen, eye twitching and muscles tense as he delivered the phrase she always dreaded: 'I've been posted…'

'Maybe not ever,' he quipped.

'Ooh, now you're talking.' She kissed him again, then freed herself from his grip and plunged her hands deep into the sink, feeling for the cups and cutlery that lurked under the suds, wanting to get a head start on the washing-up.

'Seriously, Poppy, I've been having a good old think. I reckon when this year is up, I should think about signing off. Then we can stay around here, the kids won't have to be uprooted from school and I won't have to go away again.' He turned to look at his wife over his shoulder.

'God, that sounds perfect. I'd love it. But it's a lot to consider, love – we'd lose the house, obviously, and you'd need to find a job.'

Martin nodded; he had thought of that. 'I'm sure I can get something, looking after a fleet in some company or a garage. I get casual offers from people that I meet all the time – apparently my military training and willingness to put up with the most shite conditions make me an attractive prospect!'

'Who knew?' Poppy mocked.

'Not me.' He grinned. 'Or of course I could always set up my own business, open my own garage or whatever…' He let the idea dangle and glanced at her, trying to gauge her reaction, before returning his stare to the pan.

Poppy abandoned the washing-up and turned to face him. 'That'd be great, wouldn't it? I could go back to hairdressing if need be, just while we get set up. Ooh, Mart! I'd love to see you with your own business. You could have "Cricket and Sons" over the door!'

'Or "and Daughters",' he corrected.

'Only if you're planning on setting up a flight school for our little pilot. She's quite determined.'

Martin laughed. 'She'll have to be. I think I'll see what

surprises this year has in store, but I might do the sums, see what it would take and how far we could get with my gratuity. It wouldn't be huge, but if we were careful and had another income coming in, it might just be doable.'

'Are we having another baby?' Peg shouted as she pulled a chair from the table and sat with her legs tucked up underneath her. Neither parent had heard her approach in her green-and-blue striped socks.

'Another baby?' Poppy laughed.

'Yes. I heard Dad say something about surprises this year and the last time you said you had a big surprise for me, we got Maxy! I don't mind if we are, but I'd like a girl this time, called Katniss.'

'No, darling, we're not having a baby and I can almost guarantee that if we did have one, we wouldn't be calling it Katnap or whatever.'

Peg rolled her eyes before burying her head in her colouring book, concentrating on keeping the pink pen within the lines.

Martin chuckled. 'I've got one kid that wants a new baby,' he whispered from the corner of his mouth, 'and another doing his level best to make sure I can't get within four feet of my wife!'

Poppy smiled and thought back to the previous night. Max had woken several times, only settling when ensconced in their bed. It was not quite the evening of passion they had planned.

'Oh, I don't know, you seemed to do okay in the Max-free interludes.'

'That was just me getting started.' Martin grinned at his wife.

'Better get them tucked up early tonight then, Romeo.' She flicked the water and suds from her fingers in his direction.

The door bell rang.

'I'll get it!' Peg jumped off her chair and ran towards the front door, skidding in her socks until she banged right into it.

'It's Aunty Jo!' Peg announced as their neighbour entered with two boxes wrapped in Christmas paper balanced in her arms.

'Are they for Maxy and me?' Peg pranced from foot to foot.

'Peg, don't be rude!' Poppy yelled as she released herself from her husband's grip. She smiled at her daughter, knowing how much fun it was to receive a gift when you thought there were no more in the offing.

Jo shook her head, sending her cascade of dark, glossy curls shivering down her back. She winked at Poppy. 'Actually, no, Peg, these are for Mummy and Daddy.'

'Oh.' Peg kept her smile in place. 'Can I open them for them?'

The two women laughed at the little girl who refused to let her excitement flag.

'Course they're for you, darlin'.' Jo handed the box on top to Peg, who screeched up the stairs, 'Max, wake up! We've got a present!'

Max immediately started to wail. Smoke rose from the eggs in the pan and Peg screamed in excitement as she peeled back the red-foil paper to reveal a pair of roller boots. The alarm began pipping its herald.

'It's a bloody madhouse!' Martin yelled from the kitchen as he opened the window and Poppy began whizzing a tea towel in a helicopter motion below the smoke alarm.

Jo opened the front door and worked it back and forth to try and dilute the smoke. She laughed, happy to be a small part of this chaotic, noisy family.

With Peg content to roll up and down the hallway, oblivious to the irritating rattle of her wheels, and Max diligently counting all his new dinosaurs back into the box from which they had spilled, the three adults sat and sipped at strong tea. The remnants of fried egg sandwiches and sloshes of ketchup littered the plates on the coffee table in front of them.

'When's Danny back then, Jo?' Martin missed his friend and football buddy.

'Ten weeks tomorrow. I can't wait.' Jo beamed.

'It'll be good to see him.' Martin nodded.

'He's had enough, Mart. To be honest, I don't think he's had the best tour and what with all these cuts, he knows he'll be turned around quite quickly and back out again, somewhere. He's seriously thinking of signing off.'

'Sounds familiar.' Poppy sipped at her mug.

Martin sat forward, resting his elbows on his knees. 'It's because it's tough now, Poppy: houses falling apart, too few of us stretched, posts gapped. And the jobs that need doing don't disappear; it just means that with fewer people we all work harder and longer, so you don't even have time to think. Danny and I won't be the only ones thinking of jacking it in. It's a shame, they're losing good men, trained men, but still spending money on recruiting and trying to think of the next big thing. If only they were more efficient and a bit smarter, there'd be fewer people leaving and we'd keep the skills we need.'

'I think people must be having this same conversation on every patch in the country,' Jo said. 'I was talking to some of our old neighbours up in Catterick and everyone is saying the same. Trouble is, there aren't that many jobs once you get out, not now. It's a bloody shame. I don't want to move

– I love my house. Neighbours are a bit of a handful though.' She smiled.

'That's funny.' Poppy sat up straight. 'I feel exactly the same!'

The women were quiet for a second.

'God, if you moved, I'd really miss you, I'd miss the kids.'

Poppy reached over and patted her mate's leg. 'And they'd miss you.' She felt the familiar pang of guilt that Jo had not fulfilled her wish to become a mum when it had come so easily to her. 'Mind you, even if we moved, we'd still see you.'

'Yeah, but it wouldn't be the same.' Jo took a gulp of tea.

'No, I know. But let's not worry about that – you've got Danny back in ten weeks! That's so exciting.'

'Yep, you're right. I wonder how much weight I can lose in ten weeks?'

'Lots, if you stop scoffing biscuits and fried egg sand-wiches!' trilled Peg as she whizzed past the back of the sofa on her roller boots.

Poppy felt her face colour and tried not to notice as Martin's shoulders shook. 'More tea, anyone?'

'I'm getting a new pet, Aunty Jo,' Peg shouted from the hallway.

'Are you? I thought Mummy said no?' Jo looked quizzi-cally at Poppy.

'She did, but Daddy said YES!' Peg shouted.

'She'll give me heart failure, that child, or at the very least send me grey.' Poppy smiled.

Martin pulled a face. 'In fairness, I was put on the spot a bit.'

Jo laughed and addressed Peg's back as she scooted past. 'So, what pet are you getting?'

'A guinea pig – called Katniss!'

'Piss piss!' Max shouted from the rug.

Martin felt a new wave of giggles about to erupt. 'Maybe not Katniss, Peg,' he suggested. 'I thought you wanted to call it Toffee?'

'I did, that's the name that me and Jade came up with, but I prefer Katniss now.'

'Piss piss!' Max shouted again, this time looking at his dad to see if it would get the same reaction.

'I think we're going to go with Toffee.' Martin made the decision; he couldn't have Max shouting that out every five minutes.

'Shall we go today, Dad, and pick him up?'

'Let's do it tomorrow, Peg.'

'Okay!' she shouted as she thundered past and hit the front door. 'Ouch!'

The three adults held their cups still and waited to hear if Peg would pick herself up.

'I'm okay!' she wheezed and stood up ready for another run.

'How much is a guinea pig and all its gubbins going to cost me?' Martin asked as if only just considering the cost.

'A bloody fortune and it serves you right!' Poppy laughed.

At bedtime Martin read Peg and Max *The Gruffalo*, complete with growly Gruffalo voice and squeaky mouse impression. Poppy had tried to do their favourite story justice during his absence, but knew that she didn't come close. Well, as long as they were occupied...

She let the shower run and placed her hand under the warm water. Smiling in the mirror, she felt very lucky. They had been together for over half their lives and still the spark of excitement at the prospect of physical contact hadn't waned. 'You are one lucky girl, Poppy Day. Very, very lucky.'

'Love and luck…' She heard her nan saying her favourite expression, pictured the day she had teased her about getting serious with Martin Cricket. They were sitting opposite each other at the little table in the kitchen, her nan with a roll-up perched between her fingers and a cup of stewed tea in its saucer.

'So, do you love him, Poppy Day? Does he make your tummy go flippy and your face all smoochy?'

'No, Nan, yuk!' she had shouted, although that was exactly how he made her fourteen-year-old self feel.

'I thought you was best mates, you and Mart? And that's no basis for a boyfriend! You're supposed to argue like cat and dog, not be best mates! What kind of a future will that lead to?' Dorothea winked at her granddaughter. 'I'm teasing you, darlin'. I wish you both all the love and luck in the world.'

Poppy smiled into the cascade of water. 'It's been a lovely future, Nan. But you knew it would be, didn't you?'

The hot water ran over her head and body. They had a big day tomorrow, a new addition to the family. She decided to try and feel pleased about the arrival of Toffee the guinea pig; after all, Peg was beside herself with happiness. Maybe she *would* take care of it herself; maybe Poppy wouldn't be lumbered with mucking out a bloody guinea pig as well as everything else that fell under her remit in this house. She laughed. Fat chance.

'Working nine till five…' Poppy sang loudly as she worked the soap into bubbles between her palms.

Three

'Wake up, everybody!' Peg shouted as she jumped up and down on the landing. 'It's today! And we are going to get our new pet!'

Poppy yawned, put her head under the pillow and groaned. 'This is all your fault,' she mumbled. 'You are the worst husband in the whole wide world.'

Martin reached across under the duvet and smacked her bottom. 'That's as maybe, fat arse, but I'm the best dad in the world!'

Poppy smiled into the mattress despite his insult. He probably was the best dad in the world, at least according to the very excited little girl who was running amok on the landing.

Martin jumped out of bed and fastened his dressing gown around his waist. As he opened the door, Peg jumped on him, knocking the wind out of him.

'Blimey, Peg, you nearly pushed me over!'

'I can't help it, Dad. I am so excited!'

'So I gathered. Look at you, all up and dressed.' Martin kissed her cheek.

'I've been ready for ages. Can we leave in a minute and get there when the shop opens?'

'Sure we can. I'll just have a quick shower and grab a cup of coffee. What time is it now?'

'It's nearly five o'clock!' Peg announced.

Poppy raised her head from under the pillow and squinted at the digital clock on Martin's bedside cabinet. Peg was right. Poppy laughed and pulled the duvet over her head, leaving the early morning excitement to the best dad in the whole wide world.

After much coaxing and a few tears, everyone went back to bed for an hour or two. So it was at a much more respectable 8 a.m. that the Cricket family gathered round the dining table for breakfast, with Radio 2 providing the background noise.

Poppy poured juice for Max while Peg shovelled Cheerios into her mouth. She was in too much of a rush to bother swallowing before loading up her spoon for re-entry and her cheeks bulged.

'Peg, *you* look like a guinea pig. Eat nicely please,' Poppy instructed between coffee sips.

Peg gulped her breakfast. 'Can it just be Daddy and me that goes to get Toffee?'. She concentrated on stirring her cereal. This lack of eye contact was enough to alert Poppy.

'I think we'll all go, Peg. It'll be nice for Maxy to see the animals.'

'Max told me he didn't want to go because he thought it might be boring,' Peg mumbled with her mouth full.

'Max said all that?' Poppy looked at her daughter quizzically.

Peg nodded repeatedly.

'Well, after he told you that, he told *me* that he didn't want his big sister making up things that he had said just to get her own way.'

'Diggerduck! One... two... three...' Max shouted as if in confirmation. His words were a little confused, but there was nothing amiss with his counting.

31

Poppy watched Peg's lip curl in dislike at her suggestion. She knew her daughter well enough to guess that if she was left to her own devices and under the very pliable watch of her dad, they would end up with a guinea pig, cat, dog, fish, goat and any other beast that Peg could persuade Martin she couldn't live without. One look at their little forlorn and hopeful faces and Martin would willingly load them into the car, turning their three-bed terrace into a stinky petting zoo. Poppy was not about to let that happen.

Martin stood by the table holding the mail. His fingers stilled and his eyebrows knitted as he pondered an envelope that looked unfamiliar. It caught his eye, standing out among the pizza flyers, taxi leaflets, bank statements and sales literature for a stair lift.

'This one's for you, from...' Martin lifted the envelope to his face and squinted at the postmark that sat in wiggly lines over a beautiful, tropical bird. 'Looks like St Lucia! Who the bloody hell is writing to you from St Lucia?' he quizzed.

'What am I, psychic? How do I know? Open it!' Poppy nodded at the flat blue letter in his palm.

Martin used the stubby end of his index finger to prise open the envelope, then teased out the thin sheet.

'Come on, the suspense is killing me!' Poppy gripped her mug with both hands and stood facing him.

Martin's expression was solemn. 'Jesus.' He pulled a chair from the dining room table and lowered himself onto it. 'This is a weird one, Pop.'

'What is it?' Poppy watched as a crease appeared on the top of his nose.

'It's from some bloke, says he got your address from Cheryl.'

'What bloke? Who's she been giving my address to?' Poppy laughed a little nervously and pulled a face at Peg. If her mum was involved, it probably wasn't anything she wanted to be part of.

Martin read the letter slowly, lowered the sheet of paper and then raised it again for a second read. He looked up at his wife. 'He says he's your uncle.'

'Well, it's obviously a mistake. I haven't got an uncle. My nan's sister Dee was married, so I suppose her husband was my uncle, but he died a long time ago and I never met him. They lived in Canada; she still does.'

Martin took a deep breath. 'He says he's your uncle; Uncle...' He was silent again as his eyes scanned the words and he digested the information. 'I don't know what to make of it. He says Dorothea was his mum.'

Poppy snorted her laughter through her nose. 'That's ridiculous! It's obviously some kind of wind-up. Don't you think my mum would have mentioned that she had a brother! It's a joke, or one of them "Please send me your bank account details and pin number so I can randomly give you some of my inheritance and I promise not to rob you, honest!" Just bin it, Mart.'

He gathered up the letter again and reread it one more time. 'It doesn't sound like a wind-up. He says his name is Simon and he's only a bloody vicar!'

Poppy placed her coffee cup on the table and gripped the back of the chair. Her nan's words flooded her brain with clarity. It was like watching a replay on a screen. She pictured the residential home in which her nan had lived, could see the bright light coming from the neon strip in the hallway, could smell the disinfectant that coated the shiny floor. Poppy had been tired that day: Martin was in Afghanistan and she had been about to leave for home. She'd bent forward and kissed her nan's forehead.

'Goodnight, Nan. Sweet dreams.'

Her nan's voice had boomed against her back, urgent and deliberate. 'Simon. His name was Simon.'

Simon. Simon. That was what she had said and Poppy remembered it like it was yesterday.

'You all right, Poppy? You've gone really pale.' Martin's words drew her into the present.

Poppy slid onto the chair and let her shoulders slump.

'This is so weird, Mart. Years ago, when she was in the home, Nan told me she'd had a baby and she said his name was Simon. I thought it was just her dementia talking, you know what it was like. She told me so many things, including that she'd played the violin with the band on the *Titanic*.' Poppy smiled at that memory. 'But I remember this clearly and it struck me at the time that she was quite with it. She definitely said his name was Simon. I remember... Simon.'

'Bloody hell, Poppy. So you think he's kosher?'

She nodded. 'Yes. And I seem to remember her talking about St Lucia as well, but I can't quite recall what she said. It'll come to me.'

Poppy took the sheet of paper that Martin slid over the tabletop and there it was. She read the information and reread it. He had apparently tracked down her mum and written to her, and Cheryl had given him Poppy's address as the best contact. *Bloody typical.* Her stomach flipped; she felt confused with a frisson of excitement at the idea of this new man in their lives. No matter how unrelated, she couldn't help but think that if this Uncle Simon could track her down, then maybe so could her dad...

'What am I supposed to do now?' Poppy asked.

Martin shrugged. 'You don't have to do anything at all, but if I were you, I'd call him. It's exciting, having family you didn't know about – and in St Lucia! Fancy that! It's in the Caribbean, isn't it?'

Poppy nodded. 'I think so. Just think, Mart, all them tropical beaches with soft, powdery sand.' Poppy closed her eyes and pictured lying on one in her bikini.

'You should call your mum first, find out what it's all about.'

Poppy looked at her husband. He knew how she dreaded contact with Cheryl.

'Ooh, love, just think, he might be a multi-millionaire with a mansion and a great big boat!' Martin laughed.

'I doubt it, he's a bloody vicar!'

'Boat! Three… four… ' Max had a tendency to echo any word that caught his interest and throw in some figures for good measure.

'My clever numbers boy.' Poppy kissed her son on the cheek. 'I suppose you're right, Mart. I should call him.' She hesitated. 'You'd think my mum might have called me before giving out my details.'

'Really? You know what she's like…' Martin let this trail.

Poppy got the message loud and clear. After all these years of lack of interest and poor judgement, did she really expect her mum to change?

Martin was right of course.

Poppy ran her fingers through her hair and gathered it into a ponytail before securing it with one of Peg's elasticated pink bands. 'I lived with my nan my whole life. I can't believe she had a son that I knew nothing about.'

'It must have been before she married Wally,' Martin surmised.

'I suppose so.' Poppy twisted her mouth and reached for her mobile phone. Although she knew it would be the same time of day in Lanzarote, Cheryl sometimes worked all night at the bar and slept all day.

Martin looked at his watch. 'Err… same as here, I think, at the moment. Give it a go. She can always ignore the call.' He raised his eyebrows at her; they both knew she would do so without a moment's hesitation.

Poppy closed her eyes and ran her palm over her face before punching the screen to locate her mum's number. She hated calling her; was never sure of the reception she would get. She flexed her fingers and blinked at the screen.

'S'all right, I'm here.' Martin tried to reassure her.

'Can I tell Cheryl that I'm getting a pet?' Peg piped up.

'We'll see,' Poppy whispered. It struck her like a tiny dagger, every time Peg referred to her mum as Cheryl and not Nan, although she understood, perfectly; Cheryl was a vague and distant character in the kids' lives. Nan was a term that Cheryl had in no way earned, quite unlike Granny Claudia.

''Ello.' Her voice was gruff, irritated.

'Mum?'

'Is that you, Poppy?' Cheryl's tone lifted slightly.

'Yes.' Poppy sighed. Who else in the world would call her 'Mum'? Although as the point of the call was to enquire after an uncle that had appeared from nowhere, who knew what other skeletons lay in the cupboard?

'Everything all right, love?'

Poppy heard the unmistakable sound of a flint sparking, probably igniting the first cigarette of the day.

'Yes. Fine. Is this a good time to talk?' Poppy hoped it wasn't and that she could end the call. Put it off till later.

'Yeah, go on. Me and Frank aren't up yet, but he's snoring like a bleedin' whale and I can listen.'

Poppy cringed. She had no idea who Frank was, but she could picture him: another fat, sweaty, boozing lech. She had met enough of Cheryl's 'Franks' throughout her childhood to know the type.

'Right. It's just that we got a letter today. A letter from St Lucia…'

Poppy paused, hoping that was enough information to prompt her mum's response. Apparently it wasn't.

She heard her mum draw deeply on her cigarette. 'Oh yeah?' She sounded uninterested.

Poppy continued. 'From someone called Simon? Apparently you gave him my details. He says he's my uncle. Your brother.'

The penny dropped. 'Oh that,' Cheryl said, as though they were discussing something of no consequence. 'Blimey, that was a turn-up for the books, wasn't it? Fancy Dot getting up to no good with a black man, dirty cow. And him being a vicar! I nearly wet meself laughing! I wonder, what would he have made of her and Wally – don't think they ever went into a church, apart from when they were dead!' Cheryl started one of her cackling laughs that quickly turned to wheezing and pretty soon she was emitting a throaty cough.

Poppy held the phone at arm's length, wanting to distance herself from her mother's germs and comments. Eventually she pulled the phone back towards her ear. 'So what happened, Mum? Apparently he sent you a letter?'

Cheryl wasn't finished. 'Yeah, something like that. It was a while back. To tell the truth, I can't be arsed with it, Poppy Day, but I thought you might like to hook up with him. I figured, I've managed my whole life without a brother, particularly some Holy Joe – don't reckon I have the need of one now. Can you imagine? I'm a bit too far gone for saving. Unless you think I could become a nun – what d'you reckon, Frank? Shall I become a nun?'

Poppy couldn't make out the growl of words that the recently awakened Frank issued at the suggestion. 'Did Nan never mention it to you, Mum? I seem to remember her saying something to me before she died about a baby and his name was Simon, but as I said to Mart, I thought it was just her dementia talking. It's quite amazing, isn't it?'

'If you say so, love.' Cheryl took another drag on her ciggie. 'How's your lot?'

My lot... Poppy wondered if her mum could actually recall their names. She looked at her blond-haired boy, pushing a piece of toast around the table as if it were a vehicle; at her husband standing close by, concern etched on his face, waiting to mop up the fallout that inevitably followed any contact with her mother; and at Peg, who was mouthing 'Tell her we're getting a pet!' She smiled at all the family she needed, all the family that she had ever needed.

'They're wonderful, really wonderful. I'll let you go, Mum. Speak soon.'

'Oh. All right, love. Merry Christmas.'

Poppy closed her eyes. It was January the second. 'Yes. Merry Christmas.'

Martin sat down next to his wife. 'Well, that was quick. Did you learn anything?'

Poppy ran her fingers over the fine script of Simon's handwriting, hoping that he was part of a family that made him feel safe and secure and that he was loved by someone in the way that she loved Martin; unlike Cheryl, who sadly had neither. Maybe Martin was right: it was exciting.

'I learnt that my mum hasn't changed a bit, her latest

beau is called Frank and apparently he snores. Oh, and my uncle, her brother, the vicar who she has no interest in seeing, is black. That about sums it up.'

Martin laid his hand over his wife's. 'Wow!'

'Yep,' Poppy confirmed. 'Wow.'

Four

Peg raced ahead into the store as Poppy and Martin strolled at the pace of the pushchair-free Max, who was following slowly in her wake. By the time they caught up with her, she was chatting to Jackson, who was resplendent in his uniform polo shirt and baseball cap; he was apparently an expert on small pets, if the badge on his shirt was anything to go by. Poppy caught the tail end of Peg's introduction.

'So, any of them would be good, really. By the way, my mum's uncle is black too, but I've never met him and he never actually met his mum, who is dead now, because he was born out of wedlock.' Peg smiled.

Poppy stared at Martin. *Out of wedlock?* Where on earth had she got that?

Jackson turned to Poppy with a look close to fear in his eyes.

'Hi, Jackson.' Poppy repeated the name on his badge. 'Sorry about my daughter, she is full of useless bits of information. The important thing is, we are here to get a pet.'

'Yes, she said.' He glanced briefly at Peg. 'Although I'm not sure we can help.'

'No? Oh, that's a shame. We thought it would be quite straightforward.' Poppy looked at the rows of cages and tanks that seemed to be crammed full of tiny animals all wanting to come and live in their house. She wondered if Peg had offended him in some way.

'It *is* usually quite straightforward, but we don't have otters, badgers or baby lion cubs here.'

'Peg!' Poppy shouted. 'We've told you, a guinea pig or nothing. Sorry, Jackson.'

He shrugged; it obviously wasn't the strangest request he'd ever had.

Peg bounced a pet ball she had found on the floor. 'I was only asking!'

Peg had to be prised away from Toffee at bedtime. He was apparently the best thing she had ever had, ever! 'Even better than Maxy!' Poppy and Martin decided to ignore the last bit.

Poppy sat on the sofa with her head on Martin's shoulder. The lamplight made everything look cosy. He poured them both a large glass of wine, which they nursed as they chatted, their stockinged feet stretched out and resting on the coffee table.

She stroked her husband's forearm. 'This is nice.'

'Oh, it's more than nice. It's everything. When I'm away, I dream of sitting on this sofa with you next to me, sharing a bottle.'

Poppy snuggled closer. 'I feel sad that Nan couldn't tell me about her baby sooner, couldn't tell anyone.'

Martin nodded. It was sad.

'I would have helped her find him, or something, I don't know. Or at least tried to make her feel better about everything.'

'I don't think there would have been a lot you could have said, love. She must have carried it with her always.'

'I know and I can't imagine what that must have been

like. If I think of not seeing Maxy, God, even the idea of it is horrible. It must have ripped her in two.' Poppy gulped her wine, enjoying the warmth it produced in her throat and chest. It soothed the ache that had appeared suddenly, at the idea of not being there every night to tuck her son into bed and every morning to kiss him when he stumbled into her arms, crumpled and groggy from sleep.

'Do you think that's why she was a bit…' Martin verbally tiptoed, trying to find the right word. 'Eccentric?' he settled on.

Poppy smiled at him, knowing he had wanted to say 'loopy'. 'Who knows? It can't have helped, can it? Keeping secrets like that can't be good for anyone and if she was hurting as well for all those years… That's enough to send anyone a bit eccentric.'

'Are you going to contact him?'

'I think so. I just don't know what to say. I'm working up to it.'

'Do it now! While you've got some Dutch courage.' Martin clinked his glass against hers.

'Oh, yes, that'll be good, me half cut. He'll think I'm as bad as me mother.'

Martin laughed. 'You are in no way, not one single bit, like your mother.' He shuddered at the comparison.

'I think I'll wait a bit, Mart, before I call him. Get my head round the idea and think about what I should say. It feels like a big deal and I want to get it right.'

'It is a big deal!' he confirmed. 'It's not every day a new uncle turns up.'

'You don't think there are more of them waiting to leap out of the woodwork do you?' Poppy looked aghast at the prospect.

'Well, if there is, mate, we are definitely going to have to start budgeting better for Christmas. All those pairs of socks and chocolates can really mount up.'

Poppy laughed. 'I think that's what Danny's got waiting for him when he comes home. Jo's bought up half of Marks and Sparks.'

'It must be rotten not having kids to buy for when all you wanted was to be a mum,' Martin said.

'I know; rotten for both of them. I feel sorry for her really. I've told her that you can't have everything and that she and Danny are lucky: no sicky kids in the middle of the night, no early starts when all you want is another five minutes in bed. They can be spontaneous! Go to the cinema or even on holiday. We can't do any of that. I said she was lucky in some ways.' Poppy sipped her wine.

'And did she believe your lies?' Martin pulled her towards him.

'I don't know.'

'You wouldn't swap broken nights and early starts for a day without them, would you?'

Poppy thought again of Dorothea having to give up her little boy. 'No. No, I wouldn't, Mart, not one single day.'

'Poor Jo.'

'Yep, poor Jo.'

They both jumped as Toffee moved in his cage; they had forgotten he was there. They giggled as they hugged each other; a hug that led to kissing and kissing that led to them creeping up the stairs and pulling the chest of drawers across their bedroom door, which they routinely did whilst simultaneously shedding their clothes and giggling into their palms.

Poppy left Martin snoring and quietly descended the stairs, knowing she wouldn't be able to nod off until her chores were finished. The kitchen needed a bit of a tidy; she liked to plump the cushions before she went up so it was just so in the morning; and she wanted to put the rubbish in the wheelie bin. She laid out Peg's clean uniform on the dining table, ready for the first day back at school, and placed her little rucksack next to the front door. Martin was going to take her in tomorrow as per her request. Poppy didn't mind a bit, she knew the novelty of having her daddy home wasn't going to wear off anytime soon.

Poppy slipped into the bathroom and ran the shower, letting the water run over her head. Poor Jo. She felt a jolt of sadness for all the things her mate missed by not having kids. It seemed unfair that there were women like Jo who longed for children and women like Cheryl who conceived with ease but then didn't want them when they arrived. There was so much her mum missed. Simon would be one more thing to add to the list, along with family birthdays, Christmases and a place in her children's hearts.

Poppy was distracted, thinking alternately about Peg's packed lunch, the mysterious Simon and the fact that he lived in a warm, sunny climate on the other side of the world while *his* mum had never left London. She wondered if Dorothea would have liked to have gone somewhere hot and exotic.

Suddenly, her thoughts crystallised. With clarity and poise, she stood upright and held her breath. For there, beneath her soapy hand, sitting in the gap between her breast and her armpit, was a little lump.

It made her jump, so odd and unexpected was the discovery. She ran her hand over her breast and shoulder, before snaking back to where it was sited. Yes, there it was. Her heart skipped a beat.

'What the...?' she murmured into the steam.

Poppy felt it beneath her fingers, squeezed it and skimmed it with the flat of her hand, making sure she hadn't imagined it, seeing if it might move. It didn't. She then checked on the other side of her torso, hoping to find the little mound mirrored on the opposite side of her body, making it nothing out of the ordinary but simply a little part of herself that she had previously been unaware of. Hidden. Like one of Jupiter's regularly revealed new moons, or the flabby whale-fish discovered in New Zealand at the bottom of the ocean – always there, just undiscovered. Maybe this was like that, a little nub that had always been present but that she had somehow missed, nothing to worry about.

She raised her arm above her head as her hopeful fingers systematically explored the white skin beneath it, inching across the area from her chest to her ribs. Poppy swallowed the disappointment. There wasn't one on the other side. Nothing, no matter how vigorously she searched.

Instinctively she went back to the lump. She felt a little faint and realised that she was still holding her breath. She exhaled and leant her head on the shower door.

This little thing, no bigger than a baked bean, was large enough to leave her shivering inside the cubicle despite the water temperature, which was if anything a fraction too hot. It was a small nodule but it left Poppy feeling sick with foreboding. The bean-sized lump was already casting a shadow the size of a boulder over her and her family.

Poppy turned off the water and climbed out of the shower cubicle, then wrapped herself in the one big bath towel they owned, a huge sheet that had been a present from Claudia the previous year. She wiped the steam from the mirror and stared at her reflection.

45

Instantly, Poppy saw a face looming over her shoulder. Her nan's face. She was smiling and gave a little nod before she spoke. 'The world keeps turning, girl. Life goes on.'

And Poppy knew, just like that. She knew exactly how the story of this little lump would unfold. She touched her fingers to the node and gazed at the mirror as Dot disappeared into the ether. Her nan was right: the world would keep on turning, no matter what.

Poppy turned and looked around the empty bathroom before placing her hand on the space in the mirror where her nan had appeared. She let out a deep sigh.

Five

Philip Grant OBE, 72, passed away peacefully at home. Devoted husband of Jenny and father of Kate and Emma. Philip was an ex Royal Marine and lifelong supporter of the RNLI, which is where we would like donations sent instead of flowers. Thank you for all your kind wishes at this time.

Poppy wondered what Philip had died of. It irritated her when they didn't say – not that it was any of her business, she was just nosey. She folded the paper and left it on the table with the out-of-date gardening magazines and the ten identical copies of the local glossy, which was full of adverts for boutiques and flooring shops and included an article on how to make your own bird feeder out of a pair of tights and some leftover stuffing. Her name was flashing on the new hi-tech system in the surgery. She was to report to Room 4, apparently.

Poppy gathered up her coat and scarf, which kept the winter chill from her skin, and made her way along the corridor, noting the garish royal blue carpet squares and yellow walls.

The door to Room 4 was ajar. 'Hello! Come in!' A cheery voice beckoned her inside.

Poppy hadn't met the lady doctor before. She was smiley, rosy-cheeked and make-up-free. She looked to Poppy like the type that would wear hand-knitted jumpers, take brisk walks and pack a flask of soup for the occasion.

'Hi there, Mrs Cricket. I'm Dr Jessop, what can I do for you today?' She cut to the chase. No matter how friendly, time was of the essence. There was a roomful of people out there, some snivelling into damp tissues and others with hacking coughs, all waiting to see their name up in lights.

Poppy dumped her coat, scarf and bag on the floor as she sat down. 'Oh, well, it's probably nothing, but I've found a lump. Just here.' It was Poppy's turn to cut to the chase. She pointed through her shirt to the space just behind her bra strap.

'Oh, right. Do you mind if I have a look?'

The smiley doctor sat forward as Poppy undid the buttons and shrugged her left arm from her top. She placed her hand behind her back, exposing as much of the area as possible.

'I'm just going to have a little prod, if that's okay?'

'Sure.' Poppy smiled, embarrassed.

Dr Jessop rubbed her palms together before laying her hand on the lump and pushing at it with her index finger. Poppy watched as her smile slipped a little.

'And you noticed it when?' The doctor's fingers pushed, patted and pushed again, then felt the skin around it.

'Couple of days ago, when I was in the shower. I mean, it's weird, really, I shower every night and yet I've never felt it before.'

'Is it causing you any pain, weeping at all?'

Poppy shook her head. No and no. 'It's a little tender around it, but that's probably where *I've* been having a prod.' She gave a small laugh as she borrowed the doctor's phrase.

'I don't like the look of it,' the doctor stated, quite matter-of-factly, 'but nothing to worry about, not at this stage. Let's get it looked at by an expert and we can go from there. How does that sound?'

'Sounds fine.' Poppy had so many questions, but they all

felt a little premature, embarrassing. Suppose it turned out to be nothing? She would wait.

The GP tapped at her keyboard. 'I'm referring you to the breast cancer clinic, just to be on the safe side. The process is all quite joined up, so I'll be kept in the loop and they can see you in…' She ran her finger across the screen and clicked her tongue against her teeth. 'Ten days. Shall I book that for you?'

Poppy nodded. *Breast cancer clinic… Holy shit.* 'Yes, thank you.'

The words 'breast cancer clinic' had tripped off the doctor's tongue, but even hearing them spoken out loud filled Poppy with a cold dread. She decided to keep it to herself. No point causing a fuss, not with Martin only just home and going back to work with his unit and Peg starting a new term. She'd tell Martin when it was all over.

'Mum!' Peg shouted the second Poppy placed her key in the door. 'Come and see what Toffee can do!' She grabbed her mum's hand and ran with her to the corner of the dining area, where Toffee's monstrous cage, the guinea pig equivalent of Center Parcs, had pride of place.

'Kneel down here.' Peg pointed to the floor next to where she crouched. Poppy did as she was told and knelt in front of the cage. She watched as Peg held a sliver of carrot through the bars. 'Right, Toffee, come on, remember what I taught you, say "din-dins"!'

Poppy collapsed on the floor in a heap, rendered helpless with laughter. She clutched at her sides and laughed until her tears pooled.

'It's not funny, Mummy! I've been teaching him since I got in from school!'

'You've been teaching him to speak?' she managed through her giggles.

'Yes! And he can say "din-dins" and "goodbye".' Peg folded her arms across her chest, infuriated by her mum's response.

Martin came in from the garden. 'What's so funny, girls?'

'Mummy's being a bit mean to me.' Peg pouted.

'I'm sorry, love, I can't help it.' She looked at her husband. 'Peg has spent the time allocated for her homework teaching Toffee to speak and apparently he can now say "din-dins" and "goodbye".'

Martin sniggered and leant on the table. 'Well, that is wonderful. I've always wondered how I can make my million! We have a talking guinea pig, whoohoo!' He clapped his hands. 'I'm phoning the BBC right now.'

'I hate you both.' Peg jumped up and flounced from the room, then vaulted up the stairs and slammed her bedroom door.

Poppy trod the stairs and knocked as she entered Peg's bedroom. Her little girl was curled on top of the duvet, facing the wall. Poppy sat on the edge of the mattress and stroked Peg's back.

'I'm sorry I laughed. I think it's wonderful that you have the patience to teach Toffee to talk.'

Peg rolled over. 'I was really good all day today, Mum, but I still wasn't picked to be register monitor.'

'Oh well, that doesn't matter, love.'

Peg's bottom lip trembled. 'It matters to me.'

'Come here.' Poppy gathered up her daughter and hugged her into her chest. She winced as Peg's small hand came within inches of the lump that sat like a secret between them.

'It'll all be okay, Peg. Going back to school, new term,

Daddy coming home, all of that stuff can make you feel a bit out of sorts, but it will all be okay. Everything will settle down, you'll see.'

'Promise?' Peg sniffed and wiped her nose on her mum's shirt.

'I promise.' Poppy closed her eyes and hoped that she wasn't lying.

* * *

Ten days later, Peg was still exhausted from being back at school, bodily shocked at having to get up early every morning and concentrate for six or so hours a day. She and Max were already tucked up in bed, leaving Martin to eat his supper in peace and Poppy to get on with the washing-up, her arms immersed up to her elbows in the suds.

Martin tucked into his shepherd's pie with relish. 'This is lovely, Pop. I really missed your cooking while I was away.'

'Blimey, the food must have been bad!' She laughed.

'Don't put yourself down, you're a smashing cook. Even if your repertoire is a bit limited, what you do, you do really well.' He beamed at her as he filled his mouth with mashed potato.

'Thank you – I think.' She narrowed her eyes at him. 'I can't work out if you are being nice or having a dig.'

'What have you done today?' he asked, casually, as he always did, only half listening to her response.

She answered in the same manner. 'Oh, you know, took Peg to school, dropped Maxy with Jo, went to that dentist appointment I told you about...' She turned away from him: easier to lie without looking him in the face.

'All okay?' he enquired as he reached for the bottle of

ketchup that he would quite happily slather over any and every dish of cooked food.

She nodded. *Yes, all okay. They took a biopsy and it hurt and I had a scan and gave some blood. They'll call me in three to ten days and give me the results. Even being in the building made me feel really, really scared. I'm really scared, Mart.*

'Do you want some pud?' she asked, brightly. 'I've got some ice cream, I could open a tin of peaches to go with it?'

'See! And there's you saying you aren't all cordon bleu! Peaches and ice cream would be lovely.'

Poppy reached for the sauce bottle. 'I assume you don't want this on your ice cream?'

'No, of course not. I don't need to disguise the taste of that.'

'You cheeky sod!' She swiped at the back of his head with her cupped palm.

'Tell you what, why don't we Skype Simon after tea? Shall I look and see what the time is in St Lucia?' Martin was animated.

''Fyalike.' Poppy felt nervous. She watched as, between mouthfuls, Martin opened his laptop on the table. Almost immediately the Google result showed that it was half three in the afternoon.

'Come on, Pop, that's a good time, let's do it!'

'I don't know...' She squirmed, biting her bottom lip.

'I'm right by your side. If you feel uncomfortable at any point, then we can cut the connection, make out it was a technical problem. And if you don't like him or he's a weirdo, we need never contact him again!' Martin placed the last of his supper in his mouth and pushed the meat and mash-smeared plate away from him.

Poppy knew he wasn't going to give up. 'Okay, then.' She

combed her fingers through her hair and pulled her T-shirt sleeves down, then ran her tongue over her teeth.

Martin opened the Skype site and tapped in the details Simon had sent, asking to be accepted as a contact. Simon was obviously prepared, keen and online; it came back with an almost immediate yes.

'Oh God! Supposing he's a right religious nutter or something?' She pulled a face at Martin.

'Then it's Plan A, remember? We end the call and say it was a technical fault. This'll be easy. You ready?'

Poppy shook her head, but Martin clicked on the contact anyway and before she had a chance to panic, the call was being answered.

And just like that, there he was. Her uncle. Smiling at her from St Lucia. Poppy felt an inexplicable wave of sadness that she was unprepared for: what wouldn't Dorothea have given to be connected to her son via a couple of clicks, just once in all those years.

He looked like a big man, with a wide smile showing perfect teeth, and hair that sat in braids that reached his shoulders. He was wearing a white T-shirt that showed off his muscled neck and chest. Despite being a couple of years older than Cheryl, he looked a lot younger.

Simon shook his head and when he spoke, he too sounded quite choked with emotion. He beamed at her from the screen. 'Well, well, well. I must admit, Poppy, I am feeling quite nervous!' His voice was slow and deep.

'Oh God, me too.' Poppy swallowed and regretted using the word God – was it okay when talking to vicars? She didn't really know. 'You sound a bit American.'

'Ah, Canadian actually. That was where I grew up and went to school.'

'Was it cold there?' Poppy felt the spread of a blush. *Was it cold?* She didn't know why she'd said that! She wiped her hands on her arms to remove the cool layer of sweat from her palms and gulped to moisten her dry mouth. Her nervousness was palpable.

'Yes, sometimes very. Bit different to here.' Simon leant back and moved to the right and Poppy could see the lush green of spiky plants and palm trees against a bright, blue sky. He was sitting on a veranda of sorts.

'Oh wow! That looks beautiful!'

'It is.' Simon came back into focus. 'And you guys are in Wiltshire?'

'Yes, it's cold and dark right now, night time. Do you know Wiltshire?' Again she shook her head, feeling as if she kept saying the wrong thing.

'I went to Bath and then Stonehenge once and you are near there, right?'

Poppy nodded. He had been that close to her home… 'Yes, very near.'

Simon laughed. 'Ah, I knew it wouldn't be long before Little Miss Nosey appeared.' He beckoned with his hand and up on the screen popped a little girl with cornrow braids, large, clear eyes and a smile that split her face in two. 'This is Matilda,' he announced.

Matilda pushed her face close to the camera so she filled the screen, which made Poppy and Martin laugh. 'Hi, Matilda, how old are you?'

'Nearly ten,' she whispered.

'Hey! We have a little girl, Peg, she's not far off your age.' Poppy felt herself relax for the first time: talking to a little girl was something she was well practised at.

'Can I see her now?' Matilda peered into their room.

'She's tucked up in bed. It's quite late here and she's got school tomorrow.' Poppy smiled.

'Me too.' Matilda beamed before running out of view, her curiosity satisfied.

'Isn't this something, Poppy? Technology, eh?'

Poppy nodded. No need for Plan A; talking to Simon was easy, he was far from a weirdo and she was fascinated. 'I'm so glad you got in contact with us, Simon. It's lovely.'

It was his turn to nod. 'Yes, it is lovely. Unexpected and wonderful!' He clapped his hands together and they all laughed.

'This is Martin. My husband.' Poppy stretched out her palm towards Martin.

Martin came into view and waved. It was his turn to feel a little awkward.

'Hey, Martin, how you doing?'

'Doing great – apart from the Spurs at the weekend, not the best result.'

'Well I'm an Arsenal fan, so you won't hear any complaints from me!'

'You are? What a shame, I was just beginning to like you.' They both chuckled. 'How come you support Arsenal?'

Simon considered this. 'I think my mum and dad, despite having whisked me off to Canada, wanted me to retain some of my Britishness. I'm a Londoner after all, thanks to Dorothea.'

'It feels really weird hearing you talk about my nan.'

Simon sighed. 'It is weird. Strange for me that you knew my birth mother. I have so many questions, I have to stop myself from bombarding you with them.'

'You can ask me anything!' Poppy meant it.

Simon hesitated. 'Do I look anything like her?' His voice was quieter.

Poppy stared at him. 'You look familiar and so I suppose yes, a bit.'

Simon exhaled and pinched the bridge of his nose. 'Ain't that something? I wish my wife were here. She's the one that got the ball rolling, made the first enquiries. She's just nipped out, she'll be mad to have missed this momentous occasion.'

'There'll be others,' Poppy confirmed. 'Why don't you call later in the week, when she's with you and we can have a proper catch-up.'

'I'd like that very much. God bless, Poppy. Bye, Martin, and thanks both, it means the world to me that you got in touch.'

Poppy waved goodbye to her uncle and just like that, he was gone.

They sat back in the dining chairs. 'That was bloody surreal.' Martin spoke for them both. 'He seems like a really nice bloke, apart from being a Gooner.'

'He does, doesn't he?' Poppy agreed. 'I can't believe we're related, but it's true what I said, he does seem familiar, and there's something about the way he looks.'

'And not too vicary,' Martin added.

'No, not at all vicary, in fact quite normal really. It was lovely when he said "God bless", wasn't it? Special.'

Poppy wondered if Matilda was his daughter or his grand-daughter. She couldn't get over how Simon looked so much younger than her mum; maybe that was what a life of Jesus instead of gin did for you. She laughed as she considered whether she should recommend it to Cheryl and imagined her mother's two-word response.

Six

Dr Jessop called and left a rather chirpy message asking her to 'nip in'. Poppy was delighted at the lack of urgency in her tone.

She pushed Max through the light drizzle, which was melting the very last dregs of snow that lay in thin grey clusters on the verges and kerbs. She wandered up past the shops, waved at a mum from school who was out walking her dog and nodded at the man who owned the kebab shop as he unloaded cans of drink on cardboard pallets from the back of his van.

Max laughed and counted out loud. 'Two... three... four... six...'

Poppy patted the plastic roof of his pushchair. 'That's close enough, Maxy.'

In the warmth of the surgery waiting room, she watched Max fall asleep in his little anorak and blue wellies and rocked the handles to keep him dozing. Finally her name flashed up and she entered Room 4 with a sense of déjà vu. Dr Jessop wasn't quite so smiley today and there was no hint of the jovial tone that had brightened her phone message. This did nothing to ease Poppy's nerves. She watched the doctor's eyes widen at the sight of her little boy. *Yes, I'm a mum.*

Poppy took in the bland, box-like room. Its curtained-off area was so small that despite the attempt at privacy, its very proximity to the doctor and her desk made undressing a little uncomfortable. She scanned the poster on the wall, a sketch of the human body without skin. Its veins, organs and bones were exposed. She wondered if that was how medics viewed people – as nothing more than a collection of tubes, pouches, pumps and liquids. It probably made their jobs a little easier.

There must have been some preamble or wider discussion, but Poppy wasn't interested in that. Only one sentence stuck in her mind: 'You have cancer.'

Her thoughts flew to the hundreds of people she knew who had been given a similar diagnosis. 'Poor old Mrs Collins, she's got cancer.' 'Heard about Jake's dad? He's got the big C. It's not looking good, poor thing.' 'We're trying to raise money for Jane at work, she's got cancer.' The last three words whispered through pursed lips. 'She just lost her mum… Cancer.' 'My nan died… Cancer.' The list was endless. All those people for whom she had felt a flicker of sadness as she'd received the news – offered incidentally at the school gate, in the supermarket or over the phone – but without really caring. They had a disease that felt remote from her life. Only now it wasn't, now it would be underlining her every thought and lurking in every corner.

I have cancer. I have cancer. Cancer. That can't be right, not cancer, not me! This is something that happens to other people, like car crashes or flooding. This can't be happening to me. I don't believe you. I don't.

It didn't matter how many times she repeated it inside her head, it still felt unreal.

Dr Jessop was informative, businesslike, and it helped. There was no room for emotion or panic: she made the whole thing sound almost commonplace.

'They are going to perform some further tests and we will

go from there and decide on what will be the best course of treatment for you. I'm referring you to an oncologist, who will be your primary care point, but I'm still here. The thing you need to remember, Poppy, and I say this to all my cancer patients, is that this is new to you and very shocking, but the team that will care for you do this day in and day out. You are in the very best hands.'

Poppy nodded but took little comfort from her reassurances. She was stunned and quite unable to ask the hundred questions that battered her lips.

'Here's my number, call me any time and I will get back to you as soon as I can if I can't take your call immediately.'

Poppy took the little slip of paper with a telephone number scrawled on it and nodded again.

'The breast cancer clinic will call when they have your other results. We are not quite in panic mode yet, you know that, don't you?'

And for the third time in as many minutes, Poppy could only nod.

She walked home slowly. The man who owned the kebab shop was placing his 'Open' sign on the grass verge; he smiled and waved. Poppy stared at him, unable to reconcile the fact that in the half hour since she had last seen him, her world had changed; changed with the utterance of three words. *You have cancer.*

As Poppy and the sleeping Max made their way up the path towards home, Jo spied them from her sitting room window. She raced to the front door and shouted across to her friend.

'Cuppa?'

'Sure!' Poppy smiled and fished in her bag for her key. Jo disappeared and reappeared seconds later with her cardigan over her arm and her phone and keys in her hand. Poppy had really wanted to lie in a darkened room alone and plan the conversation she would have with Martin, but life wasn't like that, it didn't make allowances, not even today.

'You look knackered, mate,' Jo observed.

'I am a bit.'

Jo patted her arm as the two entered the house. 'Tell you what, you sit down and I'll make us a nice drink.'

Poppy nodded. *Lovely*. A nice cup of tea was the cure for most ills, but not today, not for this. She felt a bit third party, shocked, and yet chose to carry on as normal, delaying the moment of impact for as long as possible.

Martin was collecting Peg from after-school club today. Poppy relished the moments of silence as she sat on the sofa while Jo pottered in their kitchen. She let her eyes drift over their home. Home. Where they lived. A little family with all their belongings safely under the roof and pictures of them smiling on the walls. Home, where a trampoline sat in the back garden that they bounced on in celebration of new babies, new teeth and new years. She tried to imagine this little house without her in it, but couldn't.

Don't be silly, dramatic; it's a disease, like the flu. You'll just have medicine and get better and then run that race in a pink T-shirt, grateful for having won.

'To tell you the truth, Poppy,' Jo called from the kitchen, 'I'm really fed up. Danny's being a right tosser.'

'Oh?' Poppy focused on her friend's words, glad of the distraction.

'He's being really off on the phone and I keep making suggestions, things we should do when he gets back, and he's just like, *whatever*... It's driving me mad. I know it's tough for him, but it ain't exactly a picnic for me, stuck here.'

'You should talk to him.' Poppy sipped at the mug of tea Jo had placed on the coffee table in front of her; it was too hot.

Jo laughed. 'It's easy for you and Mart, that's what you would do, but it's not like that for us, we don't talk about anything. We just muddle through and hope it's all going in the right direction and we only talk when we argue. That's how we move things forward and I know that sounds like shit, but that's how it's always been.'

Poppy grimaced. It didn't sound like much fun.

'You're so lucky, you know.' Jo nodded at the photo of Poppy, Martin and the kids on the wall.

In some ways. Poppy smiled, tightly.

'Mart's one in a million, Poppy.'

'Well, we've had a lot of years to get it right, I suppose. We kind of grew up together and so there's no drama, he's just always been there and we've always been together.' She was aware that sounded a little smug. She smiled as she heard the noisy duo progressing up the path. 'Talk of the devil!'

Peg ran up. 'Aunty Jo! Would you like a makeover?'

'Oh, well, I hadn't planned on one, but I think I could probably do with new lipstick?' Jo pursed her lips. 'What do you think?'

'I think yes!' Peg clapped her hands and raced off to find her make-up bag. 'I'll chuck you down some tissue and you can wipe that old colour off. It makes your teeth look yellow anyway.'

Poppy placed her hands over her eyes. 'Jo, what am I going to do with her?'

Jo laughed. 'I don't know, mate, but I don't think the diplomatic corps will be calling up any time soon.'

'I'm going to be a pilot!' Peg yelled from upstairs as she

rummaged in her cupboard, locating her collection of lipsticks and brushes.

Martin whipped off his beret and smiled at Max, still asleep in his buggy, his fat little legs hanging down. He had been wheeled into the lounge and parked in front of them.

'Look at him, proper zonked out.' Martin chuckled and returned to the hallway to collect the mail.

Poppy stared at her son, wistfully, framing the memory forever. 'I know how he feels.' She yawned.

Jo reached out and lightly touched Max's hair. 'They are even more beautiful when they're asleep, aren't they?'

Poppy noted the resigned tone in Jo's voice. 'They are,' she agreed.

'I wonder what ours would have looked like.' Jo stared at the sleeping Max and didn't seem to require an answer. 'D'you want a coffee, Mart?' she whispered.

'Yes, cheers, Jo, that'll be lovely. It's been quite a day. What's up with my missus? You on strike?'

Martin stood in the doorway of the lounge, shuffling the stack of mail, scanning the logos and text of each envelope before placing it at the bottom of the pile.

'Ha! I love how you think it's my job to make the drinks! Actually I was just going to offer everyone some toast, as I haven't even thought about tea yet, but you can whistle now.'

'Get in the kitchen, woman! Toast is what we need.' He pointed towards the kitchen and winked at his wife. Then he turned to Jo. 'Heard from Danny?'

Jo exhaled through bloated cheeks and shook her head. 'Don't ask. He's driving me bonkers.' She tapped the spoon against the side of the mug and reached into the fridge for milk, comfortable in her neighbour's kitchen.

'How long now till he's back from his holiday in the sun

and can drive you bonkers in person?' Martin asked. He was keen to defend his mate, who was probably struggling on tour, no doubt missing home and wishing his view was anything but the barren, dusty landscape that lay outside his tent.

'About six weeks or so.' Jo, oblivious to his dig, placed Martin's mug of coffee on the sideboard.

The toast popped up and Poppy went to fetch it. She laid it on the breadboard and reached for the butter knife that was staked into the carton.

Max yelled to alert everyone that he was awake. 'I'll grab him!' Jo eagerly swooped on his buggy.

'Peg, toast!' Poppy shouted up the stairs as she cut the slices into triangles. She placed them on two small plates and set them on the table.

Clutching her lipsticks and brushes, Peg took a seat at the table; Jo joined her, with Max on her lap. Max grabbed the toast and began tearing at it with his front teeth.

Poppy felt the room spinning; she gripped the chair to steady herself. 'I'm really sorry to be rude, Jo, but I think I'm going to go and have a lie down, I don't feel too good.'

'That's fine. Are you all right, mate?' Jo settled Max on the chair and reached for her cardigan, phone and keys. 'Actually, you don't look great. Think you're coming down with something?'

Poppy shrugged. 'Maybe.'

'Can I do anything, get you some paracetamol, look after the kids?'

'Thanks, honey, but we're fine.' Poppy wanted her to go so she could lie down.

'I was thinking of heading off anyway,' Jo lied. 'I'll leave you lot to it.'

'But I need to do your lipstick!' Peg wailed.

'Tell you what, Peg, I'll come back tomorrow and we can finish off then, okay?'

'S'pose.' Peg thrust her bottom lip out to show her disapproval.

It was early evening and the kids were tucked up. Martin, having washed up the tea things, went upstairs and sat on the bed where his wife lay bathed in the honey-coloured glow of the lamplight.

'How you feeling, babe?'

Poppy sat up. 'Bit better now, thanks. Sorry to leave you lumbered, I just felt crappy.'

'Reckon you've been overdoing it. Maybe it was more of a shock hearing about Simon and your nan than you let on. I still don't know what to make of it all.'

'Me either,' Poppy agreed. 'It's weird, isn't it?'

'I'm a bit worried about you.' He ran his fingers over the bare arm that poked from under the duvet.

Poppy took his hand in hers as she sat up straight and supported herself against the pillows propped behind her. She gave a small cough. 'I went to the doctor's today...'

'You did?'

'Yes.' Poppy scanned the ceiling, mentally searching for the right words.

'You all right?' He sounded a little impatient, irritated to have been left out of the loop.

'Well,' she swallowed, 'there's something we need to talk about—'

Martin jumped up and punched the air. 'I bloody knew it! I knew it! You've been a bit of a pain in the arse these last few days and I sat on the loo earlier, trying to think of how to make you happier, and it clicked. After what we'd spoken about with Peg, when she thought she was getting a baby brother or sister. And we have been rather frisky since I got back.' He kissed her hand. 'I thought to meself, Poppy's not miserable, she's worried!'

'Mart—'

'No, it's all right, babe, I know what you're going to say – it's very early days, but you think you're up the duff, don't you?' He sank down onto the carpet by her side of the bed and placed his head on his palm, propped up by his elbow. 'It'll be bloody brilliant. Don't worry about the space or money, we'll figure it all out, we always do, right? If it's a girl, she can go in with Peg and if it's a boy, then we can move both boys into the big room and Peg can go into Max's room. She'll kick off, but I'm sure we can sweeten it with a splash of pink paint and a few cushions!'

'Martin, please.'

He sat back on his haunches. 'What? Too excited too soon? I know, but I can't help it. A baby! Oh, mate, this'll be the making of us. It'll all be fine, it always is with us. Peg will go nuts and Maxy will be the big boy – imagine that. He can teach it how to count, if nothing else!'

Poppy shook her head. 'I'm not pregnant.'

Martin stared at her, still with his grin fixed. It was a little while before he spoke. 'No?'

'No, love.'

He sat back on the carpet and folded his arms across his chest, leaning against the wardrobe and looking confused and slightly embarrassed. 'Blimey, I thought that was what you were going to say. I would have sworn...' He stared at his wife. 'So what was the doctor's all about then?'

Poppy studied her fingers as they fidgeted in her lap. 'I'm poorly.'

'Well I guessed at that much, you silly moo. You don't go to the quack if you're feeling great, do you?' He gave a small snort of laughter, trying to lighten the mood; already his breathing was coming a little too fast. The vein on his neck pulsed. 'Is it... period business?'

Poppy gave a small laugh in spite of herself and the gravity of the conversation she was trying to have. *Period business.* They'd been together since they were fourteen and yet he was still shy, awkward at having to mention or observe this most basic of bodily functions. She went quiet, unable to locate the words that hovered on her tongue.

'No, it's not period business.'

Her tongue stuck to the dry roof of her mouth. She practised the words in her head. 'It's cancer, Mart. I've got cancer.' That sounded too blunt; maybe it should be 'They think I've got cancer,' and give him a small ray of hope on which to focus. She looked at the worry etched on his face. It didn't matter what she said or how she phrased it, she was going to shock him, upset him and smash the serenity in which he thought they lived. *How? How do I do that to you, my love?*

Max let out a wail from his bedroom. 'Maxy's awake!' Peg shouted from hers. 'It's okay, Maxy, Mummy'll be in in a sec!'

Poppy smiled and closed her eyes for a second and she saw it, saw how she would shift in an instant from wife to patient, from lover to invalid and she didn't want that, not yet.

'I've got some fluey bug, apparently.'

'Oh no! You should have said earlier. Can I get you anything?' Martin was already standing and making for the door. Busy, preoccupied as ever, this was their life.

'You can go get that Maxy!' She smiled at her man.

Martin nipped across the floor and kissed her on the

forehead. 'You should have said you weren't well. Tell you what, you nod off and shout if you need anything. A good night's sleep and you'll feel as right as rain. Don't worry, just go to sleep. Ssssshhh…' He crept backwards out of the room.

'I'm sorry about the baby thing, Mart.'

He looked back at his wife. 'Don't be. I'm happy with the practising!' He winked at her and went to grab the crying Max.

Poppy stared at the back of the closed door and wished that she *could* wake up feeling right as rain, without the stone of anxiety sitting in her stomach and with her mind free from the worry about what the future might hold.

Seven

Poppy sat in the large consulting room with its examination couch and wide desk with two armchairs positioned in front of it. She was grateful that Jo had agreed to sit with Max, who had been sleeping soundly on his beanbag when she left. He would only have been grumpy if woken. She was also thankful to be by herself. Alone, she was able to keep her emotions in check, stay calm. With someone she loved by her side, she would have been concerned about them and unable to concentrate on what was being said, unable to freely ask the many questions that filled her mind.

She looked at the wooden-framed photo on the desk. His wife, she assumed. A beautiful woman with a dark, glossy ponytail that Poppy was sure would swish this way and that as she sauntered – this stunning lady could rarely have cause to hurry, after all. Looking like that, she must surely lead a charmed life. The woman beamed into the lens, revealing perfect white teeth behind the full cupid's bow of her top lip. Two boys of similar ages, maybe three and four, each with a thick dark cap of hair, stood behind her. They were wearing matching stiff white shirts and had her mouth, but smaller, and studious eyes, maybe the eyes of their dad. Poppy wondered why the picture was facing out and not towards the chair that would shortly be occupied by the consultant she had come to see, Mr Ramasingh.

Perhaps it was a reminder to those whom he addressed that he too was a family man; perhaps it was meant to show that he understood and recognised that his words, casually issued, had far greater implications than the mere explanation of numbers and ticks on the charts to which he referred. Maybe. Or maybe a previous nosey patient had turned it round for a gander and forgotten to turn it back. This filled her with instant dread: supposing he thought she had done it? She toyed with the idea of repositioning it, but then the door opened and she heard his voice in the corridor behind her, and that of a female.

'What can I get you?' The woman sounded chirpy, a little flirty and familiar.

Mr Ramasingh's reply was thoughtful; he was in no hurry to get to Poppy, who sat counting the seconds, clasping and unclasping her hands as she sat in front of his desk.

'Oh, the usual please, Gill. Chicken or tuna on wholewheat or whatever and if they have them, a couple of those little blueberry muffins, or cranberry, and a coffee, large.'

'Coming right up!' Gill laughed.

Poppy heard the soft tread of Gill's shoes as she walked along the corridor. Mr Ramasingh pushed the door wide and Poppy saw his mouth straighten into a thin line and the crinkle leave the outer edges of his eyes as his smile slipped into something closer to a frown.

'Hello, Poppy. Sorry to have kept you.'

She blushed, feeling strangely shy in front of this man who was probably, in some corner of his mind, thinking about his tuna on wholewheat and his blueberry muffin.

'How are you?' he asked as he took up his seat and placed a file upside down on the table in front of her.

Poppy considered her answer. Gone were the days when

she casually offered 'Fine' in response to everything. 'Fine. I'm fine.' She had recited the phrase throughout her child-hood, even when it was far from the truth. Her memory was peppered with the avoidance of honesty when it came to enquiries about how she was faring. Embarrassment and fear were equal partners, forcing her to skirt around the issues.

But not any more. It was one of the freedoms afforded her by her new situation. She could be honest, she had nothing to lose and she was far, far from fine.

She took a deep breath. 'It's hard to describe how I'm feeling; it changes throughout the day and night. Most of the time I feel frightened and a bit sick, but I might only be feeling sick because I'm so frightened and not because of the erm... you know.'

Mr Ramasingh nodded. 'That's understandable. Take another deep breath: it's a good thing to do. You'll be surprised how much it helps. Just getting your breathing under control can make you feel a lot better, less afraid. It's okay.'

Poppy felt a flicker of relief. *It's okay*. That's what he'd said. Was it a clue? Was it all over before it had even begun? She smiled at the thought.

The consultant placed his elbow on the desk, cupped his clean-shaven chin with his left hand, and with his right tapped at the keyboard of his computer. He was handsome, with thick dark hair that was cut into a neat crop. His wide eyes were hidden behind the square black frames of his glasses. She found it hard to guess his age; he could be a fit, healthy fifty or a not so fit thirty, someone who'd had a tough paper round.

Poppy watched as he studied the screen before knitting his hands into a little basket and placing them on the desk in front of him. He looked her straight in the eye and for his direct gaze and blunt delivery, she was grateful.

'I have looked at all your test results and have shown them to the team here. I'm afraid that it's not good news, Poppy.'

And just like that, any small flicker of hope, any tiny flame of reprieve was extinguished and Poppy knew immediately that telling the kids was now unavoidable. This was her overriding thought – not what the horrible disease might do to her, but that telling her family would bring sadness and illness to their door. What would she do? Tell Martin first? Yes. Yes of course, then Granny Claudia. Then what? Sit Peg down on the sofa, or maybe take her for a walk. Wherever she told her would become a place forever tainted for them both. Should she be honest, open? How much to explain to her little girl? Max was probably too little to take in much of anything. *Oh God.*

'No?'

'No.' He shook his head. 'I have studied the results of your biopsy, scans and blood work. And we can see from the tests we have performed that your cancer is not the one isolated tumour that we had hoped for.'

'Oh, that's a shame.' She cringed at her words, inadequate and child-like. Poppy was struggling.

'It *is* a shame.' He smiled at her. 'You have a number of tumours, not just the one that we have located in your breast. Do you know what that means, Poppy?'

She shook her head; no, she didn't know what any of it meant.

'It means that you have metastatic breast cancer. It has spread.'

He watched as the information filtered into her brain. He gave her time to mentally catch up.

'Where has it spread?' she eventually asked.

Mr Ramasingh again offered the words slowly. 'It has spread to your bones.'

'My bones?' Poppy took a moment to replay this in her head; it didn't make any sense. 'How did it get in there? I don't understand.' She had pictured her lump as the bad thing in her body, but was unable to think of other lumps inside her bones.

It was Mr Ramasingh's turn to take a deep breath. His voice was soothing, calm and steady. Poppy had quite forgotten he was waiting for his lunch.

'Cancer can be complicated. It is made up of millions of cells and sometimes those cells can break away from the original tumour and travel to the bones in different parts of the body, through the lymph or blood system.'

'Is this what has happened to my cells?' she asked, picturing the cells as tiny blob-like creatures riding in pedalos around her bloodstream.

'Yes.' He gave one nod.

'So what do I have to do to get better?' Poppy wanted to show him her resilience, give him faith that she would fight. 'I'll take any medicine, do chemotherapy or whatever and I'll work really hard at it. I'm not afraid of getting stuck in and doing what I need to.' She smiled at him, feeling like an interviewee for a job she desperately needed, trying to convince him to take a punt on her.

Mr Ramasingh's fingers drummed lightly on the tabletop. 'We will make a plan for your treatment, Poppy—'

'That's good, thank you,' she interrupted.

'There are things that we can do to minimise and manage your pain and to slow the progress of the disease. We will start your chemotherapy as soon as possible and we will keep monitoring your progress with scans and X-rays, to see how the treatment is progressing.'

'Well that's good, but I don't want it slowed, I want it gone!' She gave a small laugh, embarrassed at having to state the obvious.

Mr Ramasingh looked away from her, concentrating on his computer screen, and a wave of fear shot through her stomach and ricocheted around her bowels. She felt her back stiffen and listened with her mouth agape to what he had to say.

He stared at her once again. 'I need to tell you, Poppy, that given the type of cancer you have and the stage at which it is at, we can only *treat* it. We cannot cure it. I'm very sorry.'

'So you are saying...' She felt confused and a little light-headed.

'We can offer you a palliative care programme that can help you in the everyday, but we can't cure it. I am sorry.'

'Can't cure it now, or...?' She had to ask.

'Can't cure it ever.'

Poppy was quiet for a moment. The doctor again waited for her to gather her thoughts.

'I'm thirty-two,' she stated, as though he might have missed the fact, or as if this new information might make him rethink his diagnosis.

'Yes.' He nodded. 'I know.'

'Is that your wife?' She nodded at the picture.

'Yes, yes it is.' He smiled.

She pictured her own family again, all of them at that precise moment, going about their regular day, unaware of the drama unfolding inside these four walls, unaware that this information was going to change their lives too. 'I... I don't want to be rude, Mr Ramasingh, but is there any point in me going to see a different doctor? Another consultant that might be able to help me?'

Mr Ramasingh leant forward. 'You are not being rude at all and I will tell you what I tell every patient of mine who asks me that exact same question when given this news. I *wish* there were a doctor who could give you a better prognosis and could make this disappear. I would refer you to them in a heartbeat. But it is my belief that your disease is advanced and incurable. Mrs Cricket, I truly wish I could say otherwise.'

The two sat in silence for a second or two more. Then Poppy stirred and sat up straight. 'So, what am I supposed to do now?' she whispered.

A few minutes later, Poppy wobbled her way across the car park, opened the driver's door and slid into the car. It started to rain. She watched the fat splotches hit the windscreen and trickle down. It felt like the world was crying and she was glad.

'Oh God.' She exhaled.

Poppy turned her face to the window and remembered when she and Martin were little. She couldn't remember a time when he had not been present, offering words of solace, a warm palm in which to rest her own or the gift of a cola bottle when finances allowed. Her other half, her friend.

'I'll always look after you, Poppy Day.'

Gripping the steering wheel, she rested her head on her knuckles. 'Oh God. Please... please...'

They had agreed to Skype Simon at 6 p.m. Poppy brushed her hair and gave her lips a slick of gloss before spraying herself with a spritz of her signature perfume, Angel by

Thierry Mugler; it had always been her favourite. She remembered boarding the plane for Afghanistan and naively trying to take a bottle on board.

'You know it's not smellavision, right?' Martin chuckled.

'I know.' She nudged him with her elbow. 'But if I smell nice, I feel good and that makes me more confident.'

They sat close together in front of the laptop, which they had placed on the dining table.

The first connection failed and Poppy was surprised to feel a sense of disappointment. It wasn't as if she knew this man, her uncle, not really. But on the second attempt there he was, beaming as usual. They continued chatting where they had left off, enquiring about each other's weeks and asking respectively about Peg and Matilda.

'Ah, here's my wife,' Simon announced, extending his arm out of sight.

Poppy sat up straight and stared at the screen and then a lady came into view. A white woman in her early fifties, with mousy-coloured hair, a fresh, sun-kissed complexion, clear eyes and a smile that rivalled Simon's.

'Hello!' The woman waved enthusiastically, her voice a lovely sing-song. 'I'm Kate!'

Poppy waved back and couldn't help but return the smile.

'Isn't this wonderful?' Kate enthused. 'I mean, the whole thing – finding each other, not just the Skype thing, although that's pretty brilliant. We use it a lot. I have two children in the UK, well, not children, grown-ups really. My son Dominic and his wife are in Sussex and my daughter Lydia is in London, she's an artist.'

'Oh wow, I was always pants at art,' Poppy said.

'Oh, me too.' Kate chuckled. 'Always too busy reading. Books are my thing. Do you read, Poppy?'

'When I can, but it's hard to find the time. My kids are little – well, one's little and one's demanding!' She liked chatting to Kate, liked the fact that they didn't know she was sick.

'Ah, inquisitive ones are the best kind. Talking of which, I hear you've met our foster daughter, Matilda?'

'Yes, she's gorgeous.' *Foster daughter?* Poppy could not have called that.

'Oh, she really is, keeps me on my toes.' Kate clasped her hands under her chin. 'And we are about to become grandparents! Dominic's wife, Fiona, is expecting, so it's all very exciting; not for a few months yet, but exciting already.'

Simon edged forward. 'Kate buys anything small that she can find and has taken up knitting – the poor child.'

Kate nudged him. 'Oi! I'm getting better.'

'I think I'm too young to become a grandfather,' Simon said, though he looked far from concerned.

'Rubbish, you are absolutely ancient.' Kate leant into her husband and Poppy saw him nuzzle her head. They were clearly in love and it was nice to see.

'And Martin, Simon tells me you are a soldier?'

'Yes, for my sins.' Martin blushed, conscious of Simon's status.

Simon chuckled loudly. 'I don't think it works like that! Who are you with?'

'The REME, the Royal—'

'Electrical and Mechanical Engineers!' Simon finished.

'The very ones.' Martin nodded. 'How long have you been vicaring?'

Poppy laughed at this new adjective.

Simon laughed too. 'Oh, all my life really, but formally for nearly thirty years.'

'Wow, and do you have a church?' Martin's interest was genuine.

'Yes, I do now and we run a mission for kids and people who need a bit of help up at a place called Dennery, not far from where we live, a ten-minute drive inland.'

'That sounds amazing.' Poppy thought of all the times in her childhood when she could have done with a bit of help. Having people like Kate and Simon to turn to would have made her life a whole lot better. 'I'd love to see it.'

'Well...' Simon leant in and his face loomed large on the screen. 'Kate and I wanted to talk to you about that.' He glanced at his wife, who smiled encouragement. 'We hope this isn't too soon or too forward, but we would love to invite you and Martin over. May we send you some tickets?'

Poppy sat back and placed her hand on her chest. 'Oh God! I don't know, I...'

'Wow!'

She and Martin spoke simultaneously.

'You don't have to decide now, obviously,' Kate gushed. 'But have a think and let us know. Tickets are cheaper to buy here than in the UK and you wouldn't need to spend a cent once you were here. We have a lovely guest room and you could just potter and sit in the sun and we could all get to know each other a bit. It'd be lovely.'

Poppy beamed, forgetting entirely about the dark shadow of sickness that hung over her future. 'I can't believe you'd do that for us! It would be amazing.'

'It really would,' Martin concurred.

'Well, we can chat about it next time,' Simon said. 'Hey, how did Spurs get on this week, Martin?'

'Sorry, what's that? Bad connection! Didn't hear the question so can't answer you, I'm afraid!'

'I said…' Simon tried to repeat the question.

'No, there it is again. Sorry, Simon, completely lost you. Mind you, next week, if our results are a bit better, I might hear you more clearly.'

And the four of them laughed, like old friends. Like family. They agreed to talk again soon.

Martin grabbed his wife by the waist and pulled her onto his lap. 'We are going to St Lucia!' He squeezed her tightly and kissed her on the mouth. 'I knew this was going to be our year, didn't I say?'

Poppy kissed him back, an aftertaste of guilt on her lips. She hated deceiving him, but hated even more the thought of shattering his happiness. 'Yes you did.'

Martin and the kids ate supper, a little later than usual, while Poppy locked the bathroom door and stepped under the shower. She could hear Peg and Max chatting and shouting at their dad. He was probably teasing them. It was good to feel the hot, hard jets pummelling her skin. Wiping the water from the inside of the door, she studied the outline of her figure in the wall mirror opposite. She smiled. She didn't look like she had cancer, she didn't even feel particularly ill. 'What the fuck do you know, Mr Ramasinghadoodah? What do you know about me?'

Poppy felt an unexpected surge of energy force its way up through her gut and flow through her limbs. 'I tell you what you don't know about me! I got on a plane to Afbloodyghanistan without a sodding passport! I met with terrorists and I bought my man home – that's what I did! Me! So you can stick your diagnosis where the sun don't shine. I will not bring illness into this house. I won't. I'm going to win. Watch me – I'm going to bloody win!' Poppy clapped and gave a small jump as she reached for her shower gel. 'Hundreds of people beat cancer, thousands even! I'm going to St Lucia to feel that soft powdery sand slip through my fingers and the hot sun on my face. I'm going to prove you wrong. I'll take any drug, I'll do anything, but I'm not going to give up.' Poppy looked once again at her reflection. 'I will not.'

'Mama Mia – here I go again!' she sang, loud enough for the kids and Martin to laugh into their spaghetti bolognese.

Eight

At the cancer outpatients clinic, Poppy kept her eyes lowered whenever she could. She didn't want to mix with these people. She didn't want to think of herself as being one of them and she was also fearful of being spotted. She knew how whispers worked in the military community and she was afraid of having her deceitfulness exposed. A couple of women were accompanied by women of similar ages to them – friends, Poppy assumed. Their conversation was jovial, intended to distract. An older man sat looking miserable, next to his wife, whose demeanour was similar. She couldn't blame them, this was hardly a fun day out. A young guy sloughed off his leather jacket and practically jumped into the chair as he chatted to the nurse like an old friend; maybe he was. Poppy was fascinated by his shiny, bald head and missing eyebrows; he reminded her of a mannequin.

She smiled at the picture Jo had just sent of her with Max at the soft-play centre. He was waist-deep in multi-coloured plastic balls and was clearly loving his adventure. Good old Jo. She hadn't pried or suspected a thing when Poppy had told her she was going to a routine hospital appointment.

The busy nurse settled Poppy back into a reclining chair and gave her a stack of dog-eared magazines before placing the IV cannula in her arm; it was attached to a pump that would push the drugs into her. Poppy couldn't help but stare at the plastic apron, gloves and goggles that the nurse wore, wondering how toxic was this shite they were about to feed into her.

Another nurse tucked a blanket around Poppy's legs before making her way along the line of similar chairs, like a worker bee on a production line. Poppy glanced at the pouch that dripped poison into her veins. She closed her eyes and began planning how she would break the news to Martin. She knew she couldn't delay any longer but she was dreading the sledgehammer she was going to bring down on their perfect year. She closed her eyes and feigned sleep – anything rather than face the reality of where she was and why.

A full week later and Poppy still hadn't found the right moment. The better she felt, the longer she felt able to deny the fact that she was ill. She was happy, seemingly unaffected by her first round of chemo. She'd spent the best part of the week in cleaning overdrive, scouring the kitchen floor with such regularity that Peg had pointed out their house smelt like a hospital. She'd defrosted the freezer twice and had even run a bleach-dipped toothbrush between the tiles to clean the grout in the bathroom.

Whenever she had the house to herself, she sat on the sofa and propped the laptop on her knees. Flexing her fingers, she typed in the words 'cures for cancer'. This threw up a whole host of articles claiming that her type of cancer was nigh on impossible to cure. The medical papers, stats and figures were frightening. She took a deep breath, cleared the search and started again. Delving deeper into cancer blogs and testimonials, Poppy read about a woman who had seen her tumours shrink after eating nothing but a particular mushroom found in Brazil; she made a point of remembering the name, wondering how she might get hold of some.

She devoured page after page of first-hand accounts by people who swore they had been healed by eating vast amounts of kale or tons of asparagus; others had watched their tumours disappear under the hands of a dancing shaman. She read about retreats in California and Mexico, learnt about self-healing, spiritual healing, crystal healing and more. She read of women who had been cured after turning to Jesus and others who had reversed the progress of their disease through yoga, meditation and the odd Gregorian chant. In every spare moment, when Poppy wasn't cleaning, she scoured the internet, reading obsessively about cancer, its causes and cures, and seeking out the opinions of those who were experts in both. The information was plentiful and confusing.

One day she found a blog written by a cancer patient in Australia and there was one particular phrase in the woman's diary that resonated: *You always read about that million-to-one chance, the person that makes it against all the odds, and I figure, why can't I be that million-to-one person? Why not me?* Poppy switched off her computer.

'That million-to-one person... why not indeed?' She looked up to see her nan standing at the foot of the stairs. She looked thoughtful. In the seconds before her nan faded from view, Poppy saw a flicker of a smile around her mouth.

She walked into the bathroom and paused in front of the mirror. She opened her shirt and ran her hand across her chest, over her ribs and up her arms; her fingers lingered on the little dot where the needle had punctured her skin, then continued, across her neck and down over her breasts to the flat of her abdomen. This looked like her body, felt like her body. It was hard to reconcile the healthy-looking outer layer with what was going on inside.

Bones, how do I get you fixed? She stared into the mirror, picturing her skeleton. She saw it grey and fractured as the bastard little pedalos sailed up and down her blood rivers, tossing their dirty toxic cargo of broken cells as they travelled. Still Poppy hadn't cried. Shock, Dr Jessop had informed her. Poppy had only nodded; again, placing her fate in the hands of those who knew better than she. If smiley doctor said it was shock, then shock it was. If Mr Ramasingh said it was incurable, well... that was something she would not accept. She would show him, show them all. She did however submit to swallowing the cluster of drugs they had prescribed for her, daily and without debate.

Next morning, Poppy woke bright and early, with a feeling of optimism in her stomach. It felt a bit like starting a diet or a new regime. She was motivated and positive. She might just be that one in a million. She placed the collection of pills on her palm and, looking at the shiny, colourful display, she counted them, like Max would. 'One... two... three... four...' She smiled at the thought of her little counting boy.

'Bisphosphonates,' she said out loud, verbalising this new word in her vocabulary. She replayed in her mind what Mr Ramasingh had said about what they were for: 'to slow down the process of bone breakdown while allowing the production of new bone to carry on as normal. Bisphosphonates can strengthen existing bone and reduce the damage caused by the cancer in the bone.'

So be it, thought Poppy as she threw the pills onto the back of her tongue and drowned them with water. She pictured them bashing into the bastard little pedalos and blasting them to harmless smithereens. 'Ha! Take that!' She smiled at her reflection.

Walking the recycling box to the end of the path, she saw Jo in her pyjamas and slippers doing the exact same thing.

'Good morning, lovely! God, it's chilly!' Poppy pulled her sweatshirt around her shoulders.

'You need a bit more meat on your bones. You can have some of mine,' Jo quipped. 'Are you dieting, Poppy? I'd definitely say you've lost weight, but you don't need to, honestly, mate.'

Poppy cringed. She was now able to pull her jeans down without undoing the zip and she didn't like it one bit. 'I'm not trying to lose weight. I've just been so busy, I forget to eat sometimes, and all that rushing around doesn't help.'

'I wish I could forget to eat.' Jo lifted up her pyjama top to show her friend her more than ample tummy.

Poppy laughed. 'I think the bloke at number ten just choked on his cornflakes!'

Jo turned to the house a couple of doors down and did it again. Poppy snorted her laughter.

'Ooh, I know what I meant to show you.' Jo raised the phone that nestled in her palm. 'Look what my sister sent me. The loveliest pictures of her and the kids.' Jo opened the image and handed her mobile to Poppy. It was a fabulous picture of them laughing. 'She got this London photographer who came to the house. He usually does all the actresses and whatnot and you should see the others, they're all like this. Not cheesy or too formal, but the best photos I've seen. You should think about getting the kids done. It wasn't too pricey.'

That was a light-bulb moment for Poppy. That's what she should do, get some photographs taken and capture the now.

'Have you got his details?' she asked.

'He's called Paul Smith and he's based in Greenwich, in London, but he'll come out to you. And apparently he is drop-dead gorgeous, which is a bonus!'

Poppy nodded. 'Send me his number.'

Sipping her coffee at the table, Poppy waited for the day to begin in earnest. She liked the idea of having photographs taken, something a bit more formal than the hurried snaps they captured on phones and loaded onto the laptop, where they simply sat, unlooked at. She had very little to remind her of her own childhood, other than a few blurry shots from her childhood home. This gave Poppy an idea.

Later that evening, while Peg did her homework and Max coloured in a picture at the table, trying to copy his big sister, Poppy stood at the stove stirring chilli. Martin arrived home from work.

'Hello, did you get my boxes?' Poppy asked.

Martin walked past her and smacked her bum. 'Well, yes, it's nice to see you too, my beloved!' He nodded and pointed to a large white carrier bag on the dining table.

Poppy turned the ring down to a gentle simmer and wiped a splodge of the rich sauce that had splashed from the pan onto the worktop. Then she took the bag up to their bedroom and pulled the boxes from their packaging. They were perfect, one lilac and the other dark blue, just the right size and each with a sturdy lid. Encased in a tiny metal rectangle on the front of each was a small sliver of white card on which to write the contents. Poppy opened the drawer in the side table and pulled out one of Peg's black felt-tipped pens. She held up each box, writing first 'Peg' and then 'Max' in the spaces.

'Dinner's ready!' Martin called up the stairs, interrupting her task.

Poppy smiled. She'd known he wouldn't be able to resist taking over if she left the kitchen for long enough.

'Coming!' She placed the boxes neatly in the bottom of her wardrobe and trotted down the stairs. The next stage would just have to wait.

Poppy was halfway down when she let out a loud, guttural yell. It left her body without warning. It was instinctive and primal and it not only scared her but Peg and Max too. Both kids ran to the foot of the stairs, their eyes wide as saucers. Peg placed her hands on her little brother's shoulders and pulled him to her as Poppy staggered backwards and leant on the wall, unable to get a breath. The pain in her breast-bone was so acute it had literally knocked the air from her. She was aware her face was contorted, but could do little to control it.

'Oh shit,' Poppy panted. She laid her head against the wall and slowly, slowly was able to catch her breath. Her whole body shook. It was the first time she had experienced a pain so all-consuming that it was the only thing she could think about, a pain that hijacked every nerve in her body and left her weakened, trembling and afraid of when it might return. She stared at her children, who looked equally scared.

Martin came out of the kitchen. 'What on earth was that noise?' He looked from his kids to his wife, who was hovering on the stairway. Her skin had turned grey and was covered with a fine mist of sweat. 'Christ! What's the matter, love? What happened?' He climbed the stairs with his arms outstretched, not sure where to touch or how to help.

Poppy took a couple of deep breaths and laughed as she addressed the kids, wiping the tears and sweat from her eyes. 'I'm so silly! I tripped and I think I hurt my back! I'm fine now though. What a stupid mum you've got!'

'Stupid and a bit noisy!' Peg shook her head in disdain and made her way back to the table, where a hot bowl of chilli and rice awaited her. Max toddled after his sister.

'Are you okay?' Martin's brows knitted in concern.

'I'm fine! Don't know what that was, my back just twinged, must have twisted it.'

Poppy ignored the look of panic that Martin shot her as she sidled past him. She took up her place at the table and did her best to eat, ignoring the tremor of the fork in her right hand.

Nine

It was the morning of Poppy's hospital appointment. She was dreading discussing the progress of the treatment so far. She had hardly slept and now wandered around the kitchen in her rubber gloves, looking for something else to scrub. The hob had been given a good going-over and she had emptied out the cutlery drawer and washed it thoroughly, before polishing the knives and forks and replacing them in their size-appropriate trays.

Martin came in and opened and shut the fridge. What he was hoping to find in there, God only knew. 'Cor, you were fidgety last night, my little super-scrubber. Think you might have had ants in your pants. Lucky ants.' He kissed her as he walked past.

Poppy noted his trackie bottoms and T-shirt. 'Sorry, love, I had a restless night, don't know why.' She found the little lies were easy to pile on top of the bigger ones. 'Why don't you go for a quick run? Max's soundo and Peg won't be up till I call her; it'll do you good. Go on, go running in them there hills!' She pointed out of the window.

'I feel guilty going for a run and leaving you cleaning.'

'Go!' she shouted. 'I'm fine, honestly. Go get some fresh air.'

'Sure you don't mind?' Martin asked as he reached for his trainers from the cupboard under the stairs. He straightened up and kissed her hard on the mouth. 'See you in a bit.'

She turned her back and poured disinfectant on her cloth, which she then wiped over the bin.

'Poppy?'

'Yep?' She looked over her shoulder.

He spoke from the front door. 'You sure there's nothing on your mind? It's not like you, tossing and turning all night. Was it your back again?'

Poppy dug deep and produced her brightest smile. 'No! I'm fine. Now go running while you have the chance. No one likes a fat soldier, Mart!' She hurled the tea towel in his direction.

He ducked and laughed as he closed the door behind him.

After breakfast, as soon as Martin and Max left to walk Peg to school, Poppy sank down onto the sofa and closed her eyes. She felt tired, very tired. Smiling and laughing her way through the days was proving harder than she thought. She looked at the photo propped against the wall, of her and Martin on their wedding day. It showed them in their best outfits, sipping Guinness through a straw from a shared pint glass. They looked happy, making up for what they lacked in white lace and flowers with a deep, devoted commitment.

Her nan had told her it was the difference between wanting a wedding or a marriage, which had foxed Poppy at the time: what was the difference? Now, all these years later, Poppy knew exactly what she meant. Their marriage was built on an unshakeable foundation of love and dedication. Both were secure in the knowledge that they would be there for each other no matter what, through the good times and the bad, in sickness and in health... And in that second, Poppy knew that she had to tell her husband. She held her shaking hands inside each other and practised what she might say.

She would tell him the moment he got back from the school run. There was no easy way to do it, but she knew she had to dig deep, find her courage and give him the facts as she saw them. Those facts being that this was a challenge, but that she would win. She was determined. Gathering the paper from the hall floor, she opened it and lifted the small print to her face.

Emily Grace Manson, called by the angels at six weeks. Baby sister in heaven of Joe and Billy. Private family ceremony. Know, Emily, that for the brief time we had you, you were loved.

'Ah, bless her heart.' Poppy sighed. She picked up the pad and tore two strips of paper from the bottom sheet. On the first she wrote:

Your first word, Peg, was 'Mumma'! I was very happy that you picked me to say first, and you've been saying it ever since! I hear your little voice in my head when I am not with you and it makes me very happy. Xx

On the other she put:

The day we brought you home from the hospital, Maxy, was a real adventure. Peg had decorated the lounge with strips of coloured paper and balloons! We had only ever called you Max, but as we put you in her little arms so she could hold you, she kissed you and said, 'Welcome home, Maxy! ' and that was it, it stuck! Xx

Poppy folded the two strips and placed them in her pocket. Martin came home singing, he was in a great mood. His earlier run had done him good.

Max sat on the rug and loaded his digger up with Lego bricks before dumping them into a box using the scoop. This task would keep him busy for an age.

'Do you need a lift into Salisbury today? I could drop you on the way to work.'

'No, I'll jump on the bus.' She smiled. She had told him she was going for a manicure and a spot of shopping. Max was off to toddler group and the mum of one of his friends was going to hang on to him until she got back or Martin finished. Poppy wasn't really sure how long it would all take.

'Why don't we have a coffee and a catch-up before you go to work?' she asked, casually, planning on holding the mug but not drinking anything, as per her hospital appointment instructions.

'Can do, love. I'm not meeting the warrant officer until later. I know, let's really push the boat out and have a biscuit as well.' He reached for the digestives and shook them in her direction. 'Living the dream, Pop!'

'You're easily pleased.' She beamed, hesitating. Then she took a deep breath. 'Mart?'

'Yes, love?' He waited for her to speak.

Poppy felt her stomach flip with nerves, still unsure how to begin.

The front door bell rang.

'Bugger it,' Poppy muttered under her breath as she made out Jo's outline through the glass. She sighed and opened the door, searching for a smile. It quickly faded, however, at the sight of her friend. Jo's face was streaked with mascara, her tears running like liquorice stripes down her cheeks. Her eyes were red and swollen and her mouth quivered.

'Oh, Poppy!' Jo fell against her friend, who wrapped her in her arms and patted her back, like she did the kids.

'Hey, it's okay, love. It's okay,' she soothed.

'No, it isn't okay, nothing is. I don't know what to do!'

'Come and sit down. What's the matter?' Poppy steered her towards the sofa and watched as her friend, seemingly weakened, slumped down onto the cushions, shredding the damp kitchen roll that she twisted in her fingers.

Poppy felt her heart hammering in her chest. Had something happened to Danny? It was a constant unspoken fear for them all. Poppy thanked God that Martin was home. She braced herself, ready to hear Jo's news.

Jo shook her head. 'I just can't believe it. I can't.'

'Can't believe what?' Poppy coaxed. 'Have you had a shock?'

'A bloody shock? I should say so. I keep hearing his voice, telling me over and over, and it won't sink in, it just won't. It's not bloody fair.'

Poppy sighed. 'Whose voice? What's not fair, love?'

'Life! Life's not bloody fair!' Jo sounded angry.

Poppy ran her tongue round her dry mouth. 'Have you heard from Danny?'

'Yes. This morning, earlier. He phoned, the fucking coward.'

Poppy sat up straight, shocked to hear Jo's language and sentiment. Maybe it was the shock. 'He phoned?' It didn't make any sense. If he was hurt...

'Yes, can you believe it, ten years of marriage thrown away with a bloody phone call. He said being away has given him time to think. I could have screamed. All I've *got* is time to think, too much time! I could kill him, I could. He's a fucking coward, couldn't wait till he got home and pay me the courtesy of a face-to-face conversation. That's all I got – a muffled phone call, no doubt with half of Bastion listening in. All these years, trying for a baby, it was all I ever wanted and they said it probably wasn't me and now those years are behind me, what a waste. Too fucking old and he took those years from me!'

All thoughts of her illness flew from her mind. Poor Jo. Her lovely mate did not deserve this. 'Jo, you need to calm down and tell me exactly what Danny said.'

'He said he wants a divorce, said he hasn't been happy for a while and that I should pack up my stuff before he gets back as he's given up the quarter.'

'Shit!' Poppy sat back and rubbed her face.

'Yes.' Jo nodded in agreement as she unfurled the remnants of her tissue. 'Shit.'

Martin skulked out of the kitchen. 'Think I'll leave you girls to it.' He gathered up his jacket and beret and left the house.

Two hours later, Poppy lay in the austere, echoey room in her blue hospital gown. She was on a narrow, white, fixed bed that looked part kitchen counter, part supermarket conveyor belt. Above her hovered a large white machine that reminded her of something you might see at the dentist's or in one of those vintage episodes of *Star Trek*, like the ones she'd watched in her youth.

'What the bloody hell am I doing here?'

'All okay, Mrs Cricket?' A robotic-like voice floated through the speakers.

Poppy gave the thumbs-up and felt her cheeks flush. She had forgotten there were speakers and a microphone and that a team in the adjacent room could hear her every word. She closed her eyes and thought of Jo, poor Jo. One phrase stuck in her mind: 'Now those years are behind me, what a waste.' Poppy felt strangely thankful, knowing that not one second of one day had been wasted in her life with Martin. He was the best thing that had ever happened to her, her other half, to whom her heartstrings were joined. She remembered him striding across the playground at school one Valentine's Day. He had marched across the tarmac, ignoring the taunts and jibes of their classmates, and delivered a huge padded card of a kitten in a wine glass, with the words 'I Love You' emblazoned across the top in swirly gold script. She still had it somewhere, probably in the loft gathering dust along with her other treasures. She hoped something similar would soon happen to Jo; hoped she would find someone who would make her feel like the most important person in the world, the way Martin did her. Poppy didn't need diamonds the size of ice cubes or kidney-shaped pools; she knew what it was to be loved and that gave her riches beyond compare.

The CT scan was finally done and Poppy waited in the reception, feeling a little like she had a chill. She asked the lady behind the desk to call her a taxi; she didn't feel up to the bus.

The taxi dropped her outside the house. Poppy paid the driver in silence. She was in no mood for small talk. Martin was home and Max was playing in the hallway when she put her key in the door.

'Where have you been?' Martin shouted from the kitchen.

'I lost track of time and then I went for my beautician appointment and felt really awful, bit fluey. So I didn't stay, I just came home.' She gave a feeble smile.

'I've been worried sick!' He dried his hands on a tea towel. 'You didn't answer your phone.'

'Oh God, sorry, love. I'm out of battery. I didn't mean to worry you.'

'Well you bloody did!' He shook his head. 'You don't look well,' he noted, his voice softening.

'Hello, my lovely boy,' she cooed, reaching down to stroke her son's head. Suddenly, she bent over and clutched her stomach. 'Oh God, Mart, I need to get to the loo!' Her tone was urgent.

'God, are you okay?' Martin rushed forward.

Poppy shook her head.

'It's okay, love, up you go.' He picked up Max and stepped away from the bottom of the stairs. Poppy did her best to make it to the bathroom, moving as fast as her aching bones would allow.

She shoved open the bathroom door with her elbow as she pulled her coat up and tore at the buttons on her jeans. 'Christ, no!' She nearly made it.

Martin ventured upstairs ten minutes later, to find his wife sitting on the bathroom floor, her back against the radiator. She was naked and wrapped in a large towel, and she was crying. She had used the showerhead to hose herself down in the bath and her clothes were in a heap in the corner.

'Can you throw them away please, Mart?' She prodded the pile with her foot.

'Throw them away? Can't I just wash them for you? I don't mind.'

'I mind. Please throw them away.'

'Okay, love, will do.' Martin bent down and retrieved the sodden pile. He fought his gag reflex. 'I'll be back in a sec to get you into bed. What on earth do you think it is? Should I call the doctor?'

'No!' She was adamant, shaking her head through her tears. 'It's just that horrible bug still. I don't want to give it to the kids.' She retched once more as though she was going to be sick, but nothing came.

True to his word, Martin came straight back to the bathroom. 'Come on, let's get you into bed and get you toasty.' He hooked his arms around her back and lifted her until she could lean on him.

'Mart?'

'Yes, love?'

'I'm sorry.' Poppy took a step outside of the bathroom and then turned, aghast. 'Oh God, no. Mart, I need to go back on the loo, now, right now!'

'Okay, okay!' He tried to calm her panic while guiding her onto the loo and for the second time in the short while she had been home, she nearly made it.

Spent, Poppy lay under the duvet shivering and wondering how she was ever going to find the strength to tell him. There was the quake of fear in her stomach. She didn't feel like a person in a million, didn't feel like she was winning. If anything, she felt the exact opposite.

Ten

The bell rang at a little before one. Peg ran at the front door, skidding along the hall floor in her socks and smacking into it. She slid onto the ground then jumped up and opened the door to a man standing with black boxes of equipment around his feet and what looked like folded-up umbrellas under his arm.

'Are you okay?' He looked concerned, having heard the bump from the other side of the door.

'Yep, I always do it, I'm not very good at stopping.' Peg studied the man in his boots, jeans, white T-shirt and sunglasses. 'You've got a lot of perfume on,' she commented.

'It's aftershave.' He smiled at her.

She wrinkled her nose. Same difference.

Poppy came down the stairs and stared at the man on the doorstep. Jo was right: drop-dead gorgeous.

'Poppy?' He removed his glasses and stepped forward.

'No, I mean yes... Come in, or get your things... whatever...' She was surprisingly flustered.

Paul strode into the hall and grasped Poppy's hand in a firm handshake; she tried not to stare at his tanned, muscled arms. She felt a little weak and wasn't sure she could blame that entirely on the bastard pedalos.

'Knock knock!' Jo shouted through the open door.

'Thought I'd come and help, or watch, or whatever...' Jo too went a little gaga.

'I'll just grab my stuff.' Paul smiled and motioned to his car, which was parked with the tailgate lifted.

The moment he left the house, the two women collapsed on each other in a fit of giggles.

'Blimey, Poppy, who cares what the photos are like. This will be the best afternoon we've had in a long time!'

Martin came down the stairs carrying Max. The two were in their best clothes, Martin wearing a suit with a stiff white shirt underneath. Max's hair had been brushed into a side parting; he had proper shoes on, and the collar of his shirt, which was just like his dad's, was poking over the top of his navy jersey.

Peg had spent the best part of the morning painting her nails for the occasion, a concession by Poppy in exchange for Peg agreeing to wear her navy and white dotty dress that was saved for best. Her hair hung in a glorious red-brown curtain, with her newly trimmed fringe looking just right.

Poppy had thought long and hard about what to wear. She finally settled on her dusky blue cotton top, which had a layer of silk in a slightly darker shade over the top. It was floaty and flattering and she loved the colour. Two long strands of multi-coloured beads completed the look. She'd put her hair up, leaving tendrils hanging loose around her face. She wanted to appear sophisticated and older, so that when Peg and Max looked at these pictures in later years, there might be less of a sense of her having been marooned in time. Poppy swallowed the sob that threatened. Determined that today of all days she would remain cheerful.

Paul moved the coffee table from the middle of the room and arranged a series of vast umbrella-like shades and screens.

He stood with his camera in one hand and light meter in the other, measuring and clicking at the blank wall.

'My Aunty Jo said she thought you were really fit, do you think you're as fit as my dad? He's a soldier and he can run up and down the hill with his rucksack on his back and he can lift me over his head.'

Paul stopped clicking and stared at Peg. 'Erm... I'm not sure. I think your dad is fitter than me and definitely a lot braver.'

Peg smiled, more than satisfied with his response. Jo, on the other hand, turned red and decided to nip back next door to cringe in private.

Poppy and Martin sat straight-backed on the sofa with Peg between them and Max on his dad's lap. Paul began to click, and every time he did, the flash to the right of him fired.

'I'm going to be a pilot!' Peg yelled quite suddenly.

Paul stared at the little girl, not quite sure how to respond. He settled on 'Cool.' Keen to get back to snapping, he chatted to them all, trying to relax them and get the shot he wanted. 'Max!' he called. 'What have I got?' He held up one of Max's diggers in his free hand.

'Digger!' Max shouted, and he clapped, beaming. Paul clicked. The whole family laughed, and he clicked again.

'Relax a minute, folks.' Paul studied the images stored in his camera.

Freed from their poses, Martin sat back on the sofa and Max climbed up his torso and patted his head like a drum. Poppy reached over and hugged Peg, who threw her arms around her mum's neck.

Paul looked up and grinned. He snapped, and snapped again. And again.

The Crickets looked wide-eyed at the photographer, who had seemingly caught them unawares.

Paul rested on his haunches and spoke to Poppy and Martin. 'Can you do me a favour?'

Poppy nodded and peeled Peg from her neck.

'I want you to almost make as if I'm not here. I want you to relax and chat. Martin, are you comfortable in that suit?'

'Nah, mate.' Martin pulled at the sleeves and twisted his head, jutting his chin.

'Then make yourself comfortable,' Paul instructed.

Martin jumped up. He didn't need telling twice. He took his jacket off, undid his top button and rolled up his sleeves. They slumped back down on the sofa and Paul carried on snapping.

'Glad I bothered ironing that shirt!' Poppy joked. Martin bent forward and kissed her nose. Click.

'Yuk!' Peg shouted and covered her eyes, as was her habit whenever they kissed. Click.

'Yuk!' Max echoed as he pulled off his jersey and put it on his head, then threw it on the floor. His hair was mussed and stood up at right angles, as if he had just woken up. Click.

Without warning, Peg leapt from the sofa and ran upstairs, appearing moments later with her neon-green tutu over her frock and her googly-eyed deely boppers on her head. 'Now I'm comfy!' she said.

'Give me strength!' Poppy laughed as she pulled the band from her own hair, letting it fall in loose waves over her shoulders. They were only vaguely aware of the camera working in the background.

'Ooooh! We forgot Toffee, he's a part of our family!' Peg jumped up again.

Poppy and Martin roared with laughter. Peg dashed to the palatial cage in the corner, plucked Toffee from his sawdust and fussed over him on the floor. After a moment or two, she sat down between her parents, beaming.

'My Barbie accessories!' she announced. She held Toffee in the air to reveal her pet dressed in a mini tiara, with a pink plastic handbag held against his paw and four blue plastic stilettos perched on his little claws.

And it was in that second – as Poppy and Martin saw the guinea pig outfit for the first time and looked at each other and laughed, as Max reached up to pet Toffee, as Peg tipped her head back on the verge of giggles, and as Toffee stared straight into the lens with an expression that said 'Help!' – that Paul Smith, photographer to the stars, got the shot he wanted.

'And that, Cricket family, is a rap,' he said, winking at Poppy.

Having recovered from the hilarity of their photo shoot and all in agreement that it was one of the best days they had ever had, *ever!*, Martin and the kids, with tummies full of crispy bacon sandwiches, rested in front of the television. Poppy nipped upstairs for her shower. She stripped off, still laughing as she flicked the tap on the shower. She removed her make-up in the mirror, watching as the mascara and lipstick slid from her face and onto the tissue paper which she then dropped down the loo. She felt tired. Bracing her arms against the sink, she sighed and hopped into the shower. She reached for her vanilla-scented gel, squeezed a blob into her palms and inhaled the glorious perfume as she worked up some lather against her skin. 'That bloody guinea pig!' She chuckled to herself as she pictured again the little blue stilettos.

Taking her shampoo bottle, Poppy covered her palms and began to massage the suds onto her scalp.

The two things happened simultaneously.

As Martin came into the bathroom to grab his pyjamas

from the hook on the back of the door, Poppy lowered her hands and stared at the clumps of hair that sat like wet, tawny animals in her palms. She felt her knees go weak as she gazed at them. The shock rendered her speechless as she slumped forward.

'What, Poppy? What's the matter?' Martin pulled open the shower door and stared at his wife's face, contorted with tears.

Poppy sank down to the shower floor, raised her knees and rested her head on them. Her hands she kept clenched tightly shut. Martin crouched down and placed his hand on her back. She jumped as if she'd been cut.

'It's okay. I'm here. I'm right here.'

'I can't do this, Mart,' she whispered.

'Can't do what? What's going on? Are you hurt? Is it your back again? Talk to me, Poppy.' He sounded angry, panicked.

'I'm sorry. I'm so... sorry! I thought if I kept busy, I could stop it, but I don't think I can and I'm really scared,' she stuttered.

'What are you sorry for? What's going on?' He reached into the cubicle and peeled her hands from her sides. 'What the fuck?' He stared at the wet clumps of hair that she dropped into the tray by her feet.

Martin's breath came heavily. 'What have you done? Are you shaving your head? For God's sake, tell me, Poppy. You're scaring me now.'

'I've got cancer.' She stared at the floor; the water ran in steady streams from her chin and elbows. Her voice was level.

'What?' He must have misheard.

'That's what's wrong with me.' She lifted her face and looked at her husband. 'I've got cancer.'

'When? How? I don't...' Martin swayed as the strength left his core and his bowels went into spasm. He sank down at the edge of the shower tray floor. The water soaked his head and shirt. He tried to catch his breath. It was some seconds before he reached up and flicked the shower tap to the 'off' position.

The sounds of Poppy's crying and his breathing seemed extraordinarily loud. She wished he'd turn the water back on again.

'I don't understand.' He shook his head and wiped the water from his face with the back of his hand.

'When I went to the doctor's before—' she started.

'Before when? You went where?'

'Before, a few weeks ago. I told you I went to the GP's. It was because I'd found a lump.' She looked at the floor.

'You what?' he snapped as his chest heaved with all that it was trying to contain.

'I found a lump, Mart.'

He stared at her. His head twitched as if it had been struck, his mouth hung open. 'You found a...?' He needed it repeating. Though he'd heard her with perfect clarity, he still hoped he had got it wrong.

'A lump. Just here.' Poppy's hand flew to the space between her breast and armpit, a small area that was now as familiar to her as her face.

'And you didn't tell me?' He placed his hand across his mouth as his eyes widened.

She shook her head and closed her eyes. 'No.'

'Why didn't you tell me? I'd have come with you, sorted it out.'

'That's *why* I didn't tell you. I didn't want you to get in a state and start worrying until I knew we had something to worry about.'

Martin ran his tongue over his lips. His voice was quiet,

his speech slow. 'And do we, Poppy? Do we have something to worry about?' He looked like a child, pleading as he edged closer to her.

She nodded and leant forward, resting her face on his shoulder, inhaling the scent of him. 'Yes, Mart. Yes we do.'

He pulled away from her, his face inches from hers. 'Are they sure it's cancer?' He was struggling.

Poppy nodded.

'And the thing is, Mart...' She swallowed. 'They don't think I'm going to get better.'

'I feel sick,' he murmured as he fought to stop the rise of bile in his throat. 'I feel like I've been punched in the gut. I don't believe it.'

Martin stood slowly and left the bathroom.

Poppy scrambled from the shower and wrapped her head in a white towel and her body in another. She opened their bedroom door. Martin was standing stock still, facing the window. He had his back to her and he didn't turn round. She pictured the hair that had come away from her scalp, weightless, like nothing, as it slipped through her fingers free of its anchors.

Poppy crept from the room. She jostled Peg up the stairs and kissed Max as she got her sleepy boy into his pyjamas and laid him in his bed. 'Night night, sleep tight, my darlings.' She blew kisses from the landing and walked back into their bedroom, closing the door behind her.

Martin was where she had left him, staring out into the dead of night. Poppy sat on the bed, pulled back the duvet next to her and patted the space by her side. 'Come here, Mart.'

He turned and looked at her, staring as if seeing her for the first time.

'Come on, come and lie down,' she coaxed.

Martin reluctantly lowered himself down next to her on the bed, his actions stiff and unnatural, and she drew the duvet over his shivering form. She sat sideways and crossed her legs, resting her hands on her knees. As she stroked his chest beneath the covers, it reminded her of when they'd first got together. The simple joy of sharing a bed with someone she loved had been overwhelming. Poppy would wake in the dark and watch him sleeping, careful not to disturb his slumber. She would watch his mouth twitch and his eyelids flicker, until eventually, when daylight penetrated their room, he would open his eyes and reach for her and hold her tight, keeping her safe from all that lay beyond the bedroom door.

She laid her head on his hip. 'The consultant I've been seeing, Mr Ramasingh, is the best, apparently. If anyone can help me, he can. He came up with a treatment plan for me and he's monitoring how it's going. You can come with me if you want.'

'It will all be okay, won't it, Poppy?'

Poppy closed her eyes and considered her words with care. 'Whatever happens, it will all be okay. We will get through it.'

'I don't know what to say to you. I'm trying to take it all in, but I can't. It's like I'm having a dream, a really bad dream.' He spoke to the wall, facing away from her.

'Just hold me then.' Poppy eased back the duvet and lowered herself into the warm space, wriggling down the bed and pulling at his shoulder until he twisted and she was in his arms. She felt her muscles relax against the solidity of his body. There they lay until morning, pressed together, matching each other breath for breath.

Eleven

'Here's Mummy,' Martin said as Poppy came down the stairs in her pyjamas the next morning. She had combed her hair back over the bald patches and tied it up in a scrunchie. He was looking at her in a way that she had never seen before, with a combination of fear and disbelief, as if he were committing her every move to memory, petrified that she might disappear in a puff of smoke. She could only smile and nod in his direction, reassuring him with her gaze. *It's okay, darling. I'm not going anywhere. Not yet...* He looked ahead of her footfall, wanting to remove objects and clear her path, as though she were made of glass. Poppy realised it was this sort of treatment she had been hoping to avoid, knowing in that instant she had made the leap from wife to patient.

They had agreed to talk to Peg that morning, before Poppy went into hospital for more therapy. It would give them the whole weekend to answer any questions and calm her before school on Monday. Poppy dug deep to find a smile and tried to make it as sincere as she could. They had decided to give her a watered-down version of the truth, a baseline onto which they could add details as time and circumstances required.

Peg sat on the sofa with her bare feet resting on her dad's leg. They were watching the Cartoon Network. Scooby-Doo was in a hurry. Peg chuckled as Scooby stood flailing his arms and legs, which were a blur. He stopped, gulped and looked straight at them as he realised that despite his efforts he wasn't going anywhere at all – that darn tin of spilt grease! Martin reached for the remote control and the screen gave a tiny flash before disappearing into a black dot in the middle of the TV.

'Daaad! I was watching that!' Peg kicked her feet against him in protest.

'I know, but Mummy and I want to have a word with you.'

'Oh God.' Peg sat up on the sofa and folded her arms across her chest. She looked and sounded like her great-grandma, Dorothea, and it made Poppy smile.

Poppy sat on the coffee table, opposite her daughter, and took her chilly little toes between her hands.

'There is something that I need to talk to you about, sweetheart.'

'Is it sexy stuff?' Peg asked as she flicked her fringe from her eyes.

'Sorry?' Poppy blinked.

'Is it babies and sexy stuff, because I know all about that already.'

'You do?' Poppy asked, while Martin coughed and shifted uncomfortably in his seat.

'Yes.' Peg sighed. 'Jade McKeever had a book about where babies come from and I know it's seeds and eggs, so you don't need to explain it to me.'

'Why am I not surprised?' Poppy asked. 'But no, it's not about that. The thing is, I went to the doctor's a little while ago and I am not very well.'

'What's the matter with you?' Peg was, as ever, direct.

'I have a problem with my blood and my bones and I am going to go into hospital in a few days, only for a day or so, so they can sort it out a bit. And then I will feel a lot, lot better, hopefully less achey and not so tired.'

'What sort of problem is it?' Peg's nose twitched.

'It's a really horrible bug and it's a bug that is going to make me very poorly and make me feel like rubbish, which is pants.' Poppy grimaced. 'It might make me feel weak and sleepy and all sorts of yucky things. So Daddy will pick you up from school more and maybe do a bit more of the shopping and cooking, that kind of thing.'

Poppy waited for her daughter's next comment, but it wasn't what she expected.

'Can you or Dad get me some little cartons of Ribena? Jade McKeever has them for break time and I'd like some too.'

Poppy nodded. 'Yes, sure.'

Peg hopped off the sofa and went to collect Toffee from his cage.

Poppy looked at her husband, who shrugged.

It turned out to be like any other Saturday, where the hours flew by twice as fast as they did on a weekday. They ate ham and pickle sandwiches and crisps from plates which they balanced on their laps for lunch, Max had a nap mid afternoon and Martin pottered in his garage, doing goodness knows what. Poppy wiped down the surfaces in the kitchen ten times and washed the same mugs and plates at least four times before drying them and stacking them in the cupboards, ready for use.

Aunty Jo dropped by, much to the delight of Peg, who insisted on giving her an impromptu makeover. Afterwards, as Poppy and Jo sat on the sofa – the remnants of blue eye shadow and a generous smear of red blusher still shockingly visible on Jo's face – Martin thundered down the stairs, nearly slipping off the bottom step in his socks.

'I've had a great idea!' he announced.

'Oh God, what now? I can think of several times when

you've said that in the past and on one occasion you actually got me arrested!' Poppy laughed.

'Yes, my sweet, but you were never charged, and that's the difference.' He winked at his wife. 'Why don't we have a party?'

Poppy curled her top lip. 'What, now?'

'No, in a few months – in the summer!' He was grinning like a kid.

'What kind of party, love? The kind where Peg sits on the stairs and watches everyone get drunk and you wee in a cupboard?'

Martin laughed. 'No, the kind where we hire the hall in Bulford and fill it with balloons and bunting and get a band in, do a really nice buffet, invite all our friends and all the kids' friends and have a bash that they will never forget!' He was brimming with energy.

'Like the wedding reception we never had?' Poppy asked. 'Only don't expect me to wear a silly white frock or anything.'

Martin beamed at her. 'Exactly. Like the wedding reception we never had. What do you think?'

Poppy pictured the kids dressed up, her and Martin laughing with their friends. 'I think you better give them a ring and see what dates they've got free. The whole thing, mind, Mart, not half the hall roped off like they do for kids' parties. I'm not sharing my special do with the over-sixties' dinner club or the Brownies' indoor Olympics!'

Martin clapped his hands together and went off in search of the local directory.

'Looks like we're having a party, mate!' Poppy smiled at Jo.

'I'll come back for it from wherever I've moved to.' Jo swallowed at the horrible thought of having to start over.

'Oh God.' Poppy placed her hand on her friend's arm.

'You better had. It wouldn't be the same for me if you weren't there and I've a feeling his lordship will have you on balloon-blowing duties.'

'My pleasure. Ooh, I think I might treat myself to a new outfit. I've got to grab every opportunity I can – the chances of meeting husband number two while wandering around Sainsbury's are pretty slim!'

'Oh, I don't know, I've seen you eyeing up that bloke on the fish counter!' Poppy raised her eyebrows at her friend.

Peg came down the stairs with her hairbrush and a collection of ribbons and sparkly clips. Jo groaned and looked at Poppy. Clearly her transformation wasn't quite complete.

'I know we're joking, but in truth it's all a bit soon for that. I don't know how I'd ever trust anyone again.'

'You will, mate, when the right one comes along.'

'How do you know when the right one comes along?' Peg asked as she arranged her hair accessories on the table.

Poppy laughed. 'You know because your tummy goes flippy and your face goes all smoochy. Isn't that right, Jo?'

'Yep, that's the way!' Jo smiled at her friend. 'And you know, don't you, that I'll come back whenever the kids need minding or you need shopping, or anything, anything at all. Just pick up the phone, Poppy, and I'll be here in a flash.'

Poppy smiled, feeling very lucky to have a friend like Jo.

Poppy had spent the day constantly glancing at Peg, who she had to admit seemed fine, despite the news of her mum's horrid, lingering bug. She ran her daughter's bath and sat on the floor while Peg splashed and chatted. She had been told to expect a delayed reaction, questions out of the blue, but so far, nothing. Though she was concerned that Peg might be bottling things up, she was in truth relieved not to have to deal with that reaction and those questions.

When she and Martin went to bed that night, they were both thinking about Peg.

Martin clicked off the bedside lamp and reached for his wife. Poppy pulled herself across the mattress until she lay with her head on his chest and his arm around her back and shoulder, cradling her to him. They liked to snuggle like this and when she drew away from him to seek out the cooler, uninhabited side of the mattress, they both knew that was their cue for sleep. It was one of the many habits, little rituals that they had fallen into over the years.

'She seems okay,' he whispered into the dark, his eyes not yet fully adjusted to the blackness.

'She does, but we'll need to keep an eye on her. She'll probably have some questions once she's consulted the oracle that is Jade McKeever and had her head filled with all the gory details. I guess we'll have to use the dreaded c-word at some point, but all in good time.'

'Maybe. Should we tell the school, do you think?'

'What, that Jade is more knowledgeable than the *Encyclopaedia Britannica*? I'm sure they already know,' Poppy quipped.

'No, clever clogs. About you.'

Poppy shook her head. 'No. Not yet.' She thought about the dinner lady who had contracted leukaemia a year or so ago, remembered the fundraisers, the vast, signed cards, the looks of pity and the gossip at the school gates. She wasn't ready for that, any of it. 'I don't want to tell them because then it makes it real and I don't really think it is. I keep expecting to get a phone call from the health centre telling me that there has been a bit of a mix-up and they'll expect me to be angry, but I won't be. I'll just be happy and relieved.'

'I feel the same. I still can't take it in.' He squeezed her tight. 'How are you feeling?'

Poppy heard the clammy sticking of his teeth to his lips. Even asking this made him nervous.

'I'm okay.' This was the truth; at that point, she was okay.

'I was thinking…' Martin stopped.

'Thinking what?' she prompted.

She heard him sigh, felt his chest rise and fall beneath her cheek. 'I was thinking that most people meet when they are much older than us and then have so many years together.'

'Mmnnn.' She didn't know where he was going with this.

'Well, maybe we met when we were so young so that we could have as much time as possible together. Or maybe *because* we got together when we were so young, we have kind of speeded things up and that's why you are ill now, when you're still only young, almost like ahead of your time.'

Poppy moved her face against his skin. 'I don't know how or why it all happens, Mart. All I know is it has. It is what it is and I know that I love you and that's all that matters really, isn't it?'

He nodded and kissed her scalp. 'Yep. That's all that matters.'

She changed tack a bit. 'Simon and Kate seem happy, wonder how long they've been married?'

'Don't know, but fancy them inviting us over! I still can't get over it. It's incredible.'

Poppy smiled against his chest. 'It really is.'

There was a pause while both considered the practicalities involved in making a trip to the Caribbean.

'Do you think you're allowed to travel, Poppy? I don't know how it works.'

'Me either, love. We're both on a bit of a steep learning curve here.' She kissed his neck.

'Yep, we are that.'

Poppy lifted her head and raised her shoulder, preparing to scoot over to her side, but Martin held her fast. 'Stay here.' He almost pleaded.

Poppy woke to the sound of the bedroom door creaking open. It was early and as usual she had tossed and turned into the wee small hours with her cogs turning and her body aching. Yet now, with the creep of day making its way under the curtain and across the wall, she could quite happily sleep until lunch time. It was always the way.

Peg, trying her best to be silent, kicked the bottom of her parents' bed, muttered, 'Oops, sorry!', half pulled off the duvet that snagged on her foot, and whispered loudly to her dad as she knelt on the floor beside him, landing with a thump on her knees. Poppy lay still, with her eyes closed, listening. She was hoping she could go back to sleep before Max woke and, still squashed and warm from sleep, demanded cereal, dinosaurs to count, his digger book and Mr Tumble on the telly – not necessarily in that order. Her mouth twitched into a smile at the thought of her boy.

'Daddy?' Peg tried to whisper but instead spoke at her normal volume, just with a rasp to her voice. She hadn't quite grasped the concept.

'What, Peg?'

Poppy felt Martin lean up on one elbow and heard him reach for his watch. 'What is it, love?'

'I need you to get up and take me into Salisbury.'

'Right now?' he asked, his voice still with its morning's gruffness.

'In a little while will be okay. I need to get to the shops for when they open.'

'Okay. What do you need to buy?' Martin yawned and stretched. Poppy heard his back crack as he twisted. The mattress springs creaked as he swung his legs off the bed and she heard him put his dressing gown on. She loved this man and wondered how many dads would be so appeasing and not bark that it was early, come back later, five more minutes... But he was no ordinary dad and this was no ordinary situation. He was the dad of kids whose mum had cancer. Cancer. It was as if now it had been spoken there was no way it was going to stay hidden. Like a sleeping bag that once removed from its little sausage-shaped bag was almost impossible to get back in. Or like an image so graphic that it sat in your mind for perfect recall, no matter how repellent.

'I need to go to Smyths. It's important.'

'Well, if it's important then we better get a wiggle on. I'll have a quick shower and meet you downstairs in, what, ten minutes?'

'Thank you, Dad.' Poppy heard the relief in Peg's tone.

'I'll tell you what,' Martin said as he rummaged in the drawer for socks, pants and a T-shirt, 'why don't we go to McDonald's and get breakfast? Don't tell Mummy!'

Poppy smiled into her pillow as Peg gasped with joy. A McDonald's breakfast was a rarity.

'What about Maxy?' Peg asked. Poppy screwed her eyes shut, overwhelmed by the love this little girl had for her brother, not wanting to receive a treat if he did not.

'I reckon you'll find him a little something in Smyths, don't you?'

Peg squealed as she scampered from the room. Martin sat back on the mattress and placed his hand on the curve of his wife's hip as he leant over and kissed the side of her face.

'What d'you suppose that's all about?' he asked.

'I don't know, love, but thank you.' She turned her head and kissed his stubbly chin.

'Peg seems okay,' he offered.

'Yes, she does. It said in one of the leaflets I was given that kids often adapt better than adults, partly through lack of understanding but also because, until the worst happens, it's all a bit unreal.' Poppy had devoured all the literature she had been given. The advice was seared into her mind. 'We can give her more details when she asks for them or if we need to; it's important we go at her pace, drip-feed her the information. That's what my leaflet said. We're not to overwhelm her or lie to her. I guess the right thing lies somewhere between the two.'

Martin kissed his wife once more before he headed for the shower. 'That leaflet can fuck right off,' he said as he shut the bedroom door.

For some reason this made Poppy laugh. She giggled into her pillow and then, quite without warning, her laughter turned to tears. And there she lay, with a seemingly never-ending stream of tears meandering like a little tributary across her nose and cheek and pooling in a cold, wet patch on her pillow. It was as if now she had started she couldn't stop. She sobbed, pushing her face into the pillow as if this might stem the flow, but it didn't. Thankful that she was alone, with no one to witness her distress, she curled her legs up towards her body and wrapped her arms around her shins, trying to make herself as small as possible.

* * *

Poppy eventually roused herself and decided to make the most of her time alone with Max. With Peg and Martin in Salisbury, the two pottered in the back garden for the best part of the morning. Resplendent in his bright blue wellingtons, Max ran around the grass until he got dizzy and fell down in a heap, then scrambled up and repeated the performance.

'Don't hurt yourself, Maxy!' Poppy smiled at her happy little boy. She slowly gathered up stray leaves and twigs, snipping at the dead heads of her flowering tubs and collecting all the waste into an old, cracked bucket that she had saved for the purpose. She worked slowly, her movements laboured.

'Is that you, Poppy?' Jo called from over the six-foot fence that divided their gardens.

'No, I'm a burglar, but when I saw the state of the garden, I decided to have a little tidy-up!' Poppy replied.

'Very funny!' Jo gave a small snort of laughter. She was finding it hard to find anything amusing as she packed up the house, dismantling all the reminders of her marital home. 'I could do with a burglar like that: this place looks like a swamp. Not that I care. I'm not doing a thing before I move out, I'm leaving it all to the D.I.C.K.H.E.A.D.' She spelt out the last word, conscious of Max's mimicry skills.

Poppy heard a dragging sound seconds before Jo's head appeared over the top of the fence.

'What are you standing on?'

'An old recycling box!'

'God, be careful.' Poppy could see her friend's balancing act ending in disaster.

Max pointed up towards her, holding his car. 'Tractor, Jo Jo!'

'I see it, Maxy!' She waved at him.

'Am I having the little man this week?' Jo looked eagerly at Max.

Poppy thought about her hospital appointment. 'Actually, mate, I have one day that might be good...'

'Fab, let me know!'

'Will do.' Poppy smiled.

Jo wobbled and grabbed at the fence. They both laughed.

Poppy heard the car pull up outside, followed by the burble of Peg's chatter as she ran up the path.

'That's Peg home! See you in a bit.' She watched as Jo's face fell, wishing she too had a family charging up the drive, homeward bound.

Poppy pulled off her gardening gloves as she entered the house through the kitchen door. Peg was beaming. Martin, however, looked almost ashen as he raised his eyebrows in greeting.

Peg thundered up the stairs, taking two at a time.

'You all right?' she asked. She ditched her muddy gloves under the sink and pulled off Max's wellies, whereupon he immediately raced back into the garden in his socks.

Martin gave a smile and a small nod with his lips tucked over his teeth. It was his fake smile, the one she had seen him use throughout his life. It was a smokescreen, convincing to everyone except her, who knew him too well.

'I was just saying to Jo that she could have Maxy one day this week.' She caught his eye and he smiled.

'Yes, that's a good idea,' he muttered as he watched her from the doorway. 'Here he is!' Keen for the distraction, he scooped up his son and lifted him high into the air before planting a kiss on his face. 'We got you a pressie, Maxy.'

Walking over to the table, Martin retrieved a large plastic digger truck, complete with JCB stickers and monster-sized wheels, which the little boy counted. 'One… two… three… four!' Max wriggled to the floor and tried to pull the vehicle from its cardboard backing. Martin dropped to his knees to help and before too long, Max was shuffling around the floor on his knees, pushing the truck with one hand and making an engine noise by blowing out through his lips. 'Digger!' he shouted sporadically, just in case anyone was in any doubt.

'So what was the big drama? What did she need to buy?' Poppy asked as she filled the kettle and flicked the switch.

Martin drew breath to answer, but before he could find the words, Peg was in front of them, standing at the bottom of the stairs.

Poppy gazed at her daughter, who had a plastic stethoscope around her neck, a little white bag with a red cross on it under her arm, a natty little white headscarf also with a red cross on it, and a blue-and-white-striped dress that was a couple of sizes too big for her.

'I can look after you now, Mummy, and make your bug better. I'm a nurse.'

Poppy stared at her little girl, speechless, overcome with love for this child of hers, and with sadness, for all that she instinctively knew she would miss.

Twelve

Poppy went through the now familiar routine. Staring at the others in the outpatients unit, with their sunken eyes and unhealthy pallor, she wondered if she looked the same. The burble of the radio in the background soothed her; it was good to hear life going on as normal.

She called Martin when she was ready to go home. He drove up to the front door and jumped out, opening the passenger door.

'I brought you a blanket.' He stood holding their picnic rug in his hands.

'Thanks, love.' Poppy felt obliged to place it on her knees. Martin drove slowly home as Max slept in his seat.

'Does it hurt?' He winced as he navigated the traffic lights and looked straight ahead.

'No.' She answered truthfully. 'It's weird, but not painful.'

Martin glanced to his left to check her expression. 'I'm so glad. I've been worried sick.'

'I don't feel great though. I feel a bit fluey.'

'It's okay, we'll have you home in no time and I can tuck you up on the sofa and drive you nuts by fussing over you.'

Poppy gave a small smile and closed her eyes, allowing herself to snooze, rocked to sleep by the rhythm of the car.

When she opened her eyes again, they were home. Martin

had opened the passenger door and was attempting to lift her from the seat.

'I can do it, love. I'm fine,' she whispered. 'You don't have to lift me. Get Max first.' Her whole body shook as if she had a chill.

Martin rushed Max inside and came back for his wife. Leaning on him, she walked slowly up the path and into their little home, which had the lamps glowing, the heating on and the cushions plumped. Poppy thought it was the nicest sight in the whole wide world. Max opened his eyes and beamed at his mum, happy that she was in front of him.

'What kind of treatment makes you feel a shed-load worse than you did before you had it? What kind of medicine is that, for God's sake?' Poppy laid her head on Martin's shoulder as he rubbed her back.

'I don't know, love, but we've got to trust those that tell us it's for the best, haven't we?'

'Yes, we have.' She reached out and squeezed his hand.

'Do you think it's working, Poppy? Do you think it's… shrinking everything?'

She nodded. 'I hope so.'

Martin went to collect Peg from school. Poppy took the opportunity and reached from under the blanket to pull the receiver into her hands. She closed her eyes, hesitating. She needed to talk to someone. She needed help and she needed someone to help Martin. There was only one person whose calmness and wisdom would bring her the comfort she needed. She punched in the digits and listened to the ringing tone.

'Hello? Claudia? It's me…'

After she put the phone down, Poppy trod the stairs and replayed Claudia's words: 'I want to come over to Larkhill right now, but I don't want to interfere. I won't rest until

I've seen you, my precious girl.' Poppy went into the bedroom, took the memory boxes from the bottom of her wardrobe and carried them slowly downstairs.

She placed the boxes on the table and lifted the lids. Into Max's she put a photograph of him at two weeks old, asleep on his beanbag. On the back she wrote:

One of your favourite places to nap! Mind you, Maxy, you can nap anywhere! X

Alongside it she added a small white button with a duck on it. Poppy had sewn it onto a two-inch square of white hankie, on which she had written, in her tiny, neat script:

A button from the little cardigan you were wearing when we brought you home from the hospital. You were tiny and gorgeous! I was so proud of my brand-new little boy that I thought I might burst. Xx

Into Peg's box she put an acorn along with a note that read:

You found this acorn when we were walking up by Woodhenge. You were so excited, do you remember? Convinced you might have an oak tree growing in your bedroom if you watered it enough! No oak tree, Peg, but still a lovely thing. xx

Poppy recalled the acorn lying in the palm of her little girl's hand, and the way she had run ahead, eager to get home and find an empty yoghurt pot in which to plant it. 'Come on, Mummy!' she had called out over her shoulder. There was no time to waste.

Next to go in the boxes were the little plastic identification bracelets that had been put round their wrists and ankles as soon as they were born, each with the date and their name, 'Baby Cricket'. Holding them between her thumb and forefinger made her smile. She closed her eyes and remembered the first time she had fed each of them, watching as their rosebud mouths sought her and gorged until milk trickled down over their rounded, sleepy cheeks.

The bell rang. Poppy opened the front door and Jo rushed in. 'God, Poppy, I'm having a right panic. I move out in ten days and I feel sick if I think about it.'

'You'll be fine, mate,' Poppy said. Jo had found a little cottage in Marlborough to rent. 'It's not that far. We'll still see you all the time.'

'I guess. It just feels like the end of an era.' Jo tried unsuccessfully to stifle a sob as her tears welled. 'I still can't believe it. All those bloody nights spent sitting in, waiting for a call or cleaning the house even though he wasn't coming home, trying to keep my mind off the loneliness. I loved him, Poppy, I really did. But I don't know that he ever loved me, not really.'

'I'm sure he did, Jo.' Poppy had decided to give Danny the benefit of the doubt. 'And I know this is an awful time for you, but it will pass, mate, everything does.'

Jo sniffed and wiped her eyes as she walked over to the table. 'What you doing with these?' She stared at the boxes.

Poppy sat down and pulled a chair out for her friend and neighbour. 'I'm making memory boxes for the kids.'

'What are they?'

'Just boxes that I put little things in to remind them of me when they are older. Photos, notes, that sort of thing.'

'Ah, that's lovely.' Jo paused. 'Won't you just be able to show them that stuff yourself?'

Poppy looked at her dear friend and swallowed. 'I don't know. I've got cancer, mate. Inoperable bloody cancer.' And just like that, she had said it out loud, and surprisingly it was easier than she'd thought.

Jo stared at her friend in silence, allowing the words to filter through to a place of understanding. Then she placed her head in her hands and sobbed, loudly.

That evening, Poppy sat in front of the laptop and drew her cardigan around herself, practising what she needed to say. It felt so much easier in her head and the idea of saying the words out loud to Simon and Kate was daunting to say the least. But Martin was reading Peg a story and this was a good opportunity.

Kate answered the call. Her sunny face appeared on the screen. 'Hello, Poppy! I was only telling someone today in Super J, our local supermarket, about my niece Poppy. It feels really nice knowing there are more members of our family out there, and you're the only niece I have. My sister has a boy, Luke, but you are my only niece – how great is that? The more the merrier, I say. Safety in numbers and all that. All okay? Have you had a chance to think about your visit? We can't talk about much else, we're very excited.'

Poppy smiled. 'Us too and we would really love to come and see you, Kate—'

Kate interrupted, giving a little clap of her hands and bouncing in her chair. 'Oh, that's wonderful! I'll get Simon to email you dates and details and we can make a plan. My friend Natasha is coming over with her bloke, some American musician she's picked up, can't wait for that! But other than her week, we are completely free.'

'The thing is, Kate...' Poppy exhaled.

'Yes, lovey?'

'I'm not very well.'

'Oh, you poor thing, sorry to hear that. Well, look, don't let me keep you, we can chat anytime. But please have a good nap, drink plenty of fluids and see how you feel. Do you think you've picked up a little bug?'

Poppy smiled at Kate's lovely mothering nature. She envied Dominic and Lydia and could only imagine how idyllic their lives must have been, growing up with a mum like that.

Telling Kate was even harder than she'd feared and the first thing Poppy did when she shut down Skype was seek refuge in the obituary pages.

Joy Roberts, 68, stepped off this mortal coil with dignity. Joy spent her last days at Hawthorne House, surrounded by her friends. Widow of Jack, mother to the late Julian Roberts. Joy was an educator, a Justice of the Peace and a lifelong member of the WRVS. You helped so many, Joy, and you will be sadly missed by all.

Martin came down the stairs, treading carefully in his socks to avoid the creaky spots. This meant that both kids were asleep.

'Both nodded off?' Poppy asked from the sofa with her legs tucked up underneath her.

'Yes. Peg before we even got to the end of the chapter – not like her. She usually stays awake in case I miss a bit of the story out or, God forbid, misread a sentence.'

'You've got to be up early to catch her out.'

'Don't I know it. Our little pilot.' Martin stood in front of his wife. 'Did we hear you talking to Kate?'

'Yes. I told her.'

'That can't have been easy, love. What did she say?'

'Oh, just what you'd expect. She was shocked and sorry, but not too gushy. I really like her.'

'That's good, and you still think we should go? Think you'll be up to it?'

'Yes I do. I want to go, Mart.' She looked up at her husband, her gaze determined.

'Then let's make it happen.' He sounded equally committed. 'What you got there?' Martin reached under the cushion and pulled out the folded newspaper.

'Poppy! Not the bloody obituaries again!'

She sighed and patted the space next to her on the sofa. 'I'm interested in them.'

'What's interesting about people you never knew?' He shook his head as he sat down next to her and she unfurled her feet, placing them on his warm lap.

She shrugged her shoulders. 'In a weird way it gives me comfort. I like to read how loved these people were. Their lives weren't wasted, were they, if they were loved?'

Martin cupped her foot in his palm and rubbed the skin back and forth, watching it rise in a wrinkle against his thumb. He didn't mention her fat veins that sat like bloated sausages under her skin, standing proud of her ankle and instep. 'I guess not.'

'And also...' She swallowed. 'If I am reading about people that have died, it means I am still here, while they are not. I'm beating them. Aren't I?'

'Yes, my love, you are.' Martin stared at her foot, still unable to have that conversation. 'I guess I don't want you reading them because I'm worried it'll make you sad.' He spoke the truth, staring at her feet, incapable of meeting her gaze. His voice was gruff, his eyes reddened, tired.

'Christ, Mart, I'm so full of sadness right now, reading the obituaries in comparison is bloody light relief!'

'I'm sorry you're full of sadness. I wish I knew how to make it better. It's hard for me too, but you being unhappy is the last thing I want.'

Poppy pulled her feet from his grasp and sat back on the chair. 'Hard for you too? You haven't got a clue! And it's nothing to do with what you do or don't want!' She had raised her voice. 'There are lots of things *I* don't want,' she snapped.

'I know that. I'm doing my best.'

'Well maybe your best just isn't good enough!' Poppy's frustration flared. 'I hate the fact that I'm stuck here and I can't do anything properly and the house is turning into a pigsty!' Poppy flung her arm in an arc to indicate the lounge that, to the untrained eye, bar a couple of toys scattered on the floor, looked immaculate. 'I hate the fact that my every waking moment is taken up with feeling this shit and I hate that you get to stay with them and watch them grow and I don't!'

Martin was shaking. 'I hate it too! I fucking hate it! I hate the obituaries and I hate the fact that you have had to tell Peg and Claudia and Jo and Kate and God knows who else. And I hate the fact that you are leaving me. And I hate the fact that you excluded me. Christ alive, we've been through everything together and you didn't say a bloody word until you had to. It was dishonest and I hate that!' He sank down on the floor and tried to control his shaking frame.

They both sat for a minute or two in silence, letting their anger dissipate and their words settle like a fine dust around them.

Poppy eventually rose from the sofa and knelt down beside

him on the cool, laminate floor. Martin reached out and pulled her into his chest, cradling her against him. He closed his eyes. He made a silent pledge to try and look at things from her perspective, no matter how hard. They sat in silence for a while longer until the storm had passed.

Poppy pulled herself free from his grasp. 'We need to cope with this, Mart. We have to, for our sake and for Peg and Maxy's sake. You know that, don't you?'

'I know.'

She turned to face him. 'What's the first thing you remember, Mart?'

He sighed and thought about it. 'Dunno really. I remember being in primary school and we were allowed to wear home clothes, but you came in that day in your uniform. I now know it was probably cos you never had anything else to wear and you got a lot of stick for it. I remember that day quite clearly. I wanted to go and punch that silly cow who used to pick on you – Jackie—'

'Sinclair. Jackie Sinclair.'

Poppy would never forget her name or her angry, accusing tone as she fired barbed comments and spit-laden insults in her direction. 'Why are you wearing your uniform today, Poppy? Is it because all your clothes have got fleas like you?' Jackie's cronies had giggled in the background, fascinated by the vicious taunts and relieved that they weren't in the firing line. Jackie was as usual, buoyed up by their support. 'Did you hear me, Fleabag? Why are you wearing your scuzzy uniform? Didn't you know it was home clothes day? Don't you have any home clothes?' Poppy remembered the questions coming at her like bullets in quick succession. The onslaught far too fast to think of a good retort other than the truth. No, she didn't have any home clothes that would pass muster. She had felt like she was outside of her body, watching herself blinking rapidly with her arms folded across her chest as though this might deflect some of the attack. It didn't. Jackie's words cut through her defences and embedded themselves in her memory where they were permanently lodged, even now, over twenty-five years later.

'Yeah, that was it – Jackie Sinclair.' Martin nodded. 'God, you've got a good memory. And I remember our school trip to the zoo.' He smiled.

'Same.' Poppy nodded, shaking her head to rid herself of the memory of her crappy packed lunch that defined her crappy life. 'The point is, Mart, you don't remember being two, do you?'

'Two? No, course I don't!' He shrugged.

'And neither do I.'

Martin's face dropped as he realised where this was heading.

Poppy was silent, picturing her little boy's chubby fists clutching a digger or a dinosaur; her little counting boy, her two-year-old. 'Max won't remember me, will he?' She searched his face for the honest answer.

'Course he will!' he backtracked.

'No, no he won't. You just said.' She shook her head. 'Not properly.'

'He will, Poppy. It will be different for him. I'll keep you in his head and show him pictures and tell him stories. Blimey, you don't think Peg'll shut up about you for a minute, do you? We will keep you with him, always.' Martin swallowed.

'He will read about me, read things like this.' She pointed at the obituary page. 'And our story, he'll only need to click a few pages on the internet and our story is there, for always. Do you remember all the fuss way back then? Arriving back on home soil and seeing those banners – "Well Done, Poppy Day" and "Welcome Home, Martin!" Imagine that? All for me, for us.'

'And all them articles calling you a hero!' Martin beamed.

'It all seemed so unreal! Like it was nothing to do with me. And a bit embarrassing, really. A hero? Nah. Just doing what was necessary to get my man back. It feels like a long time ago.'

'Not to me, Poppy. Sometimes it feels like yesterday. I don't ever stop thanking my lucky stars for what you did for me.' He smiled at his wife. 'And that'll be wonderful for Maxy and Peg to read about. They will know how amazing their mum was, not only because of what I'll tell them, but from what others will tell them too.'

Poppy nodded and slumped back against his chest. It would have to be enough; it wasn't as if she had any choice in the matter. She watched Martin cough and breathe deeply, realising that since this whole horrible thing had begun he still hadn't cried.

Thirteen

Poppy stood in front of the shower and flicked the tap, listening as the water hit the tray. Raising her arms, she tried to summon the energy to take off her clothes. She closed her eyes and breathed deeply, knowing that this morning, like last night, she didn't have it in her to step into the cubicle and wash herself. Instead, she turned the tap off, rinsed her face, cleaned her teeth and began slowly gathering up the pants, socks and discarded pyjama bottoms from the bathroom and bedroom floors. She'd shower later. She stood on the landing with the laundry basket in her hands, taking a minute to rest before she attempted the descent. She hated how physically weak she felt.

'Bastard pedalos,' she whispered.

Cocking her head to hear better, Poppy sighed at the unmistakable sound of crying that came from Peg's room. Placing the basket and its grubby contents at the top of the stairs, she walked back and tapped on her little girl's bedroom door.

'Can I come in?'

There was no reply.

Poppy listened to the shuffling of the duvet, the sniff and then the deep breath that belied the age of the girl who opened the door. Peg greeted her mum red-eyed but grinning, knowing already how to paint on a mask that told the world

all was well. It was a mask that would get her through the
darkest of days and a mask Poppy knew only too well. Her
daughter's bravado sent a jolt of love through her veins.

Peg pulled the door wide and bounced back into the nest
of duvet that she had only just vacated.

'Are you okay?' Poppy leant on the chest of drawers with
her arms folded across her chest.

Peg nodded and picked at the embroidered pattern on her
quilt.

'It's just that I thought I heard you crying.'

Peg sat up and used the heels of her hands to plug her
eyes. 'I'm sorry, Mum. I'm having a bit of a sad day and I
don't know why.'

'Oh, love, you're allowed a bit of a sad day. We all are.
Is there anything I can do to help? Anything you want to
talk about?' Poppy recalled the advice: she was to let Peg
ask for information and guidance. Far better that they went
at her pace.

'Not really.' Peg looked up. 'It's just that I'm trying really
hard at school, I'm trying to talk less and I'm still not register
monitor. Mia-Rose has had three goes and I haven't been
picked once!' And just like that, another wave of tears broke
their banks and cascaded down Peg's cheeks.

Poppy knelt on the carpet next to the bed. 'Do you know
why you haven't been picked, Peg?'

Peg took a deep breath and shook her head. 'No.'

'I do,' Poppy said. 'You haven't been picked because Mrs
Newman is a miserable, bitter cow.'

'Mum!' Peg gasped, before breaking into giggles that shook
her whole body. 'You said "miserable cow"!'

'It's true, Peg, Mrs Newman is a bloody miserable cow.
What is she?' Poppy smiled as Peg lay back on her mattress

and fought for breath through her laughter; it was wonderful to see.

'She's a cow!' Peg placed her hand over her mouth and closed her eyes, unable to believe the conversation she was having with her mum.

'That's right. I want you to remember that just because someone holds a certain position or is in charge, it doesn't mean they always know best or that they are smarter than you.'

Poppy saw an image of Major Helm, Martin's former reporting officer, who she had butted heads with when trying to bring Martin home from Afghanistan. She hadn't allowed his rank slide to curtail her behaviour. What had she said to him? 'I am not "every other army wife". I couldn't give a shit about coffee mornings and convention!' She remembered the look he had given her, part furious, but also confused, unable to comprehend her lack of deference.

'Okay, Peg?'

'Okay, Mum.'

'That's my girl. But you are not to say that word again – promise?'

'I promise.' Peg beamed, tears abated. Her smile was now genuine, the kind that caused her nose to wrinkle and her eyes to shine. 'I get upset about Jade McKeever sometimes as well...' Peg plucked at her duvet cover.

'Why? I thought she was your best friend?'

Peg shrugged her shoulders. 'She is, but sometimes...' She hesitated.

'Sometimes what, love?'

'Sometimes she's a bit mean to me.'

Poppy took her little girl's hand into her own. 'Well, all I know, Peg, is that best friends are kind to each other, not mean. They look out for each other and they make each other happy.' She thought of her own childhood best friend, Jenna, and how she used to burst into their little flat like a ray of sunshine.

Poppy had been happiest when in the company of her girl friend and could only picture the two of them slumped on the single bed in her bedroom, laughing uncontrollably until they cried and one or both had to scurry to the loo. No matter what topic, whether boys, music, make-up or something far less important, she and Jenna found almost everything hilarious. Poppy knew she had never laughed in that way before or since.

'Did you and your best friend ever fall out, Mum?' Peg asked, hopefully.

Poppy shook her head. 'No, never. Not properly, maybe the odd disagreement, but it was always sorted out before one of us had to go in for our tea.' She declined to mention that their lives were now so far apart that their closeness existed only in memory. She and Jenna were proof that life was lived on the spin of a coin, where one small decision could determine a path from which it was often impossible to deviate.

Peg sighed. 'Sometimes I cry if I think about Jade being mean to me.' This too she addressed to the duvet.

'It's up to you who you choose for your friends. But if I was going to give you a bit of advice, I'd say that if Jade is mean to you and makes you cry, then I think maybe you need to find a different best friend, don't you?'

Peg nodded.

'Now, go get showered and off to school we go!'

Peg nodded. 'I'm quite excited.' She raised her shoulders and bared her teeth. 'It might be my turn to do the register today!'

'You never know, my love.'

Poppy clumped down the stairs, pausing halfway to catch her breath. She could hear Martin laughing with someone in the kitchen. She looped her hair behind her ears and patted the back of her head to make sure the bald patches and clumps of shorter hair were hidden. She was surprised to see that it was Danny leaning on the cooker with a mug of tea in his hand. He had been back from Afghan for a little while but still had the unmistakable tan that started at his T-shirt sleeves and was darkest at the back of his neck.

'Hello, Poppy. Hope it's okay, just nipped in for a cuppa with Mart.' He looked at her sheepishly, unsure of the reception he could expect.

'Course it's all right. We're not taking sides, are we, Mart?' Poppy looked at her husband.

'No, course not,' Martin confirmed.

'No, we aren't,' Poppy continued. 'But if we were, Dan, we'd say that dumping your wife via the telephone after all those years of marriage was a really shitty thing to do.'

Danny exhaled through bloated cheeks. 'That's fair enough, Poppy, but there was a bit more to it.' He scratched his scalp. 'I was in a hurry.'

'You were in a *hurry*?' Poppy couldn't keep the disdain from her voice.

'I met someone a while ago, through work, and I was kind of seeing her while Jo and I were still married for a while...'

'Did you know about this?' Poppy rounded on Martin, who shook his head and splayed his palms.

'No, he didn't, no one did,' Danny said.

Poppy stared at Jo's husband and tried to find the words. 'Blimey, Danny, that is really nice work.' She thought of her friend, who had done nothing but keep a nice home and wait for his return. 'As I said, we don't take sides in this house, but if we did, I would tell you that you are a nasty little shit-head who has caused a lot of unnecessary pain for someone that really didn't deserve it and I would tell you to get the fuck out of my house. If we were the type to take sides, which we are not. Are we, Mart?' With that, she swept past the two men and proceeded to stuff the laundry into the washing machine, without looking up.

Danny placed his mug on the work surface. 'I think I'd better...' He indicated the wall of the house next door with his thumb.

Martin nodded.

They heard the front door click shut as Danny closed it behind him.

Poppy stood upright and looked at her husband. 'What?'

'Nothing!' Martin held his hands above his head in surrender. 'I didn't say a word.'

'Good.' She pecked him on the cheek as she walked past. 'And if you want to talk to your unfaithful, stupid, dickhead friend, I'm not stopping you. You can just do it next door. I couldn't look Jo in the eye if I'd entertained him in here, like it was all okay, which it's not.'

Martin nodded and picked up Danny's mug, which was nearly full.

'Don't be too long!' she bellowed at his back, feeling inexplicably angry at him, even though he had been as much in the dark as she had.

That afternoon, Poppy sat in the car, refusing to display her blue badge, seeing it as yet another reminder to everyone that she wasn't well. This was not something she was happy to share with the world just yet; doing so would feel like losing part of the fight. She decided instead to take her chances with all the other illegally parked parents, so she sat just beyond the school gates with the window down, waiting for Peg to come trotting across the playground. She missed picking up her little girl and had gathered all her energy to make the trip.

She reached for the newspaper on the passenger seat and read while she waited.

Lizzie Innes Bishop, 39. We are sad to announce that Lizzie lost her battle. Beloved wife of Clinton and mum to Jonah and Phoebe. Lizzie's mantra was 'run with it!' and she did, every step of the way. Keep running, we'll miss you, Lizzie.

Poppy swallowed the lump in her throat. Thinking about Jonah and Phoebe, she hoped they were okay, these two children that she didn't know. She crammed the paper into the side pocket of her door and her fingers touched on a small, flat, square packet, a leftover gift from some fast-food chicken in a box. Unfurling a wet wipe from its pouch, she proceeded to give the dashboard a good wipe over, before starting on the cubby behind the gear stick, as good a time as any to have a little clean.

Peg appeared and stood a few feet away from the car on the pavement. She didn't see her mum instantly, as she was deep in conversation with her friend and mentor, the one and only Jade McKeever.

'But it's *true*, Jade,' Peg pleaded.

Poppy watched as her little girl twisted handfuls of her skirt into her bunched-up fist. 'For tea we have sweeties and cake and marshmallows and lemonade!'

'What, *every* night?' Jade looked at her quizzically.

'Yes, every night.' Peg nodded.

'Don't you have to have vegetables and meat and stuff?'

'No, not in our house. We can have anything we want and it's always sweeties!'

'Why don't you get really fat then?' Jade smirked, with her chin jutting forward and her faux diamond earrings glinting in the sun. Poppy hated the way Jade used her body language to intimidate her daughter.

Peg considered this as she looked down at her own skinny, bruised legs. 'Because when we have finished eating, my mum gives us a magic tablet that gets rid of all of our fat so we can have the same again the next night.'

'I don't believe you, Peg fibber-fox! You are such a liar.' Jade stuck her face right into Peg's.

Poppy felt a red tide of anger rise within her. Yes, Peg was fibbing, but the way Jade sneered in such close proximity to her daughter's face was horrible. And judging by the look of resignation on Peg's face, it wasn't the first time she had been subjected to such an assault.

'But it's true!' Peg looked close to tears.

Poppy mustered all her energy, sprang out of the car and strode towards her daughter. 'Hey, Peg! How are you?'

She watched as her daughter tried her best to find a smiley face. 'I'm fine!' It tore at Poppy's heart to hear Peg resort to the phrase that she herself had used so often during tough times.

'Good, good.' Poppy patted her hair. 'And how are you today, Jade?'

'I'm fine too, thank you.' Jade smiled sweetly.

'Great!' Poppy beamed. 'I was wondering, Jade, it's been a while since we've seen you, why don't you come over for tea sometime?'

Jade gazed at Peg's horrified expression. 'I would love to, thank you, Mrs Cricket.'

'You are welcome. It's Peg's birthday soon, we were going to invite you over anyway. I'll give your mum a ring.' *I'll show you, Jadebloodymckeever!*

Jade narrowed her eyes at Peg and smiled as she ran towards her mum's car.

Peg was quiet on the back seat of the car.

'You okay, Peg? You're a bit quiet.'

She nodded. 'I don't want Jade McKeever to come to my house for tea.'

'Why not? I thought she was your best friend? It'll be a good chance to show her Toffee!' Poppy looked back over her shoulder. 'And I know we said only a family celebration for your birthday, but it'll be nice to have a little birthday tea in advance, don't you think?'

Peg shrugged and sank down on the seat, unable to find the words.

Peg's mood didn't seem to have improved overnight. It was time to get her up and off to school, but, unusually, her bedroom door was closed. Poppy knocked.

'Peg?'

'Go away!'

Poppy twisted the handle and spoke through the gap. 'Go away? That's not quite the welcome I was expecting! Can I come in, please?'

Peg didn't answer; Poppy took this as approval and slipped inside the door. The smell of ammonia was overpowering. Poppy casually drew the curtains and threw open the window. 'Let's let the day in, shall we? No point living in this beautiful place and not appreciating the view.'

Peg, with her gaze averted, gave a little nod.

'When I was little, I only had a tiny window high up on my bedroom wall and even if it had opened and I'd been able to reach it, it looked out on grubby concrete walls and someone else's washing! Can you imagine?'

Peg ignored her, clearly not in the mood for a chat.

Poppy tried a different tack. 'How did you sleep? Did you have any sweet dreams? Any bad ones?' She sat down on the edge of the duvet and tried not to stare at the pyjama bottoms and bath towel that had been rolled into a damp ball and shoved under Peg's desk.

'Mummy?'

'Yes, my love?'

'Is it my fault you've got this horrible bug?'

'Oh, Peg, darling. God, no, it's not your fault! Whatever gave you that idea? No, of course not. It doesn't work like that, Peg. It's no one's fault and you can't catch it, they don't know why I got it, it's just really bad luck.'

Peg tried to sniff back the tears that slid down her nose and over her cheeks.

'Oh, Peg, come here, darling. It's okay. It'll all be okay. Let me cuddle you.'

'No!' Peg was adamant.

Poppy let her daughter cry and sat quietly by her side.

'Why did you think it was your fault, Peg?'

'I heard you say I was going to give you heart failure or turn your hair grey, and so I thought I might have made you poorly. And I know I talk too much, but I can't help it, I've always got something I want to say.' Fresh tears now fell.

'Oh, Peg, I don't remember saying that, but if I did, I was only joking.' Poppy bent low until her daughter had no option but to look her in the eye. 'You are the best thing that I have ever done, you and Maxy, the very best things ever. You make me happy; every single day you make me happy. Even when you are not here, just the thought of you makes me smile.'

Peg gave a brief smile.

'That's more like it.' Poppy kissed her. 'Don't ever forget it, Peg. I would not change one single thing, not one, because being your mum is something I would not swap for all the tea in China, and you know how much I like tea, right?'

Peg laughed.

'And don't ever stop talking. I could listen to you all day.'

'Sometimes you do!' Peg sniffed and wiped her nose on the back of her sleeve.

Poppy laughed. 'Yes, sometimes I do and those are the best days I have. I don't ever want you to keep things bottled up, my darling. Come and talk to me or Daddy anytime, or Granny Claudia or Jo. There are lots of people you can talk to if anything is bothering you, ever. Okay?'

Peg nodded.

'Mummy?'

'Yes, Peg.'

She bit her bottom lip. 'I did a wee in my bed.'

'Oh, my darling girl, everyone wees somewhere they shouldn't at least once and no one minds a jot. How about I run you a nice warm bubbly bath before school and you can have a soak and a splash while I strip your bed and get things cleaned up? How does that sound?' Poppy kissed Peg's scalp.

'Sounds good, Mum.' Peg allowed herself a small smile.

Poppy bent over the running taps to swirl the strings of bubble bath that sat on the surface of the water. It happened in an instant. She felt the breath stop in her throat as a stabbing pain shot along her spine. 'Shit!' She lowered herself onto the loo and tried to steady her breathing. Her tears came suddenly and without warning. She was in too much pain to be brave.

* * *

The day of the birthday tea arrived, bright and sunny. Poppy worked diligently, giggling as she did so. She carried bowls and packets from the kitchen, removed wrappings, shook out ingredients and artfully arranged vibrant displays on their dining room table. She took photographs at every stage, so that she could later pop them into her daughter's memory box. The final picture was a selfie, of her in front of the table, over which she scrawled:

The world's greatest mum!

As instructed, Martin finished work early and collected Jade and Peg from the school gates. The two little girls hopped into the back of his car.

'How's your dad, Jade? I've known him for a long time.' The two men had gone through training together.

'He's okay, thanks.'

'That's good to hear.'

'I can't wait for my tea. I'm starving!' Jade enunciated the last word and fired it in Peg's direction like an arrow. Peg was strangely quiet.

'Peg says she's got a guinea pig that speaks!' Jade piped up.

'Yes, that's right,' Martin replied, without any hesitation or trace of a smile. 'He can't say much, mainly "din-dins" and "goodbye", but he doesn't like talking to strangers, only Peg's really good friends, so he might not say anything tonight.'

Jade stared at Martin, unable to think of a single response. Peg sucked in her cheeks and smiled into her lap.

Poppy opened the front door and greeted the two girls. 'Hello, ladies! How was your day? Hope you are feeling hungry!'

Jade stood in the hallway. 'I think our house is a bit bigger than yours,' she said as she dropped her school bag and coat on the floor.

Poppy bit her lip.

Jade marched into the lounge and halted at the sight in front of her.

The table was set, but not in any way that Jade McKeever had ever seen a table set before. Pink fairy lights were strung across the ceiling and hung over the table. On top of a pristine white tablecloth were glass bowls full of sticky jelly sweets in every colour imaginable; separate bowls were crammed with chunks of chocolate, and plates of shiny cookies gleamed in the light. Tall glasses nearly overflowed with strawberry milkshakes, each with a natty red-and-white-striped straw protruding from the top. Dishes of ice cream dotted with sweets and latticed with loops of caramel sauce sat at regular intervals. There were vases crammed with candy canes and liquorice sticks, and a platter piled with strawberry laces that looked like spaghetti, garnished with lollipops that fanned out from the pile. Dainty iced fairy cakes had been arranged on a three-tiered cake tower and jugs of cola with floating ice sat in wait, complete with crazy neon straws through which to sip the usually forbidden drink. All these brightly coloured, sugar-laden goodies were eclipsed however by what occupied the middle of the table: the pièce de résistance was a very grand three-foot-high chocolate fountain. Peg was in awe of it. The girls stood and watched as the rippling waves of pale chocolate undulated over the side; their eyes darted to the fat marshmallows, enormous strawberries and apple slices that sat in dishes awaiting a good dunking.

'Hope you're hungry.' Poppy, her tone nonchalant, pulled the chair from the table and gestured for Jade McKeever to take a seat. Jade, who was uncharacteristically silent, sat.

'Oh, Peg,' Poppy started, 'I was chatting to Toffee earlier and he said the usual – "din-dins" et cetera – and then, you won't believe what he said!'

Peg beamed at her mum. 'What did he say, Mum?'

'He said he'd got you tickets for a Princess Pamper day for your birthday, a bit of an early present! A special gift from him. It'll be lovely, a total makeover – nails painted, hair curled, the full works.' Poppy pulled the two shiny gold tickets from her back pocket and popped them on the table next to her little girl.

'You can take a friend, how about Amelie Smith? She's such a lovely girl.' Poppy smiled, sweetly.

'I'm her friend!' Jade practically shouted.

Poppy bent low. 'Well, that's good to hear, Jade, because any friend of Peg's is a friend of ours, welcome here anytime. And anyone that isn't, isn't!' She jumped up and clapped. 'Right, I'll leave you to it. Peg, don't forget to take your magic anti-fat tablet before you go to sleep, because you're getting the same tea tomorrow night.' Poppy wandered from the room, without so much as a backward glance.

After Jade McKeever was eventually dispatched home, Peg sat in the tub, surrounded by bubbles. Poppy knocked and entered and took up a seat on the loo, taking the opportunity to chat to her daughter.

'How's my girl doing?'

Peg looked into the foam. 'I don't think I will ever forget today, ever.'

Poppy crouched down by the side of the bath and placed a blob of foam on her little girl's nose. 'You know, Peg, you are a fabulous girl and you will become a fabulous woman.'

'A fabulous woman pilot,' Peg corrected.

'Yes, darling, a fabulous woman pilot. But the point is, Peg, if people don't love you for you, then they don't deserve to be loved at all. You don't ever have to lie or be anything other than yourself, because you are fabulous, inside and out. Promise me you will remember that, always?'

Peg nodded. 'Okay. I love you, Mum. And thank you for the Princess Pamper tickets. I'm so excited!'

Poppy stood and placed her hands on her hips. 'Well, don't thank me, thank Toffee!'

'Mum, is it true, are we getting that for tea tomorrow night as well?'

Poppy leant on the door frame. 'No, Peg, we most certainly are not.' She winked at the chocolate-smeared face of her little girl.

Fourteen

Poppy walked along the corridor and was surprised to find Mr Ramasingh sitting at his desk; there would be no waiting for him today. Martin had decided to stay in the car with Max, who was grizzling on the back seat. He'd woken in a bad mood and nothing was making him feel better. She suspected he was simply feeding off the edgy, nervous vibes that she was emitting. She was disappointed not to have Martin by her side: it would have been a chance to involve him in the process and to make her feel less secretive about the whole thing. But she was also relieved, especially after he had taken several corners at speed, beeped his horn at a couple of innocent cyclists and shouted at least one expletive at someone who he deemed was inappropriately parked. She didn't trust his firecracker nature when he was this wound up and that did little to help *her* nerves. And Max's constant crying had done little to help his mood.

'Come in, come in!' Mr Ramasingh gestured and stood, shutting the door firmly behind her. 'How are you feeling today?'

Poppy noticed that he avoided eye contact with her as he took up his seat and punched the keys on his keyboard.

She sat opposite his desk and placed her bag on the floor. 'Same, really. I keep getting a sharp pain, a painful pain, if that makes sense.' She squirmed at her lack of eloquence.

'Not all the time, but when I get it, it knocks the shit out of me.' There, that was what she had wanted to say.

Mr Ramasingh sighed and nodded. He opened the large brown cardboard folder and extracted two X-rays, laying them alongside a sheet of what looked like graph paper.

When he spoke, his words were slow and considered. He now gave her his full attention. 'The aim of your treatment was always to try and control your symptoms, help you feel better.'

Poppy nodded. She got it: no cure. Not yet.

'We have been monitoring your cancer via the scans and X-rays that you have had.'

Poppy watched as he took a deep breath. She glanced at the empty chair next to her, convinced her nan was close by.

Mr Ramasingh continued. 'It has been nearly four months since your diagnosis and you have coped very well, but I'm afraid to say that your treatment has had little to no impact on your disease.'

'No impact?' She thought of the days spent feeling horrible, only made bearable because she believed it was helping.

'None. And that can happen, sometimes. The cancer puts up its defences and we simply can't break them down.' Mr Ramasingh knitted his fingers to make a wall.

Poppy thought about this. 'So what do we do now? More chemo? Stronger drugs? I don't mind if it makes me feel worse, as long as it does its job.' How would it be to feel lousy all the time, she wondered. Those days of diarrhoea and sickness had felt never-ending.

'No, Poppy.' The doctor removed his glasses and stared at the woman sitting across from him – the mother, the wife. He paused. 'We are not going to give you any more treatment.'

Poppy looked at the photograph on his desk. 'Why not?' She wanted it spelling out.

'Because there is very little point, and in my opinion, it will only make you feel very sick, but without the benefit of aiding your recovery.'

'So that's it?' She stared at the man who was severing her lifelines one by one. His words echoed inside her head. She thought of Peg at school and Max and Martin sitting in the car, waiting for her. She looked up at Mr Ramasingh, who was still talking.

'We will of course continue with your pain management and carry on helping to control your symptoms, but we will stop all intervention therapies.'

Mr Ramasingh reached into his drawer and produced a glossy pamphlet. 'I have some information here—'

Poppy shook her head as she picked up her bag and stood up. 'Please, not another sodding leaflet.'

A few minutes later, she climbed into their Golf, taking Martin by surprise.

'What did he say?' Martin stared at her.

'Erm... it was... Can we talk about it when we get home?' She flicked her eyes towards Max on the back seat, who was thankfully calmer now and holding a book upside down. Her voice was quiet.

'Well, just give me a clue!' Martin raised his voice.

Max kicked the back seat and let out a garbled noise. Poppy looked at her son and then her husband.

'For God's sake, Poppy.' His patience was at its limit.

Max let out a deafening wail.

'Just take me home!' Poppy banged on her thighs with her flattened palms. 'Stop going on and on!'

They drove home, the silence only broken by Poppy's

whimpers and Max's cries. She couldn't hold back the fat tears that clogged her nose and throat. Martin drove with one hand gripping the top of the steering wheel with such force that his knuckles were white, the other hand like a claw on top of the gear stick as he rammed the gearbox through its paces on the bends. Max cried and Poppy didn't blame him. She reached behind her seat and stroked his leg.

Back at home, Martin put Max in the care of his big sister and gave them a bag of crisps each for good measure. Then he followed his wife up the stairs.

Poppy sat on the bed and Martin stood in front of her. He was like a coiled spring. Her hands fidgeted in her lap as the words floated around inside her head, trying to lodge somewhere before finding their way out of her mouth. She felt flat, deflated, and exhausted at the prospect of what lay ahead.

'Right, no more messing around. What did he say?' His voice was stern.

'He… he stopped my treatment.'

'What? Why?'

Poppy looked up at her husband. 'He said there was no point. It wasn't working.'

'Can he do that?' Martin looked angry, flexing his fingers and rocking on his heels.

'Yes, and he's right, really. It wasn't making any difference and so there's no point.' Her eyes flickered from her husband to her lap.

'And you are just going to accept that, are you? Give up?' he snarled.

Poppy pulled her head back on her shoulders. 'I've been waging a war on this bloody disease and I thought I could win, but I can't, Mart. I can't.' As she spoke the words, she felt her resolve slip, her muscles loosen and her spirit flag. *I'm sorry...*

'We should see about going private, can't we pay for the treatment? Go abroad. I'll find the money somehow, whatever it costs. We should do that. I'll ask Claudia, I don't care.'

'Mart—'

'No, I mean it, let's do it. You need to go abroad and get the treatment somewhere else. What about America, don't people go there for everything? I've read about it before, and what about that kid we had that fundraising supper for at the mess? D'you remember? It was so he could go to America and have treatment. That's what we should do.' His words came in a flurry.

'Mart, please—'

'No, fuck it, Poppy! *You* may just be rolling over, but I will not let you leave me. I won't.'

Poppy stood and faced him. 'Look at me! Look at me!'

Martin stared into her face. His breath came in short bursts, as though he were running out of air. Slowly, he ran his fingers over her pale complexion, pausing at the dark, black circles that sat beneath her eyes.

'You are so beautiful,' he whispered.

Poppy laid her cheek against his palm and closed her eyes. 'If I could have anything and everything was possible, then I'd get rid of this bloody disease. But I can't and I don't think I've got much fight left in me, Mart. I'm getting tired.'

Balling his fingers into a fist, Martin spun round and punched the bedroom door, pushing his fist through the first layer of white-painted laminate and the first couple of sheets of plyboard. He pulled back the moment he punched and stared at the gaping hole and the splintered wood around it.

He fell to the floor and sat in a crumpled heap. Poppy

dropped down to crouch by his side and placed her arms around him.

Peg appeared, wide-eyed, and poked her head into the room.

'What was that bang?'

'Daddy did some karate on the door.' Poppy smiled.

Peg tutted and raised her eyebrows before going back to her telly and crisps.

The two sat on the floor in silence until their heart rates had slowed and they had stopped shaking.

'Did you hurt your hand?' Poppy whispered.

'Not as much as I hurt the door.' He gave a small, awkward laugh.

'Mart, I know that none of this is easy, but I want to talk to you about after I have gone.'

Martin stared at her, unsure of how to respond. He ran his tongue over his lips.

Poppy continued. 'I want to talk about my funeral, Mart, if that's okay.'

Martin sighed and rubbed at his nose, transferring a grey smudge of dirt from the fractured door onto his face. It reminded her of his early days working in the garage before he joined up, when he used to come home dusty, grimy and knackered. He narrowed his eyes. 'Actually, it's not okay. No.'

'Don't be like that.'

'Don't be like what?' he snapped.

'Shutting me out and making it awkward. It needs to be discussed. It's what I want.'

'Is it? And don't even start on *me* shutting *you* out.' Martin sighed, still upset that she had kept her illness from him. 'And here's the thing, it's not what *I* want, not even slightly.'

'Oh God, what now? You can't keep punching doors!'

'Can't I?' he sneered.

She ran her hand across her brow. 'Sometimes you can be a selfish bastard.' She banged her thigh and instantly regretted swearing at him.

'Is that right? Well, if it's selfish to not want to think about the person I love the most in the world leaving me here alone with two kids to look after, then yes, I'm selfish. If it's selfish not to want you involved in any way with what comes after so that I can only think of you as alive and here with me, then I probably am. When you...' He paused. 'When you *are* gone, I will face the things I have to, all of them, including your funeral, but until I absolutely have to, you are here and I will not let myself get dragged into that dark pit of shit that is waiting for me. That is how I see my life without you and I see it stretching on for ever.'

The two sat quietly for a minute or two until Martin placed his head in his hands. 'Christ, what's happening to us? I feel like we're falling apart. I'm scared, Poppy.'

'Me too.' She kissed his chin. 'But we need to stay strong, Mart. We need to keep it together because we don't have that many doors.' She nudged him with her elbow. 'Now, what always makes the kids feel better when they've been a bit upset is a big mug of hot chocolate – how about we go down, sit with them babies and treat ourselves?'

Martin nodded. 'Just give me a minute.'

Poppy kissed his forehead. 'I'll see you down there.'

She took extra care with their drinks, swirling them with cream and loading them up with marshmallows and chocolate sprinkles. They looked glorious. Poppy found a smile and carried them into the sitting room, trying to control the shake to her hands that sent a tremor through the metal tray and made the spoons jump. 'Here we go!' she announced as she set the tray on the sofa.

Peg and Max clapped her brilliance. Poppy handed everyone a mug and proposed a toast. 'To us!'

'To us!' Martin and Peg echoed.

Max held up his cup and shouted 'Three, four hot drinks!' instead.

Peg smiled from beneath the cream moustache that sat on her top lip. Poppy brought the mug to her mouth and took a sip. She ran her tongue around her mouth and took another. Martin watched as she inhaled the scent of her drink and took another sip.

'You all right, Pop?' he asked.

'I can't... I can't taste it.' She looked up at him, perplexed.

Poppy lifted a chocolate sprinkle and placed it on her tongue, letting it melt before pressing her tongue against the roof of her mouth. 'I can't taste anything.'

She stood up and wandered back into the kitchen, where she opened the fridge and scanned the shelves. Unwrapping a block of cheese, she cut a small corner and put it in her mouth, then shook her head. Next she plucked a fat strawberry, pulled the little green stalk off and bit into it.

Martin watched her from the doorway. 'Are you okay?' he whispered. She looked so preoccupied, he didn't want to disturb her.

Poppy ignored him, opened the carton of orange juice and took a swig straight from the box. On any other day he would have mocked her hypocrisy, but not today. Next she gulped down some milk. Finally she tore at a piece of ham and laid it on her tongue before swiping it off with her fingers and flinging it in the bin.

She stood with her arms braced against the work surface,

staring out at the garden. Martin came over and placed his hand on her shoulder.

'Are you okay?' he repeated.

Poppy spoke to their reflection in the window. 'I can't taste anything.'

'What do you mean?'

'I mean, I can't taste a single thing! Everything is like cardboard in my mouth. It's disgusting.' Her tone was clipped.

'It's probably just temporary.' Martin tried to placate her.

'You think?' She turned around. 'Well, that's good, Dr Mart, because with all the other shite I've got to deal with, not being able to eat anything would take the cake.'

'If you want a door to punch, there's one upstairs that already needs a bit of repairing.' He tried out a smile.

'Very funny,' Poppy snapped. She flashed a look of anger at him and swept past and up to bed.

Martin closed his eyes and threw his head back.

By the end of the week Poppy and Martin had found a fragile peace. Poppy was plagued by a deep and constant fatigue. It was almost as if she had finally allowed herself to recognise how shattered she was, now that they had both acknowledged her illness. Whether psychological or not, it didn't matter. Most days she woke with a bone-deep ache and the tiredness would wash over her and leave her dazed. Exhausted and in pain, she could not think beyond the everyday; to try and do so left her gasping for breath as a cold fear plucked at her skin. She had quit asking Martin if he was okay, sensing that it was driving him crazy.

Good days were rare, but today was one of them. She had already given the kitchen floor a good going-over and had changed the light bulb in the extractor fan. She switched off the iron and folded the last of Peg's T-shirts into their pile. They now sat next to three similar piles that she would take upstairs and put away next time she went up. She was happy to be able to do chores. It felt normal and normal was good; in fact normal was bloody marvellous. She was determined not only to get as much done as possible, but also to make plans while she was able.

Martin swooped by with a dirty oblong thing that he had removed from the Golf's engine.

'What's that?' Poppy asked as he whisked it past her and into the kitchen.

'Air filter, just giving it a bit of a clean. I was hoping you wouldn't see, I know what you are like with mess and dust.'

Martin smiled at her as he knocked the filter over the sink with the heel of his hand and blew into its little crevices.

'Actually, Mart, that's kind of what I wanted to talk to you about.' She coughed.

'Now?' He looked from her to the filter in his hand.

'Yes.' Poppy sat down.

'Oh God, what have I done? Is it too late to say it wasn't me? Because it wasn't. Or do you have evidence? Which, I might add, Peg is very good at fabricating.' He sat in the chair opposite her.

'No, nothing like that. Unless there is something you *want* to confess?' She narrowed her eyes.

'Ha! You're not going to get to me that easily. I am blame-free, I think. What's up, Poppy Day?'

'This isn't easy for me to say.' She swallowed.

Martin knitted his grubby, oil-covered fingers and rested them on the table.

'I think it might be an idea if we get some help, with the house.' She paused, taking his silence as a cue to continue.

'I've been given the names of charities and agencies that can come in and help with everything from childcare to taking me to appointments, anything really. I thought it might be a good idea?'

Martin scraped the chair across the floor. 'When I want some bloody busybodies coming into my home and sticking their noses into my family's life, I'll tell you.' With that, he grabbed the filter from the sideboard and slammed the front door on his way out.

'Well...' Poppy spoke to Toffee, who had poked his nose through the cage. 'That went well.'

Martin found her lying on the bed an hour later. She was humming and reading an article on how to decorate your home for Easter. 'Just getting ideas on how to "create the perfect environment for fun and frolics with your houseguests this Easter"!' she read from the magazine.

He shifted from foot to foot. 'I'm sorry about earlier. I guess I just don't want to think we're at that stage yet.' He addressed the floor.

'I know. But I think the more we can put in place, the easier it will be for the kids.' She was blunt, without the time or the inclination to sugar-coat their situation.

Martin took the magazine from her hand and ran his eyes over the article. 'I thought we usually just bunged the kids some chocolate for Easter and hoped for an extra hour in bed?' He laughed.

'We do, but if ever I get me that kidney-shaped pool and my ice-cube diamond, this will be how I celebrate Easter.' She turned the page to show him the image of a kitchen decked out with lilac and lemon ribbons and chicks and bunnies aplenty.

'Looks bloody horrible!' He screwed his nose up.

'Don't ever think of trading soldiering for interior design – you haven't got a clue.' She swatted him with her magazine.

'Someone seems to have got a bit of their mojo back. Nice to see some of your old spark, Mrs Bossy Boots.' He jumped onto the mattress and grabbed her around the waist.

'Maybe I have.' Poppy smiled. It had been a while since either of them had shown the slightest interest in each other physically, other than in a caring capacity. To have even the smallest flicker of sexual desire felt wonderfully life-affirming.

'Ooh, lucky me!' Martin nuzzled his wife's neck.

As he did so, she was hit by a wave of nausea. 'Oh God, Mart, sorry, stop, stop!' Poppy pushed him away and sat upright against the headboard.

'What's the matter? Oh God, did I hurt you?'

'No, I just feel really sick. I'm sorry.' She took deep breaths and clutched at her stomach.

He nodded. Not as sorry as him.

The two sat, feeling an awkwardness that was strange to them after so many years married.

Eventually Poppy found her voice. 'Claudia arrives tomorrow. I was wondering if you fancy taking me on a little trip, a day out. I've already asked her and she's happy to sit with the kids.'

Martin nodded. 'Sure. Where are we going?'

'Ah, that's the surprise.' She did her best to smile, hiding the discomfort that racked every inch of her.

Fifteen

Claudia pulled her pashmina around her shoulders as she stood on the doorstep to see them off. She had arrived, bringing with her an air of serenity and organisation, and the whole family had heaved a huge sigh of relief. Everything was okay, Granny Claudia was on hand.

She kissed Poppy and patted her hair. 'You have beautiful hair, Poppy. It was the first thing I thought when I met you.'

'It's getting a bit thin and is very patchy at the back.' Poppy ran her fingers though the reddy-brown layers, letting her fingers graze the skin of her head in places.

'No matter, it's still beautiful. Right, off you go. Hope you both have a great day and don't worry about rushing back. We are going to have a ball; it will be bliss, just me and the children. I've written them a new bedtime story and we are going to make sweets this afternoon. I used to make them with Miles and he loved it – peppermint creams, coconut ice and chocolate truffles. We shall stuff them until we feel thoroughly sick!'

'Oh, goodness, that sounds like fun. Think we might stay here instead!' Poppy smiled.

'Take care of him, Poppy.' Claudia nodded at Martin, who was putting a blanket in the front seat. Poppy kissed Claudia on the cheek and climbed into the car.

Martin indicated and pulled the Golf into the Packway.

Poppy stared at the parade of shops that catered mainly for squaddies and their families. It was busy as usual. Girls wearing skinny jeans and chunky fur-lined boots, with their hair scraped up into topknots, were leaning on pushchairs and catching up. Poppy, envying them their smiles and easy banter, wondered what occupied their minds. It felt like a long, long time ago that she had been able to natter freely without thoughts of her disease invading her every waking moment. There was, as always, a dog tied up outside the newsagent's, waiting patiently and enjoying the attention of everyone that nipped in or out.

A queue snaked its way through the door of the post office. Service wives, girlfriends, husbands and partners waited patiently with boxes and padded envelopes, the contents of which became harder to keep original. But no matter how random, the offerings would still be treasured: the currency of love, flying between the patch at Larkhill and any number of BFPO addresses.

Poppy instinctively turned to the back seat to check on the kids, but of course it was empty.

'Well this is nice, eh? No kids. We could even put the radio on and listen to a grown-up programme and not that bloody *Junior Pop Party* CD. Just think, Mart, a car journey with no Justin Bieber or One Direction!'

Martin laughed. 'I won't miss them – Justin and Harry, that is.'

But Poppy knew that he didn't mean it. She knew that, like her, he was thinking of all the car journeys he'd taken as a kid in his mum and dad's old banger, a Carpenters tape on a loop in the background. No debate, no discussion, just sitting in the back quietly, trying not to gag on their fag smoke. So different to how Peg usually jumped in the car, happy and confident and demanding her parents be her own personal DJs. God knows what she'd be like at sixteen. Poppy felt a lump rise in her throat and coughed to swallow it.

The Wiltshire countryside gave way to motorways and pretty soon they hit the North Circular, then Wembley, Brent Cross and finally the Crooked Billet roundabout, meaning they were nearly home. Home. Not home any more, but with all their childhood memories wrapped up in concrete and sitting in one postcode, London E17 would always be a place they held in great affection.

Poppy let her gaze wander over the smoke-stained chimneys, the blackened paintwork, graffiti-covered walls and diesel-splashed roads. She noticed the pockets of black dust that sat against the kerbs and lodged against the railings. And despite the unfavourable comparison with the green open spaces among which she now lived and the fresh, clean air that filled her lungs with every breath, her stomach flipped with excitement. It was lovely to be here, where her nan would forever reside and where she and Martin had met.

'Dirty, isn't it?' It was as if Martin had read her thoughts. She nodded. 'But still lovely.'

He nodded in her direction. 'Oh yes, still lovely, girl.'

Martin parked in the road outside the house and walked round the car to open the door for Poppy.

'Thanks, love. We'll just stay for a bit, have a cuppa and then make tracks, okay?'

'Fine.' He tried his best to make his smile genuine.

Poppy tried not to notice the stained sofa that sat minus its cushions on the patch of overgrown grass inside the fence; tried to ignore the piles of dog poo that had been deposited uniformly along the path. She looked up at one of the upstairs windows, which had been boarded over with a piece of plywood, crudely tacked and barely hiding the enormous crack in the pane beneath it.

A green recycling box was a third full of rainwater and overflowed with cigarette butts, empty cans of Carling and several bottles of WKD whose lurid-coloured contents had long been drained. Bugs feasted on licks of sticky sauce smudged over the sides of empty foil containers.

There being no bell, Poppy rapped on the door with her knuckles.

'She's 'ere!' came the loud shout from inside.

'Waaaaaaagh!' Jenna screamed as she crushed Poppy against her ample chest. 'Ooh my God! I've really missed you.' She kissed her friend all over her face. 'Come in, come in! Kids, make some space.'

Poppy looked down at the three toddlers, a girl and two little boys, who she hadn't seen before. They peered up at her with chocolate-smeared faces and grubby sweatshirts.

'Who are these little didders?' Poppy asked.

'Ryan's kids by his two exes. He has them every other weekend. Or should I say, *we* have them every other weekend.' Jenna twisted her mouth and curled her top lip as she crossed her eyes and poked out her tongue, telling Poppy all she needed to know about the situation.

Then Jenna narrowed her eyes, studying her friend properly for the first time. 'Blimey, you all right, Poppy? You look like shite!'

Poppy cringed. 'I'm okay.'

'Boys, come and say hello to Aunty Poppy,' Jenna barked into the sitting room.

Her two sons, Malik and Adil, who were only a year or two younger than Peg, sloped into the hallway. They had identical haircuts with intricate patterns shaved into the sides of their heads. Their large eyes shone and they smiled, showing off their dimples and beautiful mouths.

'Hello, gorgeous boys!' Poppy hugged them before handing them a stiff cardboard bag each. 'I got you some S.W.E.E.T.I.E.S – didn't realise the little ones were going to be here!' She spelt out the word so as not to alert Ryan's babies. The two boys looked at her and then each other, a little nonplussed.

'Come in, come in. Kettle's on.' Jenna squeezed Martin and kissed him on the cheek. 'Hello, mate. Boys, take the little ones upstairs and they can watch telly in your room while we chat.'

The boys, good as gold, did as they were told, shepherding the smaller ones up the stairs with kind words and hands on their little backs lest they should topple backwards. It made Poppy's heart lurch.

'They're so lovely, Jenna.' Poppy felt a swell of affection for the boys she had known since birth.

Jenna smiled. 'They are angels. Their dad has them two nights a week and he's strict on manners. They're both smart as well, doing great at school.'

'Must take after their mum then,' Poppy quipped.

'Blimey, Poppy, I don't think I did a full day from the age of twelve!' Jenna laughed as she and Poppy remembered the lengths Jenna would go to in order to miss school.

'I remember coming in from school and you'd been hiding in my bedroom all afternoon. Don't think even my nan knew you were there!' Poppy laughed.

'I was naughty, not like you, Mrs Girly Swot.'

'Hardly.' Poppy looked at the floor, not wanting to admit to having been keen at school. Even at thirty-two, she was still too embarrassed to share her love of learning.

Jenna walked ahead, giving Poppy a chance to study her.

She had gained weight: her black leggings stretched over her thighs and were almost translucent where they touched her dimpled skin. Her heels were cracked and had a purplish tinge as they slipped and slapped in her flip-flops. Her hair, once pristine, her pride and joy, was now scooped up and held fast with a wide clip. Her roots were dark and greasy, while the bleached-blonde ends hung limp and straw-like. Her skin was pale and peppered with spots; she looked to Poppy like she needed a big bowl of veg and a brisk walk in the sunshine.

'Ryan, Ryan!' Jenna yelled at her partner. He lay slumped in the armchair in front of a vast TV with his long legs outstretched and a roll-up smouldering between his fingers. The look he flashed the duo who had interrupted his morning viewing said it all. He rose slowly and placed his cigarette in the ashtray beside him, freeing his hands to grasp Poppy by the shoulders and plant a kiss on her face.

'All right, Poppy.'

'Yes, good thanks, Ryan,' she lied. Her nose wrinkled at the sour tang of cigarette smoke, body odour and food that hung in the air. It was the smell of her childhood home.

Martin held out his right hand and gave the man a firm handshake. 'Nice to see you, Ryan.'

'Yeah, you too, mate. Just catching up on the darts.' Ryan's delivery was fast, as though he was impatient to get the visit over.

Martin nodded. The feeling was entirely mutual. 'Nice one.' He sat on the sofa and the two men stared at the screen. Far better than having to find a mutual topic of conversation.

Martin stole glances at the man who now lived with Poppy's childhood mate. He had a large earring that was a wide hoop inserted into his left earlobe. Martin could see clean through it to the tattoo of a star on his neck; he wondered what the point of it was.

'Can we go and get a DVD?' Malik appeared in front of the screen and addressed his mum's boyfriend.

'Get out of the way – we're watching this!' Ryan swept his arm left to right as though he had Jedi powers that could make the boy move. It worked. Malik ran from the room.

Martin tensed and felt his bowels spasm. He remembered the way his dad would dismiss him from the room, reminding Martin that this was his house and they lived under his rules. Watching as Malik ran from the room, he saw his eight-year-old self and recalled the sinking feeling in his stomach that accompanied the idea that he had no refuge, nowhere to go and nowhere to hide, like an interloper under his parents' roof.

He hoped the day would come sooner rather than later when one of them, Ryan or Malik, packed their bags for good and went off to find a different life. Martin had only met the boys' dad once, but he had seemed like a good sort. He pictured him on all fours, crawling around the room with his sons, who were much younger then, riding on his back.

Poppy was horrified at the conditions in which Jenna prepared the tea. Every inch of the work surface was covered in something and the clutter made the large room feel claustrophobic. There was an array of cereal boxes, the kind Peg would whine for but wouldn't get, whose contents were spilled in small piles where they were placed. Empty cans of baked beans, ravioli and soup stood there with their jagged edges and dribbles of sauce running down the sides. The aluminium draining board was dull and covered in tea- and coffee-coloured sploshes. In the sink itself sat a mountain of cold, flabby oven chips and pieces of fried egg, as though someone had forgotten to switch on the non-existent waste disposal. A tortoiseshell cat with black points to his ears and three dark socks trod nimbly between the dirty plates and detritus, pausing occasionally to look up at Poppy, his expression haughty, as if to say, 'Look how I have to live...'

A clothes horse in the corner next to the radiator was draped with tracksuit bottoms and several pairs of boxer shorts. Two enormous Alsatians lay top to toe on an old duvet under the window; their hair formed a gritty mat under Poppy's feet.

'They've got big, haven't they?' Jenna flicked her head towards the dogs, who had been puppies the last time Poppy had seen them. She nodded yes, they had. *Bloody enormous.* One of them lifted his head and gave a loud, bassy bark that made Poppy jump.

'Shut up, Prince!' Jenna yelled in stereo with Ryan, who bellowed the same from his chair of power in the front room.

Prince glanced at the cat and Poppy wondered if they conversed about their woeful environment when they were alone.

Poppy grabbed an empty carrier bag, picked the food from the sink and deposited it inside. Jenna leant on the work surface and lit a cigarette, blowing smoke into the already stuffy atmosphere. Poppy then ran the hot tap, filled a sponge with water and washing-up liquid and rubbed it around a frying pan that sat on the work surface.

'You gonna do the whole house, Pop?' Jenna asked as she drew on her cigarette.

'Hmmm?' Poppy looked at her friend, distracted as though on autopilot. She laid the pan in the sink and put the sponge inside it. 'Sorry, Jen... I...' She couldn't explain her desire for order.

With tea made, the four sat in front of the large TV screen in the sitting room. The walls were bare and a layer of dust covered the shelving unit and the saggy furniture. It made Poppy sad to think of the kids spending time in this depressing environment. She had grown up poor, but this was nothing to do with money; it was about laziness and neglect, and bore no connection to the size of a bank balance. She had to almost shout to compete with the commentary and cheers from the darts match.

'Phil "the Power" Taylor, bloody legend.' Ryan nodded at the screen.

Martin gave his first genuine nod.

'It's lovely to see you, Jen.' Poppy smiled at her mate.

''Tis, mate. Been too long. Mind you, if you will live in the bloody sticks...'

Poppy smiled. Give her the sticks any time. 'It's not all bad, Jen.' She reluctantly sipped at her tea.

'I couldn't stand it. Where do you go if you run out of milk or fancy a wander up the shops?'

'We do have shops!' Poppy laughed. 'Just not on the doorstep.'

'That's the life you get if you want to play soldiers,' Ryan piped up, then went back to licking his cigarette paper and rolling it into a skinny tube.

Martin felt his jaw tighten but said nothing.

Ryan wasn't done. 'I don't know how you put up with it. Having to take orders: go here, go there.'

Martin smirked but kept his eyes fixed on Phil the Power. It always made him laugh, this reasoning from those who had never served, as though those that mocked had jobs where no one ever told them what to do, gave them instruction or monitored their progress, or lack of. He was pretty sure that even that Facebook billionaire bloke had shareholders to answer to.

'And I bet there's some right dickhead telling you what to do. I wouldn't last five minutes.'

Martin looked Ryan up and down and thought of his mate, Aaron, who had lost his life serving his country. A better man and a great dad. 'You're right, Ryan, you wouldn't.'

'Thing is, Jen, I wanted to see you, not just talk on the phone.' Poppy tried to deflect the men's conversation and decided to say what she needed to and make their excuses.

'Yeah, me too. Can't hear on the bloody phone with that thing blaring.' She used her cigarette to indicate the TV screen.

Poppy took a deep breath and glanced at Martin. 'I'm not too well, Jen.'

'There, I said you looked like shite. I bloody knew it! What's amatterwivyou?' She took a deep drag and let the smoke swirl from her nostrils.

'I've got cancer.'

'You've got what?' Jenna twisted her head in the direction of her friend.

'Cancer.'

Ryan sparked the flint and lit his roll-up as though the two were entirely unconnected.

'Oh God! That's terrible.' Jenna clutched at her T-shirt. 'Where is it?' She didn't try and stem the tears that brimmed in her eyes.

Poppy sighed. 'Everywhere, really.'

Jenna cupped her head in her hand. 'Oh Christ.'

The four sat in silence, listening to the whooping of the crowd as the tiny arrows landed with precision in the board.

Jenna spoke first. 'D'you remember the day we saw the news when Mart got taken? I'll never forget it, we just kept watching Sky, didn't we, on a loop, waiting for him to come on again. And they kept saying your name, Mart, and it was like it wasn't real. And you had to run up the old people's home to stop your nan seeing the paper cos you knew she'd freak out.' She shook her head as her tears fell.

'Long time ago.' Martin stared at the carpet, sticky underfoot.

Jenna sniffed loudly. 'So what are they doing, Poppy? Are you having chemo and all that?'

'I have had treatment – chemo and stuff – but to be honest, Jen, there's not much point.'

Jenna let her head hang against her chest and she sobbed without restraint. Her nose ran and her eyes streamed.

'It's okay, Jen.' Poppy rubbed her back.

'No, it isn't, nothing is. Everything's a fucking nightmare,' Jenna managed between bouts of crying.

Ryan seemed oblivious to his partner's distress. He took a long draw on his cigarette and twisted his earring as he addressed Martin. 'So have you, like, ever killed anyone?'

Martin stared at him. Death was not a topic he was comfortable with at the best of times. 'No, Ryan, but I've felt like it once or twice.'

And in spite of the horrible atmosphere in the miserable house in which they sat, Poppy laughed.

Half an hour later, Martin drove past the parade of shops beneath the flats where they had lived in Walthamstow. The hairdresser's where Poppy had worked was still there, only it was no longer Snipz Unisex Salon but The Cutting Station and now had trendy stainless steel fittings and a neon-lit reception desk. There wasn't a tray of perm curlers in sight.

'Blimey, that Christine,' Poppy said. 'I haven't thought about her in a while.'

Martin gave a shudder. 'Your old boss? She was a right

old sort, wasn't she. Bet she's chasing the male nurses around her care home.'

'Oh look, Sonny's has gone!' The two craned their necks to look at the mobile phone shop that had taken over the premises of their favourite café. The number of times they had sheltered from the rain there as kids, made a Coke last all afternoon in their teens and nipped in for a restorative cup of tea and a fry-up as adults. 'Good old Sonny, he was a big part of our lives, wasn't he? I didn't think about it at the time, but he was just always there, making life a bit better.' Poppy pictured him – enormously fat and always in a white apron spattered with food and drink, holding court from behind the counter. He always used to greet her in the same way – ''Ello, my darlin'! Long time, no see. How's my gel?' – and she could only ever remember him smiling.

'You're right,' Martin said. 'I used to just sit in that café sometimes because it was warm and he was so friendly. It was good to have somewhere like that to go.'

Poppy beamed, remembering the day Sonny had made her a birthday cake. It had been a crisp, blue day, but a day like any other. She had poured herself some cereal and as they had run out of milk, she'd eaten it dry in front of the telly. Spying Sonny outside the café, she had shouted at him, 'It's my birthday, Sonny! I'm nine!' He had smiled at her. 'Get away, I'd say you look at least ten! Happy birthday, darlin'.' It had made her smile all the way to school, the fact that she looked ten. By half past three she had quite forgotten it was her special day and as she sloped past the café on the way home from school, wondered why he called her inside. With her bag slung over her shoulder, she trod the small step and walked inside. There on the counter was a big fat coconut sponge with icing on the top and nine pink candles. She could see it now. How she had beamed, reluctant to blow the candles out and spoil the effect. It was the first birthday cake she ever had, and the best.

'He was a lovely man.' Poppy smiled. 'Wonder what he's up to now?'

'Dunno.' Martin shrugged.

Martin reversed the Golf into a tight spot between two vans. He looked up at the light shining in the kitchen window of his parents' home.

'Are you going to go up and see them?' Poppy asked, following his gaze.

'Nope,' he snapped. 'If I bump into them, then that's one thing, but I'm not about to start trying to win them over at my age.'

Poppy saw the twitch under his eye.

'Seeing them kids today with Ryan and the way he spoke to them, it made me feel sick. He's a bully, Pop, just like my dad, and there's not a day, not one single day I don't think about the way he treated me.'

Martin heard his dad's words, loud and clear as if they had been spoken only yesterday: 'Do what, you useless little poof? How would that work? You bloody idiot!'

'So, no. I won't be going up to see them.'

Poppy looked around at the buildings, taking in the familiar surroundings of the estate where they had both grown up. 'I feel very close to my nan here. I can picture her everywhere I look. It's lovely.'

Martin took her hand. They trod the same path that Dot and her new husband, Wally, had walked more than fifty years earlier. Poppy closed her eyes and felt the ghost of Dorothea walking by her side, young, anxious and with a heart full to bursting as she twisted the fresh gold band on

169

the third finger of her left hand and tried to take in every detail of the featureless, concrete landscape. Poppy smiled, remembering suddenly her nan's outpouring that one after-noon, at the time meaningless: 'My secret, my lovely little secret. My Simon, my little boy, my beautiful baby.'

Poppy's history was all around her. 'Poor old Nan,' she mused.

'In some ways,' Martin interjected. 'But Dorothea's face always lit up when she spoke about you. You made her so happy.'

Poppy smiled. 'And her me, mate. I don't know what I would have done without her.'

'All those times I'd walk into the flat and hear you both roaring over something stupid!' Martin grinned. 'It used to make me chuckle, it was infectious. And I'd find you sitting in that little kitchen with the kettle whistling and the windows steamed up and bacon under the grill. I thought it was the nicest place I'd ever been. Cosy.'

Poppy squeezed his fingers inside her own. 'It was, some-times, before she properly went downhill and Cheryl pissed off. When Nan was on form, I could forget about all the other crap. Do you remember at our wedding, when she went to the wrong ceremony and only realised at the end?' Poppy bent over and held her stomach at the memory. 'Oh God, only her! And she even cried during the vows and flut-tered her hanky like any good nan of the bride, only to realise when they turned around that it wasn't us!'

'Bloody typical.' Martin smiled.

In the darkening twilight, Poppy scanned the blocks of flats that surrounded them. They formed a square of sorts. Each block was identical, each balcony or walkway faced the other, meaning there was little variation, sunlight or privacy. Many of the original front doors had been replaced and the mismatched façades made them look scruffy and dated. On the walkway outside one door sat a large plastic tub in the centre of which was a gnarled, stubby brown root. Poppy found it sad that someone had tried planting something pretty but either through lack of know-how or effort had failed. She found it more depressing than if they hadn't bothered.

She let her eyes wander over the tarmac apron on which they stood, mostly now divided into parking spaces. Abandoned untaxed vehicles and the dented vans of working men sat squashed together, forming a multi-coloured metal herringbone in what used to be an open space.

She studied the grey concrete slabs daubed with graffiti and the generous stains of chemical discolouration where it had been half removed, leaving just a shadow of the anger spewed from a spray can. Many of the windows had bars over them and no amount of fancy scrollwork or bright turquoise paint could lift the gloomy message that they conveyed. One flat bore the scorch marks of a recent fire; blackened wisps snaked from behind the metal panels that had been secured over the doors and windows.

'Look at it, Mart. It's run-down, isn't it? And so dirty.'

'It always was, love.'

'Not in my mind.' She shook her head. Even the unhappiest of days would be cheered by a trip outside to the playground. The way she remembered it, the hours she'd spent sitting on the swings or hanging around the slide were always in sunshine, never in the rain or winter. As if this dingy space existed in permanent summer. She could only picture herself wearing a vest top and shorts, with brown legs and her hair shining with coppery highlights. Poppy drew an arc with her gaze. 'It all looks smaller, more cramped.'

'Maybe you just got bigger, fat arse.'

'Oi, cheeky! I was here only ten years ago, don't think I've got that much bigger.' They were both pretending, neither wanting to acknowledge her weight loss, the way her hip bones jutted against the denim of her jeans, and her jaw that now looked overly large for her face.

Martin gripped his wife's hand as they tripped across potholes and skirted crisp packets that cartwheeled ghostlike in the breeze. Martin sidestepped a blob of chewing gum and narrowly missed a pile of discarded beer cans.

He looked up towards the third-floor balcony. 'Blimey, the times I stood here and called up to you.' He brought his hands up to his mouth, curling his fingers to form a cone. 'You comin' out, Poppy Day?'

They stared at the space where she would appear, wearing her grubby school jumper, her forearms cushioning her chest as she leant over the concrete edge. 'On me way!' They both heard the reply that had echoed a hundred times around the walls. This little square of concrete had been a welcome escape from their grimy, oppressive flats, a pocket of joy in an otherwise joyless life.

'Peg and Maxy are so lucky, aren't they?' She thought of Malik and Adil and then pictured the wide-open green spaces where her children ran, the back garden in which they built dens and splashed in their paddling pool, and the sweet, clean Wiltshire air that flowed through their lungs. 'It's what we always wanted, wasn't it? To give them better than what we had?'

'Yep.' Martin nodded. 'And we have. But I was often happy here, especially when I was with you. You were all I needed, always. I didn't notice anything else.'

'Me too.' She squeezed his hand.

'Fancy a swing?' He smiled.

Poppy tucked her hair behind her ears. 'Well, we could hardly come to our playground and not, could we?'

She gathered her coat at her throat, ignoring the throb in her chest and the waves of sickness that threatened to wash over her as they quickened their pace. They edged past the clutch of cars and the row of industrial-looking wheelie bins. Despite their size, the bins still couldn't contain all the rubbish: the overflow was piled in slimy bin bags and stuffed into leaky cardboard boxes that gathered at every corner.

They paused and stared at their old playground, which was now fenced in by knee-high metal railings painted a garish shade of orange. Martin pushed open the gate and Poppy followed him in. The ground underfoot was black and spongy and had the outlines of puzzles painted on it, so worn they would only make a game frustrating, like hop without the scotch.

It was in this little square that Poppy and Martin had been free to laugh and fall in love. Childhood games, illicit smoking and teenage kissing had all taken place in this playground, their refuge. And, when he was eighteen, it was where Martin had proposed.

He walked to the centre of the space, breathing deeply and with his arms outstretched as if to confirm what his eyes were telling him. He turned a full circle. 'They took away the fucking swings!'

Poppy saw the unmistakable glint of tears in his eyes. Walking forward, she placed her hand on his chest. 'They were always dangerous. It's a miracle we never lost a finger or worse! They were old and creaky even then, Mart. It doesn't matter.'

'Doesn't matter?' He blinked as his distress spilled down

his cheeks. 'It matters to me. This was our place, our swings! Why can't anything stay the same? Why does everything turn to shit?' Martin sank down to his knees and Poppy, with her arms now wrapped around his trunk, sank too. 'I don't want the swings not to be here, Poppy Day, and I don't want you to leave me. Please, please... don't... leave... me.' He stuttered through his sobs.

Poppy cradled her man-child into her chest and stroked his hair from his forehead. 'Ssshh... Ssshh... It'll all be okay. It'll all be okay.'

Martin gripped her a little too tightly. 'It won't be. I'm losing you and it hurts so much that I can't even think about it. My stomach is twisted into a knot and I can't swallow properly. I don't want to be in this world without you. There's a big ball sitting in my throat and every time I look at you... I want to go hysterical I want to punch every single bloody door off its hinges!' He spoke through gritted teeth. 'And keeping it all in, Pop, it's really hard.'

'I know, baby. I know.' She sighed and kissed his forehead, relieved to finally see the emotion that he had been battling against for weeks.

They were both silent for a second or two. Poppy felt a deep sadness on his behalf. It was the first time she considered the fact that if it hadn't been for the kids, it would be better to be the one leaving, not the one left behind. She looked up to see a lady in a dark blue mac and headscarf walk past. She was carrying a red-and-blue-striped shopping bag, the kind Poppy hadn't seen in years. The woman scuttled past and the smell of hot fresh chips slathered in salt and vinegar wafted in their direction. Poppy inhaled the aroma. The woman turned on the path and smiled at Poppy. Poppy jumped a little and held onto Martin. The woman looked like her nan, only younger. Poppy blinked and the woman was gone.

'I don't think you will be in this world without me. I'll always be close to you. And Peg and Max, they are me and you, and they aren't going anywhere.'

Martin sniffed up his tears and wiped his eyes on his shirtsleeve. He exhaled, trying to calm himself down.

'This is where you proposed to me.' Poppy kissed his ear.

Martin nodded and sniffed again. 'I didn't plan it, not really. I just saw you fall off the swing...'

Poppy remembered the moment. She had been sitting on the swings as he leant on the post, drawing on a fag. She had swung higher and higher, kicking her legs back and forth.

She hadn't realised that after a tumble onto the floor, he would ask her marry him and her life would be changed forever. She would no longer be 'Poppy who lived in the flats,' 'Poppy with the fleas and no home clothes' or 'Poppy with the bonkers Nan.' She would be elevated to the rank of wife. And this was something her mum had never been able to achieve and her Nan had done reluctantly. The placing of a thin gold band on the third finger of her left hand had given her a security that she could only have imagined.

Martin Cricket had cupped her face in his hands and spoken in a voice so low, she had to concentrate to hear. 'I want you to marry me and I want us to live together until we get old and die.'

'I couldn't believe someone wanted to marry me!' Poppy brought them into the now. 'And I'm still chuffed that you picked me, Mart. Even now, I look down at my little gold wedding ring and I get this warm feeling in my stomach because you picked me.'

'I said I wanted to look after you always.' Martin sniffed.

'And you have.'

'Until now.' He swiped at his runny nose with his fingers.

Poppy's voice was calm, her tone measured. 'This is bigger than both of us, Mart. There's nothing you or I can do.'

She felt his shoulders ease against her chest. *It's not your fault.* They sat quietly in the middle of their playground, listening to the dog barks, door slams and engine revs all around them. The April air had lost the sharp bite of winter and whilst not warm, there was something in the breeze that hinted at the summer to come.

Martin nuzzled deeper against her, placing his ear flat on her chest. 'I can hear your heart beating.'

Poppy leant her chin on the top of his head. 'I sometimes wish I could stop it beating, Mart.'

He pulled away, trying to seek out her features in the dim half-light. 'You do?'

'Yes.' She nodded. 'Yes. I'd like to stop it and start it again in a few years, when the kids are older.' She tapped the space where his head had rested moments earlier. 'I know that this heart only has a certain number of beats left in it and that means every single one is like taking a step away from you.'

Martin sat up straight and took her hands into his own. She thought he looked young, like the Martin of her youth, when they were kids and this had been child's play.

'I love you, Poppy Day, I really love you.'

'And I you.'

The two sat entwined, listening to the sounds of their childhood echo all around them, both wishing there was a way to prevent the separation they knew was inevitable. With their heads close together and their hearts beating in unison, there they remained until the chill from the damp spongy floor beneath them crept into their bones and night threw its canopy over the remaining light.

Sixteen

Poppy was roused from her sleep with a jolt as the front door banged open. It was one of the many things she missed, now that Claudia had returned home: someone to 'ssshh....' at visitors, ensuring her rest was undisturbed.

'Only us!' Martin swooped down over the sofa and planted a kiss on his wife's forehead.

Poppy sat up slowly, ignoring the grinding pain in her spine, her dry mouth and the grittiness behind her eyelids that irritated with every blink.

'Have you had a good day, Peg?' She craned her neck to get the best view of her little girl.

Peg scowled in her direction. 'Not really. I didn't get register monitor again. Pawel Cyrekicz got it and he doesn't even know what register monitor is. It's not fair!' Peg thumped up the stairs to find solace in her bedroom.

'Oh, don't stomp off, Peg. It's your birthday tomorrow, you've got a lot to look forward to!'

'I don't care about my stupid birthday! I don't care about anything!' came the angry reply.

Poppy slowly swung her legs off the sofa. 'Mart, can you do me a favour, love?'

'Course.' He paused from unpacking the shopping and poked his head through the kitchen door.

'Can you drop me off in the village? I need to do something.'

She stood and swayed, trying to find her balance.

'Sure. Are you okay? Can I go for you, save all that running around?' He came closer and noted the steely look of determination that burned on her face. He wiped his hands on the tea towel and went off to fetch the car keys.

Minutes later, Martin pulled the Golf into the staff car park at Peg's school and unclipped his seatbelt.

Poppy gazed up at the hawthorn tree. Heavy clusters of rose-like pink and white blossom covered every branch. The gentle breeze shook the more delicate petals. She watched as they fluttered down onto the windscreen like confetti. 'Beautiful!'

'Yes, you are.' Martin stared at her craning forward to look at the beautiful display. 'Come on, I'll come with you. You don't look too clever.' He reached for the door handle.

Poppy placed her hand on his thigh. 'Actually, love, I'd rather go in on my own, if you don't mind?'

Martin saw how she tugged impatiently at the seatbelt, noted the two bright spots of colour in her otherwise pale complexion. He knew she was fired up, agitated. 'No, not at all. I'll be right here, you just shout if you need me.'

She reached over and squeezed his hand. 'I know that. Shan't be a mo.'

Buttoning up her coat, she breathed in the warm, fresh air. It felt good to be outside. She walked slowly towards the front door of the school, conscious that she was a little unsteady on her feet. She had been sitting or lying down for much of the last few days, so any movement required concentration. Inside, she crept along the corridor and paused to lean against the wall, taking in the fabulous murals painted by the kids, enjoying the people with disproportionate-sized heads and bodies and green and purple hair. She laughed at the photos of sports day, scouring every one until she spotted a picture of Peg, gurning as she completed the sack race, coming a very respectable seventh out of nine. There were little rows of bright green cress in old butter tubs and soft-cheese cartons that someone had placed on the window sills. It felt like a happy place.

Poppy thought back to the last time she had set foot inside the classroom, on parents' evening in the run-up to Christmas, before this whole horrible nightmare had begun. She had disliked Mrs Newman on sight: her pinched face, thin lips and sarcastic tone. The woman's words were there for perfect recall: 'It has been a most challenging term. Peg asks a lot of questions.' She'd given a brief, false smile. 'It really isn't a good thing.'

Poppy took a deep breath, then knocked and entered. Mrs Newman was sitting behind her desk, her mouth poised ready to say, 'Come in!' Utterly pointless now. Poppy watched as she grabbed the large bar of Galaxy and shoved it into the open top drawer, flustered.

'Ah, Mrs Cricket.' She furtively passed her tongue over her gums, gluey with milk chocolate.

Poppy nodded. At least she'd remembered her name this time.

'What can I do for you? I was just finishing up.'

'I'm sorry to come in without an appointment, but I wanted to see you.'

'Yes, yes of course. Let me get you a seat.' Mrs Newman flushed and Poppy noted the panicky haste with which she dragged over a chair. She must look pretty bad: the woman was probably worried that she might keel over there and then.

'How are you?' Her tone was clipped and in her eyes there was something that looked horribly like pity.

'I'm great, thanks.' Her lie was swift, if a little unconvincing. 'I wanted to have a word with you about Peg.'

'Of course.' Mrs Newman nodded.

'The thing is, Mrs Newman, she doesn't seem very... happy.' Poppy's voice was tight, her hands balled to stop them shaking. She found it harder than she had imagined, controlling her anger and expressing herself to the teacher.

'Well, we have had words on more than one occasion.' The woman smirked.

'But that's just it, Mrs Newman. I don't want you having words. I want you to encourage and support her.'

Mrs Newman ran her finger and thumb over her lips and pushed her chair from the desk. Rising, she placed her glasses on the tip of her nose and flicked through a pile of exercise books on a shelf at the back of the room. Selecting one, she marched back to the desk and opened it at a particular page, cracking the spine to ensure the book remained flat.

'There are some things, Mrs Cricket, that require words. This was one such thing.'

Poppy took the offered book into her hands and read the heading: *My News*. She scanned her daughter's handwriting, neat and uniform. One sentence jumped out at her from all the others: *My mum herd me cryin and made me laugh a lot when she said Mrs Newman was a misrabel cow and I laughed because Mrs Newman is a misrabel cow even though I mustn't say it again...*

Poppy looked up. Mrs Newman's chest heaved and her eyes shone with triumph. Poppy closed the book and placed it on the desk. Her words, when they came, were slow and considered.

'Here's the thing, Mrs Newman. I *do* think you are a miserable cow. I think you are petty and mean and God only knows why you are in charge of a class of kids who you clearly have no affection for. Being a teacher is a privilege and not one you have earned.'

'I beg your pardon?' The teacher's chin dipped to her chest, emphasising her large jowls.

'I think you heard me perfectly and I don't really want to repeat it.' Poppy felt surprisingly calm.

'I would like you to leave, Mrs Cricket!' Mrs Newman's voice shook.

'I bet you would. Well, there are lots of things I'd like too. Like not to be so bloody sick that I can hardly find the energy to stay awake. Not to have to think about the fact that when I'm gone, people like you will still get to see my little girl every day, even though you really don't deserve to. But mostly, Mrs Newman, I would like Peg to be register monitor. Because, despite the fact that her mum has cancer and her home life has turned to rat shit, this is the one shining beacon of hope that keeps her smiling – the possibility that one day you might bestow upon her the favour of carrying the shitty register to the school office!'

'I...' Mrs Newman failed to find a response.

Poppy stood and walked to the door. With her fingers on the handle, she turned back to the red-faced teacher, who sat aghast. 'You can go back to your chocolate now.'

She strode down the corridor feeling a burst of energy. Stopping at the collage of sports day pictures, Poppy kissed her two fingers and pressed them onto the picture of Peg.

Martin watched her come out of the building. He leant across and opened the door. 'All okay?'

'Yes! All bloody marvellous. Now drive me home!' Poppy pointed in the direction of the road, laughing.

'Yes, ma'am.' He laughed too. It was good to see the

sparkle in her eye, and whatever had occurred inside had certainly fuelled her energy levels.

Poppy was always conscious of disturbing Martin in the night, what with her frequent trips to the loo, the need for painkillers and the continual desire for less or more heat. That night, she lay on her side, keeping as still as she could, trying to cry silently into her pillow. It was no use. Martin, in tune with her every movement and monitoring each intake of breath, twist of the duvet and sip of water in the dark, noticed the tiny judder of her shoulder. It was as if he was guarding her. She clenched her jaw at the sound of the springs creaking under his shifting weight; she hadn't wanted to wake him. She heard him move the water glass across the bedside table so he could see the clock, then scratch his beard. He rolled over and placed his hand on her shoulder.

'What can I do?' he whispered, his voice pained. 'Can I get you some painkillers, love?

Poppy shook her head, wiping her tears on the pale cover that she knew would be peppered with mascara residue and need another wash. Not that it really mattered, not in the scheme of things.

Martin moved his hand to her waist and scooted over to where she lay, placing his legs inside the hollow of hers, mirroring her position and nuzzling her neck with his chin. Poppy felt a surge of love for him and remembered the first time they had slept together – teenagers who'd stolen a secret hour behind doors that didn't lock. What had he said? 'We fit together, don't we?'

'What's the matter, baby?'

Poppy sniffed and swallowed. 'Peg... Peg's birthday.'

'Yes, and she'll have a brilliant day. Everything's wrapped

and she'll love her balloons. You've worked hard, Pop, don't worry about it now.'

Martin glanced at the alarm clock. It was only 4.30 a.m., far too early to be worrying about Peg's present opening.

'It's not that,' Poppy whispered.

Martin closed his eyes against her back. He knew what was coming next but hoped she wouldn't voice what they were both thinking. He didn't want to hear it, didn't want it confirmed. He felt too tired to cope with the fall-out.

'I won't be here for her next birthday, or the one after that, or any of them. This is the last. Her ninth, that's all I got.'

He stroked the line from hip to thigh, still enjoying the feel of the curve after all these years. 'Hey, don't talk like that,' he said, soothingly. 'You never know, we might just be lying here this time next year having this same conversation. You don't know.'

'But that's just it. I do know and it's breaking my heart.' Poppy turned and twisted her body into his arms. Martin held her tight. Her tears were rare.

'It's so hard, Mart, trying to keep everything great for the kids because I think it might be the last thing they remember.' This admission made her tears fall even faster. 'And trying not to fall apart or go nuts, because that's what I feel like doing sometimes. I feel so bloody awful a lot of the time that I just want to curl up and hide under the duvet and not see or speak to anyone, but I don't have that luxury. I have to keep going and I have to try and keep things normal. Sometimes it feels like all my energy is being taken up just coping with this bloody illness and I have absolutely nothing left.'

He kissed her forehead. 'You are doing a great job. You

are making it the best for them that it possibly can be and most people wouldn't have the strength to do what you are doing. I'm so proud of you.'

Poppy placed her cheek against his skin and cried hot tears from swollen eyes that left her face and hair wet. Angry thoughts clouded her mind as she gave in to a rare bout of self-pity. 'I don't want to be doing a great job! It's so bloody unfair – why me? Why after everything we have been through is it me that has to go through this? I wish it was someone else. Someone mean or someone evil and I know that's a horrible thing to say, but I don't care. It's not fair, why did it pick me? I just wanted to have a normal little life and watch my kids grow up. That's all I ever wanted – it's not too much to ask, is it?'

Martin stroked her shoulder and let her rage exhaust itself. Eventually Poppy wriggled even closer against her husband and closed her eyes. She wanted to block out such thoughts, she wanted sleep. Inhaling the scent of him, she wished absurdly that she could crawl into him and never resurface. Soon, despite the threat of fractured nightmares, her breath fell into a rhythm and sleep arrived.

'I GOT A SCOOTER!' Peg screamed loud enough to wake the whole of Wiltshire.

Poppy rolled over and looked at her husband, then buried her head in his T-shirt. 'Something tells me she might have found her presents.'

'What gave you that idea?' He kissed her scalp. 'Are you feeling a bit better?'

'Yes, much,' Poppy lied, doing what she did best, trying to keep everyone happy.

'IT'S MY BIRTHDAY!' Peg hollered.

They both laughed as they rose slowly and reluctantly from the warmth of their bed, thrust arms into dressing gowns and rubbed sleep from their eyes.

Poppy palmed small circles on her lower back, which for some reason was particularly painful. She went into the bathroom and swallowed her morning dose of drugs. 'Try harder, little soldiers. You've got to kick the shit out of those pedalos. Do your very best.'

'All okay in there?' Martin called from the bed.

'Yep, just talking to myself.'

They descended the stairs to find Peg tearing at the ribbons on the handlebars of her scooter. Poppy bent down slowly to retrieve the length of shiny pink satin, which would go into her memory box later, with the date and a message:

This was wrapped around the handlebars of your new scooter, Peg, the greatest form of transport you have owned to date! May all your birthdays bring you joy and happiness, and know that on the day you were born I loved you with my whole heart and I always will. x

'Happy birthday, darling.' Poppy smiled from the kitchen door as Peg ran her hands over the thing of beauty that she had coveted for a while.

'Thank you, Mum and Dad. I love it! I really love it! Can I go out on it now? Please?' She was practically jumping up and down.

Martin opened the front door. 'Be my guest.'

They sat on the sofa with their first cup of tea of the day, listening as Peg tore up and down the pavement in her pyjamas and slippers.

'The neighbours are going to hate us,' Poppy said as she sat back and closed her eyes.

Peg had insisted on scooting to school and Martin had been coerced into walking alongside her with Max in the pushchair. At the end of the school day he set off early, deciding to walk the long way round and leave Poppy on the sofa. A few minutes of shut-eye would do her no harm at all.

The front door bell rang and Poppy opened the door to see Jo smiling on the doorstep and holding a large white box.

'Hey, I knew you'd come! It's lovely to see you.' Poppy ushered her friend into the hallway. 'I don't half miss having my mate next door.'

'I miss you too, and the kids. More than you know.'

Poppy noted Jo's weight loss, which suited her. She was still lacking her rosy glow, but all in good time. 'Well, you're here now.'

'How you doing?' Jo squinted to get a better look at her friend.

'So-so.' Poppy didn't want to dwell on the subject. 'The times I go to knock on your door! I forget you've gone. I don't like it, Jo, not one bit.'

'I know how you feel. It's weird being here. I see the house is all locked up.' Jo flicked her eyes to the wall next door. 'Have you seen shit-face?'

'Yep, briefly. I left him in no doubt about how I feel about the whole thing.'

'Thanks, Poppy. You're not going to believe this...' Jo took a deep breath. 'But I heard he's having a baby with his new bit of stuff. No wonder he was in such a hurry to get me packed up and moved on.'

'Oh, Jo!' Poppy put her hand on her friend's arm, knowing that this above all else would be the hardest thing to bear.

'I know. I can't get my head around it. I don't want him any more, Poppy, not after the way he treated me. I figure I deserve better. But the idea of him having the baby I wanted so badly with someone else...' Jo shook her head. 'It's killing me.' Poppy watched as her friend's face threatened to dissolve into tears. 'But I'm not going to cry today, I do enough of that at home. Today I am going to be happy because I get to see my birthday girl. Is she not back yet?'

'No, but she's on her way now. Mart's walking her home. Come through, you don't need an invite!' Poppy stood back.

Jo grazed her mate's cheek with a kiss. 'Don't go mad, but I made Peg a cake. Ta da!' Jo put the box on the dining table and removed the lid, revealing a vast pink cake covered in tiny pink marshmallows and with three sparklers sticking from the top ready for lighting.

'Oh my God, look at that! Did you really make it, Jo?'

'Yep! It's taken me all day, but I bloody love that Peg and I can't wait to see her face!' Jo smiled.

'She is one lucky girl.' Poppy admired the fondant creation, ignoring the grinding pain in her joints and the slight blurring that was obscuring her vision. 'Thank you, Jo. It's bloody amazing. Did you hear her this morning, out at the crack of a sparrow's fart on that bloody scooter? She was making so much noise, I thought you might have got the echo over in Marlborough.'

'Ah, so that's what woke me up!' Jo laughed.

The two women were still admiring Jo's handiwork when they heard Peg clatter up the garden path and smack into the front door.

'No brakes,' Poppy explained.

187

'God help you!' Jo grinned.

Poppy opened the door and smiled at Peg, who lay in a crumpled heap on the ground. 'Come on, birthday girl, you've got a visitor.'

'It's Aunty Jo, isn't it? I saw her car. Did she get me a present?' Peg stood up and dusted down her knees.

'Peg!' Poppy remonstrated. She turned to Jo and grimaced.

'I did better than a present, I made you this!' Jo stood to one side with her arms outstretched and her palms turned upwards towards the cake.

'I LOVE IT!' Peg screamed and jumped headlong into the sofa, her squeals muffled by the sofa cushion.

'I think she likes it,' Poppy said.

Max ran in on his sturdy legs. 'Cake for Maxy!'

Jo bent down and lifted him, smothering his rosy cheeks with kisses. 'Hey, Maxy! You are getting so big! And doing good talking too, clever boy.'

'Five... six... seven...' Max added for good measure.

'Still counting?' Jo enquired.

'Yep, anything and everything. He's going to be a maths genius, this child,' Martin said with pride.

'Vorderman, eat your heart out.' Jo laughed.

Poppy lit the sparklers and Peg stared at the flickering rainbows that shot from the top of her cake. It was hypnotic.

'Don't forget to make a wish, Peg!' Martin encouraged.

Peg closed her eyes and her lips moved silently up and down, mouthing her wish. As the sparklers died and sat forlornly in their sugary pink base, she sighed. 'I did a wish for you, Mum, so that you could stop being sick in the night.'

Poppy caught Martin's eye, both of them unaware that their daughter had been privy to her trips to the bathroom in the dead of night. 'Thank you, lovey.' She was genuinely touched.

'And the reason I could wish for you was because the other thing I *would* have wished for has already come true.'

'Oh? What's that, love?' Poppy asked as the cake was cut and heaped into bowls.

'You are not going to believe it, Mummy, but Mrs Newman made me register monitor! When she made the announcement, I listened like I do every morning and I always look down so she can't see how sad I am when I am not picked. But today she said it! She said, "And the register monitor is... Peg Cricket!" She even got my name right. And I know you are not supposed to, Mum, but I couldn't help it: I ran up to her desk and I put my arms around her neck and I gave her the biggest cuddle you can imagine. I squeezed her so tightly that her glasses popped off. I told her it was the third best day of my life, after getting Toffee and Daddy coming home for Christmas.'

'What did she say when you said that?' Poppy was curious.

'She said, "Hard work and persistence pays off."' Peg beamed, still unable to believe her luck.

'Ain't that the truth.' Martin winked at his wife as they tucked into birthday cake.

Poppy forked a spoonful to her mouth but declined to eat it at the last minute. She couldn't muster the enthusiasm for something that looked so exquisite but turned to sawdust the moment it touched her tongue. She placed the tiniest morsel in her mouth and swallowed the crumbs that stuck to the dry husk of her throat. 'Mmmm... this is lovely.'

Seventeen

Two days later and the excitement surrounding Peg's birthday had dwindled. Poppy's mood was not quite so jovial as she drummed her fingers on the arm of the chair, waiting impatiently for Mr Ramasingh. Martin had insisted on accompanying her to the clinic and despite her protestations, she knew she needed him to lean on, in every sense, although his presence made her even more nervous. The room was a tad chillier than usual, making the white walls and grey blinds seem even more austere. She decided this was probably a good thing; she couldn't picture what kind of art or knick-knack would be appropriate for the conversations that flowed across his tidy desk.

'Ah, good morning, good morning, Poppy. and nice to meet you at last, Martin.' Mr Ramasingh shook hands with Martin and took up his position. 'You look tired,' he noted as he tapped into his keyboard.

Poppy liked the way he avoided small talk. There was no verbal meandering: he was straight to the point and she knew where she stood. 'I am. I'm not sleeping too well and I keep being sick. And I've had terrible diarrhoea, but that seems to have calmed down a bit, thank God.'

The doctor nodded. 'You need to take your anti-sickness medication, and do you remember what I told you about sleep? You are not to worry about the clock on the wall, you have to listen to the clock in here.' He placed his hand over his heart, or at least where his heart might be. Peg, who maintained that people's hearts were always exactly in the centre of their chests, would have said about six inches too far to the left. 'You need to listen to what your body needs and if it needs sleep, sleep! Nothing else matters as much as getting through the day and having the best rest you can get.'

Poppy nodded. It was easy for him to say, with his beautiful wife at home to pick up the toys and cook the supper while he was here trying to fix people. Who did he think was at home with her, performing wifely duties? Martin was brilliant, doing all he could, but it wasn't easy juggling his job and caring for her and the kids.

It was as if he read her mind. 'We can get you some help, you know, if you need it.'

Poppy shook her head. 'No. No, we're fine, thanks.' The last thing she wanted was another row with Martin over busybodies poking their noses into their business. Martin squeezed her hand.

'I wanted to ask you something, Mr Ramasingh.' She sat forward in the chair.

'Fire away.' He stopped tapping and placed his clasped hands on the blotter in front of him.

'Am I allowed to go on holiday, abroad? My uncle lives in the Caribbean, St Lucia, and wants us to go over.' She bit her lip, desperately wanting him to say it was okay.

'Well, if you feel up to it, yes. You would have to take some precautions – make sure you have enough medication with you, and you'll need good health insurance, which can be ridiculously pricey. And you must take care of those bones of yours. Don't forget, they are weakened, Poppy, and you

191

don't want to go breaking anything abroad. But all that said, if you feel you want to and are able to, then why not!'

She beamed. 'Why not!'

'And you are going too, Martin?'

'Yes. It will be good to get away. A new environment, a bit of sunshine...'

'It will be good.' The doctor nodded his agreement. 'It's easy to forget, when all the focus is on your wife, just what *you* are going through. I know I've mentioned it before, but we can put you in touch with a team of specialists who will do anything from helping with form filling to just giving you an ear to talk to.'

Martin nodded. 'It is tough,' he almost whispered.

It was Poppy's turn to squeeze his hand.

Mr Ramasingh coughed. 'I remember when my wife died, it happened so suddenly that it was like having the rug pulled out from underneath me. I actually envied people like you, who had some time to plan, put things right, be together.'

Poppy reached for the photograph that sat on the doctor's desk. How she had envied this beautiful, beautiful woman. 'This wife here? She's dead?' Tears began spilling from her eyes.

'Yes. Six years ago. A brain aneurism. It was very sudden.' Poppy heard the catch in his voice.

She slumped back in the chair and placed her hand on her chest. Her sobs came loudly and with such force, she had to fight for each breath. 'Does everyone have to fucking die?'

Mr Ramasingh couldn't help the spurt of laughter that left his mouth. He removed his glasses and rubbed at his eyes as he shook his head. Martin too saw the funny side and let his shoulders shake, while simultaneously trying to comfort his wife. Eventually, Poppy's lips twitched as well.

'Oh, Poppy, that has made me laugh! And in answer to your question, yes! Yes they do, each and every one of us!'

They drove home almost in silence. Martin didn't comment on Poppy's swollen, red eyes and face streaked with tears, but instead stole furtive glances at her as he took left-hand corners. He parked in front of the house and ratcheted the handbrake, but neither of them made any attempt to move. Their breathing slowed and the windows fogged, creating a bubble around the two of them. Both stared ahead, in silence. It felt cosy and peaceful. When Martin did eventually speak, his voice was husky, as if he'd just woken from a long sleep.

'Do you ever want to ask him how long you've got, Poppy?' His question came out of the blue. It was somehow easier to discuss these things in the car, leaving their home free of some of the echoes.

She shook her head. 'No. I think it's best I don't know.'

'Really?' he asked, wondering if having a timescale would make it easier or harder.

Poppy nodded. 'I think if I knew, then I might just give up.'

'Don't ever say that!' he shouted. 'You must never give up. This is all about getting as much time as possible for the kids, for me. You owe us that.'

'I *owe* you that? What's that supposed to mean? Are you blaming me for this, Mart? You think I would choose this?' She punched her chest.

He pinched his nose and rested his elbows on the steering wheel. 'No. No, I know you would never choose this and I'm sorry. I just hate the way Mr Whatshisname is so positive, so smiley and matter-of-fact. I know I should be more like that, but, truth is, I feel like I'm drowning and it's exhausting.'

'Tell me about it.' She unclipped her seatbelt and walked slowly up the path. Her sympathy was a little thin on the ground today.

Jo had made a huge chocolate cake, covered in thick frosting, much of which was around Max's face.

'Cake!' Max announced as they walked into the hallway.

'I can see that!' Poppy bent down and picked up her boy, which was becoming increasingly hard for her to do. She carried him to the sofa and flopped down with him on her lap.

'What have you been up to, Maxy? Have you been a good boy for Aunty Jo?'

Max nodded. 'Toffee did a poo-poo.'

Poppy laughed at her son's rare sentence. 'Do you know what, Max? I think you know exactly what is going on and you just choose to stay out of it, in your own little world. And honestly, mate, I can't blame you. Not one bit. Sometimes I wish I could hide from the real world too.'

Maxy held up his favourite little digger for his mum to kiss, which she duly did.

Jo came through from the kitchen with mugs of tea and two large slabs of chocolate cake. Poppy groaned inwardly.

'How did you get on?' Jo asked eagerly as she forked the sponge into her mouth and washed it down with a gulp of strong coffee.

'Okay. Not much to say really. Nothing new. Thanks for looking after Maxy at the last minute, mate. Mart could only finish a bit early to come and collect me, which is fair enough. And thank you for our lovely cake too – you've been busy!'

'We had great fun. He is such a fabulous kid, Poppy. He just smiles and chatters – he's so happy. We let Toffee run around on the rug and he did a poo and Max thought it was the most hilarious thing.' Jo smiled.

'You will stay in their lives, won't you, Jo? Look after them, be there if they need someone to talk to? They've got Mart and Claudia, of course, but someone my age will be good for them.'

Jo was choked with emotion. 'I will love them for you, Poppy, always, and I'm honoured that you'd ask me.'

As she prepared for bed later that evening, Poppy stood and stared at her reflection in the bathroom mirror. She looked sick. For the first time she realised it must now be obvious to anyone who glanced at her through a window or met her in the street. She had started to notice how people looked the other way or crossed over to avoid her and that made her feel like one of the afflicted. Her chest was concave; her skin, which had taken on a greyish hue, was taut, stretched over her skeleton without the layer of fat that had given her her shape. She hated the way her body looked. She smiled at the irony of it: she had disliked the curve of her hip and the slight bulge of fat on her stomach her whole life and yet now she would happily swap her skinny form for her old self. Her teeth looked large in her mouth. Black circles sat beneath her eyes and her hair was lank, thin.

She swallowed the handful of drugs that had become her habit and cleaned her teeth. Spitting into the sink, she recoiled at the globs of blood spattered around the plughole. She ran the tap and swilled the water with her hand; out of sight, out of mind.

Reaching down, she plucked the box of tampons from the shelf behind the loo and shoved them in the pedal bin, trying not to think of all they represented: making babies, having babies, the cycle that meant life. 'I won't be needing those again.' She smiled, kidding herself that she had found the one advantage to being sick, refusing to allow the painful truth to permeate, that her body was failing, shutting down.

Eighteen

'I am so excited!' Peg jumped up and down on the sofa in her new frock. The floaty skirt billowed around her as she bounced and the sequined bodice caught the light and shimmered, making her look like a human glitter ball.

'Peg, take it off! You've got three weeks to go and you'll have it ruined if you put it on every single day until then. People will think you are turning up in an old rag.' Poppy sighed.

'But I LOVE it so much!' Peg jumped higher and higher, fluffing the skirt with her hands.

'I know, love. But we need it to stay white for as long as possible. You don't want to get it dirty, do you?'

Peg shrugged her shoulders, not fussed really whether it got dirty, so long as she could wear it.

Martin laughed from over the top of the paper, delighted that the fifty quid price tag he had ummed, ahhed and sweated over had turned out to be worth every penny. To see Peg that happy was something he would pay any price for. The party had turned out to be a wonderful idea, for which he took full credit. The buzz of the planning was giving them all a lift. Even Poppy, though she looked frail and a little green around the gills, had got some of her vitality back.

'She's all right in it, Poppy,' he commented.

'Oh, is that right? Well that's good then, Peg, you can just ignore me and do what your dad says.'

Martin tutted in response. He was in no mood for another bickering session.

Poppy picked up her phone as it buzzed on the counter top. 'Ooh, I've got a text message from my mum!' Martin watched as her face lit up; she reminded him of Peg. The moment the message was opened, the light disappeared from her eyes.

'Oh,' said Poppy, 'she says she can't make it, but hopes we have a "GR8" time.'

'Hey, that's Cheryl, queen of text speak. She always was a teenager at heart.' Martin tried to lighten her obvious disappointment.

'Urgh.' Poppy shuddered, thinking of her own teenage years and her mum coming home in the early hours smelling of booze and sex.

'Have you spoken to her, Poppy?'

'No. I mean yes, but not properly, not about, y'know...'

'Does Cheryl know about your bug?' Peg enquired matter-of-factly between bounces.

Martin raised his eyebrows; they couldn't have a conversation without Peg sticking her oar in.

'No, lovey, not yet. I haven't had a chance to tell her.' Poppy scrolled through her messages, avoiding eye contact with Martin, who knew it was more a case of avoidance than lack of opportunity.

'Well you better get that sorted!' Peg advised.

Martin chuckled. 'For once your daughter is right. You better get that sorted.'

'GR8. That's all I need – both of you telling me what to do.'

'It's for your own good, Poppy Day!' Peg shouted, using her dad's name for his wife.

'Right, that's it! Go upstairs and get that bloody dress off – now!' Poppy raised her voice.

The letterbox flap banged against the door.

'I'll get it!' Peg skidded across the floor in her pink socks en route to the stairs. She came back holding a small stack of mail and sat with it on her lap, flicking through the envelopes.

'Give me that!' Poppy grabbed the bundle from her daughter's lap. 'Don't make me tell you again – go and get that dress off and hang it up in our room. I am confiscating it until the party!'

'No, no, Mum, please! Let me hang it up in my room so I can see it,' Peg pleaded.

Poppy pushed her forehead with her thumb and forefinger as if to relieve some unseen pressure. 'Okay, but if you so much as remove it from its hanger, that's it, you will have to wear one of your old dresses and that one is going back to the shop!'

Martin winked at his daughter as she marched past with her arms folded. Peg winked back; she knew her dad wouldn't let this dress go back to the shop.

Poppy sorted the invite responses into a separate pile from the bills and pizza flyers and tucked her legs up underneath her. This was one of the best things about having a party: reading the acceptances, scanning the notes. She selected one, placed her finger under the sticky flap and pulled out the reply slip.

'Oh, fab, Rob and Moira Gisby are coming! I didn't think they'd travel all the way down from Scotland, but they are.' Poppy read the details. 'They are going to stay with Rob's brother who lives in Andover, so that's handy. It'll be lovely to see them, Mart.'

'It will.'

Martin gave a small smile, remembering the role Sergeant Gisby had played in bringing him home from Afghanistan, the support he'd given Poppy. He tried not to think about it too much, but at the mention of Rob's name he was back in that hotel room in London, newly freed and with one hell of a mess going on inside his head. Rob had found him distressed and aggressive, yet his tone had been kind: 'You don't need to say sorry, son. You've been through a lot. And call me Rob.'

Poppy drew him from his musing. 'Claudia can make it, which I knew already, and she is offering to pay for the food. Honestly, that woman – what would we do without her, Mart? I've told her it's all taken care of, but she is always trying to make our lives easier. I love her, Mart, I really do.'

He smiled. They all did.

'Jenna and Ryan are coming but are leaving the boys behind. They're going to make a weekend of it and stay in a B&B.' This she uttered quickly, as if that would make the information more palatable.

'Yay!' Martin raised his fist half-heartedly.

'Don't be mean, Mart. Jenna is our mate.'

'I know, but that knobhead she's with… I can't stomach the bloke. He thinks he's a bloody gangster, but he's just a lazy git.' He pursed his lips.

'Blimey, you've got to learn to stop holding back – what do you really think of him, Cricket?'

Martin smiled. 'I can't help it, Poppy. He is not a very nice bloke and I don't want him at our do. I don't want him near Peg and Max and I don't want him dipping into our guests' pockets and helping himself.'

'What a thing to say! Just because he's lazy and you don't

WILL YOU REMEMBER ME?

like him doesn't make him a criminal.' Poppy laughed in spite of herself. 'Oh God, you haven't invited Danny, have you?' She suddenly thought about what might happen if Jo were to bump into him, especially with a few glasses of plonk inside her.

'No, thought it best not to, in case Jo is in handbag-swinging mode.'

'Who's in a handbag-swinging mood?'

'Oh, here she is – Batfink with her supersonic sonar!' Martin shouted as Peg came down the stairs.

Poppy and Martin laughed at their daughter, who didn't know who Batfink was but decided it wasn't necessarily a compliment.

Poppy waited until everyone was occupied – Peg in front of the telly and Max with parking all his diggers and trucks in a neat row, ready to be counted. Taking her mobile phone into the kitchen, she pressed the screen to connect to her mum.

'Yep?' It was a bloke's voice.

'Can I speak to Cheryl please?'

'CHERYL! PHONE!' the man bellowed, without another word to ask who was calling or to offer any pleasantries.

Poppy heard her mum's cackle getting louder, until she finally breathed into the phone, part wheezing, part laughing.

'Hello?'

'Mum, hi, s-sorry to interrupt you, are you working?' Poppy experienced the usual stammer of nerves.

'Yeah, but that's all right, love. I've got one punter passed out on the floor and another one trying to do the flamenco in his undies – it's bloody chaos here!' She chuckled, clearly enjoying every second of the non-stop party that was her life.

'Can you go somewhere a bit quieter, Mum, so you can hear me properly?' More to the point, so Poppy didn't have to listen to the raucous shouts, screams and clapping that filled the background. There was a second or two of silence and Poppy heard the creak of a whining hinge.

'That better?' Cheryl asked.

'Much, thanks. I wanted to talk to you, Mum...'

'Fire away.' Poppy could tell Cheryl was speaking from the side of her mouth. She couldn't remember a single occasion when her mum had spoken to her without reaching for or sparking up a fag. Just the idea of it made Poppy feel nauseous.

'All okay with you, Mum?' Poppy was stalling.

'Not bad, love. And you?'

This was her chance. She sighed. 'Not great, actually, Mum. I just wanted you to know that I've been diagnosed with cancer.' She could think of no other way to phrase it.

'Oh shit, Poppy. You all right?' Her mum drew on her ciggie.

No! I'm not all right. I've just told you I've got fucking cancer! 'Yes, I'm okay, just wanted you to know...' Even now, at the age of thirty-two, Poppy could not be honest with her mum. Whether it was to spare her the emotional turmoil or simply because she couldn't bear to hear her sympathy and regret expressed too late, she wasn't sure.

'Are you having treatment?' Cheryl asked, her voice wobbling. Was she crying?

'Yes, all that, Mum. I'm fine, as I said. I just wanted to let you know.'

'Where is it?' she asked.

'My breast, kind of...' She hated discussing the specifics, it made her picture it and she tried to avoid that.

'Shit. There's loads they can do now, Pop. It's not un-common, is it?'

'No, I guess not.'

'Have you lost your hair?' Poppy smiled at her mum's biggest concern, something that now seemed so incidental in the scheme of things.

'No. A few clumps, but that's it.' Poppy closed her eyes.

'Oh well, that's a blessing.'

'I guess. I've been thinking a lot about things...' Poppy swallowed and closed her eyes. 'And I wanted to ask you something.'

'What?' Cheryl sounded a little impatient.

'I... I wanted to ask you who my dad was.' Poppy gripped the phone with both hands, trying to stop them from shaking.

'Jesus, Poppy, not that again!'

Poppy felt her cheeks flush, awkward and embarrassed as ever at the topic. 'It's important to me.' Her voice was quiet.

'Well, it shouldn't be! You are a grown woman, you've got Mart and your own kids now and to be honest, I'm not even sure myself. I was young, free and single; things happened.'

Poppy cringed at her mother's admission.

'If you need me to come over, you just shout. I mean it.' That was Cheryl's way of ending this uncomfortable call.

Poppy twisted her mouth at her mum's words. What had Claudia said? 'I want to come over right now, but I don't want to interfere.' And not long after, she had appeared. That was the difference.

'I will. I'll speak to you soon, Mum.'

'Look after yourself. I love you, Poppy Day.' This was a rare admission of how she felt. Cheryl ended the call.

Poppy leant on the cupboard door and looked at the worktops, which were sticky with food, and the dirty upturned cups in the sink. She held the phone in her hand and imagined what her nan's reaction would have been, had she just received the news. She heard her voice loud and clear. 'You are a tough cookie, Poppy Day; you was brought up that way. Stay strong for them kids and remember, life goes on.'

Poppy felt warmth spread through her body as though she was being hugged from the inside out. It felt lovely. 'I miss you, Nan. I miss you so much.'

And just like that, Poppy was crying, as she always did. So much regret, so much anger and those three little words from her mum served as both a balm and a dagger. She suspected they always would.

'I love you too, Mum,' she whispered into the air.

Later, Martin drove them to Amesbury; a big Tesco shop was needed. As was often the case, he bumped into a couple of his colleagues in the car park. Even on Saturday, a precious day off, it seemed they needed to talk about work. Poppy gave them a little wave and left them to it.

She walked slowly ahead, pushing the trolley up and down the aisles, using it as much for support as anything else as she looked for food for the week. It was as if she was on autopilot, automatically reaching for the same brands and same products week in and week out. Her menus didn't vary and neither did the kids' snacks, which she tried to keep as healthy as possible. Sometimes she struggled to think of something different to serve them. They seemed to be on an alternating rota of chilli, roast chicken, egg and chips and spaghetti bolognese, with fajitas as a Saturday night treat.

At least her recipes were simple; she was confident that Martin could reproduce them, so if nothing else, the kids' meals would remain consistent.

Poppy kept her eye open for anything they might need for St Lucia and was on the lookout for a couple of large jars of pickles and relishes for the buffet. They had decided to get all the sandwiches, quiches and sausage rolls made by the caterers that ran the hall, but it worked out cheaper for them to provide all the extra bits, nibbles and so on. Poppy collected three large jars of pickled onions that were on special offer and placed them in the trolley next to the after-sun lotion.

'Oh God!' a woman gasped.

Poppy looked up to see one of the mums from Maxy's parent and toddler group coming in the opposite direction. She wished she could remember her name... Finn's mum, that was as close as she could get.

Finn's mum stopped and parked her trolley alongside Poppy's. She put her hand on Poppy's arm. It's... well... I don't know what to say! It is lovely to see you, really lovely!' She looked a little tearful and swished her long blonde hair over her shoulder to get a better view.

'Oh!' Poppy was taken aback by the intensity of the woman's greeting. She had sat opposite her once or twice while shaking a tambourine and singing 'Twinkle, Twinkle', but they were hardly good buddies. 'Thank you. It's lovely to see you too!'

The woman stared at Poppy, taking in her face and letting her eyes rove over her body. It made Poppy feel awkward. Her face flushed.

'How's Finn?'

'Oh, Finn? Yes, yes, he's fine. And... yours?' The woman clearly couldn't remember Max's name.

'Max? He's fine too, lovely, actually. He's big into numbers, counting everything and anything. He's not too fussed about words, but my philosophy is that they'll all have caught up by the time they're eighteen. No one walks around a nightclub boasting about when they took their first step or said "ta", do they! And hopefully by then they'll all be dry at night!'

'Yes, quite.'

The woman continued to stare and Poppy wondered if something had happened to her face. Was she bleeding? Marked? She checked her nose and wiped at her mouth.

'Forgive me...' Finn's mum shook her head as if waking from her stupor. 'I shouldn't be staring. It's just that it's rather a shock to see you.'

Poppy took a deep breath. 'Oh, yes, I know. I look a bit rubbish. I've lost a lot of weight and my tablets make me look a bit crap.'

'No, no, it's not that. Oh God, no. It's just that we were told at parent and toddler group that you had died!'

'I'm sorry?'

'Ginny Wilson, Ross's mum, was told by Alice Morgan, the one with the campervan and daughter who's a coeliac, who I think heard it from Abby, that you had died of cancer, quite suddenly. We were all devastated, of course – are devastated... were... Gosh. How awkward, but marvellous, of course!'

Poppy stared at the woman, open-mouthed, but couldn't find the words. She glanced up the aisle and saw Martin walking towards her. Their eyes locked and he sped up. 'You okay, love?' His eyes darted briefly to the woman on his right.

'I want to go home.' Her voice was very quiet.

'Can you walk to the car?' He placed his arm across her back, worried by her expression.

Poppy nodded. Abandoning the trolley without a second thought, she wanted to get as far away from Finn's mum as possible. They made it to the car before Poppy started crying. Huge sobs racked her body and her face twisted with uncontrolled distress.

'What's up, love? What on earth happened?' He leant over and wiped her tears from her face.

'That woman... she thought... she thought I was dead. The whole of Maxy's toddler group thinks I'm dead!'

'What a silly cow. I'm not having anyone upset you – shall I go and have a word with her?' Martin ground his teeth together.

Poppy shook her head. 'No, please, just stay here with me.'

'I won't go mad, I promise. I just want to set her straight on a few things. The stupid cow!' He was angry.

Poppy looked up. 'No, Mart, don't. It'll make me feel worse if you get mad at her. I can't cope with that.'

'Okay, okay. We'll just sit here for a bit.' He switched on the engine and put the heater on, trying to stop her shaking.

Poppy hid her face in her hands and cried. How could she explain to her husband that she wasn't upset because of what the woman had said, but because one day it would be the truth; she would be dead. And after it had happened, Finn's mum would carry on going to Tesco, and Mart would still chat to his mates in the car park, and Max would go to parent and toddler group, and life would carry on without her as if she had never been there. She would be just like all the other women that she could picture, whose names she could no longer recall – people who suddenly weren't around any more because cancer had taken them away from their families. The thought of it made her feel so very empty and sad.

Martin smoothed her hair from her face. 'Would you like to go for a little walk? Or we could go for a coffee somewhere?'

Poppy took a deep breath. 'No thanks. I don't want to do anything and I don't want to see anyone. Can we just go home?' She smiled as she blotted at her tears.

Poppy spent the afternoon lying on the bed. She opened the laptop and grinned at the subject-line in her inbox, *your chosen photo's, edited as promised...* Poppy called for Martin and the kids, who ran up the stairs. Martin sat next to her and Peg and Max crowded in behind.

'Oh my word!' Poppy opened the slideshow and watched, as the bright, clear pictures from their photo shoot appeared one by one on the screen.

'Maxy!' Max leant forward and touched his little finger to the screen.

'It is, it's you!' Poppy kissed him.

Poppy and Martin had selected their favourite snaps a while ago and now, as they studied them, every image drew gasps from Poppy and claps from Peg, each one better than the last. Poppy gazed at the faces of her family, laughing, smiling and chatting. Captured perfectly, for always.

'I never realised we were so good-looking!' Martin quipped. 'Are you pleased with them?'

Poppy could only smile and nod, her throat clogged with emotion. These were the pictures that her grandchildren would be shown; this was how she would be immortalised. Peg would tell her children the story of Toffee and his star-ring role. Her grandchildren would shake their fringes from their foreheads and wrinkle their noses as they touched her face and asked 'Who's that?'

They were better than she could have dreamt. She felt

happy that, for years to come, these would be the images by which people would remember her.

Thank you, Paul Smith.

The last photograph came onto the screen and the whole family shouted their laughter. It was a close-up of Toffee in all his finery. The Crickets pointed and roared with laughter until their tears came.

'That one is going up on the wall!' Martin announced.

It gave Poppy an idea. Martin, as requested, deposited their old photograph albums on the bed. Poppy smiled as she leafed through them at her leisure. They seemed to have been keen, years ago, to catalogue their every event, snapping at will. But the novelty had obviously worn off, as there were a disproportionate number of photographs of them with the kids when they were babies, but few as they grew. And poor old Maxy had half the number of entries that Peg had when she was little. Poppy selected one or two precious pictures, removing them from the sticky film that trapped them. The newborn Peg asleep on her mum's chest; Max at nine months, nudey-dudey in the paddling pool, held by his dad under the arms as he kicked up splashes of water, spraying himself and anyone and anything in close proximity. He grinned gummily at the camera. She carefully turned over the photographs and wrote on the back of each one – the date, the subject and how much she loved them, then and now – before placing them inside the kids' memory boxes.

Turning the pages, Poppy came across some shots of her nan. One showed Dorothea on her wedding day, standing in a white satin wedding dress in her mum and dad's back garden in Limehouse. Poppy had never known her great-grandparents, Joan and Reg, but she knew for a fact this was their garden. Dot had told her often enough. The young

Wally had his arm around her waist and she was laughing at something in the distance. She looked beautiful. Poppy plucked it from the album and decided to give it to Simon. There was another shot of an older Dorothea in their little kitchen in Walthamstow, taken in the late seventies; she was holding a cup of tea and smiling into the camera. The table was set and she was sitting next to a little plate piled high with fondant fancies – must have been a celebration of some sort. It was before dementia had claimed her and her expression was reminiscent of the girl in the wedding photo. Poppy decided to take him this one too.

Poppy thought how strange it would be for Simon to see pictures of the woman who had given birth to him and whom he had never known. The breath stopped in her throat when she pictured Max being in the exact same position in years to come. Poppy plucked a photo of her son and sank back on the pillows, holding it against her cheek.

Nineteen

It was a glorious summer afternoon. Poppy sat in a chair in the garden and let the sun warm her skin; she rolled up the sleeves of her white shirt and lifted the hem of her jeans to expose her shins, wiggling her bare toes against the grass. Closing her eyes, she listened to the bird song. It was a moment of calm before the madness of the weekend took hold. She flipped open the laptop and read the email from Simon and Kate. They had attached their tickets to travel, all confirmed for ten days' time. She felt a rare bubble of excitement at the prospect of going away. It would be perfect: just the two of them, with time to talk and hold each other in the sunshine. Maybe they would sit on a beach and sip fresh pineapple juice under a tree – or maybe she had seen too many movies.

She must have dozed off in her chair because she woke with a start when the front door banged shut. She stretched, eased herself into an upright position and made her way into the sitting room.

'Hello, darling, have you had a good day? Bet you're excited – it's our big weekend!' Poppy clapped.

Peg stomped across the room, hung her cardigan and bag on the bannister and said, without preamble, 'What's for tea?'

'Oh yes, I'm fine thanks, Peg, and how was your day?' Poppy slumped down onto the sofa, exhausted by even the slightest exertion.

'It was okay. Dad's gone to the supermarket. He said I had to watch Maxy.' Peg cleared the table of the pile of laundry that awaited folding and pulled out her reading book.

Max roamed around the rug with a car in each hand.

'Oh, good girl.' Poppy nodded at her book. 'Would you like me to listen to you read?'

'If you like.' Peg didn't look up.

'What's up, love?' Poppy could tell there was something on her daughter's mind.

'Nothing.'

Poppy decided not to pursue the topic, figuring that sometimes Peg needed to be left alone with her thoughts, just like she did.

Several minutes passed while Poppy read the local paper.

In memory of Dusty, our much-loved Parson terrier, who went to sleep and didn't wake up. He has been a loving, faithful companion to Marion and David. Dusty, we know you are now in doggy heaven, chasing rabbits again and running free. Goodbye, our little mate. You made our house a home and we will miss you every time we put the key in the door.

Peg sat with her eyes on the page and her finger following the words. 'Mum?'

'Yes, love?'

'Sometimes you can do something and it seems like a good idea and so you do it, but then when you think about it after you've done it, you realise that it might not be such a good idea after all, but because you've done it, it's too late to undo it, no matter how much you wish you could.'

Poppy stared at her little girl, unsure if she was being asked to confirm or discuss the statement. Instead, she said,

'Well, that's true, but at least if you are ever in a situation like that, you can talk to me or Daddy about it, right?'

Peg nodded and turned her attention back to her reading book.

Almost on cue, the phone rang. Poppy reached out and listened to the stranger's voice on the other end. 'Yes, I'm her mum... Oh hello, Jane... Yes, yes, I've seen you at school...'

Peg put her head in the cradle of her arm on the table and waited.

'Oh... Oh, I see... No, that's fine, no problem... Righto, Jane. My husband, Martin, will pop over later and thanks so much for contacting me. I don't know – kids!' Poppy gave her false laugh and hung up.

She walked over to the table and leant on the chair. 'Peg?'

Peg reluctantly looked up.

'That was Maisie's mummy. Is there anything you want to tell me about your scooter?'

Peg looked up at the ceiling and considered her answer. 'It got stolen.'

'It got stolen?' Poppy repeated, incredulous. 'When?'

Peg swung her legs back and forth and picked at the corner of her book. 'At lunch time.' Her cheeks were scarlet.

'How do you know?' Poppy was intrigued.

'I saw it get stolen.'

'You did? That must have been scary! Did you tell a teacher? Did you call the police?'

Peg shook her head. 'No, I was too shocked!'

'I bet you were. Seeing something you love get stolen is definitely shocking. Who stole it?'

Peg opened and then closed her mouth, her lips twisting to form sounds which she then rejected. She suddenly looked up at the TV, which as usual was fixed on the Cartoon

Network. Max was playing in front of it on the rug, paying it little attention.

'Batman,' she announced.

'Sorry?'

'Batman took my scooter.' Peg looked at her lap.

'What, the *actual* Batman? Blimey, I must say I'm shocked. I thought he was a force for good, not a scooter nicker. And who knew he was hanging around Larkhill! I didn't even know he ventured that far from Gotham City.'

Peg sucked in her cheeks, unsure if laughter would be appropriate right now.

'Peg, what happened to your scooter? Truthfully. I don't care about the scooter, but I do care about lying. It's the worst thing.'

Peg sighed as her bottom lip trembled with tears. 'I swapped it.'

Poppy nodded. 'So I heard. At least that's what Maisie's mum said. What did you swap it for?'

Peg hesitated for a second. 'A pencil sharpener that looks like a rabbit.'

'A pencil sharpener?' Poppy couldn't keep the shock from her voice.

Peg nodded, enthusiastically. 'A cool pencil sharpener that looks like a rabbit.'

'In exchange for your scooter, your birthday present?'

Peg nodded and chewed her bottom lip.

'You know that was a silly thing to do, right?'

'Yes, Mum. But it made Maisie very happy.' Peg smiled.

'I bet it bloody did.' Poppy sighed and rubbed at her eyes. 'Daddy is going to go and get your scooter back tonight. You can't do things like that, Peg.'

'I didn't know if I was going to be in trouble or not.

Jade McKeever said it would make Maisie pick me for her gang.'

'Oh, good God, Peg, please stop listening to Jade Bloody McKeever, who, believe it or not, does not have all the answers in the universe. And what gang? Maisie has a gang?' Poppy pictured the blonde girl with her hair in bunches and a penchant for frilly white ankle socks – hardly mobster material.

Peg nodded. 'They go to the back of the climbing frame and share sweets and Maisie gives out dares like making Phoebe say "I've seen your willy" to James Hillman in the dinner queue.'

Poppy stared at her. 'You want to be part of a gang that says "I've seen your willy"?'

Peg shrugged. 'Sometimes I do.'

Poppy gazed at her little girl. Sometimes even she was lost for words.

* * *

It was Saturday, the day of the party. Poppy was once again taking refuge in the back garden, finding the house, as she often had recently, a little claustrophobic.

Peg had her bath at 10 a.m. and put her new white dress on, along with her glittery pumps and her self-chosen plastic tiara. Poppy was still recovering from the purchase of the tiara and cringed every time she saw it. She had stood in the shop, presenting her daughter with an array of subtle pale roses that she could affix with a clip to the side of her head.

'No, Mum! I want this!' Peg had pointed at the hideous creation.

Poppy had hoped she was joking. Sadly, she wasn't.

215

Peg finished the whole ensemble off with a thick smear of lurid pink lipstick, which was quickly transferred onto her dad's face, her own arm and the corner of a cushion on the sofa. Now she stood in front of her mum on the grass and twirled around with her arms held out. The sun glinted off the sequins on her dress. Poppy smiled at her daughter, who literally sparkled.

'You look like a princess.'

'I feel like a princess, Mum!' Peg said, before commencing her next set of twirls.

After running and jumping all day, including a brief stint on the trampoline to see how high her skirt would go, Peg had fallen asleep in the same attire at 3 p.m. She woke up in a crumpled heap, with her tiara askew, looking like a drunken partygoer in the early hours trying to find her way home. Now, two hours later, as the Crickets prepared to gather in the lounge and wait for their taxi, Peg glided up and down the hallway on her scooter, with the skirt of her frock flowing behind her.

'I love parties!' she boomed as she rattled by. 'Ouch!' She hit the door, still not having quite got the hang of stopping without brakes.

Martin led Max down the stairs.

'Oh, Maxy, you look so cute!' Peg cooed at her little brother. He was especially adorable in his turned-up navy trousers, new trainers, tiny white shirt and blue waistcoat that sat snug over his rounded tummy.

Max couldn't look up quite yet; he was busy counting the stairs.

'You look nice too, Dad,' she added for good measure, although as far as Peg was concerned, a dark suit was a bit boring. She wished he had followed her suggestion and dressed as a superhero.

Poppy stood in front of the mirror in the sitting room and ran the brush through her hair for the fifth time. Having decided to leave it loose, the best she could do was make it shine. She pulled out the clumps that had gathered in her hairbrush and rolled them into a ball before throwing them in the bin. She had always been slim and, since having the kids, comfortable in her shape, but tonight, with her newly bony décolletage and greyed skin tone, she wanted to be as covered up as possible. She had chosen a rose pink water-silk frock. It might have been prim, with its high neck and nipped-in waist, covered buttons on the long sleeves and double cuffs, were it not for the kick to the bottom of the knee-length skirt and the layers of net in a slightly darker pink that protruded from the hem. Her kitten heels and silver-embellished clutch bag gave her the air of a fifties siren.

Martin stood at the bottom of the stairs and stared at his wife. 'Oh God, Poppy...' He swallowed the lump in his throat. 'You look... you look absolutely beautiful.'

She turned and looked at him over her shoulder. 'Thank you.' Loving his sentiment, even if she didn't quite believe it.

'Dad! Give it to her now!' Peg abandoned her scooter and jumped on the spot.

'You think?' Martin teased his daughter.

'Yes! Go on, Dad!' Peg stopped jumping and pushed her tiara back up onto the top of her head from where it had slipped.

Martin lifted Max and the three gathered in front of Poppy.

'What's all this about then?' Poppy was curious and slightly embarrassed.

'Well, we can't get you a kidney-shaped pool and it ain't raining, so you can't go out dancing in it...'

'Wouldn't want to anyway, it'd ruin me frock!' Poppy laughed as she smoothed the skirt with her palm.

'But we did get you a diamond.'

'A really, really big one, Mum. The size of an ice cube!' Peg was beside herself, squeezing her fingers into little fists.

Martin reached into his pocket and produced a square silver box tied with a ribbon.

Poppy sat on the sofa as Max climbed up next to her. She pinched the end of the ribbon between her thumb and forefinger and removed it, putting it to one side for safe-keeping. It would go in Peg's box of lovely things with the date and details written on it.

She carefully opened the box and there, nestling inside, was a ring of huge proportions. The vast diamond sat inside an oval of smaller diamonds. Each of them caught the light and sparkled furiously. It was indeed the size of an ice cube.

Poppy laughed. 'Oh my word!'

She wasn't sure how she would wear it. It looked heavy. Thankfully, as she lifted it from the box, she realised it was as light as a feather.

'It's solid plastic, Poppy, but don't worry, I've added it to the insurance.' He winked at her.

'It cost six pounds, Mummy!' Peg yelled with excitement, despite standing less than a foot from her mum.

'One ring for Mummy!' Max chirped, before scrambling off the sofa to find a digger to cling to.

Poppy felt the breath catch in her throat. 'It's beautiful, the most beautiful ring I have ever seen. I love it!'

'I told you she wouldn't like a smaller one.' Peg folded her arms across her chest, victorious.

'Give it here.' Martin took the shiny bauble from her hand and dropped down onto one knee. He took her left hand in his and kissed her fingers. 'Will you marry me, Poppy Day?'

Poppy ran her fingers through his hair, her handsome man. 'I'd marry you today and every day.'

The two stared at each other, feeling the current of love and understanding flow between them. Both thought of their wedding day, the drinks in the pub, his mum tight-lipped with disapproval, hers pissed in the precinct and missing the service. Both thought of the journey that had led them to that point and both wished the outcome was going to be different.

Martin slipped the ring onto the third finger of her left hand.

Poppy flexed her fingers. 'It looks lovely, doesn't it?'

'It really does,' Martin echoed.

Twenty

The taxi pulled up outside the hall and Poppy could hear the beat of music – Abba. She gripped Martin's hand as nerves filled her stomach. The team at the hall had been busy: pink and white balloons sat in clusters in the corners of the room and around the stage where the DJ stood behind his decks. There was a huge banner strung over the buffet table, saying simply, 'Poppy and Martin'. The food was plentiful and varied. There were piles of sausage rolls and neat sandwiches with the crusts removed, slices of quiche and bowls of coleslaw and potato salad.

'It all looks brilliant!' Poppy beamed at her husband.

'Here you go, madam.' One of the bar staff leant forward with a small tray on which sat two flutes of champagne.

Martin took one and sipped at it eagerly. 'Thanks, mate.'

Poppy held the delicate stem between her fingers and, raising the glass to her mouth, made as if she were taking a drink. She couldn't drink alcohol, not on top of the multiple drugs that were daily engaged in the anti-pedalo mission.

Martin smiled at her and bent close, whispering in her ear, 'I'll swap it for apple juice, how about that?'

She nodded. 'Thank you.'

Poppy saw Claudia in the far corner. She looked beautiful in a dark green silk coatdress with her hair pinned up and just the right amount of jewellery sparkling at her neck and wrist. When Poppy caught her eye, Claudia rose and swept towards her.

'You look lovely, Claudia.'

'Oh, you can talk! You look like a film star!'

'Oh, bless you.' Poppy kissed the woman who had become her kids' granny and her own substitute mum. 'Have you seen my new diamond?'

'Ha! Have I seen it? Peg has shown it to me several times. It's a whopper, isn't it?'

Poppy looked down at the huge rock. 'It is that.'

Claudia leant in towards her. 'Word of warning, darling. I wore it for ten minutes and it turned my finger green. Beware!'

The two women laughed.

Claudia placed her arm across Poppy's back. 'Now, don't get mad, I cleared it with Martin. I know you didn't want me to help with the food, but he agreed that I could treat you to a cake.'

'Oh, Claudia, you didn't have to do that!' They had decided not to bother with a fancy cake – besides, it would have blown their budget. Instead they had ordered individual cupcakes for everyone, which would double up as pudding.

'I know I didn't have to, but I wanted to. Come with me. I do hope you like it!' Claudia clasped her hands under her chin.

Poppy let Claudia hook her arm under hers and steer her to the back of the hall. There, in the middle of the square table, sitting on a silver plinth atop a pristine white cloth, was the most extraordinary cake she had ever seen.

It had three tiers – the bottom was dark chocolate, the middle milk chocolate and the top white chocolate – and the surfaces of all three were blemish-free and glossy. Each tier was decorated with chocolate shapes: white chocolate on the bottom, milk on the top and dark in the middle. It looked shiny and inviting, far too nice to cut. Not for the first time, Poppy lamented the state of her taste buds.

A chocolate flag stood proudly on the top, with 'Love and Luck' written inside the most beautiful scroll; her nan's mantra. Poppy was touched that Claudia had remembered. At first she thought each tier was adorned with a coordinating ribbon, but these were in fact also made of chocolate. How the edges had been made that sharp and the lines so perfect, she had no idea.

'Look at the shapes,' Claudia urged.

Poppy peered more closely and saw that what at first had looked like discs were in fact images. There were silhouettes of Peg and Max, regimental medals that Martin had been awarded, the REME insignia, tiny images of Stonehenge and even a quill and ink bottle to represent the time she'd spent masquerading as a journalist. Some also carried the date.

'Oh, Claudia! It's beautiful. It really is. I don't know what to say, but thank you!'

'It's from Plum Patisserie, all the way from Mayfair!'

Poppy had of course seen their pictures in magazines and read the articles, but she never thought in a million years that she would have one of her very own. 'Plum Patisserie! I feel like a bloody celebrity!'

Claudia nodded. 'And so you should. I wanted only the best for you tonight.' She beamed at Poppy's reaction.

'I can't believe you did that for me, for us. It's perfect.' Poppy let her eyes rove over the balloons, ribbons and decorations. She saw Peg dancing alone under the glitter ball, swirling in a circle until she wobbled. 'It's all perfect.'

'Poppy!' Martin shouted from the door.

Poppy looked up as he beckoned her over. By his side she saw their dear friend Rob Gisby and his lovely wife.

'You go and chat to everyone!' Claudia urged before heading off to join hands with Peg under the glitter ball.

Poppy walked as quickly as she could over to where they stood. Rob had aged but was still smiley, with eyes that crinkled at the sides. His moustache had gone grey. She flung her arms around his neck and held him tight.

Rob patted her back. 'Hello, Poppy Day. What have you been up to, girl?'

Poppy pulled away and saw the flicker of shock in Rob's eyes. She knew she didn't look well. Even tonight, with the mask of make-up and a liberal sprinkling of glitz and glamour, there was no denying that she was sick.

'It's so lovely to see you, Rob – to see you both.' She kissed Moira on the cheek.

'He loves you, Poppy Day. We wouldn't have missed this for the world.'

Poppy smiled at Moira's soft brogue, it was soothing.

'And I love him, but don't tell him, will you?'

Moira patted the side of her nose. 'Shan't say a word, hen.'

'How are you feeling?' Rob looked worried. Martin had obviously filled him in.

'Tonight, Rob, I feel like a million dollars!'

'And you look it too.' He smiled.

Poppy laughed. 'You never could lie to me, but thank you anyway. Are we dancing later?'

'You bet.' Rob rubbed his hands together at the prospect.

'Hope you've got plasters for where he'll tread on your toes!' Moira added as she and Rob walked towards the bar.

Martin snaked his arm around Poppy's waist and pulled her towards him. 'Isn't this brilliant?'

'It really is.'

'I love you, Mrs Cricket.'

'I love you, Mr Cricket.'

They kissed – to the sound of retching from Peg, who rolled her eyes in their direction and mimed being sick.

'Aaaaagh! Oh my God!' Jo screamed as she walked in. 'This looks awesome! And look at Peg and Max!' She pointed at the kids, who were now chasing each other around the dance floor.

'You look gorgeous.' Poppy hugged her mate, who was vampish in her red lipstick and black satin dress that skimmed her hips and clung in all the right places.

'Oh, I don't know about that!' Jo shook her head, sending clusters of dark curls cascading over her shoulders.

'Why are we so bad at taking compliments?' Poppy wondered.

'She's right, Jo. You look fabulous,' Martin chipped in. 'Danny must be mad.' Poppy raised her eyebrows in his direction.

Jo squealed, pivoted on her high heels and sauntered off to the bar, where a group of Martin and Danny's mates stood clutching their pints and admiring the woman walking towards them. She turned to look back at Poppy and bit her bottom lip, her confidence fading.

Poppy made a shooing motion with her palm. 'It'll do her good to get chatted up a bit,' she said to her husband from the side of her mouth.

Jenna and Ryan were late arrivals. He looked decidedly uncomfortable. Poppy noted the twitch of his fingers and the sweat that sat in little beads on his upper lip. Strange how he wasn't nearly so cocky when faced with at least thirty blokes who all earned their living from 'playing soldiers'. It made Martin smile. Jenna had made an effort and dazzled in her floaty silver tunic and matching silver heels. Her hair was wild and her red lipstick gave her whole outfit a lift. Poppy grinned at the sight of her mate looking much more like she used to, spirited and ready to take on the world.

The music played and people danced; beer flowed and food was eaten amid squeals of laughter and the babble of conversation. Martin accepted the many drinks offered to him, until he sported his soppy beer grin and swayed whenever he was stationary.

Poppy felt exhausted. It was only nine o'clock, but she was struggling, fighting the waves of fatigue that washed over her. She was determined to stay until the end. She nipped into the loo and popped two painkillers on her tongue.

'Please, just give me a break tonight.' She stared at her reflection and pleaded with the nasty cells, hoping they might stop pedalling, just until she could get home to bed. She wanted at least one dance with her husband.

The loo in the cubicle flushed and Moira walked out, adjusting her bosom inside her black velvet coatdress.

'Are you okay, hen?'

Poppy wondered if she had heard her plea. 'I'm tired, Moira, really tired. I just wish I had a bit more energy.'

Moira rubbed the soap between her palms into a lather and rinsed her fingers under the hot tap. Poppy handed her a paper towel.

'Thanks. You know, Poppy, I think you are amazing. I always have.'

'I don't know about that, but thanks, Moira.' She looked at the floor, unable to take her own advice on accepting a compliment.

'What can we do to help you? Anything at all?' Moira's concern was genuine and touching.

'Nothing, I'm afraid. Nothing at all. I'm just so glad you came.'

Jo burst into the loo. 'I've found her! Here she is!' She swayed slightly and her voice was loud. The Bacardi Breezers were obviously kicking in.

Jo held Poppy's shoulders and steered her back into the hall to shouts and claps. Poppy hadn't known she was being looked for.

Martin stood on the stage and held the microphone in his hand. 'Can you come here, Poppy?'

'Oh God, he's not going to sing, is he?' She laughed along with their guests as she made her way to the narrow steps that led up to where he stood.

Poppy gripped the handrail, taking each step slowly, one by one. Martin saw she was having difficulty and indicated to Rob, who handed him up a chair. He placed it next to him and led his wife by the hand until she sat, looking out at the sea of faces, their family and friends. Claudia stood at the front with Max on her hip and Peg leaning against her. Poppy gave Peg a little wave.

Martin tapped the microphone, making it whistle, before bringing it up to his mouth. 'Blimey, I'm not very good at speeches.' He stuck his fingers in his collar and pulled it to release imaginary steam.

'Get on with it!' one of his colleagues yelled from the bar.

'Yeah, thanks, mate, I will.' Everyone laughed.

'It's been... it's been a bit of a year since I got back from tour.' Martin swallowed and raised his eyes to the crowd, who were absolutely silent. 'I think it's what you might describe as a real rollercoaster. I was trying to think about what I should say tonight and I realised that our whole lives have been a rollercoaster, ever since we were kids.' He stopped and shook his head. 'We seem to have lurched from the highest of highs to the lowest of lows, and back again. But we have always been happy, because we have each other. I didn't know what the future held when I married Poppy all them years ago, but I knew we'd always be all right because we had the most important thing – a deep, unshakeable love.'

Poppy looked up at her husband and nodded.

Martin coughed and continued. 'That love has been the glue that has kept us together, for richer or poorer, for better or worse, in sickness and in health.'

Martin paused and the sobs could be heard around the room; women and men alike, catching their breath and swiping at noses and eyes.

'And I want you to know, Poppy Day, that I wouldn't have changed a single thing.'

He bent down and kissed his wife on the lips.

'So, ladies and gentlemen, would you please raise your glasses to my bride, my wife and my best friend – Poppy Day!'

Shouts of 'Poppy Day!' rippled around the room like a shockwave, followed by the chinking of glass and clapping.

The DJ turned up the volume and 'We Are Family' belted out of the speakers. As everyone had already abandoned their chairs and were now in close proximity to the dance floor, they danced. Martin and Poppy gazed at the crowd of smiling people, at their friends, loved ones and children, who were all bopping and singing and having a ball. It was perfect – exactly what they had both dreamt of.

Poppy turned to her husband. 'Thank you, Mr Cricket.'

Martin bent down and kissed her.

They left the stage and Peg ran straight at her mum, holding her tightly around the middle.

Poppy hugged her back, laughing at the enormous tiara that sat majestically on her little girl's head. 'I love you, Peg.'

'I know.' She smiled up at her mum.

Martin grabbed Poppy around the waist and pulled her towards him, more roughly than she was used to being handled. She swallowed the nausea that rose from her stomach. It wasn't his fault, this was how he used to hold her, pawing at her, before she became something delicate. In a way, she was glad that for tonight at least, one of them had forgotten that she was ill.

'Here she is – my girl.' He swung her round and crushed her to him. She tucked her lips in, trying not to inhale the beer fumes. 'You look bloody gorgeous,' he whispered in her ear. 'How about we slope off to the loo and I help you kick off that frock?'

Poppy gave a false laugh. 'Mart, I can't. I don't feel that good. I feel really sick and a bit wobbly.'

He let go of her and took a step backwards, looking embarrassed. 'Of course, I knew that.' He put his hands in his pockets and walked backwards into the crowd.

'But we can still have our dance?' she shouted as she lost sight of him. 'Shit!' she muttered under her breath.

She looked from left to right. Peg popped up in front of her, her cheeks flushed from jumping up and down.

'Where's Dad gone?' Poppy asked. 'I want to have our dance.' *And then I can go home.*

Peg shrugged. 'He might be drinking more beer and getting more drunk with his mates?'

Poppy laughed. 'Yes, he might be. You go and see if he's at the bar and I'll check the loo.'

WILL YOU REMEMBER ME?

Peg dashed off through the crowd.

Poppy sauntered across the hall, looking cool and unhurried, successfully masking the fact that each step required monumental effort.

The male and female loos were adjacent to the entrance, either side of the cloakroom where everyone had stashed their coats and other items. Poppy shivered. With no meat on her bones, she felt the cold more than she ever had. Though it was warm in the hall, she wanted her pashmina.

Placing her hand on the panel of the door into the cloakroom, she noted the sticky fingerprints that were smudged on its shiny surface; it could do with a wipe over, she thought. She smiled at her cleaning obsession. She was still smiling when she pushed on the door and looked up. The first thing she saw was Jo's hand, splayed against a dark suit jacket. Her smile widened – she'd been right! *You go, girl!*

She noted Jo's hair, falling sideways in a curtain, her head twisted to the side to avoid the nose of her beau, whose own head was bent at the opposite angle. Jo was stooping slightly in her heels; the man she was kissing was a couple of inches shorter than her. This information, these facts, hit Poppy's brain in nano-seconds. It was in one more blink of an eye that Jo leapt back and put her hand over her mouth, and in that same blink of an eye, Poppy realised that the person Jo was kissing was Martin. The same Martin who had just publicly declared his love for her in front of all their friends and family.

She felt her legs buckle. The strength that she had conjured to get her through the evening finally evaporated as she slid down the door. She opened her mouth to speak, but nothing would come.

Martin wheeled round and dropped to where she sat slumped on the floor. 'Oh Christ, Poppy!'

229

'Claudia...' Poppy managed.

Jo stepped over them and ran from the hall.

Martin bent low. 'It's okay. I'll go and get Claudia and we'll get you home. It's okay.' His breath came fast and shallow.

Her words, when they came, were so quiet he had to put his ear to her mouth to hear. 'Get your fucking hands off me.'

Claudia turned the heating up in the car. She could see that Poppy was shaking as she bundled her into the passenger seat. She clipped Max into his seat and settled Peg next to him.

Poppy could hear a single note ringing in her ears. But she knew she had to keep calm – no one close to her at that point deserved to witness the rage that boiled inside her.

'I didn't want to go home yet, Mummy! I haven't danced enough and I didn't have any of that special cake!' Peg whined.

'I've got some cake at home,' Poppy croaked.

'But I wanted that chocolate cake with the pictures on and the chocolate ribbons, and Max did too, didn't you, Maxy?'

Max's head lolled on his chest. He was shattered.

'Well, I'm sure it will turn up at the house and you can have some when it does.' She spoke into the back of her knuckles, which were stuffed into her mouth, her elbow propped on the door.

'Maybe Aunty Jo can bring—'

'Shut up, Peg! For God's sake, just shut up! Christ, it's incessant. I just need a moment of bloody quiet. It's only a cake and she is not your aunty, just an old next-door neighbour!'

With that one statement, Poppy had managed to make her daughter cry and Claudia gasp – it was so much more than just a cake.

'Don't cry, darling.' Claudia spoke to Peg, who whimpered on the back seat.

Poppy looked out of the window and despite trying to focus on the hedgerows and houses that whizzed by, she could only see Jo's splayed hands, her fingers arched into Mart's jacket, their heads twisted at opposite angles. She couldn't make the picture go away.

Twenty-One

Poppy walked straight through the house and into the back garden. She wanted some fresh air. She ran her hand over the trampoline and thought of the times they had bounced on it as a family. She heard his words as if he had spoken them yesterday: 'There is nowhere on earth that I would rather be than right here, right now. It's going to be the best year, Poppy. I just know it.'

Poppy looked up into the dark windows of the house next door. What was going on? What had she missed? Were they seeing each other? And if so, for how long? Her stomach constricted without warning and she vomited where she stood. The watery release splashed from the edge of the trampoline and hit the front of her pretty dress – not that she cared. She didn't care about much as she wiped her mouth with the back of her hand.

Shivering despite the warm summer evening, Poppy trod the stairs and lay on the bed in her clothes. Her tears when they came beat a steady path, a tiny river that flowed over her nose and across her chin and pooled onto her water-silk frock, leaving a damp stain.

Claudia crept in and hovered by the bed. She removed Poppy's sparkly heels and lifted the bottom of the duvet to cover her toes and calves. 'You stay here. I'll get Max to bed and see to Peg. They'll be fine. Do you need anything, darling?'

Poppy shook her head. The image of the two of them reappeared at every blink of her eyelids.

Claudia dug deep to find a smile as she traipsed down the stairs. Max had fallen asleep on the sofa, still in his finery, and Peg was kneeling beside Toffee's cage.

'It's okay, Toffee. Come on, let's have a cuddle. She doesn't mean to shout at us. Daddy said it's because she's feeling poorly and we have to be as good as we can.' Peg held her squeaking guinea pig under her chin and stroked his fur across her skin. She whispered into his chubby belly. 'I liked the old Mummy that wasn't poorly. I think this new Mummy can be a bit of a meanie.'

'How about I see if I can find us some cake and I whip us up a mug of hot chocolate?' Claudia offered.

Peg shook her head. She wasn't in the mood.

Once Peg was tucked up and Max was sound asleep, Claudia checked again on Poppy, who hadn't moved. She crept down the stairs and sat on the sofa. 'What a bloody mess.' She sighed, trying to think of a solution to this most horrible of situations.

She must have dozed off, because a key in the lock woke her. She sat up straight and faced Martin, who stood in the doorway. He looked terrible: his hair was dishevelled, his jacket hung over his shoulder and his face was twisted in the ugly grimace of someone who'd been crying. It was hard to recognise the beaming man who had given the heartfelt speech earlier.

'I was worried about you,' Claudia blurted out, truthful and neutral as ever.

'Is she okay?' he asked, blinking his red-rimmed eyes.

'Not really, no.'

Martin sat on the edge of the sofa. 'It's like a nightmare. I can't believe it!' His tears welled up again.

'What happened?' Claudia's voice was soft.

Martin shook his head. 'I left the stage and I felt ten feet tall, so happy.' He swallowed. 'I kind of grabbed at Poppy – it seemed like a good idea, I just wanted my wife, no one else.' He shook his head. 'But of course it wasn't. I'd had too much to drink and I was heading for the loo. I went into the cloakroom, got the wrong door and Jo was standing there.' He pinched his nose and closed his eyes. 'She said something about my speech, said it was moving, I can't remember what. She came towards me and I thought she was going to give me a hug, but she kissed me and I kissed her back and it just happened.'

'Just happened?'

They both looked towards the door. Neither of them had heard Poppy come down the stairs.

'Poppy, I—' He stuttered.

'Don't speak to me!' Poppy's voice shook with emotion. 'Are you having an affair with her?' Her hands were so tightly clenched that her nails drew half moons of blood on her palms.

'What? No! No.'

Poppy didn't know what to believe. Everything she'd thought she could rely on, everything she thought she knew had been erased with one tilt of the head.

Neither she nor Martin noticed Claudia slide off the sofa, go into the kitchen and shut the door.

'Do you love her?' Poppy whispered

'No! Of course I don't, no! It wasn't love, just a bit of comfort, someone familiar that wanted me.' He looked at the floor.

'There is no "of course" about any of this.' Her chest heaved. 'I waited my whole life for tonight, my whole fucking life for a party, my wedding reception! How could you do that to me, to Peg and Max?' Her voice was shrill, her vocal chords taut with emotion.

He shook his head.

'When I think about the sacrifices I made to get you home...' Poppy bent and wept as the words left her mouth. Martin stood and placed his hand on her back, feeling the knobbles of her spine under the thin covering of skin. She flinched as if she'd been struck. 'Don't you touch me! Don't you dare touch me!'

He stood back and twisted his palms together. 'I don't know what to say. I'm sorry. It was the first time someone had been nice to me in a long time. I don't know what to say to make it better. Tell me what to say!'

Martin put his fist to his mouth to try and stop his shakes.

Poppy sat on the sofa and took off her plastic diamond. 'The first time someone had been nice to you? You poor old thing, Mart. Well, I hope it made you feel better.' The sarcasm dripped from her lips. 'I can't believe I sat here a few hours ago and you got down on one knee and proposed to me! Proposed to me in front of the kids – and then you did that? With Jo, my friend – she *was* my friend.' Poppy's whole body shook at the admission. 'I'll fucking kill her!'

'I'm sorry. I had too much to drink and I felt good and then it just happened.' He spoke to the floor.

'Stop saying it just happened! That doesn't *just* happen, you make it happen or you let it happen! Sticking your tongue down someone else's neck and letting them hold you doesn't just happen!' As soon as the words left her mouth, she retched and then vomited, like she had earlier. This time it landed on the floor. Neither of them made any attempt to clear it up. 'I *saw* you... I saw you, Mart.'

'Poppy, please...'

'We are done, Mart. We are done.' Poppy stood up and pulled away the hair that was stuck to her chin with vomit. 'Get a bag together and get out. Just go.'

'Where?' he asked.

'As if I fucking care!' she screamed. 'I bet if you head off now, you can make Marlborough within the hour.'

'I don't want to go to Marlborough,' Martin retorted, his voice shaky. 'I don't want to go anywhere. I want to be with you. Supposing you are ill? I need to be here for the kids.'

Poppy stood on the bottom stair. 'Well I don't want to be with you. And we've got Claudia here – the kids don't need you.'

'You are my whole world, Poppy. You and the kids are everything... and I'm losing you.' He sniffed and gulped. 'Maybe... maybe I felt a bit relieved to know that there ... there might be some kind of life for me, after...'

Poppy felt her chest cave. 'Are you kidding me? Are you saying you have a future with Jo after I'm dead?'

'No!' he shouted. 'That is absolutely *not* what I'm saying. But the feeling of happiness, for one second, that filled my gut... For once it wasn't about you or the kids, and that... that... gave me some hope.' He sighed heavily, rubbed his hand through his hair and mumbled at the floor. 'I'm not explaining this very well.'

'You're bloody right you're not!' Poppy shouted back. 'And if you think you are coming out to St Lucia, you've got another thing coming. I'm going on my own and I'll be gone for ten days, so you'll have plenty of time to practise that feeling of happiness in your gut that is nothing to do with me or the kids!'

'Poppy that's not what I meant, please...'

'Save it, Mart!' She was adamant.

She took another couple of stairs before turning back and addressing him again.

'Do you remember Mr Collins who ran the chippy in the precinct?'

Martin gave a small nod. Of course he did. Mr Collins had served him his tea at least four nights a week throughout his childhood.

'Do you remember when he got married to Marcia who worked in the café, just three months after Mrs Collins died? There was uproar, it was all people on the estate talked about. "Bit soon, isn't it? Do you think they've been carrying on for long?" Well I tell you what, Mart, you take the biscuit – at least Mr Collins waited until his wife was actually dead.'

'I only want you. I've only ever wanted you.'

'Well you've a very funny way of showing it. Fuck off, Mart, and close the door on your way out.'

Poppy spent the next day in bed, mentally and physically exhausted.

Claudia ferried cups of tea up and down the stairs, followed by mugs of soup; anything that she thought might tempt her to eat. She drew the curtains and cracked open the small window. 'Bit of a breeze might make you feel better.'

'Kids okay?'

'Oh they're great. Resilient little creatures at the best of times.'

'This feels like the worst of times.' Poppy sat up, propped against her pillows.

'It probably does,' Claudia agreed.

Poppy liked that she didn't try to sugar-coat their situation. 'I keep seeing them together. There was a second or two when they didn't know I was there.'

'You have to try and not keep picturing it. It's only torturing yourself.' Claudia folded a clean towel and placed it on the shelf in the wardrobe.

'I wish I could switch it off, but I can't. I keep wondering what would have happened if I hadn't walked in, how far they would have gone. Or worse, supposing Peg had walked in?'

'She didn't though.'

Poppy swallowed another wave of sickness. 'I never ever thought this could happen to us. I thought we were solid, rock solid.'

Claudia sat on the mattress. 'Poppy, I love you, you know that. And I think Martin is an idiot, but—'

'I don't want to hear the but!' Poppy sighed.

'But,' Claudia continued as if she hadn't spoken, 'this cancer has come along like a sledgehammer and smashed everything you used to be able to rely on to pieces. You said he wasn't very good at talking about it – goodness, he only cried for the first time when you went back to Walthamstow, isn't that what you told me?'

Poppy nodded.

'He had a moment of madness and even though it's nothing to do with me, I think it would be a huge mistake to throw away your entire family life for the sake of a silly second or two. Especially for Peg and Maxy, who have a lot of heartache ahead of them.' She let this linger.

'I know you are right about Peg and Max. But I don't know that it *was* just a moment of madness. It might have been going on for a while, behind my back.'

Jo's words echoed in Poppy's head: 'You're so lucky, you know. Mart's one in a million.'

'I feel like an idiot, and the worst thing is, I'm not in a position to fight her, Claudia. I'm not in a position to fight anyone.'

'Then don't, Poppy. Make it easy for everyone.'

Peg bounded into the room. 'You've got a visitor!'

Poppy felt her stomach flip. Had Jo turned up?

'It's Toffee!' Peg pulled the plump guinea pig from behind her back. 'Here he is.'

Poppy sat up and Peg placed the furry little puffball on the duvet. 'Hello, Toffee, thank you for coming to visit me.'

Peg gave him a little nudge until he was closer to Poppy. She stroked him as he sat still, trembling. Poppy wasn't sure if he was afraid or delighted to be there.

'Hey, Toffee, did Peg tell you I shouted at her last night?'

Peg nodded.

'The thing is, Toffee, sometimes when you get grumpy or angry you shout at someone because you are feeling mad, even though the person you are shouting at hasn't done anything wrong. And that's what happened. Peg's mum is very sorry for shouting at the wrong person.'

'Toffee says he understands that, Mum.'

'Well thank you, Toffee, for being so grown-up and gorgeous.'

'Is Daddy the person you wanted to shout at? Is that why he's not here?'

'Yes,' Poppy answered.

'I don't like you and Daddy fighting.' Peg looked tearful.

Poppy sighed. 'I know. It's just sometimes it feels like that's the only way to get something sorted out.'

Peg retrieved her pet and nuzzled him under her chin.

'Couldn't you just write to each other or sort it all out nicely over a cup of tea?'

Claudia smiled. 'Out of the mouths of babes...'

'Mummy, your phone is buzzing.' Peg handed the vibrating phone to Poppy.

It was a text, from Jo.

Poppy pictured her and Mart again as she opened the message and read her friend's apology and request for contact. She switched off the phone and placed it face down on the bedside table. She was torn between not wanting to see her ever again and relishing the prospect of telling her what she thought of her face to face, venting all the words that swirled around her head and interrupted her sleep at three in the morning.

Twenty-Two

Poppy was sitting on the bed, reading the obituaries again.

Mabel Jean Cunningham died peacefully in her sleep, aged 101. Much-loved sister, wife and mum, nan, great-nan and great-great-nan. Sleep tight, Jeanie, you were one in a million and we shall miss you.

'A hundred and one? Mabel Jean, you lucky, lucky lady.'

She had readily agreed to Claudia's suggestion that she go and stay with her in Oxford for a few days, to try and get some clarity back into her thoughts. They were leaving any minute. She tried not to think of the last time she had visited, at Christmas. It had been perfect: the kids full of turkey and chocolate and sleeping soundly upstairs; her and Mart nestled on the sofa in front of a roaring fire, glasses of ruby red port in their hands. She couldn't remember a time when her life had seemed more perfect.

Now she was running through the list of extra things she might want to throw in her bag to take. She heard Martin's voice downstairs. After all the years of smiling every time she heard him speak, and longing to hear his words whenever he was away, it felt alien to her that this morning she was acutely embarrassed at the prospect of having to interact with him. She closed her eyes and took a deep breath. This would require a lot of strength and her reserves were already running low.

Her phone buzzed. Poppy retrieved it from her handbag and opened the screen. She groaned loudly. 'That's all I bloody need.' Cheryl had apparently booked a flight over for a few weeks' time.

'Come down, Mummy. Daddy's home!' Peg shouted up the stairs.

'Shit.' Poppy ran her fingers across her forehead. She picked up the holdall and went downstairs.

Her eyes went straight to Martin, who stood by the kitchen door and looked dreadful, hovering awkwardly like a stranger who hadn't been invited to sit. His two-day beard growth made him look scruffy. His eyes were bloodshot, with two dark circles beneath them, the result of fatigue and night-time ponderings. His shirt was crumpled. He glanced at her and gave a small, nervous smile; hesitant, gauging her reaction.

'Right then, we'll be off. Daddy will look after you for a couple of days.' Poppy found it easier to talk to him via the kids, no matter how cowardly. 'Be good, Maxy, and you too, Peg. Make sure you give me a shout at Granny Claudia's every evening after school. I want to hear exactly what you've been up to.' Poppy gave the brightest smile she could muster. 'I love you both soooo much!' She hugged and kissed her children, then climbed into Claudia's Mini.

Claudia pulled out of their road and past the parade of shops. 'I've left a big lasagne for tonight and other bits and bobs in the freezer, so all he's got to do is get them out the night before and then heat them up for supper. I've given him instructions. They'll be fine.'

'Thank you,' Poppy whispered as her tears fell. 'I can't believe this bloody mess.'

'It'll pass, darling. Everything does.' Claudia nodded sagely, keeping her eyes on the road.

Poppy stared out of the window. 'Am I doing the right thing?'

'You mean meeting Jo?'

'Yes.'

Claudia sighed. 'I think it's up to you, but anything that moves things forward has to be a good idea. I can't bear the idea of you carrying lots of anger around in you, it can't help anything.'

'No,' Poppy agreed. 'It can't.'

'Next stop Salisbury, then?' Claudia asked.

Poppy nodded, too apprehensive to say anything.

The windows of the Salisbury branch of Costa were fogged up. Unusually for the time of the year, the door was closed. The day had unexpectedly thrown down a summer shower and the pavements, which still held heat from the early morning sun, steamed slightly. Shoppers and tourists, caught out by the deluge, crouched low under shared umbrellas, wearing flimsy, inappropriate clothing and open-toed footwear, hardly what was required in a downpour. Inside, however, and with a perfect view of the entrance, Poppy was toasty and dry, wrapped in a warm fug of coffee and cinnamon.

At the creak of the door, she looked up from her frothy cappuccino, but it wasn't Jo. Instead, a young mum fumbled with the handle, reversing in as she tried to negotiate the door with her bottom, dragging behind her a pushchair laden with bags and with a soggy toddler clinging to her hand. Ordinarily Poppy would have jumped up and gone to her aid, opened the door wide, helped, but not today. Today she had to concentrate, in position, ready.

Poppy had thought long and hard about what to wear, hating herself for how much she agonised over every detail. She had scraped her hair into a neat ponytail before releasing it and redoing it, twice. At the back of her mind was the thought that Jo had seen her daily in her pyjamas, crumpled from sleep as they chatted over the doorstep; she had helped Poppy with her up-do for a mess dinner once, while Poppy had sat there in her Spanx and dressing gown; and she had even perched on the corner of the mattress when Maxy was only hours old, with Poppy in a right state, her face pale, her hair stuck to her head with sweat, her stomach cramping with heavy loss. Today, that intimacy was disregarded. Jo had gone from ally to enemy. It had taken mere moments to wipe out five years of friendship: one splayed hand against his back, her head cocked to one side to avoid his nose, her dark curly hair falling in a curtain over her shoulder... Poppy blinked to rid her mind of the image. Today, the embers of her fury needed no stoking.

The door banged open. She peered over her coffee cup; her hands held the mug up to her lips, forming a pyramid that half hid her face. Her eyes flickered in recognition. Poppy watched as Jo ran her fingers through her wet hair and brushed raindrops from her black jersey and the thighs of her jeans. It felt odd not to beam out a smile, jump up and wave 'Over here, mate!' like she would have before. Poppy observed how Jo scanned the faces, saw her flinch when her gaze finally fell upon her. She noted how she walked slowly towards the table, her pace hesitant, measured, as if she was nervous, scared.

So you fucking should be. Poppy swallowed the thought.

Jo placed her bag on the floor, her purse already in her hand. 'Can I get you a coffee?' Her voice was barely more than a whisper.

Poppy shook her head and raised her mug in response. 'I'll just...' Jo indicated the counter and walked away.

Poppy exhaled and realised she had been holding her breath. Her jaw hurt from being clenched for the last however many minutes. She could hear Jo's sing-song tone as she ordered her latte and it made her stomach flip. How dare she sound normal, happy and nice?

It was a minute or two later that Jo scraped the chair across the wooden floor and took up her position opposite. She looked haggard and tired and Poppy felt a flush of euphoria that she wasn't her usual shining self.

When Jo spoke her voice quavered. 'I don't know what to say to you, Poppy. I've been sick all morning with nerves.'

Poppy looked up into her face. She gave a small smile. *What, Jo, sicker than me? Hope your nerves clear up soon.*

'Well, you don't have to say anything, you just have to listen.' Poppy was aware of the curl of her top lip and the harsh cockney inflection to her words.

Jo nodded quickly, causing her face to wobble.

Poppy's voice was calm. 'I'd waited my whole life for my wedding reception, Jo.' She paused. It was odd to hear herself saying her friend's name with such disdain. 'It was a big deal for me. But you know that, don't you?'

Again Jo nodded.

'And the sad thing is that now, when I think of it, I can only see you and my husband in the cloakroom, locked together.'

'It was nothing, Poppy. I swear to you. It was just a moment, it was nothing!' Her words tumbled out, as though she expected to be halted at any moment.

'Nothing?' Poppy shook her head. 'How dare you say it was nothing? He is my husband, we have a life, a history and you have damaged it. That day was a symbol of what we had achieved, how far we had come.' Poppy stopped, briefly pictured their dingy Walthamstow flats from years ago, the pub on their wedding day. 'But I can't think about Peg in her special frock or Maxy dancing on the spot with his little waistcoat on, not even the bloody buffet, none of it. It's like it's all disappeared and all that is left is that image of you and him.'

'I'm sorry.' Her voice was a whisper.

Poppy shook her head; she didn't want to hear sorry. 'And the worst thing, the very worst thing is that I am dying. I am dying, Jo, and you know that.' Poppy beat her flattened palm down onto the tabletop. Two women on the adjacent table looked over in the direction of the noise.

Jo's tears came now, falling over mottled cheeks and into her twitching mouth.

Poppy wasn't done. 'All my kids will have is the memory of me, the idea of me. And that party was supposed to make special memories. Instead, they saw me crying and had to leave before they got any cake.' Poppy gritted her teeth as she remembered her beautiful cake. 'They heard me screaming at their dad and that made them cry. You took that wonderful memory away from them and you took that day away from me.'

'I'm so sorry...'

Poppy looked out of the window and mentally reloaded, aware of Jo's snivelling into a paper napkin.

'Are you having an affair with my husband?'

'No!' Jo looked Poppy in the eye, emphatic.

Poppy sighed, gathering her thoughts as she stared at the woman sitting opposite her, the woman who knew everything about her; everything. The woman she had sat and counselled over Danny. Poppy rubbed her brow. 'I have felt sorry for you, worried about you! You've eaten at my table, sat my kids on your lap and given them baths.' Poppy shook her head as these thoughts formed images in her head. 'I never, ever in a million years would have thought that you'd have done that to me, to us. Especially not now.'

'I love you, Poppy. You know that. And the kids.' Jo let her head fall on her chest and gulped air that seemed to fuel her distress. 'You know how I feel about them. They… they were the closest I ever got to being a mum.' Jo continued to address the table. 'I miss them.'

Poppy remembered their conversation only weeks ago, how she'd asked Jo to be part of Peg and Max's futures: 'You will stay in their lives, won't you, Jo? Look after them, be there if they need someone to talk to?' Poppy watched now how Jo's face crumpled as she cried without restraint. She felt the tiniest fissure appear in her armour. It was true, Jo did love the kids. 'I will love them for you, Poppy, always,' she'd said, and Poppy believed her, even now.

Poppy felt her heart rate slow. She was calmer now. Peg and Max would need all the friends they could get. Would it be so hard to forgive Jo for their sakes? She drew breath to speak, but as she did so, the image of Jo's hair came into her head, falling sideways in a curtain, her head twisted to the side to avoid his nose, the two of them meeting at opposite angles. It was as if she had seen it only a second ago: Jo stooping slightly in her heels, her hand on Martin's back. It was enough to fuel her anger once again. Gathering her bag, she stood abruptly and yanked her coat from the back of the chair. 'Well they don't miss you. The only thing they will remember about you is that you upset their mum.'

Jo looked up with eyes red and swollen, her breathing

erratic, fingers fidgeting with the napkin that had rolled itself into little worms beneath her fingers. 'Poppy, I—'

'No, save it, Jo. There is nothing you can say that can make up for what you have done. And trust me, if I ever see you within five feet of my family, any of my family, ever again, you'll regret it. And remember, I have absolutely nothing to lose.'

Poppy saw Jo's eyes widen as she turned on her heel and swept from the café.

She walked along Butcher Row, her vision blurred by the rain and the tears that misted her eyes. Her hands shook as she punched her fingers into the screen of her phone.

'I'm ready for pick-up,' she mumbled, when Claudia, who was parked round the corner, answered the call.

Without warning, the ground rushed up towards her as a man's voice echoed in her ear. 'Are you okay? Oh God, I think she's fainted...'

She felt the cold pavement graze her cheek and welcomed the blackness that removed her from the world.

Twenty-Three

Poppy had insisted on getting a taxi to the airport. The cost was the last thing on her mind; she would have given her last penny not to have to spend hours in the car next to Martin. She could hardly bear to look at him, let alone sit in such close proximity. No matter how hard she tried, she couldn't dilute the bitter taste of anger that filled her mouth.

She had packed as though he had never been invited. His newly acquired trunks, sandals and pile of T-shirts were still in their carrier bags, abandoned on the bedroom floor. He hovered guiltily in the corners of the room, too afraid to interact and trying to make himself small, invisible. This suited Poppy just fine. She had deliberated long and hard over the email she'd sent to Simon and Kate and after four deleted attempts, in which she'd tried to sound upbeat and perky, had decided to be as honest as she was able. *Martin and I are having difficulties and I will be travelling alone. I hope you understand.*

Their reply indicated that they did indeed understand, but couldn't she put the ticket to some use?

Poppy looked up from her seat in the departure lounge, her hand luggage by her side, to see Peg standing in front of two tall male pilots. They were dressed in their full regalia, complete with shiny shoes, and peaked caps sitting squarely on their heads. Poppy strained to hear the conversation.

'So, yes, I'm going to be a pilot too.' Peg nodded.

'That's good to hear. Are you going to join the RAF like I did?' one of them asked. 'That can be a good route to becoming a pilot.'

'No, I don't think so. My dad's a soldier and he says the army is the best and the RAF is for softies and lightweights. But I might – does it pay you a lot of money?' Peg's head was tilted back on her shoulders so she could converse face to face.

Poppy cringed and sank low in her seat.

The men laughed. 'The money's not bad,' the other pilot piped up, 'but not as good as British Airways.'

'British Airways? Right, I'll remember that.' Peg nodded again.

'We've got to dash, but safe flying, Peg.'

'You too!'

The men saluted Peg, who returned the honour. She came over and plonked herself down in the spare seat next to her mum and pulled out her magazine.

'Who were you talking to?' Poppy asked.

'Oh, just some other pilots,' Peg answered dismissively, without lifting her nose from the article on ten ways to wear long hair this summer.

Poppy smiled at her confident daughter, who had insisted on wearing her summer sandals, floppy hat and heart-shaped sunglasses to the airport.

She declined to answer the calls from Martin as she waited for the gate to be called and it was surprisingly easy to delete his text messages without reading them. She was in no mood to hear the same wailing apology issued in any number of variants. Every time she heard his words of remorse she saw the image of him and Jo locked together in the cloakroom.

His eyes were closed, her hand on the small of his back and despite his previous words of explanation, he looked far from coerced. The memory of it made her feel physically sick; she suspected it always would.

Poppy was aware of the hum of noise around her. She watched excited families chasing each other, hauling bags on wheels behind them and popping into Boots for last-minute bits and pieces. She felt detached, unable to engage in the here and now, unable to focus on anything but the finality of her illness. It clouded everything. She couldn't even think about her marriage, or about anything practical. *It's like I'm sitting next to a giant ticking clock*, she thought. *And I just want to scream loudly to make it stop.* Everything had become meaningless, spoiled because of what lay ahead.

Peg's shouts drew her into the present. 'Can we, Mum? Can we? Can we?' She bounced on her seat and pointed at the buggy that had stopped by their side.

Peg loved the kudos of sitting in a buggy and being driven to the gate, waving and smiling at everyone they overtook. Poppy, however, hated the attention and tried to hide her face. She insisted on managing the stairs alone and didn't look back as she laboriously climbed the steps of the jumbo jet. Clipping her seatbelt into place, she kicked off her shoes and turned to look at her travelling companion.

'Are you going to watch a movie, Peg?' Poppy flicked through the in-flight magazine. 'Look, they've got *Cloudy with a Chance of Meatballs 2!*'

Peg sat with her back ramrod straight, her eyes fixed on the screen in the back of the seat in front. 'I'm not going to watch a movie, Mum. I'm going to watch this for the whole journey.' She pointed at the moving map that held her attention, running her finger over the aeroplane graphic. 'I'm going to make out I'm flying it all the way.' She traced the path it would follow. 'I'll take it over the sea and I'll land it here in St Lucia.' Peg tapped the screen and looked at her mum and grinned.

'How does it feel, Peg, to think you might fly a plane like this one day?'

Peg drew a sharp intake of breath. 'Oh, Mum. It feels... brilliant!'

Poppy stared at her little girl and for a fraction of a second she saw her daughter older. Her hair was pulled into a tight bun. She was wearing a white short-sleeved shirt with epaulettes on the shoulders and despite her age she still had the same open grin and clear eyes, and a smattering of freckles remained across her nose.

'I'm so proud of everything that you will do, Peg.' Poppy turned to the screen in front of her, unable to face her daughter, not wanting to douse this happy moment with more tears.

'Is this your first time on a plane too, Mummy?'

How to answer? Poppy felt a wave of sadness as she pictured the last outbound flight she had taken, thinking of the man she had headed out to save and trying to reconcile the way she felt about him right now.

'No. Actually I've flown four times before; two planes out and two back.'

'Was that when you went to bring Daddy home?' Peg whispered.

'Yep.' She nodded. 'As Daddy says, a long, long time ago.'

Poppy closed her eyes and gripped the arms of her seat. She remembered the smell of nervous sweat lingering inside the plane, being packed in like lambs in transit and the naked fear of being launched into the unknown.

'And Daddy didn't know you were going to see him at his work, did he?' Peg leant towards her mum, animated.

Poppy shook her head. 'No that's right, he didn't.'

'Daddy said you went to bring him home because no one loved him as much as you and no one wanted him to come home as much as you did.'

Poppy could only nod.

Peg kicked her legs back and forth and chewed her bottom lip. 'Did you love him more than anyone else, Mum?'

'Yes.' Her voice was softened with emotion. She knew what came next.

Peg gave a small cough. 'But you don't love him more than anyone right now, do you, Mum?' Her eyes were wide as she waited, hoping for her Mum's denial of this fact.

'I don't know, Peg. It's complicated.'

Peg sighed; it wasn't quite what she hoped for. 'If Daddy needed you to go and get him back right now, you would go and get him, wouldn't you, Mum?'

Poppy watched her daughter's chest heave.

'You don't have to worry about things like that, my love. He's not going anywhere.' Poppy patted her daughter's arm. Neither commented on the evasive nature of her reply.

Poppy sat in silence, replaying the journey to Camp Bastion over and over in her head. Knowing that her overriding thoughts had been of her husband, mentally reaching out to him, assuring him that she was on her way. Peg's questions had made her think, what would she do now, given the same set of circumstances?

Poppy remembered the mix of emotions she'd felt when she arrived in that hot, dusty place, driven on by the single desire to find Martin and bring him home. She opened her eyes and sat forward, shocked at the situation in which they now found themselves, still unsure of the level of his betrayal. She never would have thought it, not her Mart, not in a million years.

When they touched down at Hewanorra Airport, Poppy held Peg's hand tightly and they breathed in the hot Caribbean air. The second thing she noticed was the bright, bright blue of the St Lucian sky, a colour she had never seen before. It made everything beautiful.

'Look, Peg!' Poppy pointed into the distance. 'Palm trees.'

They stood in the slow, winding queue, fanning their faces with their passports as they snaked their way out past customs. After retrieving their one shared suitcase, which Peg pulled along on its wheels, they ventured out into the bustle of the airport. It was busy. Taxi drivers jostled for position whilst shouting greetings or insults, depending on the recipient. Holiday company reps stood in bright suits, holding up colour-coordinated clipboards. Bored kids, waiting in the heat for relatives, ran and fought among the feet of the travellers.

'It's so bright, Mum. It's making me really squinty!' Peg threw her head back and practically closed her eyes.

A tall, wide-shouldered black man with braided hair that fell to his shoulders and wearing khaki board shorts and a white polo shirt stepped forward. He stretched out his large hands and pulled Poppy towards him.

'Hello, Poppy. It's lovely to meet you in real life.' His voice was a rich, deep baritone. 'And you must be Peg.'

'I am Peg!' She sounded surprised.

Poppy stood back and studied the man, her uncle. It was a moment of clarity, bizarre and comforting. In the flesh he was more handsome than the grainy image on Martin's laptop had suggested; he was smiley and he had Dot's eyes.

'That's so weird!' she gasped.

'What is?' Simon asked

'You do look like her – my nan, Dorothea.'

'Do I?' Simon clung to the words, as sweet as nectar.

Poppy nodded. 'Yes! Despite being black and a man, you do, you look a bit like my nan.'

Simon laughed and scooped up their suitcase as though it were featherweight. 'Come on, let's get you home. There's a cold drink waiting for you.'

'That sounds lovely.' Poppy smiled, feeling quite at home within two minutes of meeting this man. Her deep fatigue was eclipsed by the excitement of having arrived in a new country; it gave her spirits and body a lift.

'How was your journey? Are you feeling okay?' Simon paused and studied Poppy's face.

'My mum's got a horrible bug; she throws up in the night. But I haven't got it,' Peg trilled as she looked overhead at the palm trees.

'Oh, I see.' Simon was unsure how to respond.

Poppy shrugged. 'That about sums it up!'

Peg piled into the back of Simon's jeep, while Poppy slowly climbed up into the front seat, every move requiring super-human effort.

'You okay?' he asked again.

'Yes, and please don't worry about me; I look worse than I am. I just need a drink and a spot of rest and I'll be right as rain.'

'Is that your way of telling me to stop asking if you are okay?' Simon smiled.

'In a word, yes.' She smiled back at her uncle.

The two newcomers gazed with fascination at the land-scape that whizzed by to either side of the steep, meandering road that led eventually to their destination, Rodney Bay. Locals by the roadside nearly all raised a hand in recognition of Simon, who smiled and waved back. Poppy stared at the rickety verandas where families congregated to chat and eat in the sunshine. The thick tangle of jungle vegetation was glossy with raindrops, and crabs the size of frisbees scurried off the road and into the undergrowth at the sound of the engine. More than once Simon had to slow right down in order to veer round a resolute goat, tethered to a tree and standing defiantly in the path of the car.

Peg sat forward and ran her hands over Simon's braids, letting them fall through her fingers. 'Your hair is a bit like girls' hair, isn't it?'

'Is it?' Simon laughed.

'Uh-huh.' She was quiet for a second. 'My friend Jade McKeever has been to Majorca and she said it was very hot. Is St Lucia like Majorca?'

'Hmmm, I don't know, Peg, I've never been to Majorca. But it's hot here, so I expect that is the same.'

'She bought these really cool friendship bracelets back and I'd like to buy some from my holiday.'

'Ah, well I'm sure my wife can help you out there. She's a bit of an expert at shopping!'

'I can see bananas growing on a tree!' Peg screamed.

'That's where all bananas come from, Peg.' Simon chortled. Poppy liked his low, patient tone.

'Not in our house, they don't. Ours come from the supermarket,' Peg informed him.

Simon let out his deep, throaty laugh.

'Do you still like your wife?' Peg was on a roll.

'Yes.' Simon chuckled. 'I like her very much.'

'My mum and dad don't like each other very much at the

moment, that's why *I'm* here and not my dad. They used to, but they had a big fight and my mum told him to piss right off and he did.'

'Ah well, these things have a funny way of working out, Peg,' Simon said.

'I know, but it's complicated.' Peg sighed.

Poppy looked at her lap, speechless. Peg had not only told Simon all their business, but she'd said 'piss' to a vicar.

Peg wasn't done though. 'Jade McKeever says it's because one of them has done sex with someone else, but I'm not sure.'

Poppy felt her face go scarlet. She turned to the back seat. 'Well, you can tell Jade McKeever that's not always the case, Peg. And just to clarify, neither your dad nor I have done sex with someone else.' She looked at Simon and smiled. 'Not quite the opening conversation you were expecting, I bet.'

'No, not really. I thought I'd be pointing out our volcanoes – the Pitons – and naming trees!'

'I'm sorry,' Poppy said, cringing.

'Don't be. It's been quite an education. You feel like family – you are family!' He grinned.

'Shall I call you Uncle Simon?' Peg asked.

'You can call me anything you like!'

'Apart from Katniss, I bet – I'm not allowed to call a new baby Katniss or my new guinea pig Katniss, even though I really wanted to.'

'You've lost me!' Simon glanced at Peg in the mirror.

Poppy turned to look over her shoulder again. 'Tell you what, Peg, let's see if you can be quiet until we arrive, okay?'

Peg mimed zipping her mouth shut and threw the imaginary key out of the window.

'She can call me Katniss if she really wants to,' Simon said.

Peg beamed from behind her sealed mouth and bounced on the seat. She liked her new Uncle Katniss, very, very much.

'You mentioned on Skype that you and Kate hadn't been married long?'

'That's right. She loves to tell the story, so I won't steal her thunder.' Simon smiled his wide grin at his niece. 'It's coming up for four years.'

He turned his jeep into a steep winding driveway that led up to their home. The pale pink single-storey building appeared to sit on stilts, leaving a cool shady area below the house. A white wooden trellis formed the front wall to a terrace that ran the length of the property and it was covered in bright red hibiscuses in full bloom.

'This is so beautiful!' Poppy climbed out of the jeep and shielded her eyes as she looked beyond the garden and out to the sea in the distance. 'I can't believe I'm here! Thank you, Simon. Thank you so much.' She smiled at him.

'No, thank you. It means the world that you came.' He lifted the suitcase and made his way towards the house.

'Hello, hello! Welcome, welcome!'

Poppy turned in the direction of the voice that came from the front terrace of the house. Kate looked unmistakably English – a middle-aged lady with shoulder-length mousy brown hair and wearing cropped jeans and a floral shirt. She bounced down the stairs, waving a tea towel and grinning.

'And this is Kate!' Simon said, with obvious joy in his voice.

'Hello, Kate.' Poppy opened herself to Kate's embrace, relishing the hug that lasted a fraction too long: Kate's way of acknowledging her illness.

'Oh, Poppy, it's so lovely to meet you in real life. And you must be Peg!' Kate bent down to Peg's height.

'Yep.' Peg nodded. 'I'm going to be a pilot.'

'How wonderful!' Kate clapped her hands together. 'Think you might fly back to St Lucia one day?'

Peg nodded again. 'Yes, I think I will. I might work for British Airways as the money is quite good. I'll bring my dad to visit if you like!'

There was a second of silence as the adults quietly recognised the unintended accuracy of Peg's words – that Poppy would no longer be alive when Peg was old enough to fly.

Kate changed the subject as Simon carried their case inside. 'I've made a lemon drizzle cake, my specialty – hope you like it! Who's hungry?'

'Me!' Peg's arm shot up in the air as though she were in school.

'Ah, here she is!' Kate turned to greet the little girl who had suddenly appeared among them. 'I knew the mention of lemon drizzle cake would draw you out! Poppy, Peg, this is Matilda.'

'Hi!' Matilda stood in front of Kate with her hands reaching back and gripping her jeans, a safety blanket of sorts.

Kate caressed Matilda's head. 'You and Peg are nearly the same age. Why don't you go and show her the chickens?'

'Sure.' Matilda reluctantly let go of her denim anchor and walked towards the back of the garden. 'Come on.' She beckoned to Peg.

Poppy and Kate watched as the little girls slipped into step, side by side.

'Are Kate and Katniss your mummy and daddy?'

'Why do you call him Katniss?' Matilda laughed loudly.

'Because he said I could,' Peg replied matter-of-factly.

'They are *kind* of my mum and dad...' Matilda started to explain.

That was the last they heard as the conversation was taken out of earshot.

'How are you feeling, Poppy?' Kate looked concerned.

'Tired, but fine.'

'And we are not to keep asking her if she is okay – isn't that right, Poppy?' Simon shouted as he came back into the garden.

Poppy laughed.

'Do you fancy a rest? Your room is all made up and you've had a long journey.' Kate was sweet, kind, motherly.

'No, but thanks. I'd love a cup of tea though and a bit of your famous lemon drizzle cake!' Poppy hoped she could get the cake down.

The three sat on the terrace sipping tea as the heat slipped from the day.

'I still can't believe I'm here.' Poppy stared at the sea, amazed at how easy it was to wake in one country and go to sleep in another.

'Simon is so pleased to have found you.' Kate patted his hand.

'I am indeed. Kate encouraged me to look for my birth family. I don't know if I'd have had the courage if she hadn't suggested it.'

'He had a gap in his life, a knowledge gap that needed filling.' She smiled at her husband.

'Yes, I did,' Simon agreed. 'My adoptive parents died within a year of each other a couple of years back and it got me thinking. I was sad not to have located Dorothea before she died.'

'She was an amazing lady, really. My lovely nan – just an

ordinary woman, or so I thought. I had no idea that she had this life before she had my mum.'

Simon rested his arms on the table. 'It was a hard letter to write to Cheryl.'

No one commented on Cheryl's lack of interest.

'I'd managed to trace the place of my birth to a mother and baby home in Battersea, London, which I vaguely knew about from my parents. But the records were sketchy. I already knew who my father was because my mum – my adoptive mum – had been told by one of the nuns at the home that he was Solomon Arbuthnott, a St Lucian. She never forgot his name. But it was harder to get Dorothea's details. There was a great deal of shame in being pregnant and unmarried, especially in a mixed-race relationship; it was very different in those days.'

'In some ways,' Kate whispered, acknowledging that the two of them had also faced prejudice.

'How did you two meet?' Poppy asked as she sipped a glass of cordial Kate had poured her.

'Oh, Kate came here as a tourist and I lured her in!' Simon laughed.

'You hardly lured me in! I met him on a beach – that's true. He was with Matilda, who was tiny; gosh, so tiny.' Kate paused, smiling at the memory. 'Matilda gave me a shell, which I still treasure and Simon invited me up to the mission in Dennery, a suburb back towards the airport on the road you just came from.'

Simon picked up the thread. 'The mission is still running, but I spend most of my time fundraising for it now. It's entirely dependent on donations and sponsorship and I quickly realised that I couldn't run it full time as well as keep it going financially. So there's a team there now, looked after by Fabian, who's been there since the beginning. I still visit nearly every day, but I'm no longer stripping beds and washing pots.'

He beamed at Kate, who continued the story.

'I went up and visited him and the kids he was looking after and fell in love with him and the place.' She paused and stared briefly at the horizon. 'It was a tricky time in my life,' she said quietly, then turned to face Poppy again. 'I went back to the UK and stuck it out for a couple of years, but I couldn't get him out of my head. Then one day, completely out of the blue, he turned up on the doorstep of my house in Cornwall – our house in Cornwall now. He smiled at me, took my hand and that was that!'

'I haven't let her go since,' Simon said.

'And as I told you, we are soon to become grandparents!' Kate grinned. 'My son Dominic and his wife Fiona are having a baby! We know it's a little boy and they want to name him Noah. I can't wait, but whenever I talk about him, I cry!' She fished up her sleeve for a tissue to blot her tears.

Poppy smiled. 'That's so exciting – a little boy! It'll be great. You must miss them all.'

'Yes, I do. But it's more than that. Noah is a symbol of all the good things I wished for my kids. He will be very precious.' Kate blew her nose.

The two girls reappeared and took up their seats at the table. They held hands. Firm friends already. Matilda was nearly a year older than Poppy and therefore an object of fascination and someone to be emulated.

'Do you know Jonty Mantiziba?' Peg asked.

Matilda shook her head. 'No, I don't think so. Does he live in St Lucia?'

'No, he lives in England. He's in my class, but he's black too.'

Simon laughed loudly. 'Not all black people know each other, Peg.'

'I know that, Uncle Katniss!' Peg sounded incensed. 'I just wondered...' She drummed her fingers on the table.

'Why don't you two get your costumes on and I'll take you to the beach for a dip!' Kate suggested.

'Yeeeeees!' They clambered off their seats and rushed inside.

'Did you ever meet Solomon Arbuthnott?' Poppy asked, hoping that Simon had met at least one of his birth parents.

'Yes, yes I did.' Simon looked at the table and paused. 'Do you think Dorothea ever thought about me?'

'Knowing her, I'm sure she did. She seemed a little preoccupied for most of her life and maybe it was you she was preoccupied with. Of course I've thought about that a lot since I found out, and I've remembered certain things.'

Simon sat forward, eager to hear the details that he'd been longing for.

'It was hard watching her deteriorate with dementia. I hated it. It made me sad that she lost so much of herself.'

'It's a terrible disease,' Simon acknowledged.

'She used to say to me things like, "How did I end up here, Poppy Day? Where did everyone go?" And all I could do was mop up her tears and stroke the back of her hand. And I'd say, "I don't know, Nan. I don't know what happened." I never lied to her, never would. But it was hard.' Poppy felt her tears pool at the memory.

'Did Cheryl not help you with her care?' he asked.

'No. Not once.' Poppy was embarrassed at having to admit to these less than attractive traits in her mum, Simon's sister. 'Just before I really lost Nan to dementia, she told me she had a baby. I didn't believe it, thought it was just more of her rambling – she was convinced Joan Collins was her daughter for a while, but that's a whole other story!'

Simon laughed.

Poppy drew breath, her expression serious now. 'But I remember she said two things. One day, she clutched my hand as if she was desperate and she said to me, "I'm sitting here thinking about that other baby. I wonder what he is doing right now. Do you think he could be close by?" And I just said, "I guess so, Nan." And then she said, "He went to a good family; I made sure of that," and now it's clear to me that she must have meant you. And another day that I remember clearly, she said, "I wasn't even allowed to say his name, not ever, not once, let alone have a bloody photograph. My little boy, my Simon." And then she cried, really cried, and it was horrible to watch. All I could do was hold her hand and tell her it was all okay and that it was a long time ago. I didn't know what else to say.'

Poppy looked up and was aghast to see the fat tears that rolled down Simon's face. 'Oh God, I'm sorry, Simon! I didn't mean to upset you. I feel awful.'

Simon shook his head. 'No, no. It's wonderful! Wonderful to hear about her and to know she thought of me, said my name! It's a hard thing to describe, because I had a fantastic mum and dad, a really happy childhood. I was very loved. But it never quite goes away, that feeling that someone didn't want you.' He paused and tried to contain his tears. 'But whatever the circumstances of my birth and my adoption, it sounds like she kept a little bit of me – here.' He placed his hand over his heart. 'Thank you for looking after her.'

'Well it was easy for me, wasn't it? I loved her.' Poppy shrugged. It *had* been easy for her: her nan had been kind and funny and as her own mum was pretty shite, she had been very glad to have her in her life.

'She sounds lovely.'

'She was.' Poppy thought back. 'What bothered me the most, after she'd gone downhill, was that the people who met her when she was like that – her carers...' Poppy smiled at the memory of the fabulous Nathan, who Dorothea had taken into her confidence and her heart. 'They only ever knew her like that. They never knew she was once this funny lady, who liked to lark around and who had a spark. They never saw that. To them she was just another old person wearing elasticated trousers.' Poppy curled her toes against the warm wood of the terrace. 'I wish I could give you something interesting, tell you about her amazing career or that she climbed mountains, but that wasn't her, she was just my ordinary nan.'

Simon withdrew his folded arms from the table and wiped the residue of tears from his face. 'It sounds to me as if she did climb mountains, in her own way.'

'Oh, I nearly forgot, I brought you some photographs!' Poppy bent down slowly and reached for her handbag. Between two folded sheets of paper sat the photographs of her nan. She peeled them off and placed them in Simon's palm. She leant into him, touching the first one with her finger. 'This is Dorothea and her husband, Wally, my grandad, on their wedding day in 1962. It was taken in the back garden of the house she grew up in, in Limehouse, east London. Her mum and dad were Reg and Joan Simpson. That was her maiden name: Dorothea Simpson.'

Simon shook his head. 'This is marvellous! I can't believe it – this is what my mum looked like!' He held the picture close to his face, to better scrutinise it. 'She looks beautiful.'

Poppy smiled and touched the other photograph. 'I don't

remember being told much about that one, but it's the late seventies and she is sitting in the little kitchen in the flat that I grew up in, in Walthamstow. She was a lousy cook, apart from the odd bacon sandwich, so it was obviously some occasion if she'd gone and splashed out on a plate of fondant fancies!'

'I shall look at these over and over. I can't thank you enough.' Simon was clearly touched by her gift.

'Uncle Katniss! Look what I found!' Peg shouted as she approached the table. She was wearing her swimming costume and holding a large shell, its surface covered with nodes and tiny cracks. 'It's enormous!' she squealed.

'That's a conch shell,' Simon told her. 'The conch live in shallow waters and on the reefs and they are molluscs – like snails, but much bigger! People eat them.' He turned to Poppy. 'This one is actually from Solomon's garden.'

'It belonged to your birth dad?' Poppy asked.

Simon smiled. 'Yes. He was quite attached to it. It's very old.'

'Be careful with it, Peg,' Poppy admonished.

'If you hold it up to your ear you can hear the sea,' Simon said to Peg.

Using both hands, Peg duly held the shell up to her ear and concentrated. She was silent for a second before her eyes widened. 'I can! I can hear the sea!' she shouted.

'I told you.' Simon winked at Poppy.

'Which sea is it I'm listening to?' Peg asked with her nose wrinkled.

'I think it's any sea you want it to be.'

Peg nuzzled the huge shell against her face. 'I think it's the sea at Bournemouth, where my dad took me and Maxy for a walk on the sand.'

Poppy felt a wave of longing for her little boy, wishing she could hold him in her arms right now.

'If Dad and Maxy are in Bournemouth and I can hear the sea there, they might be able to hear me!' Peg shouted.

Poppy and Simon laughed.

She moved the shell around so her mouth was near the opening. 'Hello, Dad! Hello, Max! I'm here in St Lucia, but I can hear your sea. Can you hear me? If you can, give my love to Toffee.' She then blew a kiss against the pearlescent pink mouth of the conch.

Poppy put her head in her hands. 'I think my daughter is the only person in the whole wide world who would think of communicating across the globe by conch shell. I don't know where she gets it from.'

Twenty-Four

When Poppy woke up, it took a second for her to remember where she was. When she did remember, she smiled and closed her eyes, feeling a sense of relief that she was here in paradise and there was a whole day ahead of her in which she could do as she pleased. Peg's side of the bed was empty. Poppy stretched her aching bones and stared at the sun streaming through the window. It was wonderful to wake in natural heat: no glug of radiators or whir of fans, just the warmth of the sun as it permeated the walls and filled the room. She sat up and looked out at the vibrant green garden with its spiky palms, lush plants and fiery red blooms. A proper Caribbean garden.

Swinging her legs to climb from the bed, she was immediately anchored by a sharp pain in her lower back. 'Jesus H. Christ!'

She sat back against the pillows, unscrewed the lid of her little pill bottle, counted the capsules into her palm and hurled them down her throat. 'Do your worst, boys,' she said, visualising the bastard pedalos. There wasn't one part of her body that on one day or another didn't cause her discomfort. It was exhausting.

There was a light rap on her door.

'Come in!' Poppy did her best to sound comfortable and

calm. She didn't want to worry anyone more than she already had.

Kate popped her head into the room. 'Morning, Poppy. Did you sleep well?'

Poppy ran her hand over the pale lemon quilt and pushed her head into the heavily starched pillowcases with little sprigs of lavender embroidered on them. 'Kate, in a room as beautiful as this, it would be very hard not to.'

'I'm so glad you like it! I tried to make it lovely for you.' Kate straightened the towel that hung on a hook on the back of the door.

Poppy cast her eye over the whitewashed dresser where a glass vase sat displaying a single white tropical bloom. 'Well you succeeded.'

'Do you feel up to breakfast? We are all on the terrace. Peg was up bright and early; she and Matilda are already quite inseparable!'

'Give me a mo, I'll be right out.'

Kate closed the door as Poppy sank back into the bed and took some deep breaths. Mr Ramasingh had said that it was good to get her breathing under control and that it might actually help her pain. At this stage, she was willing to try absolutely anything.

Some minutes later, she stepped out into the bright, beautiful morning to find Peg and Matilda sitting opposite each other, clapping hands in a rhythm. They were clapping their own and then each other's hands alternately, which Peg found hard to master. But rather than find this irritating, Matilda dissolved into giggles every time Peg got it wrong. Poppy wished sweet-natured Matilda could be her full-time guru and not Jade Bloody McKeever.

'Mum!' Peg caught sight of her out of the corner of her eye. 'Uncle Katniss made me pancakes and bacon and banana, it was like breakfast and pudding on the same plate and I ate every bit.'

'Wow, that sounds yummy.' Poppy slid into the chair next to Simon's at the table in the centre of the terrace. 'Look at that view!' she exclaimed. Her mouth dropped open as she took in the jungle-clad mountains and the way their silhouettes led her eye in a V down to the crystal-clear blue water, which sparkled with sun diamonds in the distance. 'I'd never get sick of looking at that.'

Simon's eyes twinkled. 'I feel blessed every single day.'

'I can see why!' Poppy beamed.

Simon smiled at her. 'I was thinking, we might do a bit of gentle exploring today. I could drive us to a great beach not too far from here. It's only a couple of steps to get on the sand and then when you've had enough, I'll drive you home. We can have a good chat en route.'

'That sounds lovely.'

Kate placed a bowl of pineapple and mango in front of her, cut into bite-sized chunks.

'Well, this is the life!' Poppy ate as much as she could, feeling a twinge of guilt that Martin and Max were so far away.

Peg jumped from her chair and planted a huge smacker on her mum's cheek, before she and Matilda ran back into the house, opting to stay at home and play. They had a grand plan to paint each other's nails in the afternoon and learn a dance routine.

'They get on well,' Simon commented as he pulled the car out onto the lane. 'Peg is lovely and affectionate, you must be so proud of her.'

'I really am,' Poppy beamed, subconsciously touching her fingertips to her cheek where the echo of Peg's kiss lingered.

'I bet Cheryl spoils her rotten.'

Poppy squirmed in the chair. 'Not really.'

'Oh?' Simon sounded surprised. 'Is that because she lives overseas? I expect it's difficult to see each other a lot.'

Poppy took a deep breath. 'It's more than that. She's not really that interested. It was the same when I was growing up. She never touched me, ever. Never brushed my hair or gave me a cuddle, nothing. She was fairly crap on all fronts really.'

'Are you close to her now?' Simon asked, hopefully.

Poppy shook her head. 'No, the opposite, sadly.' She felt ashamed at the admission.

Simon seemed troubled by her words. 'Have you *ever* been close?'

'No, not that I can remember.' Poppy wasn't sure how much she should divulge. It still hurt, even at the age of thirty-two, to admit that her mum had been pretty rubbish in every way. 'I don't think she could be bothered with me; I was more of an irritation. I was frightened a lot of the time as a kid. She'd come in late, very drunk...' Poppy rolled her hand in the air, as if to say, 'You can guess the rest.'

'That must have been tough for you.' It was a scenario Simon knew only too well from running the mission.

Poppy breathed in. 'Well, yes, but your normal is your normal, isn't it? And I didn't really know any different. I had Dorothea, of course; luckily she was more of a mother to me.' She paused and looked at Simon, feeling a flash of unease that Dorothea had got to mother her, but not him. 'But as a mum myself, I find it hard to understand Cheryl's choices sometimes. In fact, not sometimes, all of the time.'

271

'Does she see Peg and Max?'

'Only occasionally. She doesn't really figure in their lives. But they've got Granny Claudia, who they've adopted and I love. Her son and I were close friends, but he... got killed.' Poppy pictured the moment, a decade earlier when the car bomb that could quite have easily taken her life too, robbed her of her friend and Claudia of her son. Poppy sniffed as if to rid her nose of the metallic scent of blood that filled her nostrils every time she remembered the carnage.

'Even the way Claudia treats me makes me feel angry with Cheryl, makes me realise what I've missed. I haven't seen Cheryl since my diagnosis and I know I'm going to have to, but I'm dreading it.' Poppy picked at her fingernails, agitated. 'She's coming to see me when I get home. I've managed to put off proper contact until now, but she's booked her flight apparently. It's strange to think it might be the last time I see her – strange because I don't feel overly distressed by the idea. All my sadness is taken up over leaving the kids and, to be honest, there's not a lot left over.'

'That's understandable. It's a difficult conversation to have with your parent. I can only imagine.' Simon flicked the indictor and turned the car off the main road and down a lane. It was dark where the large fronds hung over the road and formed a green canopy through which the sun could only glimpse.

'It will be difficult, but maybe not for the reasons you think.' Poppy thought for a moment about what she wanted to say to her mum. 'I feel like it's my first and only chance to tell her exactly how she has made me feel my whole life. What it felt like to have a mum that lied to me, never followed through and then abandoned me. It was shite and I still feel angry towards her, especially now I'm a mum and my head is full of what is best for Max and Peg, always thinking about what's best for them.'

'I feel sorry for your mum.'

'You do?' This wasn't quite the response Poppy had expected.

'Yes. Look what she has missed! You are an amazing girl and Peg is one in a million.'

Poppy smiled. Yes she was, one in a million...

'Imagine passing up that opportunity because you couldn't say no to a drink. That's very sad.'

It is sad, but it was sad for me, going to school in dirty clothes, going to sleep hungry.

'Do you want to punish her in some way?' Simon was direct.

Poppy looked up towards the trees. She hadn't considered it in this way, until now. She shrugged her shoulders. 'I dunno, maybe a little bit.'

'I can understand that too, but I think punishing her would make you feel better only for a very short time and it would make her feel bad for a very long time, maybe for the rest of *her* life. You don't know that she doesn't already feel bad – none of us knows what battles anyone else is fighting.'

'Ha! Tell me about it!' Poppy's response was a little sharper than she had intended.

'I know you know that.' Simon hesitated. 'But sometimes it's not fair to unburden yourself just to make yourself feel better. It'll be her that's left and what purpose will it serve? It might be better to leave your hurt behind, let it go. But of course it's up to you.'

'I suppose I've been looking forward to clearing the slate, leaving nothing unsaid.' It sounded a little indulgent, even to her ears.

Simon smiled at her. 'No one can tell you what to do, but I guess my advice would be to think very carefully about the words you leave Cheryl with. It will affect you both.'

He pulled the car up into a gravel clearing next to a group of trees and set off with confidence through the copse. Poppy followed in his wake, descending the sandy path. Simon turned and took her arm. 'Nearly there.'

She trod slowly over large rocks and the odd knotty branch. It was worth it. One more step forward and she found herself in paradise. The bay was horseshoe shaped, on a gentle incline that allowed the crystal-clear blue water to lap its shore. The fine sand was undisturbed. The trees of the wood behind them cast gentle shadows and shady pockets over the beach. Mother Nature had dotted palm trees where the jungle met the sand. It was perfect.

'This is where I brought Kate the first time I took her out. I figured if this didn't make her fall in love with St Lucia, then nothing would.'

'It obviously worked!' Poppy chuckled.

'Yes, eventually. I thought I'd lost her when she went back to England, but I couldn't get her out of my head. And like anything, if you are meant to have it, it will come back to you.' He beamed.

Poppy thought of Martin, wondering if he was going to come back to her – or, more specifically, if she would let him.

Simon lowered himself onto the sand. Poppy hesitated and stood staring at the spot next to her uncle.

'Do you need a hand?' He looked up, concerned.

She shook her head. 'No. I'm fine. It's just that I've waited my whole life to lie on a tropical beach and feel the soft powdery sand slip through my fingers. It was one of my wishes – and here I am! I can't quite believe it.' *And I always thought I would do it with Mart by my side, in a land where I could have anything and everything was possible.*

Poppy sank down next to Simon and pushed the long sleeves of her shirt up over her arms, letting the heat of the sun kiss her skin and soothe her bones. She dug her toes into the warm sand and raked it with her fingers. As she allowed the gentle wind to lift both her hair and her spirits, she watched the small waves breaking on the shore with a gentle roll, the rhythm of which could have sent her to sleep. Her fingers chanced upon two beautiful shells. One was about an inch long, bleached white and with its ends shaped to a perfect point. The other was like a tiny scallop shell, with a stunning striped pattern running along its ridges. She dropped them into her top pocket, one for each memory box.

'I know you are right about my mum, but these thoughts, these memories, they don't just go away because I have decided to forgive her. The way she treated me shaped me, had a profound effect on my life, and if I hadn't met Mart, I hate to think how I might have ended up.'

Simon twisted to face her. 'Think about that, Poppy. You hate to think of how you might have ended up if you hadn't met Martin, got away and started a new life.'

'That's right.'

'But Cheryl never knew the joy of that, did she? And it doesn't sound like she ended up with a Martin to show her a different way of life either. That's sad on both counts.'

'Blimey, how did you get so smart? Or are you merely defending your sister?' Poppy joked.

'Gosh, my sister... that still sounds so odd to me. I grew up as an only child and to find I have a sibling at my age is a huge deal.'

'She's not...'

'Not what?' Simon prompted.

Poppy searched for the right tone. 'She doesn't take life too seriously.'

'Well that can be a good thing.'

Not if you never learn from your mistakes and life is just one big happy hour.

Both of them were quiet for a while.

Poppy sighed. 'I guess I just don't think you and Cheryl would have much in common and I wouldn't want you to be disappointed.'

Simon chuckled. 'We have one thing in common – we shared a mum, and I reckon I could talk about *her* all day and night.'

'I guess so.' Poppy sounded far from convinced. She closed her eyes and tipped her head back. 'This is heaven.'

'Well, not quite, but I'll grant you, it's pretty amazing!'

Poppy dug her heels into the sand. 'This vicar stuff – you don't seem very...' She tried to find the word. 'Preachy.'

'Would you like to me to be?' he asked.

'No.' Poppy bit her lip. 'But because I'm dying...' She took a breath; it still sounded untrue, no matter how many times she said the words out loud. 'It's made me think about stuff.'

'What kind of stuff?'

'You know, where I might go next, if anywhere.' She looked up at him and away again, embarrassed.

'Oh, *that* stuff. Well, I think about it a lot and I do believe that you go to heaven. I don't know if that's a place or a state or an idea, but I don't think this one life is it.'

'You don't?' She blinked up at him.

Simon shook his head. 'No. And I think that God is good and merciful and if you have suffered or led a good life, then you get your reward in heaven.'

'That sounds quite nice.'

'It does, doesn't it?'

'Do you think…' Poppy swallowed. 'Do you think I'll get to see my kids again?'

Simon smiled at his niece. 'I don't think you'll ever leave them.'

'Can I tell you something in confidence, Simon?'

'Of course.' He turned to her, his expression solemn.

Poppy hid her face in her hands. 'This is going to make me sound completely bonkers!'

'I'll be the judge of that.' He smiled.

'On the night I found a lump, and ever since I've been ill…' Poppy paused and looked towards the sea. 'I keep seeing my nan, Dorothea, and she kind of gives me advice. Not always by speaking; sometimes she just smiles at me as if to say it's all okay.'

Simon beamed at her and clapped his large hands together. 'How wonderful! She's telling you not to be afraid. Sounds like she's waiting for you.'

Poppy nodded. She felt a great peace wash over her. It was a comforting thought.

She watched as a young couple – a muscly black man and his white girlfriend – giggled on the sand to the left of the bay. The woman looked lovely; her curves were poured into a navy bathing suit which had large white spots on it and a pretty bow that sat just beneath her bust. They were laughing and running as they headed down to the sea. The two splashed and ducked beneath the waves, squealing like toddlers before coming together to hold and be held in the warm current. The man kissed the salt water that seemed to sparkle on her eyelids, and then peppered her face with smaller kisses. He lifted her in the water and twirled her around, causing the water to ripple and froth around them.

Poppy turned to Simon. 'Someone's enjoying the water!' She nodded in the direction of the couple.

'Who is?' Simon smiled, his eyebrows knitted quizzically.

When Poppy looked back at the sea, the couple had gone.

* * *

Kate plopped down on the terrace next to Poppy. They watched as Matilda tried in vain to teach Peg how to execute the perfect cartwheel across the lawn.

'I feel dizzy watching them.' Kate laughed.

'Me too,' Poppy sighed. 'I love seeing them together, it reminds me of my mate Jenna and I when we were young, we used to laugh all the time at anything!'

'Ah, the joy of childhood. I remember my daughter Lydia giggling like that with her friends. It's a shame, isn't it, that our adult friendships are often more constrained. I can't remember the last time my best friend and I landed on the grass in a heap.'

Poppy thought of Jo and felt a stab of loss that their friendship had been severed. 'Jo and I were close. Partly because we were neighbours, but also with our blokes away at the same time, it gave us a special bond.' She paused, remembering the early morning coffees in their pyjamas, the emergency calls when one or the other ran out of an essential, and drinking wine over the fence in the summer months. 'I miss her actually, despite what's happened, I do miss her.' It was an admission that came out of the blue.

'Have you spoken to her?' Kate asked as she sipped her iced tea.

Poppy shook her head. 'No. Not since I met her for a coffee, just afterwards. I was so full of anger that it was horrible. I was mean and she cried.' She thought about her friends words, 'I love you, Poppy. You know that. And the kids...' She felt her own tears pool. 'The worst thing is that the kids will need someone like her, and Martin too. It's not like we have a large family to call upon. She was a big part of all our lives.' Poppy blinked hard. 'Simon said something to me when we first arrived, about my legacy, what I leave behind for people I care about, and I realise that part of the reason I was so mad with Jo was that I was counting on her being there when I'd gone, being there for Peg and Max and for Mart.'

Kate coughed to clear her throat. 'So you're saying that you were mad with her for showing Martin affection, but you wanted her to be there for him after you had gone?'

Poppy nodded. 'Kind of, yes.'

'So was it more of a timing issue rather than a betrayal?' Kate kept her gaze fixed on the horizon.

Poppy laughed out loud. 'Blimey, I don't know! When you say I like that...'

Kate turned to the young mum. 'The thing is, Poppy, I know what it's like to have to rely on others to care for your kids. There was a period when I couldn't see mine,' Kate closed her eyes, even the memory of being separated was clearly painful, 'but having someone I trusted, in my case my sister, and knowing that she was there for them, well, let's just say it made everything bearable, almost.'

Poppy wanted to ask why Kate and her kids had been separated, but didn't want to pry. 'They're happy now though, aren't they?' She needed to hear that even when the worst thing happens, your children would survive.

'Oh yes, more than happy. I think the human spirit is programmed to compensate; they appreciate the happy, stable lives that they live and that's a blessing.'

Poppy watched a small speedboat dart across the vast ocean, cutting through the waves and bobbing on the foamy crests. 'Being here gives me a clear perspective on things, Kate. The sun has diluted my anger. I don't want to be jealous. I don't want it in my system.'

Kate patted her leg in a motherly gesture of love.

'Kate?'

'Yes, love?'

'Can I borrow your laptop? I want to send Jo an email.'

Kate beamed at her as she jumped up and headed for the study. 'Yes, of course. I have no doubt it will be a big relief for you both.'

* * *

It was harder than she expected, saying goodbye to Simon and Kate. Suddenly everything felt horribly final. She couldn't stop thinking about how this goodbye would be the first of many.

It was the morning of their departure. They sat on the terrace and sipped iced tea with slices of fresh lemon as Kate fussed over Peg and the snacks she was packing for her for the plane.

'I hope everything works out for you and Martin,' Simon said.

'Thank you. Being here has helped give me some perspective. I mean, he only snogged my mate, right?' Poppy tried to inject a little humour to hide her embarrassment.

Kate sat by her side. 'Take it from one who knows, Poppy,

there are far, far worse things that a husband can do.' She squeezed Poppy's hand.

Poppy got the feeling that Kate had her own story to tell. Simon smiled at his wife. Whatever Kate had been through in the past, at least she had ended up with someone who had shown *her* a different way of life.

Kate leant over and kissed her forehead. 'Things have a funny way of sorting themselves out, my love.'

'You sound like Claudia.'

'Is she a wise old bird too?' Kate asked.

'Yes. You two would get on great.' Poppy pictured the two of them on the terrace, putting the world to rights over a glass of wine.

Simon hugged Poppy at the airport. 'I'll speak to you soon. Take the very best care you can.'

'I will,' Poppy mouthed into his shoulder, thinking about how different her life might have been if Simon had been part of it for longer, the kind of father figure she had craved.

'I can't tell you how wonderful it has been meeting you and hearing all about Dorothea. You will never know...' Simon swallowed the ball of emotion that sat in his throat.

He turned and kissed Peg on the head. 'You look after your mum, okay?'

'I will. I have a nurse's uniform at home.'

'Splendid!' He beamed.

'And can you tell Matilda that I shall miss her a lot, but when I'm a pilot I'll be able to fly and see her whenever I want to, just for a cup of coffee or to paint our nails.'

Poppy smiled at her little girl's interpretation of adulthood: cups of coffee and nail painting. It made her think of Jo.

'God bless you, Poppy.' Simon held her face in his hands and kissed her forehead.

'I love you, Uncle Katniss!' Peg squeezed him tightly.

As the plane lifted from the runway, leaving the sun and blue sky of St Lucia, Poppy felt the cold creep of fear in her stomach. She was going home, back to a marriage that had nearly dissolved and a life that was ruled by sickness. This had been a wonderful escape, but she knew there was no escape from what lay ahead. As the plane soared through the sky, she looked at the clouds floating beneath them and wondered, not for the first time in her life, where heaven might be?

Twenty-Five

Martin slammed the boot and clicked his seatbelt into the clip. 'All set?'

Poppy nodded, her stare a little vacant. She was tired and freezing, having forgotten that in their time away summer would have started to give way to autumn.

'Can you turn the heating right up?' she asked.

'Of course.' Martin did so and reached behind her seat for a fleecy blanket that he placed on her lap and tucked around her thighs.

'Thank you.' She liked his kindness, always had.

'Oh, Dad, Uncle Katniss and Aunty Kate have got chickens—'

'Uncle Katniss?' Martin interrupted as he fished in his wallet for the car park exit ticket.

Poppy watched the barrier release them into the early morning. 'It's a long story,' she said, gazing out of the car window as they sped away from Gatwick. She had forgotten that the colour here would be grey. She closed her eyes, holding on to the memory of the bright blue St Lucian sky that had made everything that sat against it infinitely more beautiful, even her. The weather, the change of scenery and the love that Simon and Kate had shown her had allowed her to put her illness on hold. Now she felt it picking up the pace with a vengeance and it scared her.

Peg was excited and talking quickly. 'And Matilda and I fed them every day and collected the eggs, but I wouldn't eat them because I only like eggs from the supermarket and not from a chicken's bum.'

Poppy and Martin both laughed and the sound made a tiny crack in the silent brooding that filled the car.

'Matilda is going to come and live in London when she is big and we are going to be best friends and we are going to go and see One Direction and get our hair braided and we will both look after Toffee and I'll share him with her, he can be our joint pet.'

Toffee won't be around then. Poppy swallowed the thought, and the ones that followed.

'That sounds like fun. But what about Jade McKeever, I thought she was your best friend for ever and ever?' Martin winked at his daughter in the rear-view mirror.

'We will *all* be best friends, all three of us, but they will both like me the best and I will like them the same, but they won't like each other as much as they like me.'

'It sounds complicated,' Martin conceded.

'It is, Dad.' Peg sighed. 'It is.'

Martin smiled. He glanced at Poppy as he navigated the roads, following the signs to the M3. 'You look lovely, you've caught the sun.'

Poppy was grateful he didn't mention the whites of her eyes, which had taken on a distinctly yellow hue, or the way her skin had shrunk around her eye sockets, giving her a skull-like appearance. The blush of her tan certainly served as a distraction.

She nodded. 'I can't wait to see Maxy. I've missed him so much.'

'Claudia's spoilt him rotten, but he's missed you. We both

have.' He let the statement hover like bait on a rippling pool, hoping to reel her in.

Poppy looked to the back seat. Peg's head was slumped on her shoulder. She had stayed awake all through the flight, determined to follow the route inch by inch, but exhaustion had finally overtaken her and now at last she slept.

Poppy continued to gaze out of the window at the fields and hedges, lorries and cars that they passed. 'I did a lot of thinking while I was away,' she began. 'And some of the things Simon said made a lot of sense.' She watched as Martin's arms tensed on the steering wheel. 'I can't deny that what happened has changed things between us, Mart. Maybe it's only changed them a little bit, but it has. It shocked me and I was hurt.'

Martin shook his head, almost unable to bear hearing this again; confirmation that he had screwed up. He didn't need it saying: he knew it already. He thought about it last thing every night and first thing every morning.

Poppy sighed. 'But the thing is, life's too short. Far too short in my case, and I can't let it be something I carry with me for however long I've got. I don't have the energy for it and I'm sure you don't either.' She was staring straight ahead now. 'So I think it's best if we build a bridge that takes us from where we were to where we are going. We have to make the best of what we have left, for the kids' sake as well as ours. We've been through too much, Mart, to fall at the last hurdle. And Peg and Max deserve better. Much better.'

Martin nodded and swiped at his nose and eyes, trying to focus on the road ahead through his tears.

He sniffed loudly. 'I've been thinking too. I know you wanted to talk before, and make some plans, and you were right. It was selfish of me not to see that it's important to you. I understand that need to put things in order—'

'I'm not so sure.' She interrupted him. 'I've decided I'm not going to concern myself with any ceremony that you might or might not want to have.' She cast her eyes over her shoulder, making sure Peg was still fast asleep. 'So you can do what you like. It doesn't matter, not to me. This is what matters – the here and now. And actually all anyone has is the present, right now, just this one single moment in time.'

'I want you to know, Poppy, that I will always put the kids first. Whether I leave the job, go out on my own...' He exhaled, controlling the tears that threatened, knowing he would take that journey alone. 'Whatever happens, they will always have a stable, happy home. I will make it the best I possibly can so that they will have a haven, something we never had till we made our own. It will be different for them. We started it together and I will finish it on my own. I won't let them down, ever.'

'I know that, Mart. I've always known that.'

Poppy reclined the seat and fell into a deep and restful sleep.

When she awoke, she was in Wiltshire. The spiky palms had been swapped for rounded trees, the sand and dust for grass and gravel, and the hot sun in a bright blue sky for wisps of cloud that hovered in a grey light. It was beautiful.

'Granny Claudia!' Peg banged on the window, then leapt out of the car and threw her arms around her gran's legs. 'I missed you! But I flew all the way there and all the way back. I was practising for when I'm a pilot and I loved it. I could see above the clouds and I could see the whole sea and I wanted to fly the plane right there and then, but they wouldn't let me.'

'Well, they must be idiots. I'm sure you would have done a fine job!' Claudia ran her fingers through Peg's hair.

'That's what I said!' Peg stood with her palms turned upwards as if to say, 'Go figure!'

Poppy climbed the stairs and knelt down by the side of the bed where Max slept. She watched the rise and fall of his rounded tummy. 'Oh, Maxy! Look at you,' she whispered. 'I missed you, my beautiful boy.' She kissed her fingers and touched them gently to his rosy face.

As she turned to leave, Claudia appeared in the doorway with a mug of tea. 'Here you go. You look so tired, my love.'

'I am a bit. Thank you for my tea and thank you for looking after them so well.' Poppy kissed her on the cheek.

'Digger! Three… four… five… Hello, my mummy.' Poppy handed her drink to Claudia and with difficulty lifted her baby boy from his bed, covering him in kisses. 'Hello, Maxy! You're awake! I have missed you so much.'

'Muuuum!' Peg shrieked from downstairs. 'We need to go on the trampoline to celebrate being home!'

'Tampoline now,' Max offered as he wriggled free from Poppy's grip.

Poppy looked at Claudia and grimaced. 'Bloody marvellous. That's just what I need.' She pulled her pashmina over the shoulders of her shirt and vest, needing the extra layer. She gripped the bannister and made her way down the stairs, taking each step slowly and deliberately.

Martin hovered by the trampoline. 'Peg wants to celebrate.'

'Quite right too.' Poppy forced a small smile.

'And you, Granny Claudia – you have to come on too!'

'I think I'll watch. I'm too old and creaky for trampolining.' Claudia grimaced at Peg, who stood in the middle of the black, springy circle.

'That makes two of us,' Poppy whispered as she tried to

287

haul herself up onto the trampoline. Martin shoved her from behind – undignified, but it did the trick.

Martin lifted Max on and watched as he raced around in a small circle then fell down, laughed and tried to stand again.

Poppy looked at their little family and thought about the last time they had bounced in celebration, only eight or so months ago, when, so full of optimism for the coming year, they had jumped and laughed, before collapsing under the winter sky.

'The question is, Cricket family, how many jumps? I think we should let Mummy choose.'

Poppy caught the flicker of concern that crossed his brow. She gave him a small smile. *I'm okay, I can do this.*

'Well, I think two.' She stroked her chin.

'Two? No way!' Peg yelled. 'It has to be at least seven!'

'Seven?' Poppy gasped. 'You are kidding! What do you think, Daddy?'

'I say we split the difference, let's go five!'

'FIVE!' Peg yelled as she bounced, quickly reaching and surpassing the agreed number.

Max sat on the trampoline in front of his sister, giggling as he got tossed and flung about in the wake of her jumps. Martin trod tentatively, trying not to trample on anyone.

Poppy suddenly turned to look at Claudia, a stricken expression on her face. 'Claudia…' she mouthed.

Claudia rushed forward and stood at the edge of the trampoline, reaching up to try and help lift Poppy down, but she couldn't quite manage it.

It was the first time Claudia had seen Poppy cry like this in front of the kids. 'Whatever's the matter, love? Are you okay?' She reached up again and grabbed at Poppy's arms, awkwardly trying to get her to the ground. The bouncing made it hard for her to get a grip.

Martin looked over and could see something was wrong. 'Everyone keep still! Hold onto Maxy tight, Peg, don't let him go until I take him from you in a minute. Okay?'

Peg nodded. Her desire to bounce had gone and this felt a bit scary.

Martin waded to where Poppy had slumped. He gripped her arm, worried. 'What's the matter? What's happened?'

Poppy shook her head and fought for breath through her tears.

'Poppy! This isn't like you,' Claudia coaxed. 'How can we help? Have you hurt yourself?'

Poppy sat on the edge of the trampoline and placed her face in her hands. 'I've wet myself.'

'Oh, darling. Poppy, darling! I'll go and fetch your dressing gown.' Claudia ran into the house, trying to locate something that would spare her blushes and shield her from the children.

Martin sat down next to her. 'It doesn't matter, it'll be okay, love.'

'It won't, Mart. The reason I wet myself is because I can't feel my legs. I can't feel much at all.'

Peg handed Max to her dad and sat on the other side of her mum, who was now lying on the edge of the trampoline. She reached out and took her mum's hand inside her own. With her head on Poppy's shoulder, her voice was clear and calm. 'Don't worry, Mummy. Do you remember what you told me? Everyone wees somewhere they shouldn't at least once and no one minds a jot.'

Poppy wrapped her arms around her little girl and cried even harder.

Twenty-Six

Poppy opened one eye and noted the bright, white ceiling. Next she opened both eyes and saw a plastic tube floating above her, connected to what, she wasn't sure, but probably some part of her. There was a window to her right with white vertical blinds, pulled shut. A piece of machinery beeped in the distance. She couldn't instantly remember where she was: not St Lucia, but not home either. The mechanical beep got louder and she realised she was in hospital. The Great Western Hospital in Swindon, to be precise. Thankfully, she was in a quiet side ward, and the only other bed was un-occupied.

She remembered being on the trampoline and Martin standing in front of her on the grass with Max in his arms. He had looked afraid. When he spoke, his voice had been tight, panic-stricken.

'I'm going to call an ambulance, Poppy. Okay?'

She thought she might have nodded. No argument. *Okay.* She needed help and she knew it. The ambulance men had been red-faced and jolly, making jokes and being overly familiar. It was all part of their practised banter and designed to put the patient at ease. Poppy had smiled weakly but really just wanted silence. When was that? Today? Yesterday? Last week? She had no idea. Her throat was dry.

'Hey, hello, sleepyhead.'

She turned her head slowly to see Martin, who was sitting in a green vinyl wing-backed chair by her side. He looked crumpled and tired.

'Are the kids okay?' Her voice sounded weak, reedy.

'They've got Claudia at their beck and call, a big bowl of popcorn and *Despicable Me 2* on DVD – they are more than fine. I spoke to them a little while ago.'

Poppy smiled. She could hardly keep her eyes open.

'Go back to sleep, love. I'll be right here when you wake up.'

Poppy looked at the end of the bed and there, standing in front of her, was her nan, Dorothea. She was wearing her favourite soft pink jumper and her navy blue slacks. Her hair looked neat and she was smiling.

'Hello, Poppy Day.'

'Hello, Nan. What you doing?' Poppy was so pleased to see her.

'Oh, just checking in on you.'

'I met Simon. I stayed with him. He's lovely.'

'I saw. He *is* lovely, isn't he? Takes after his dad.' Dorothea's eyes misted over.

'Am I dead?' This suddenly occurred to Poppy.

'No, Poppy Day, not dead. Just dreaming, my darlin'.'

'I'm scared, Nan.'

'Course you are. That's normal. But there's no need to be, I promise. And you know I don't make a promise easily, don't you?'

Poppy nodded. Yes, this she knew. 'I'm worried I won't go home again...' Poppy felt a sob building in her throat and the sting of tears at the back of her eyes.

'Don't you cry. No need, my girl. You're going home in a couple of days.'

'Promise?' Poppy mouthed.

'I promise.' Dorothea patted her toes.

'I don't want to leave them – Peg and Maxy.'

'I know, but you won't leave them, not completely. You can keep an eye on them. Trust me.'

'You seem happy, Nan.'

'Oh I am! All I ever wanted was a garden. I never got one, but I longed for one even so. Simon's dad always thought it was amazing how you could take a tiny seed and, with a little bit of care and attention, watch it grow into something strong and beautiful. That's what I do here.'

'Are you lonely, Nan?'

Dorothea laughed loudly, tipping her head back and shaking it. She looked to her right, as if gazing at someone in the wings. 'Oh no, my girl. I'm not lonely, not for one second.'

'I'm going to miss so much.' Poppy felt her tears fall and soak into the pillow, leaving a hot wet streak against the side of her head.

'Listen to me, my girl. You may not see the sun every day, and the moon won't shine on you, but I promise you will still be in the light, everlasting light. Remember that and remember that I love you, Poppy Day.'

Poppy nodded. 'I love you.'

'I love you too.' Martin replied to his wife's words, spoken suddenly and strongly. He beamed and held her hand, feeling the ropes of discord slip away.

The next morning, Mr Ramasingh appeared at the bottom of her bed. 'Ah, Mrs Cricket, looking tanned and lovely, I see. How was St Lucia?'

'Wonderful.'

'Good, good. But now you're not feeling so hot?'

Poppy shook her head.

'I've had a look at the tests they ran when you came in and there's a couple of things going on. Firstly, you have quite a lot of calcium in your bloodstream. Hypocalcaemia, which with your type of cancer is quite common.'

Poppy pictured the bastard cells in their leaky pedalos.

'Have you been feeling sick and drowsy, excessively thirsty, a bit confused?'

Poppy nodded.

'Yes, well, the good news is that we can administer fluids intravenously and after a couple of days on a drip we can flush the calcium from your system and you will feel a lot better.'

'Good.' Poppy smiled.

'The other thing that's happening is that because your bones are damaged, your spine has become weakened and is compressing.' He pushed his open palms together, as though he were playing an imaginary squeeze box. 'This is causing the numbness in your legs. Are they any better today?'

Poppy nodded. 'Yes, it comes and goes.'

'Okay, Poppy, we'll get you hooked up and once we get your calcium levels under control you will feel significantly better. Rest up and I shall be in to see you tomorrow. Okay?' He beamed.

'Okay.' Poppy did her best to return his smile.

Poppy heard Peg's voice before she saw her. Propping herself up on her pillows, she smiled and closed her eyes. She knew Peg liked to wake her with a kiss.

Peg bounded into the hospital ward, full of beans and full of chatter; she had lots to report, having been back at school for one whole day. Poppy peeked from beneath her lids and was happy and relieved to see that Peg wasn't alone. She was holding a woman's hand and that woman was her Aunty Jo.

Poppy opened her eyes. The two women stared at each other in silence; neither could say who smiled first.

'Hello, mate,' Jo offered.

'Hello, mate,' Poppy replied, acknowledging that that was indeed what they were – friends. Friends who at different times had needed each other and friends who needed each other right now.

Without saying another word, Jo pulled the chair closer to Poppy's bed and took her hand into her own. The words of Poppy's email sat behind their eyelids, *we are lucky to be in each other's lives, you can never have too many people that have got your back. This is especially true for Peg and Max who will need you, Jo.*

Peg was delighted to report that Jade McKeever had loved her friendship bracelet from St Lucia, even if she wasn't quite so keen on being best friends with the mysterious Matilda, who she had no intention of letting join their club, no matter how cool she was or her ability to chase a naughty chicken into its pen.

'And look! I made you a card!' Peg thrust the folded piece of paper under Poppy's nose. On the front was a drawing of Poppy sitting on the edge of the trampoline with a large pool of yellow beneath her. Peg had drawn an arrow to the puddle and written the word 'wee' just in case there was any doubt.

'Thank you, Peg. Very creative. I love it.' Poppy smiled and showed the picture to Jo, who laughed. This was definitely one for her memory box.

'I think Jade missed me when I was away, Mum. I don't think she liked hanging around with Maisie.'

'Who, Maisie the hoodlum who runs the "I've seen your willy" club?'

'Mum!' Peg giggled and climbed onto Jo's lap.

'The what club?' Jo clutched her chest in horror.

Poppy laughed. 'It's a long story. I'm sure Peg can fill you in.'

'Jade said about when she came to tea and we had that chocolate fountain – that was the best day of my life!'

Poppy grinned. It had been worth the hassle, drama and expense.

'What's that machine thing?' Peg stared wide-eyed at the drip and its little plastic tube that snaked its way down to the back of her mum's hand.

'Oh, it's just my drip, giving me fluids and things that will make me feel better.'

'Your skin is a bit grey, Mum. You look like a statue, but a moving one.'

This made Poppy draw breath; it was how she pictured herself, like stone, crumbling from the inside out. She saw the wobble to her daughter's lip. 'I don't know about you, but I'm already missing that St Lucian sunshine!' She tried to sound perky, distracting. 'How's Max?'

'He's being a bit whiny, but Daddy said to say he is fine.' Peg looked up and bit her cheek, wondering if she'd broken a secret.

'I miss that Maxymoo, I miss you both. But it won't be forever; in fact, just another couple of days.' Poppy stroked Peg's hair.

'I told you, Peg, that it wouldn't be for long,' Jo said.

'Aunty Jo's right.'

'Have you stopped wetting yourself now?' Peg asked matter-of-factly.

Poppy saw the old woman visiting the new occupant in the next bed prick up her ears.

Jo gave a loud burst of laughter.

'Yes, for the time being, thank you.'

'Well that's good, Mum. And there is one other thing that I *know* I'm not supposed to tell you, so I won't!' Peg looked pleased with her self-restraint.

'Oh you have to tell me now!' Poppy pleaded.

'I can't, I promised. But I can say it has something to do with Lanzagrotty.' Peg hoped this wasn't too much of a clue.

'Cheryl? Oh God, when is she arriving?' Poppy looked at her friend. 'I'd forgotten all about her coming over.' It was the last thing Poppy wanted, her mum sticking her nose in.

Almost on cue, she heard the wail from the end of the ward.

'Oh, please God, no!' Her prayers went unanswered and there, trotting across the lino-covered floor in a pink neon vest, cropped denim jacket, jeans, high heels and enough gold to put Mr T to shame, was none other than her skinny mother.

Cheryl, gripping a hankie to her face, practically elbowed Peg and Jo off the chair.

Jo stood and looked at her friend. 'See you soon?'

'You betcha.' Poppy smiled, feeling nothing but relief that the awkwardness was behind them.

'Go with Aunty Jo, love. I'll see you in a bit.' Poppy gave her a look that urged her little girl to go quickly and quietly. She guessed that Martin was hovering in the corridor somewhere, hiding, if he knew his mother-in-law was coming in.

Jo took Peg's hand as Cheryl wailed loudly, 'Oh my God,

Poppy! When you said you were ill, I had no idea that you meant *ill* ill. I'd have come sooner. I mean, every Tom, Dick and Harry has cancer nowadays, don't they? It doesn't mean... this!' She waved her hand over her daughter's body, lying under a taut white sheet, attached to its drip.

Jo ushered Peg from the room.

Cheryl scraped back the chair and placed her head on the side of the mattress, exposing the black roots of her hair. She cried wordlessly, with her face in her hands and her body juddering with every sob. Poppy looked at her mother's skin: her mahogany tan was mottled with dark spots and the skin looked loose, like it might slide off her bones. It reminded Poppy of an overcooked chicken. She carried with her the pungent perfume of cigarettes and a sweet scent, applied liberally. It made Poppy gag.

'Don't cry, Mum.' Poppy thought it was typical that, even here, in this situation, she was forced to take control.

When Cheryl eventually did look up, her face was streaked where her make-up had been washed away by her tears. She rubbed at her eyes, spreading her thick eyeliner under the lids, which made her look like a panda.

'You look so bloody thin.' She sniffed.

Poppy smiled at these words from a woman who existed on liquid calories and looked as if she were in just as much need of a good feed.

'I know. Not by choice. I don't feel like eating and I've been quite sick.'

'And what's all this shite?' Cheryl pointed at the cannula in the back of her daughter's hand and all the rest of the medical paraphernalia. She shook her head and blew her nose loudly. 'I had no idea. I've known people get diagnosed with cancer and be right as ninepence within a month!'

'It just depends what sort and where it is, Mum, and I'm one of the unlucky ones.' Poppy stared at her mum, whose tears continued to fall.

'And what did you have to go gallivanting off to the Caribloodybean for? That was a stupid thing to do.'

'Because I wanted to. It was wonderful. Simon and his wife are lovely.'

'Are they now?' Cheryl twisted her lower jaw and smirked. 'And what did he have to say about you being ill? What did old Holy Joe think his God was playing at, taking a young mother from her babies? What kind of bloody God is that?'

'I did talk to him about it, actually, and it helped.' Poppy smiled at the memory of Simon's words and soothing tone.

'I can't get my head round it, Poppy Day. I just can't. I've cried all the way to the bloody airport and on the plane.'

'Did Frank come with you?'

'Who?' Cheryl looked confused.

'Frank, snoring Frank. Isn't he your boyfriend?' Poppy remembered a conversation earlier in the year.

Cheryl jiggled her shoulders and folded her arms across her chest. 'Oh God, no. Frank isn't my boyfriend. I've got a new bloke now. He's lovely, Poppy. You'd love him.'

I doubt that.

'His name's Paco; he's Spanish.' She nodded as if to emphasise the significance. 'I've got a good feeling about this one, Poppy. He's smashing.'

'Well, I hope it all works out, Mum.'

'Christ, me too. I'm getting too old for all this malarkey.'

Ain't that the truth.

Cheryl reached into her large white leather handbag and removed a packet of Marlborough cigarettes and her lighter.

'You can't smoke in here.' Poppy could hardly believe she had to say it.

'I know! But if I can see them, it calms me, knowing I can have one in a bit.'

Poppy shook her head. This was beyond her understanding.

Cheryl toyed with one of the longer gold chains around her neck. 'I've been thinking a lot about when you was little...'

Poppy lifted herself and sat higher in the bed, ready to listen.

'And the thing is, love, I don't remember much about it...' Cheryl let her eyes glaze and looked into the middle distance.

Poppy thought about what she wanted to say. *I remember it, Mum – all of it. Going to school hungry and in dirty clothes, waiting for you to come in, not being able to sleep until I'd heard you and whoever you were sneaking in shut your bedroom door.* But instead of saying this out loud, she remembered Simon's words: 'Punishing her would only make you feel better for a very short time and it would make her feel bad for a very long time.'

'And that makes me really sad, love,' her mum continued. 'I don't have any memories of taking you to the park or letting you paint a picture.'

Again Poppy bit her lip. *That's because we never did those things.*

'I suppose what I'm trying to say is, Poppy, I look at the kind of mum you are to Peg and Max and I envy you. You are a great mum, not like me. You've always been such a great kid, a lovely woman. I know I don't deserve you.' Again her tears spilled. 'And now I'm losing you and it feels like I missed my chance and it feels like shit.'

Poppy looked at her mum. 'That's cos it is shit, Mum. But there isn't a whole lot I can do about it.'

'I want you to know, Poppy, that I will be there for them kids after, whenever they need anything. They will only have to pick up the phone.'

Poppy stared at her mum, not wanting to expose the lie. Instead she again thought of her uncle's sage advice. 'Thanks, Mum.'

Cheryl wiped her face with her raggedy bit of tissue and ran her fingers through her hair. 'Anyway, I've decided that we are not going to sit here and be miserable! We are going to write you a bucket list.'

'What?' Poppy said in disbelief.

'It's where you write up all the things you want to do before... before... you know.'

'I know what it is.' Poppy tutted. 'I just can't believe you'd think I'd want to do one. Look at me! I think bungee jumping and shark diving are a little beyond me now.' She gave a rueful smile.

'It can be anything you want it to be, and I've been having a good old think. We can contact people and tell them about you and they will come and see you!'

'But I don't want anyone to come and see me.'

'Course you do!' Cheryl swatted her arm, narrowly missing the drip. 'Are you telling me if I got Gary Barlow to walk in right now and sing you a bit of a song, you wouldn't like it?'

'No.' Poppy was adamant. 'I wouldn't like it at all.'

'But you love Gary Barlow!' Cheryl sounded almost offended.

'I do love Gary Barlow, but I don't want him in here singing at me, not with me looking like this. I'd be mortified.'

'I don't think he'd mind; he's not judgemental, our Gary.'

WILL YOU REMEMBER ME?

Cheryl spoke as if she had personal knowledge. She sighed, clearly rethinking her strategy. 'What about if I got you a signed photo of the cast of *TOWIE* – that Joey Essex is lush.'

Poppy laughed in spite of herself. 'Mum, it's a lovely idea, but I don't want to be visited by a celebrity and I don't want a signed photo of anyone. I just want to get home and spend time with Mart and the kids. I want it to be as normal as possible for as long as possible.'

'Well, can I pick you up anything nice to eat? A Marks sandwich or some soup?'

'No, Mum. I wish I did fancy something, but I don't. Thanks though.'

Cheryl refolded her arms. She was out of options. The two sat quietly for a second or two.

'Actually, Mum, there is one thing you can do for me.'

Cheryl sat forward. 'Anything, Poppy Day. You just name it.'

Poppy watched as her mum's fingers twitched in her lap and her eyes darted to the packet of cigarettes that sat within her reach. 'You can tell me who my dad is.'

301

Twenty-Seven

'Ah, Poppy, good morning, good morning! Martin not with you?' Mr Ramasingh swept into the ward and sounded, to steal a word from Martin, 'jolly'. She found it more than a little irritating, like sitting next to someone on the bus who whistled when you had a headache, or having someone tell you about an unexpected windfall when you were scrabbling around in your purse for your fare.

'Not yet.'

'Good, good. How are we doing?' he asked as he studied the flipchart attached to the bottom of her bed.

'We are peachy.' She smirked.

'Mmmnn... you say peachy but your tone and demeanour would suggest otherwise.' Still he smiled and she couldn't stay irritated at him for long.

She placed her head in her hands and closed her eyes. 'If you must know, I'm well and truly fed up.'

He didn't respond, guessing there was more to come. He was right.

'I am as weak as a kitten, I could sleep all day, every day and I hurt. I really hurt. I'm sick of spending my days in pain and feeling so low.' She paused, picturing the bastard pedalos, which clearly weren't getting destroyed fast enough. 'I think I need stronger tablets to go home with, but that scares me as I'm already not very with it a lot of the time and I need to keep things as normal as possible for the kids.'

'The thing is, Poppy, this situation isn't very normal and it's no bad thing to let your kids glimpse that. It will make it less of a shock for them when things deteriorate.'

She sighed. 'I feel poorly and I hate it.'

'I'm sure you do.'

She sat upright. 'To think I used to wish for a kidney-shaped swimming pool, a diamond the size of an ice cube and the chance to dance in a fancy frock in the rain! Now all I want is to sleep through the night, not feel like throwing up every minute and be able to taste some food!'

'We need to talk about your care, Poppy. I mean, yes, I can change your tablets for you today and we can see how that goes. But there is also hospice care. Hospices are not only there for end of life; they can be used for pain relief and respite as well. Have you heard of Hawthorne House?'

Poppy shook her head.

'It's a wonderful facility and when you need to make use of it I can make the arrangements for you. If that's what you decide is best.'

'Why did this happen to me?' She let the single tear slip from her eye and made no attempt to wipe it away.

'I don't know,' he whispered.

'I am totally pissed off with it. I'm exhausted. It's not fair.' Unusually for Poppy, she cried without restraint.

'I'm afraid life is rarely fair.'

He did what he thought best in these situations and passed Poppy the box of tissues. Poppy wondered if he was thinking of his wife.

Martin padded up the ward with his hands in his jeans pocket. Poppy noted the way he peered ahead, as if nervous of what he might find. He beamed when he saw her in her clothes and sitting on the edge of the bed. Her hair was brushed and she looked considerably better than she had when she'd arrived a few days before.

'Hello, soldier, have you come to take me home?'

Martin could only nod, swamped by the realisation that he didn't know how many more times she would be coming home.

'I love you, Poppy Day.'

'Good. In that case, pick up my bag and give me your arm.'

'Do you want me to get a wheelchair?' he asked nervously.

Her look of withering disdain was all the response he needed. Martin helped her from the bed and watched as she steadied herself on his arm. They walked very slowly from the ward and neither of them looked back.

Back in Larkhill, Poppy stepped over the threshold and was delighted to see the house looking so perfect; Claudia must have been working hard.

'Welcome home, darling. Cup of tea?' she asked the second Poppy was on the sofa.

'Yes, please.' Poppy beamed at the angel woman who always knew exactly what her family needed.

Peg held Toffee up for a welcome home kiss and Max cried at yet another change in his up-and-down routine. Poppy cradled him to her on the sofa. His fat little legs dangled by her side as she rocked him. 'Sshhhh, Maxy. It's all going to be okay, my darling boy.'

Later on, Claudia took Max and went into Amesbury with Martin to do a big shop. Peg sat at the table, eating beans on toast and kicking her leg against the chair. Poppy was lying on the sofa gazing at her daughter, so happy to be home.

'Mummy?'

'Yes, Peg?'

Poppy watched as Peg toyed with the food on her plate and considered how to phrase her next sentence.

'I know that your bug's called cancer.'

Poppy drew in a sharp breath. How had she heard? Who had told her? It was horrible to hear the toxic word uttered from her little girl's mouth.

'I heard what Cheryl said in the hospital,' Peg offered by way of explanation.

Poppy hung her head, thinking of her daughter carrying the word around in her head like a dark secret. 'Yes, that's right. It's called cancer.'

Peg sighed, absorbing the confirmation.

'Jade McKeever says her nan got some cancer and she died.'

'Oh.' Poppy didn't know how to respond to that.

'And she told me that Jake Porter's dad had cancer in his lungs and he died.' Peg stirred the beans on her plate.

Poppy took a deep breath, mentally preparing for what would come next. She watched Peg hesitate, unsure whether to ask the question that threatened to leave her mouth, fearful of her mum's reply.

'And then she said that because you've got some cancer, you are probably going to die. Is that true, are you going to die, Mum?' Peg didn't lift her eyes from her plate.

Poppy gazed at her little girl, caught somewhere in that twilight time between the innocence of early childhood and the savvy pre-teens. She knew that this conversation would stay with her daughter and that every detail would be captured for perfect recall.

She looked out of the window. The sky was dark with

the threat of rain, which seemed horribly appropriate. The tinny radio was tuned to Radio 2 with the volume so low that only the bassier notes of Coldplay were audible; one of their neighbours was revving his car engine impatiently. *Life goes on…*

Peg flicked the fork and a baked bean landed on the tabletop.

Poppy knew this was the right time.

'Cancer is a funny old thing, Peg. Some people have a little bit of cancer and they can get fixed and other people have a lot of it and they can't be.'

Peg gripped her cutlery and stared at her mum. Her chest moved rapidly, in time with her breathing. 'Which is your sort?'

Poppy opened her mouth to speak and realised she was crying. Uninvited, the tears seeped from her. Peg started too. Two large tears rolled down her cheeks, followed by a whole lot more, which she made no attempt to remove.

'I have the worst kind, darling. I have a lot of it.'

Peg knew what this meant. She remained sitting at the table with her cutlery resting in her palms and her feet in their white socks no longer kicking against the chair.

'I would never ever choose to leave you, Peg. Never. But I have no choice.' Poppy fought to regain her composure and, strangely, felt a wave of calm wash over her. The prospect of no more pain, needles, drugs, hospital appointments, scans, therapies or nights spent under the harsh strip-lighting of a magnolia-painted ward suddenly seemed very appealing.

She watched the swell of panic rise in Peg's chest, watched as her little girl drew her next breath sharply, unsure of what to do or say. Peg slowly laid her knife and fork on the table and climbed down from her chair. She sat on the floor next to the sofa where her mother lay and placed her head on Poppy's lap, ready to feel the sweep of her palm against her hair.

'I know, Mummy.' Peg inhaled her mother's scent and closed her eyes.

Claudia helped Martin unload the shopping from the car and then prepared a plate of bubbling cheese on toast to be eaten by the four Crickets in front of the TV, all snuggled on the sofa under one large duvet. Poppy nibbled at hers, doing her best to emulate someone who was enjoying their grub. She knew it made everyone feel happier to see her eat.

'Look at you, you look like little chicks in a nest.' Claudia smiled at Poppy and Martin, who each had a child on their lap and a plate of food in their right hand.

'Cheep cheep!' Peg called through her mouthful of toast.

'Cheep cheep!' Max copied his big sister.

Poppy and Martin laughed.

'And, my little chicks, if you have everything you need, I am going to love you and leave you.'

'What? No!' Poppy didn't want Claudia to go.

'No panic, only for two days. I need to go to Clanfield and gather my post, check my plants and all that terribly urgent stuff. Plus I should get out of your hair, leave you in your little nest.'

'You're not in our hair. We love you, Granny Claudia.' Peg spoke for them all.

'Just a couple of days, I promise. And I love you all too, very much.' Claudia inhaled deeply, to quash the rise of emotion in her throat. 'Martin, you have my number. If you need me any sooner, shout!'

Claudia blew kisses and hopped into her Mini.

The next day, Martin was busy in the kitchen. He gripped the hot roasting tin with the floral oven glove and rattled the potatoes around in it, then lifted the tin up to his face. 'Mmmnn, if I do say so myself, I make the best roast spuds known to mankind! A pinch of rosemary, a dash of rock salt and these puppies will be good to go.'

Poppy leant on the countertop and sipped at her herbal tea.

'Jamie Oliver can only dream of making roast lamb as tender as mine and no way could he match my award-winning spuds.' Martin smiled.

Poppy let her eyes wander over their entire stock of pots and pans, dishes, sieves, spoons and jugs, which were strewn, in various states of disarray, across the work surface. The peelings of carrots and the tops and tails of sugar-snap peas were in a pile on the sink drainer, and the butter, cooking oil and at least half a dozen different jars of herbs were all lid-less and lined up on the window sill.

'I bet Jamie doesn't make this much mess.' She sighed.

'Ah, I bet he does. The difference is, Jamie probably has a team to clear it up for him.'

'Well, sadly, Mart, love, you haven't.' Poppy pulled her cardigan around her shoulders, trying to fend off the constant chill that hovered within her. She rubbed at her shoulder, hating the sharp bite of bone against her palm.

They could hear Peg's shouts and whoops of joy as she played with Max outside.

'Listen to those two.' She flicked her head in the direction of the garden.

Martin forked a crispy golden morsel of potato from the bottom of the pan and held it up to her face. 'Sure you can't be tempted? These little bits are what I call the chef's perks.'

'I'll try and eat a bit later, promise.'

Martin returned the roasting tin to the oven and started to move the pots and pans closer to the sink: stage one of the great clear-up. He looked out of the window to see Peg holding Max by the hands and swinging him in a wide circle. Max was flying out horizontally as Peg spun round, going faster and faster.

'Jesus, if she let's go of him, he'll go flying!' Martin tapped on the window. Peg didn't hear him. 'I mean it, Poppy, she's spinning him round really fast! She'll either fall and hurt them both or his bloody arms'll come out of their sockets!'

Martin tried to quell the edge of panic in his voice. He knocked harder this time and called out, 'Peg! Peg!', but to no avail. Peg was lost in the game of making her brother squeal ever more loudly. Opening the window, Martin shouted, angry now. 'Put him down right now! Before you hurt him!'

Peg, either oblivious to or ignoring the urgency in her dad's tone, shouted back, 'He's okay!'

Martin slammed the window shut and looked at his wife. 'For fuck's sake!'

Poppy put her hand on his arm and pulled him close. 'Do you remember all those times when you'd be watching Spurs on *Match of the Day* and I'd say, "Come to bed, turn that bloody telly off," and you'd say, "Five more minutes," without even looking up.'

Martin laughed. 'Yes.'

Poppy kissed his neck. 'And what did I use to do? I'd go upstairs and put on my special silky nightie and a spray of perfume. I'd slink back into the lounge and say, are you *sure* you don't want to come to bed, Mart? And you'd be up them stairs quicker than you could say "Where's the remote?"'

'God, Poppy, we've had some lovely nights, eh?' He squeezed her tight and kissed her scalp.

'We have. And the point is, you catch more flies with honey than you do with vinegar.' Poppy opened the window and watched the giggling duo, who were now on their fourth set of spins. She shouted, 'Anyone want to make popcorn?'

'Me, me!' Peg yelled, and put Max down on the ground.

Poppy watched as her little boy, rather dazed from his gyrations, wobbled like a drunk and ran straight into the trampoline.

Martin braced his arms on the sink and stood for a moment staring at the garden. 'I don't know how I'll manage on my own.' His voice was hoarse.

'You will, love. You will.'

Poppy turned as Peg burst through the door and into the kitchen, screeching, 'Popcorn! Popcorn!' She danced around the kitchen, flapping her arms like a chicken, poking her head in and out from her neck and repeating her chant of 'Popcorn!' with a decidedly West Country accent.

'She's flippin' bonkers.' Poppy laughed. 'Must take after my nan.'

Martin's lunch was as wonderful as he said it would be, even if it tasted like cardboard to Poppy, and jovial family banter flew across the table. Afterwards, Martin returned to the kitchen to try and clear away the chaos while Poppy dozed on the sofa.

Nurse Peg was on hand as ever to tend to the patient. It had become her favourite pastime: squirting water from an old bottle of washing-up liquid on to Poppy's arm, mopping it with a tissue that quickly got soggy and then wrapping the affected area in a bandage. Poppy would then lie back on the sofa while Peg placed the stethoscope on her chest, although if her heart was where Peg thought it was, Poppy was in even more trouble than she thought.

Peg thundered down the stairs and approached with her little medical bag under her arm. Her nurse's headscarf had slipped down and threatened to cover her eyes. 'Wake up, Mrs Cricket, it's time for your next injection.' Peg flipped open the lid on her square plastic case and pulled out a garish and blunt-looking plastic syringe. She twisted her mum's arm and pushed the end against the white underside, where a purple vein meandered towards her hand.

'Take your tablets!' Peg boomed in a bossy voice, before removing several Cheerios from a little plastic container and shoving them onto her mum's tongue. Poppy laughed in spite of the discomfort.

'Do not move!' Peg barked.

'If you don't mind me saying, Nurse Cricket, you are a little bit bossy and a little bit hurty.'

'That's because you are a very bad patient!' This time Peg waved her finger in her mum's direction.

Poppy laughed. 'How am I a bad patient? I do everything you tell me.' She pictured the countless Cheerios she'd been force-fed.

Peg slammed the lid shut and fumbled with the catch, trying to close it, but she couldn't make it stick. All of a sudden, she picked it up and hurled it at the ground, spilling the plastic pill bottle, stethoscope and syringe onto the floor.

'Peg!' Poppy said. 'What's the matter? Come and sit with me.' She patted the space on the sofa next to her. 'What's this all about?'

Peg's scarf had finally slipped over her eyes and she tilted her head back slightly so she could peek at her mum from underneath it. Sometimes she found it easier to speak when she couldn't see.

'You are a bad patient because you are not getting better and I am a rubbish nurse.'

Poppy gathered her little girl in her arms. 'Did you really think you could make me better, Peg?'

Peg considered this, then shook her head. Her response, when it came, was a whisper. 'No. But I just like to pretend.'

Poppy smiled at her daughter. She knew all about pretending.

'You are right, you know, I am a bad patient. I'm sorry I'm not going to get better. But I have to disagree – you are a brilliant nurse!'

'Am I?' Peg pushed the scarf back over her forehead.

'Absolutely. You always make me feel better. As soon as I see you coming down the stairs in your little outfit, I smile!'

Peg smiled too. 'Do you really think I'm a brilliant nurse?'

'I do.' Poppy kissed her cheek.

Peg placed her head close to her mum's and whispered, 'Can I give you a little operation?'

'An operation?' Poppy gasped. 'No!'

'Only a little one. I'd really like it, Mum. I could stitch it back up with cotton afterwards. I could just do one on your arm?' Peg hovered, her expression hopeful.

'Peg, I love you, but I'm not ever, ever going to let you operate on my arm.'

Peg slunk off the sofa. 'It's not fair! Jade McKeever's mum lets her use tweezers to take her own splinters out! I'm not even allowed tweezers!'

Poppy watched as her daughter stomped up the stairs,

then shouted after her, 'I hope you are going to be a happier pilot than you are a nurse – you're a bit sulky!'

Poppy smiled as Peg slammed her bedroom door.

Martin helped his wife up the stairs and switched on the shower while she sat on the bed. He bent down and removed her thick socks and helped her shed her pyjama bottoms and top. Weakened by her disease, Poppy found it hard to lift her arms, let alone soap herself, and Martin helped. He tried to make it fun, chatting and reminiscing as he let the lather build between his palms and then soaped his wife's body. She could hardly bear to look down at her naked form, with her prominent ribs, jutting hips and concave stomach. Instead, she kept her eyes fixed ahead or closed and tried to enjoy the sensation of warm water on her skin and the delicious tingle that she got from being clean. She had given up on baths. Not only was getting in and out a chore, but sitting with her bony bottom against the hard base of the bath was quite painful.

'You're a great dad. Don't ever, ever doubt that.' Poppy spoke through the deluge.

Martin paused and looked at his wife. 'Thank you. The thing is, love, I'm a good dad when I'm half of a couple, but doing it on my own scares me more than you can know.'

Poppy raised her face to the showerhead and let the water fall over her face; it was in that second that she had something of an epiphany.

Martin rubbed her down with her favourite bath towel, helped feed her arms into a warm nightie and placed clean, thick socks on her toes.

'Okay? Warm enough? Happy enough? Painkillered enough?'

Poppy nodded. 'Yes, yes and yes. Thank you.'

'I'll be downstairs if you need anything. Got to get Peg's packed lunch ready for tomorrow and iron my kit and whatnot.'

'I'm sorry I can't help you.' Her distress was as ever near the surface as she watched him juggle the kids, his job and caring for her and the house. At first, ensconced in their bedroom, she had lain there fretting, wondering if he'd stacked the dishwasher correctly and plumped the cushions how she liked them, but recently she had begun caring less and less about these details. She had much bigger things to occupy her thoughts.

'Don't be daft. Anyway, Claudia comes back tomorrow and I can skive off again.'

'There are a couple of things, Mart.'

'Name them.' He smiled as he leant on the doorframe.

'Can you put this in Peg's memory box for me?' Poppy handed him her three-quarters-full bottle of Angel perfume.

He nodded. 'That's a nice idea.'

'And can you ask Peg to come and see me and tell her to bring a sheet of paper and an envelope.'

'Righto, I'll send her in.' He blew her a kiss and went to knock on his daughter's door.

Claudia arrived as promised the following day. She had brought with her a steak and mushroom pie that she had made in Clanfield and it was now browning in the oven. Poppy savoured the scent of the rich gravy bubbling inside its golden pastry crust; she knew that would be the best part of the meal for her.

Propping the laptop on her knees, she brought up Skype and clicked on Simon's number. Kate answered the call.

'Hello, Poppy!' She smiled and waved.

Poppy watched Kate's eyes widen and her mouth form a kind of O in shock at her appearance. She knew she had deteriorated since she had left St Lucia, but it was Kate's silent reaction that told her just how much.

'How are you?' Kate's voice was soft.

'Not great.' Poppy chose the honest response.

'You don't look great.' Kate did the same. 'Things okay there?'

Poppy knew she was referring to her and Martin. 'Yes.' She smiled. 'Everything is okay.'

'That's a good thing, Poppy. And how is Peg the pilot?'

'Good! Mad as ever. We've had some very honest chats and she seems fine...' Poppy let the implications of this linger.

'Matilda is desperate to talk to her, we must arrange a time for them to chat.'

'Definitely.' Poppy nodded. 'I still can't believe we were ever there, Kate. It was a whole other world.'

'Oh, we loved it. In fact Uncle Katniss has just arrived and he'll get mad if I hog you. I'll put him on and talk to you soon. Lots of love!' Kate waved her goodbye. She appeared to shuffle to one side and Simon took up the chair at the desk in the study. It was lovely for Poppy to be able to picture where they were in the house, and their surroundings.

'Hey, how are you, Poppy?' Simon too looked concerned.

'As I said to Kate, not great.'

Simon paused and sat forward in the chair. 'Is there anything we can do?'

'I don't think there's much anyone can do.' She tilted her head to the side.

'Are you feeling peaceful or frightened? How are your

thoughts?' Simon was the only one who spoke to her in this way.

Poppy considered this. 'A bit of both, depending on the time of day or night.'

'I bet.'

'When I first got diagnosed, I thought that I'd fight, fight till the end. But quite recently I've realised it's not a battle, not at all, because that would mean that if I was properly armed and had tactics, strength and sufficient will, I might win. But I can't win, no one ever does. This isn't a battle, it's annihilation – the destruction of me.'

'Only the body of you, not you or your legacy.'

'Thank you, Simon. You are always so wise. I've finally come to understand that there is no immortality. The only variable is timing.'

'That's a good way to put it.' Simon smiled.

She smirked, rueful. 'I've read enough obituaries in my time, and it's finally sunk in.' She paused. 'So, in terms of my battle, I feel like I've lost. To fight on now seems a bit pointless, stupid. There are better ways to use up my small pockets of energy and time, both of which are now the most precious thing. Maybe they always were and I just didn't realise it. But watching Peg and Max, just watching them and enjoying them, it's everything.'

'You are right, it is everything.'

'My thoughts are quite ordered and even though I have moments of absolute despair, I'm actually okay. I see panic in the eyes of Mart and Claudia each time they poke their head around the door and peer into my face. But, strangely, I don't share their alarm. Without sounding too weird, it's as if I'm beyond the body that holds these thoughts.'

'That is truth, Poppy, right there.' Simon beamed.

'So I am going to try and enjoy my stripped-back state. I've no chores, no timescale and in one way it's quite lovely. I'm noticing my every breath, enjoying every single second of life until I draw my last.' She raised her eyebrows in contemplation. 'It's funny that, isn't it? That breath becomes everything. One more breath... That's all I can hope for, all I need. One more and then one more and then...' She shuffled to change her position on the sofa. 'Sorry, Simon, I'm waffling here.'

'It is far from waffle. You sound enlightened.'

Poppy laughed. 'Oh blimey, that'll be a first.'

'Can I ask you something, Poppy?'

'Of course, anything.'

'Can I pray with you?' Simon said, a note of cautious hesitation in his voice.

Poppy considered this and her reply was swift. 'I'd like that, Simon. I'd like that very much.'

Simon bowed his head and moved closer to the little nub of microphone. He paused and then began.

'Father, we ask you to take care of Poppy and let her find the peace that she deserves. Help her to understand that even though the sun will no more be her light by day, nor will the brightness of the moon shine on her, you will provide her with everlasting light, and God will be her glory. Amen.'

'Everlasting light,' Poppy repeated, and smiled.

Twenty-Eight

Poppy woke at five in the morning, with a searing pain that shot right though her. A pain so intense that it stopped the breath in her throat and made her whole body curl. She gripped the edge of the duvet and hoped that the fetal position might ease her discomfort. It didn't.

'Mart?' she managed.

He sat up quickly, alerted like a night guard caught napping on the job.

'Yes, love? It's okay. I'm right here.' He clicked on the lamp and in its light she saw how his chest heaved. 'What can I get you? Painkillers? Water?'

'I don't know,' she mumbled.

Martin rolled her over and looked into her face. 'Oh God, Poppy, you don't look at all well.'

'I'm a bit scared,' she whispered.

'Hey, don't be scared. You've got me, right by your side, for always. Don't be scared, my love.'

He held her tight and they waited to see who would say it first, both knowing that once this journey was embarked upon, there would be no stopping the inevitable.

'Shall I... shall I contact Dr Jessop, get her to call the hospice?' He tried to keep his voice level.

Poppy pulled back until she could see his face. Her vision slightly fuzzy, she held his gaze and nodded.

Propped on the sofa and wrapped in a duvet, Poppy waited for the ambulance, thankful that her pain had subsided, but equally fearful of when it might return.

'So will you come home tonight, Mum?' Peg asked as she sprayed the table from her mouthful of Rice Krispies.

'No, not tonight.' Poppy's words were delivered slowly.

'Daddy will take you in to visit Mummy once she gets settled,' Claudia said.

Max climbed up the sofa and sat next to his mum. He stuck his thumb in his mouth and kicked his leg against hers. It felt wonderful.

'You be a good boy for Granny Claudia and I'll see you soon, Maxymoo.'

Max pulled out his thumb. 'Three, four, five, six, Thomas Tank Engine!'

Poppy smiled at her clever counting boy. The small bag she had packed was by the front door and she was set. There was no need to go room to room, it was all there for perfect recall inside her head. Simon had been right: it was the truth. She was already beyond the broken body that she had become.

After breakfast, Claudia and Max walked Peg to school, full of plans to kick up the fallen leaves as they went to look for a couple of pretty ones to press. Poppy was relieved that the kids didn't have to watch her being loaded into the ambulance; it would only have unsettled them. But the ambulance crew were great – two smiling, positive and pro-fessional women – which gave her confidence that she was in the very best hands. Martin sat by her side as she lay strapped onto a trolley in the back of the vehicle. She let her half-closed eyes wander over the array of cubbyholes on the roof and sides, wondering what they did with all that medical booty, all those plastic packets, pouches and tubes.

The ambulance drove up the sweeping driveway to Hawthorne House. As Poppy was wheeled into the hospice, she was glad to see it wasn't very hospital-like; more like a hotel. The walls were painted in a soft yellow tone and the pictures were bold and bright. The entrance was spacious and full of light, with a wide glass canopy shielding the doors from whatever the weather might be doing. Two huge vases crammed with fresh flowers sat on round tables. She had thought the atmosphere might be a bit depressing, but it was anything but. Gentle music was piped into the communal areas and there were comfy sofas and coffee tables with magazines and coffee machines within reach. It was rather lovely. The staff were smiley and welcoming. She felt better about the kids visiting her there; it wouldn't be scary at all.

Her room wasn't huge, but spacious enough to accommodate a large bed with all the medical paraphernalia at its head. A trolley table sat over her bed and there was a small wardrobe. The one big window looked out onto the garden and a gentle breeze made the pale blue curtains flutter into the room.

'This is nice, isn't it?' Martin tried to sound upbeat.

'Nice.' She nodded her agreement as she smoothed the top sheet of the bed into which she'd already been settled.

Neither wanted to think about the wider implications of where they were or what that meant; it was too painful. Instead they took each minute as it came, silently holding hands and smiling as their world spiralled down into the dark pit that had been waiting for them ever since Poppy had taken that shower, almost ten months earlier.

Poppy's phone buzzed in her hand; it was a text from

Cheryl. She slowly pressed the little button and read her mum's words. As ever, there was little preamble, no explanation, no apology. She digested the three words and her heart lurched as her tears fell.

Martin leant forward. 'What is it, darling? What can I do?'

Poppy held the phone out to the man who had loved and cared for her since the day they had met.

'"Your dad's Sonny. X",' Martin read.

Poppy cried harder at hearing the words spoken aloud.

He shook his head. 'Sonny? I can't believe it. Do you think he knew? God, Poppy, I can see us sitting there in his café, chatting to him over our Coke.' He shook his head again. It was unbelievable to him. His jaw tensed as he thought of Cheryl and why she might have considered this good news to break at this time.

Poppy could only give a small shrug. She thought about the thousands of times she had seen Sonny throughout her childhood. He'd been to school with her mum and he'd known Poppy her whole life. She smiled and remembered his voice, always pleased to see her: ''Ello, my gel...' She closed her eyes and thought of the many nights she had spent with her toes tucked into the hem of her nightie, wondering who her dad might be. Was he a cowboy or a policeman? A prince or a film star? The countless hours she had spent scanning men on the Tube and in the shopping precinct, staring at faces that she thought might carry a hint of resemblance to her own. And all the time, Sonny, who made her bacon sandwiches and mixed her milkshakes, he was her dad. Her dad! She remembered walking to the pub just after they'd been married and Sonny driving past in his van and shouting out at them, 'Oi oi! It's Mr and Mrs!' It was the first time they had heard it and they had exploded with giggles. Sonny...

With Poppy dozing and comfortable, Martin headed off to work for a few hours. Sunlight began to filter through Poppy's window, casting a golden hue over the whole room. There was a large print on the wall opposite her bed: a chocolate-box version of a rather crude coastal scene mounted in a pale green frame. Sailors were unloading boxes of fish from a boat onto the quayside and women in long frocks and white pinnies stood talking with baskets on their arms. It was all very Catherine Cookson and certainly not what she wanted her last sight to be, when the time came. It reminded her of bed and breakfast accommodation, cheaply outfitted coffee shops and dentists' waiting rooms, which often had pictures like this screwed to the walls. Poppy smiled; the chances of anyone wanting to nick something that crap were probably very slim. She decided to ask Martin to bring in one of Max's masterpieces to place over it.

She pushed her head back into the pillow, closed her eyes and took deep breaths. She hurt. It was that familiar bone-deep ache that she could only describe as a migraine, but in her body, not her head. Mr Ramasingh had nodded and smiled at her description; he liked it very much.

Poppy opened her eyes and there, standing at the foot of the bed, was her nan, obscuring the garish print. She was smiling; she looked calm, happy and present, the nan of Poppy's youth. It was lovely to see her eyes so clear and with full recognition of what was going on; the fog of dementia had disappeared, along with the stare that used to settle on the middle distance. Poppy stretched out her left hand, reaching towards her nan. Dorothea blew a kiss from her flattened palm and disappeared as quickly as she had arrived.

Poppy felt elated and alarmed in equal measure. 'Have you come to get me?' she asked, into the ether.

* * *

A week later, Poppy watched as the light grew stronger in her room. It must be morning. She found that day and night were often indistinguishable; whether the lighting inside was bright or subdued depended on the mood and preference of the care team and now that her sleep patterns were irregular it could fool her into thinking it was any time. Not that it mattered. There were no timetables to be kept, no deadlines to be met and no consequences for being late. If anything, time was an irritation to her as she lay, waiting, within the walls of Hawthorne House. It either passed too slowly, making each hazy day last twice as long as she would have liked, or else it went too fast, leaving her in blind panic that it was too soon, too soon. *Give me one more day...*

Peg burst into the room. 'Morning, Mum!' She leant over and planted a kiss on Poppy's face. 'I see you've still got your wee-wee bag.' Peg pointed to the pouch on its little stand to the side of the bed, the tube of which curled under the sheets and into Poppy's catheter.

'I have, darling. Although, as we both know, everyone wees at least once somewhere they shouldn't and no one minds a jot!' Poppy nodded, her voice soft and slow.

Martin arrived next, his delay explained by the fact that Max was walking. 'Here's Mummy, Max! Are you going to give her a kiss?'

'No I not!' Max shook his head repeatedly. He didn't like his mum being in this room or this bed.

'It's fine. Don't make him.' Poppy smiled reassuringly at her husband.

'I think you need a bit of a position change,' Peg announced. The novelty of being able to raise, lower and angle Poppy's bed with the touch of a button had not worn off for her. She grabbed the remote control and poked her tongue out of the side of her mouth; this required concentration.

Poppy felt the top half of her bed moving upwards.

'Leave Mummy alone, Peg, you mustn't joggle her about,' Martin said, quite calmly.

'She likes it, don't you, Mum? I'll get her up a bit, it will be much better.' Peg peered at her, only inches from her face.

Poppy smiled and nodded.

'Well, not too far then,' Martin said. 'That'll do.'

Poppy was now sitting up. 'You are right, Peg, this is much better.'

Martin pulled the wing-backed chair closer to the bed. 'You should have seen her and Matilda today, playing some kind of clapping game over Skype. It was very funny.'

'I watched them doing that in St Lucia. How are Simon and Kate?'

'Sending you all of their love.' Martin held her hand.

'I'm much better at the clapping game now!' Peg chirped. 'And I've decided that Matilda is my number one best friend and then Toffee and then Jade McKeever. Matilda and I are going to be friends for ever and ever.'

Martin smiled at his wife, knowing she would be relieved to hear of the demise of Jade Bloody McKeever.

Max, who had been quiet up to this point, decided to

climb onto the bed. He placed one leg on first and, clinging to the blankets, hauled himself up. Poppy reached down and pulled him up to sit in the crook of her arm. He showed her his new toy from Claudia.

'Max's dumper truck,' he announced. 'One... two... three... four...' He counted each of the wheels.

Poppy sat back, loving the feel of his plump little body next to hers.

She must have fallen asleep and when she woke her family were gone. There was a note from Martin: *Be back in a bit, sleepyhead. xx* He had tucked it into the frame opposite her bed, which now had Max's picture tacked over it. When she had asked Max what it was a picture of, he replied, 'Digger!' She stared at the mud-coloured streaks and blobs; maybe he was more of an abstract artist.

The door opened and in strode Barbara, one of the nurses. She was a large woman, solidly built, whose forearms reminded Poppy of the hams that hung on hooks in the deli. Her brusque manner often came as a relief after the sweet, soothing tones of some of the others. It took away the emotion, made the place feel more like a hospital, and if it *were* a hospital, there was the chance that Poppy would be going home, no matter how slim.

Sofia Adams, 27, beloved only daughter of Jack and Angela. Taken by the angels. You were the light in our lives and will forever be the joy in our hearts. Instead of buying flowers, the family request that you consider carrying a donor card. May God keep you safe in his arms, Sofia.

'What you reading there?' Barbara nodded her head at the newspaper folded on Poppy's lap.

Embarrassed, Poppy moved it to the table on wheels beside her. She swallowed. 'The obituaries. I've always read them. My husband thinks it's morbid, particularly given my current predicament, but I find it quite comforting. I think it's nice to know that they weren't just patients or statistics; they were people who were loved. I like to know that people go on, by being missed, after they have... you know...'

'Died?'

'Yes,' Poppy whispered.

'Do you find it hard to say?' Barbara asked as she removed the cap from the thermometer and put it into Poppy's ear, holding it with one hand. Both were so familiar with the routine inserting of needles, swabs, suppositories, cannulas and tubes into every available orifice that neither blinked.

'Yes, I do,' Poppy admitted. 'Have you been with lots of people when they...?'

'Died?' Barbara prompted.

'Yes.'

'Yes, lots. I think it's a privilege to be with someone in their last moments.' Barbara removed the beeping thermometer, held it at arm's length, narrowed her gaze to get a better view and reached for the clipboard at the end of Poppy's bed. She drew a little X on the meandering chart, which looked like a profile of the Pyrenees.

'What's it like? What happens?'

Barbara stopped what she was doing and folded her arms. 'Truthfully, it varies. Sometimes people have been given so many drugs and so much pain relief that they slip away without really being present; they just seem to pass from sleep to death. Some relatives like this, relieved that there isn't a drama, but others feel a bit cheated, as though they didn't get the last words they were hoping for or the chance for one final goodbye.

Others, often those who've been in pain, seem to enter a space of peace and calm immediately before, and the look of relief that comes over them is quite beautiful.'

'Is it ever painful?'

'It can be.' She answered without hesitation. 'I've had one or two that have fought it until their last breath and their struggles were humbling and sad. So I guess it depends.' She straightened the chart. 'But usually it's not like that. We have medication, similar to what you are on at the moment, that takes the pain away.'

'Do some people ever forget who they are or who they are with?' This was Poppy's greatest fear, from what had happened to her nan.

'Yes. But those people are usually elderly and in the grip of dementia.'

Poppy nodded, comforted to hear that. 'Does it make you sad?' She looked up, tying to gauge Barbara's response.

The nurse paused. 'Sometimes, yes. It's hard dealing with kids and people you get close to, obviously. But the one thing I've learnt working here, seeing death very regularly, is that life goes on. We are all here for a short time and then we die. It's just what happens. Life goes on.'

'That's what my nan said to me.'

'She was right. Nans usually are.' Barbara smiled.

'It's very odd, being this ill. I can't remember what I thought about before. It was the same when I fell in love and then had my kids – I couldn't imagine not having a head full of him and them. The three of them sit behind every blink of my eyelids, imprinted there like tiny ghosts, living in my mind. And now this has taken over from them and I think about this bloody illness every second of every day; there's not a single chance to forget.'

327

'I think that's just how it is. They say it's a battle and it seems they're right. It must be exhausting.' Barbara pulled the top cover taut over Poppy's legs.

'It is.' Poppy sighed. 'I feel too old and too young both at the same time. I'm only thirty-two, for God's sake, way too young for this, surely? I know when you're really young, in your teens, you think thirty-two is ancient – like my friend Jenna's mum used to seem to me, when she was this age. I remember she had tiny lines at the top of her mouth, from her constant drawing on a fag, and no sparkle in her eyes, and she seemed really old to me. But that's not old, is it? Thirty-two – it's no age at all. They'll be saying that, once I've gone: "Oh, she was no age at all…"' Poppy gave a small laugh. 'Gone where, though? Where will I have gone? Isn't that the million-dollar question. And, come to think of it, why not the million-*pound* question—'

'I think you might be thinking a bit too much.' Barbara patted Poppy's pillow into a fat square and propped it behind her. 'Try and let your mind go blank.' She smiled and left Poppy alone to gaze at Max's artwork on the wall.

Poppy must have dozed again because the next thing she was aware of was Martin's voice.

'Gawd, we've got some weather going on out there tonight, girl. I got drenched just coming from the car park and it's hitting the pavements like bullets. Half the dirt has come out of your tubs, like someone's had a hose in there. Never seen rain like it. Still, on the plus side, it's given the car a good clean, that's saved me a fiver up the car wash.'

Poppy listened. She could tell he was nervous and upset, trying to mask his emotions with chatter.

'Funny isn't it, how every time we get severe weather, the

newspapers go into overdrive. It's always the worst we've ever had! Imagine what we'd do if we didn't have the weather to talk about or moan about. Every queue in every super-market would be silent.' His voice dropped and slowed. 'I went to the supermarket today. Walked around a bit with me trolley. I stood in front of the cereal for ages, Pop, looking at all the boxes...' Poppy heard a wobble in his tone, then a gulp. 'And I reached out for that muesli you like and it was as if I was frozen. I knew you... wouldn't be eating it, and that... that cut me in two, Poppy. The thought of not buying your cereal.' Another gulp. 'I left the trolley in the aisle and came home.'

He let out a deep sigh.

'Are you awake?' he whispered into the half-light.

She chose to stay still, lying on her side, wanting the comfort of him but lacking the energy to sit up, smile, engage.

She heard him sigh again as the plastic cushioned seat cracked and dimpled under his weight.

'Kids are soundo; I tucked them up before I left and Claudia was cleaning the kitchen. She is keeping the place immaculate – I think even you'd approve. She cleans 24/7. I think it keeps her mind off other things. Maxy ate a good tea. He had fish fingers and peas but then abandoned them when he saw the yoghurts. My mistake, I forgot what you said and let him see them! But then when he'd finished his yoghurt he went back to his peas. He makes me laugh. Peg's quiet, same really. I had a crap journey in, did I say? It's pissing down. The world and his wife are tootling along the lanes and no one seemed to be in any hurry except for me. Always the way, isn't it?'

She felt the weight of his palm as he stroked her back through the thin cotton nightgown.

'I was thinking on the way in, I wish I *had* been able to get you a real diamond the size of an ice cube and a kidney-shaped swimming pool. You've never wanted much, not like other women. No designer handbags or fancy gear. Mind you, that was probably a good bloody job on my crappy salary. You never wanted anything for yourself, did you? It would have been nice for me to be able to do that for you. I'm sorry.'

Poppy turned onto her back and opened her eyes. 'I was only ever joking.' Her voice was thin, reedy, her breathing laboured.

'Yeah, you say that...' He gathered up her fingers and kissed her knuckles, holding her hand against his mouth.

Poppy gave a small nod. 'Only ever needed you and the kids, no diamonds.'

'Good job, innit, Poppy Day?'

Poppy nodded again. 'Did you say it's raining?'

'Yes, absolutely larruping it down.'

'Can you open the curtains?' Poppy pulled herself up as far as she was able; she wanted to see the rain against the window.

Martin stood and pulled the outer curtains and ran the nets along their wire to reveal the water trickling in tiny rivers from the top of the pane to the bottom.

'Take me dancing in it, Mart...'

'What?' He took a step closer to her bed, to better hear.

'Take me dancing in the rain!' She beamed at him from beneath the sheet.

'I can't! You'll catch your death of cold, you're not well!'

Poppy laughed. 'I'm not well? Oh, really? I hadn't noticed!' she croaked. 'What does it matter if I catch a bad cold, what does it matter now? Please...'

Martin exhaled through bloated cheeks. He looked from

the window to his wife. She seemed so frail, her skin almost translucent where the light touched it.

'Oh, what the hell! Come on then.' He pulled back the blanket and sheets, shocked, as he always was these days, by the withered state of his wife's body. He unhooked her drip from its stand and gave it to her to hold. Then he fetched her coat from the wardrobe and slipped her thin arms into it before securing her scarf around her neck.

'I'll carry you.'

Poppy nodded her approval.

Martin bent down and scooped his wife into his arms like he was lifting one of the kids to bed from the car after a long journey. He didn't comment on how light she felt in his arms or the way her hip bones dug into his stomach, sharp and painful. Poppy curled her head under his chin and he kissed her scalp as they navigated the corridor, ducking into doorways and making sure they weren't seen as they made their way across the foyer.

'I haven't had this much fun since I shoplifted as a kid!' He laughed.

'Naughty boy,' she whispered.

'I might have been, if you hadn't kept me on the straight and narrow.'

Martin stood under the glass-canopied entrance with his wife in his arms. 'Listen to the rain on the roof, it's bucketing down. Are you sure you want to do this?'

Poppy nodded against him and wriggled for him to lower her to the floor. He gently moved his arms and bent over until her feet, in their thick woolly socks, rested on his shoes. With one arm clamped across her back, holding her fast as she balanced on his shoes, he lifted her slowly and inched forward, until they stood outside in the rain.

Poppy looked skywards and let the deluge drench her hair and skin. She stretched her arm out at an angle and Martin gripped it, locking their hands together. Slowly they began to waltz. Right there in the car park. As Martin grew more comfortable, he sped up. They giggled as they twirled and spun while the rain came down. He twisted her in gentle circles, watching as the droplets sat on her eyelashes and dripped from her nose. Poppy threw her head back and laughed as if she didn't have a care in the world.

Changing direction, he swooped to left and right, pulling her with him and against him, a willing partner as they slipped across the shiny tarmac under the night sky. The rain ricocheted off the ground and sparkled in the spotlights, sending silver shards of light where their feet danced. Poppy's nightdress clung to her thin frame beneath her coat and Martin felt the weight of his waterlogged jumper and jacket.

Soaked and breathless, Martin stopped moving and pulled his wife into him. 'Listen to the rain hitting the roof and the cars, it sounds like clapping! That's applause for you, my girl; my beautiful dancing partner.'

'It's the dance of my life.' Poppy smiled against his chin.

Wiping the hair from her face, he kissed her full on the mouth. 'I bloody love you, Poppy Day! I always have and I always will.'

Poppy kissed him back, a proper kiss that each would savour for the rest of their lives.

Twenty-Nine

Martin woke from his brief nap in the chair by the side of her bed. His two-day-old beard was itchy and uncomfortable, but he was not going to leave her, not for one second. She was asleep more than she was awake, but there would be plenty of time for showering and shaving, after. After. He could not bear to think of it.

'How's she doing?'

Martin jumped. He hadn't heard the nurse enter the room. He nodded. 'Fine, same.'

She walked to the side of Poppy's bed and flicked the drip, delivering all that was needed to keep Poppy calm and pain-free. She bent low and seemed to be examining Poppy's face. Her breath was rattly, each exhalation a wheezing chore.

'She seems quite peaceful. I don't think too much longer.' She smiled at him before she left the room, shutting the door slowly, almost reverently.

Martin hated the sense of relief he felt at hearing those words, wanting to stop time and spend eternity in her company and yet also wanting it to be over for all their sakes.

The tick of the clock seemed extraordinarily loud. He wished he could stop it.

He sat on the edge of his chair and smoothed the hair from his wife's forehead, stroking the paper-thin skin stretched over her jutting cheekbones. Her breath was sickly sweet and the whites of her eyes were sallow.

He whispered to his wife, 'I was just thinking, Poppy, about when we were at school. You walked past me in the dinner hall and you said, "You make me feel very safe." Do you remember? God, I thought I might burst. It was as if you'd given me the moon in a box, something so wonderful, I felt ten feet tall.' He paused, smiling at the memory, at the way she had shaken her fringe from her eyes and wrinkled her nose, just like Peg. 'Those words changed things for me. I figured that if I made someone as smart and beautiful as you feel safe, then I wasn't the useless little poof my old man told me I was. I shan't ever forget it.'

Poppy murmured something.

He bent low towards her and placed his ear next to her mouth so he could hear her words.

'I'm not ready... Mart...' she whispered.

'Ssshh... Ssshh... It's okay. I've got you, Poppy Day.' He slid his arm under her back and lay next to her on the bed, cradling her fragile form against his own, holding her fast inside his strong arms, right where she belonged. With his free hand, he smoothed her thin hair against her clammy scalp. 'I've got you, darling.'

'Don't let me go.' Her voice was a croaky whisper and each breath rattled against his chest. He fought the urge to cough on her behalf, not wanting to trigger a coughing fit in her, worried she might not recover from the effort.

'I'll never let you go. We're joined together, aren't we? You're my girl. Remember what I told you when we were little?'

Poppy found talking a struggle, but she closed her eyes and remembered his childhood words. 'I promise you, Poppy, that I will always be your best friend. It's like we are joined together by invisible strings that join your heart to mine, and if you need me, you just have to pull them and I'll come to you.' She had laughed out loud, loving the idea of their unbreakable, invisible bond. 'And if you pull yours, I will come to you, Martin. That way, I'll always know if you need me.' And it had worked, even in Afghanistan – especially in Afghanistan. She mentally smiled as she remembered Miles's amused disbelief when she'd told him that Martin was still alive. 'Poppy, you don't know that for sure' 'Oh but I do. I do know it. He pulled on my heartstrings!'

She lifted her eyes and there was her nan, standing quietly and patiently, smiling and waiting. There was someone with her. A tall man, with dark, curly hair who stepped closer and pushed his glasses up onto the bridge of his nose. Miles... Poppy tried to lift her fingers in a small wave.

Martin's voice was soft now, soothing, and it screened out the beeps of the machinery and the echoey, impersonal noises of the hospice.

'And you know, Poppy Day...' Martin paused, swallowing the emotion that threatened. 'You don't have to be afraid, because these heartstrings last forever. They stretch all the way to heaven and back.'

He felt the tension leave her shoulders. Her head, suddenly heavy, sank against his chest. He instinctively knew she was smiling. He smiled too and grazed her scalp with a kiss.

'Heaven and back,' she whispered. These were the last words of Poppy Day.

Martin didn't want to leave her. He held her tight until he felt the warmth start to slip from her body. He was vaguely aware of a nurse coming into the room and then a doctor arriving and confirming what he already knew, that he had lost his wife. As soon as the man spoke the words and filled out his form, Martin felt grief wrap itself around his shoulders like a cloak. He felt drunk, unable to think of anything clearly. His mind was jumbled with all that he had to do: collect Poppy a clean nightie, pick her up a magazine that he could read to her. Then the thoughts settled and he felt the sledgehammer to his gut as he remembered he needed to do neither of those things. 'Oh God.' He kept repeating it over and over. 'Oh God.' But it didn't help make anything seem real. He drove home in their car, to their home, but it would never be theirs again. She was gone.

He had no recollection of the journey, navigating the lanes and their turns like a robot. He stopped the car outside the house and switched off the engine. Looking down, he saw one of her hairbands on the gear stick. Gently, he eased it off and held it to his mouth and then under his nose, registering the vaguest scent of her shampoo and perfume. He inhaled deeply as his tears gathered. He cried loudly, his tears coming so hard and so fast he thought he might drown.

Claudia saw the car and drew the curtains, wanting to leave him alone for as long as possible before the kids spotted him. Once he set foot over the threshold, their lives would never be the same.

'Why are you shutting the curtains?' Peg asked from the table, where she was making a half-hearted attempt at her homework.

'I thought I'd cosy things up a bit.'

Half an hour later, Martin put his key in the front door. He was pale, with swollen eyes; a broken man.

'Daddy!' Max shouted from the kitchen.

Peg slid from the chair and walked towards him. Martin

sank down on to the sofa and Peg stood in front of him.

She clenched her fists by her sides and lifted her chin. 'How's my mum?' she asked.

Martin would never forget the next few moments. He lifted his eyes to face his daughter and placed his large hands over her tightly coiled fists.

'She is very, very peaceful now, Peg. She just went to sleep and she has stopped hurting.' Martin hung his head as the next wave of tears came flooding out.

'Is she dead?'

Martin nodded, unable to say the words.

'Will I ever see her again?' Peg's voice was small.

'I think so...' He tried his best to smile through his tears. 'One day. Your mum will be waiting for you. She loved you so much and she would never ever have chosen to leave you.'

Peg stepped forward and into her dad's arms as her tears finally came. 'That's what she told me.'

Peg sat in her dad's embrace while Max cried into Claudia's neck. He was too little to know what was going on, but he cried because everyone else was and it was quite frightening.

'I've just remembered, Dad, I have to get you something.' Peg wriggled from his lap and ran up the stairs.

Martin swiped at his face and took deep breaths, only able to picture the last image of his wife, still and pale, but beautiful, always beautiful.

Peg came down the stairs and handed Martin a pale cream envelope. 'Mummy said I had to give you this today and she said you had to read it upstairs on your own.'

Martin took it between his palms and trod the stairs to the bedroom. Sinking down onto the bed, he slipped his finger inside the flap and lifted the paper from the envelope.

Mart, my love,

*You once asked me, if I could have anything and every-
thing was possible, what would I want? And the answer to
that, my love, is simple. I would want the life I had, the
life we made. I wouldn't change one single thing.*

*My fear is and always has been that I might slip away
without setting things straight with you, Mart. I try to imagine
you without me, but I can't. So I can only imagine how
you must be feeling right now.*

'You don't know! You can never know, Poppy. I am ripped
in two!' Martin cried out, pushing the heels of his hands
into his eyes and sobbing.

*I know I said I wasn't going to interfere and I'm not,
but... You and I have shared our whole lives together and that
makes me well qualified to know what's best for you.*

*You said that you were a good dad when you were half of
a couple, and that doing it on your own scares you. So here's
what I think, Mart. When you are ready, in your own time,
what is best for you is Jo.*

*You might be surprised to hear that from me. But as you
know, Mart, I came to realise that what happened that night
wasn't just about me. My illness made things tough for lots
of people, and especially for you. Jo of all people understands
that. She loves us – all of us – and the kids love her. She
made me a promise once, that she would love the kids on my
behalf, for always. Tell her I want her to keep that promise.*

*You are a wonderful dad and you are my very best friend
– you always were. And that, Mart, is the most precious
thing of all. We had some adventures, didn't we? And I don't*

want yours to stop. Because you know, Martin Cricket, what my eccentric nan said is true. Life goes on.

Your Poppy Day xx

Martin clambered beneath the duvet and buried his head in the pillow. He stayed there for two days, until Peg knocked on his door.

'You can't stay in here forever!' She pulled back the curtains. 'Granny Claudia has made soup and she wants you to come down and have some with us. See you in ten minutes or I'm coming back again!'

Martin felt like the shell of his former self, didn't recognise the grizzled face that stared back at him. It reminded him of his time as a prisoner in Afghanistan: he remembered looking round, startled, to see who was standing behind him in the bathroom and being shocked to realise that the battered, broken, bearded face was his. This was similar.

He went downstairs with a heavy heart and pulled out a chair at the table, sitting where Claudia had placed a bowl of soup. He could hardly stand to look around the room, at their furniture and photographs, the cushions where her hand had rested and her head had lain.

'Where's Mummy?' Max called from the floor.

Martin stared at his son and his heart broke again.

'Where's Mummy?' Max repeated, louder this time.

Peg bent down and spoke to her little brother. 'I told you, Maxy, Mummy is in heaven. We've just got Daddy now, but he's not going anywhere, are you, Daddy?'

Martin shook his head and let his tears splash from his beard and into his soup. 'I'm not going anywhere.'

339

Peg picked up Max and plonked him on her dad's lap. She cradled Martin's head in her arms and the three, locked together, stood and cried.

Claudia hovered in the kitchen, all too aware of the sadness that gripped this little family unit, knowing there was very little she could do to alleviate it. She lifted the newspaper from the front door mat and sat down to read it. Popping her glasses on to the end of her nose, she opened the paper in the middle. Her eyes were immediately drawn to a small block of text:

Poppy Day, aged 32, died peacefully in her husband's arms. Wife of Martin, daughter to Claudia, mum to Peg and Max. An ordinary girl who did extraordinary things. Poppy, you are loved, then, now and always. Wishing you a fond farewell, my best friend, my wife, my love.

Epilogue

Twenty years later

The cabin was spacious. He felt a little bit guilty at having so much legroom and a big cubby for his hand luggage, when people with kids and bigger bags were easing past, making their way to the economy seats. Privilege and special treatment had never sat easily with him.

'Stop bloody fidgeting.' He stretched his legs out in front of him and tapped her fingers, which were toying with the end of the seatbelt. 'You need to calm down, you can't sit there wiggling for hours, they'll chuck you off!'

'Ha ha! As long as they chuck me off before we're airborne, I don't really mind. I can't help it, I'm really nervous. I hate flying.' She twisted sideways and reached into her jeans pocket for a boiled sweet – anything to distract her from the take-off, always the worst bit for her.

'Well don't be; it's only a plane. We'll be up and away before you know it.' He patted her hand, which felt clammy to the touch. 'Gawd, look at that! Bloody champagne now!' He nudged her in the ribs; he felt more than mildly embarrassed.

'Drink, madam?' The pretty flight attendant bent low with a tray on which sat tall flutes of sparkling plonk, orange juice and small bottles of water.

'No thanks.' She waved her hand, too nervous to contemplate holding a glass or sipping alcohol.

'I'll have hers.' He beamed and selected two of the tall flutes, sipping at them alternately.

'Thought you didn't approve?' She tutted at him.

'What? It'll only go to waste.' He winked.

The overhead speaker pinged. 'Ladies and gentlemen, I would like to welcome you on board this British Airways flight to St Lucia. We are just waiting for clearance and expect to be leaving on time. Weather's looking pretty good overhead and our journey time today will be about eight hours and forty-five minutes. So sit back and enjoy your flight and I'll update you before we make our landing at Hewanorra. On a personal note, I'd like to welcome my dad and his wife on board today. Relax, Jo, you are in very safe hands. This is Captain Peg Cricket wishing you a comfortable and enjoyable flight.'

Martin reached over and patted his wife's hand. 'See, I told you you've got nothing to worry about.'

'Martin, I've seen her trying to control roller blades and a scooter – she couldn't even open the front door without bashing into it! It's a wonder she never broke a bone or the door, and now she's flying this bloody big plane!'

'Ah, don't worry, love, she's done it more than a few times now and this thing's got a good set of brakes.' He chuckled.

'I bloody hope so.' She shuffled in her seat, then smiled at the memory of Peg's ninth birthday. Jo had driven from Marlborough to Larkhill with a pink cake on the back seat, taking the corners so slowly that a line of frustrated, beeping drivers had formed behind her in the lanes. Not that she cared; it was more important not to dislodge the marshmallows that she had spent hours icing on, one by one.

'That feels like five minutes ago Martin' Jo mused. 'Did I tell you I bumped into her old school friend, Jade McKeever? She's married to a soldier, lives not far from Larkhill.'

'Yes you did, love.' Martin smiled, knowing Jo would repeat the story no matter what his response.

'She's got four little ones under five! Can you believe it? Four? They were running riot in the supermarket, poor Jade looked exhausted. Her oldest seemed like a handful, giving out orders to the others and contradicting her mum. I think she's got her work cut out with that one.'

'Cabin crew prepare for take-off.'

Martin grinned. Peg sounded so calm and in control. *That's my girl.*

Nine hours later, Peg descended from the aircraft with her briefcase under her arm and her long, toffee-coloured hair wound up into a tight bun under her cap. She brushed the dust from her epaulettes and walked across the tarmac under the blue, blue sky.

Peg knew that Uncle Katniss, Kate and all the grandchildren would be waiting at the barrier to meet her, her dad and Jo. For the first time in years they were all going to be together for Christmas and she couldn't wait. Matilda's university term had finished and she was flying back from Canada, no doubt with a pile of marking under her arm, as usual. Peg was dying to hear about the developments between her and the gorgeous Nick. Matilda had confirmed when questioned that he did indeed make her tummy go flippy and her face all smoochy! Peg was fully expecting wedding bells within the year.

Even Maxy was leaving behind his latest leggy lovely and was flying in from New York. She was excited about seeing him, thankful that the banking world could spare him for the holidays.

Max was accompanying Granny Claudia, who had been on an art tour of New York, keen to take in Kate's daughter Lydia's latest exhibition. Peg had spoken to Granny Claudia a couple of days ago and knew she was very much looking forward to taking up her favourite spot on the terrace and nattering to Kate while Simon supplied his customary iced tea and sugar cookies. The two liked nothing better than to sit in the sun putting the world to rights and watching the comings and goings of Noah and his brother Jack as they appeared for food and a change of clothes before disappearing back to the beach to woo more unsuspecting tourists.

Whenever Peg touched down in St Lucia, her thoughts went to her mum and that very first time, all those years ago, when she had watched the plane progress across the map, her finger on the screen, making out she was flying. Peg smiled. 'I still miss you,' she whispered, 'every day.'

'Is that your plane?'

'Sorry?' Peg looked down at the little boy with glasses and a stubby, freckly nose. He was wearing red shorts and a blue polo shirt and seemed to have broken free from the crowd as he stood staring up at the shiny undercarriage of the 777.

'Is that your plane?' he repeated.

'Yep.' Peg smiled.

'What does it feel like to fly it?' he asked, his eyes wide as saucers.

Peg paused and considered this. Her mum's smiling face filled her mind. 'It feels absolutely brilliant!'

She started to walk away, eager to get to her family and begin the reunion; there was a large cocktail somewhere with her name on it.

'I'd love a plane like that!' the little boy gasped.

Peg turned and looked at him. 'You would?'

'Yes, really, really. I would show everyone in my school. Apart from Toby Patterson, who is mean to me and won't let me join his gang.'

Peg raised an eyebrow and turned on her navy heel. Removing her hat, she bent down and studied the boy. 'Toby Patterson sounds like a dickhead.'

'He is,' the boy confirmed.

'How old are you?' Peg asked.

'I'm eight.'

'Hmmm, a good age. And what's your name?'

'My name's Horatio.'

'As in Nelson?' Peg asked.

'Yes.' Horatio nodded without the hint of a smile.

'Tough break, kid.' Peg sighed.

Horatio shrugged; he was used to it.

'And you want this plane, you say?'

'I really, really do.' Horatio's face lit up.

'Have you got any cool pencil sharpeners, Horatio? Cos if you have, we might just be able to strike a deal.' She smiled and wrinkled her nose, laughing as she walked away.

Peg closed her eyes and felt the warm St Lucian sun against her skin. Bliss. She vaguely noticed the two women standing in the window of the arrivals hall, one in a soft pink jumper and navy blue slacks, the other with her reddy-brown hair looped behind her ears and wearing jeans with a neat white shirt, the sleeves of which were rolled above the elbow. Had she looked back, she would have seen that they had disappeared.